MACK MAHONEY
RACE FOR THE MONEY
Published By: C.S. Ramahon

I0634616

RACE FOR THE MONEY

is a

Mack Mahoney book

PROLOG

The uniformed customs inspector nodded politely to the attractive blonde woman next in line. She stepped up to his counter and gave him a flirtatious smile, but he wasn't impressed. He had seen it too many times before. Besides, it had been a long day. It was almost midnight and in thirteen minutes his shift would be over. It was his birthday and he knew his male roommate of 23 years was going to 'surprise' him with another party.

Acting purely on instinct, he decided to teach the skirt a lesson. He looked into her soft blue eyes and gave her his most uncompromising bureaucratic glare. The intimidation worked. Her jaw tightened perceptively. Naturally, he would have to search one of her bags to maximize her discomfort.

From the four light blue Samsonite suitcases, he randomly selected the makeup kit. He liked makeup kits. They were very personal.

"Open this one," he commanded.

Her slender fingers trembled as she flipped the latch and raised the top. It was jam-packed with cosmetics. After his long years of service, he sensed her reaction wasn't quite right. He noticed her eyes dart nervously as he skillfully removed the upper tray to check the hidden bottom compartment. He was shocked when he observed that it was filled with banded packages of freshly printed twenty-dollar bills.

That was the last thing he saw. The huge black man standing in line behind the girl struck him in the temple so hard that he instantly collapsed. By the time his head smacked the cold pavement, the couple abandoned their luggage and left the cosmetic case sitting on the counter. They raced for the door and in a flash, the black giant deftly took out the armed guard at the nearest exit and he and the girl disappeared into the night. As panic broke out inside the customs area, three strategically placed security cameras silently continued to roll.

CHAPTER 1 - MAKING CONTACT

I was laying in a lounge chair out on the deck in the mid-afternoon with my eyes closed listening to the nothingness and allowing the warm sun and gentle breeze to purify my soul. It was late August and Indian Summer was lingering well. The mountain air was brushed gently with the scent of laurel and pine. It was a good time to be alive.

My lounge chair companion was my ten-year-old Golden Retriever named Glory. Her head was laying peacefully on my chest and her breathing synchronized with mine. We were playing a game, trying to see how long we could keep our eyes closed. I've discovered that is the best way to get close to a mountain. With open eyes, it is too easy to become distracted by the splendor. Glory was as much into it as I was.

Instead of seeing the beauty, we were listening to it. There is no other sound like the high wind singing to the universe as it plays tag through tall mountain trees. The sound of a trout taking a bug off the water, a pine cone falling, or a squirrel chattering is intensified ever so much more with one's eyes closed and can punctuate a moment vividly.

We were enjoying a happy mockingbird trilling its special jazz arrangement. He was getting into it when the damn phone rang. Society had to intrude on our reverie. Glory bounced off the chair like a young puppy. I reluctantly opened my eyes but stayed there, knowing that Lukban would answer it. A few seconds later he opened the sliding glass door. With the long black cord trailing behind him and an apologetic look, he handed me the contact phone.

"It's me," I answered.

The special number is unlisted and goes through a 213 LA area code instead of the 714 Big Bear area code. Anyone calling should know who 'me' is.

There was a brief silence. "Mr. Race?"

"Who's calling?" I didn't recognize the voice.

"My name is, Smith. Mr. Raymond Benadiaz recommended you."

It was a job! "Hold on a moment, please."

I stepped into the house and checked the in-line impedance detector. The line was clear. "This is Race."

"That's an unusual name."

He had used the right code so I fed him my cue. "It used to be Racine, but someone took the 'in' out."

It was his turn. "I understand that you slay dragons."

I've always felt silly responding to the world's oldest cliché about dragon slaying, but it wasn't me that came up with it. The credit had to go to some want to-be wonder boy in a large corner office at Spooksville, obsessed with ancient Greek mythology. I was just glad they didn't make us sing the Mickey Mouse Club theme song.

Anyway, he had it right, so I countered. "Perhaps, if they're in season."

That was over with, so he got right down to business.

"We need your service, Mr. Race. Time is of the essence."

I'd worked with Benadiaz in South America, so I had a good hunch.

I pumped him. "Ray sent you huh? What's the nature of the situation?"

He hedged a bit. "I understand you speak Spanish. Is that correct?"

"Took it in high school. Perfected it during a year in South America training Fidelistas and counter-revolutionists for the Bahia' de Cochinos invasion in '61."

He grimaced. "Bay of Pigs, eh? Nasty stuff that was. How did you get away?"

I wasn't sure if he was curious, or still checking me out.

"Just luck and swamp experience I guess. A few of us made it out. It's a South American job, then?"

"No! It's a Mexico thing. We'll need at least two weeks of your time. I've been told your minimum fee is two-thousand a day plus expenses, and at my discretion—a bonus present."

I jerked him back. "A nice one!"

"Fine. It will be first class. I guarantee that. I understand you sometimes work out of San Diego. I'd like to meet you there tomorrow afternoon around five. Is that possible?"

"Where should I meet you?"

"There will be a room reserved in your name at the Half Moon Inn on Shelter Island. Is that agreeable?"

"Sure, I'll be there."

I hung up. Lukban didn't say a word. He was being his introspective self and required no explanations or justification. Communication between us wasn't usually necessary. His pensive soul-stirring eyes said it all. He has been with me for a long time and knows the nature of my work.

He has an intuitive way of knowing things about me that I had never understood. He had been a First Class Steward at the BOQ or Bachelor Officer Quarters in Key West when I chanced to meet him during an assignment. He got into a sticky situation that might have cost him the Chief's hat and I resolved it, for which he's been very grateful. We stayed in touch and when he got his twenty in, he contacted me looking for something to do. I had just acquired Cub Island and needed some help. It had worked out great for both of us, and he eventually brought his wife Maria from Puerto Rico.

I walked back out on the deck and stared across the placid lake. There is something about mountains. The wise man that said 'Mountains stand closer to God' had it right. My place is a time capsule of nature's perfection, created with love through the corridors of time. 'Cub Island' is a small outcropping of jumbo-sized sandstone and granite boulders rounded and polished smooth over the millennia by countless eons of mountain rains.

My seventy-five-year-old rock house majestically crowns this small parcel of paradise some fifty yards from the shoreline in Boulder Bay near the southwestern edge of Big Bear Lake in the San Bernardino National Forest. At a tad under 7,000 feet, the eight-mile-long sparkling blue Alpine waters of Big Bear Lake lie mostly to the northeast of my small island. In between the boulders, the citadel is sprinkled with magnificent pinion and sugar pines interspersed with mountain cedar. Sage peeks out from where it can grab hold, and lichen and green moss dot the massive boulders.

Behind the 4,000-square-foot home, a spacious redwood deck juts out over the water. Steps lead down from the deck to a private beach where ferns and grasses grow along the bank. There is a stand of white alders and one giant oak at the northeastern edge next to a barn-sized-boulder, which serves as the end of the island.

Till then, the house had been my best present ever. I got it from the very wealthy Martin Haliday. I had saved Mr. Haliday's family fortune and along with it, his only son's life. In gratitude, he had given me "Cub Island". I couldn't have been happier. Neither could my man Lukban or his wife, Maria, in whose names the title appears. In my profession, I've found it best to keep my name off of paperwork.

As I stood wondering what kind of job I was about to undertake, I rationalized that it didn't matter. Although I hadn't consciously faced it, I realized that I'd been growing bored lately. Besides, a true dragon slayer never questions the ferocity of the dragon, not the fire it breathes. What I do is just a living ... with a lot more action and danger.

As the sun dove below the mountains, the warm air became cool and nippy. I watched the sky turn cobalt and stars began to crowd the heavens until there was no more room. I remained out on the deck drinking in the atmosphere as if it were my last time, knowing that it might well be—because dragons sometimes belch very intense fire and they seldom die easy.

When I no longer enjoyed the cold, I went inside and climbed into my old four-poster, and waited for sleep to overcome my wondering thoughts and concerns. When it did, the dreams were hollow and unreal— tenuous apparitions moving about in the darkness—stalking through my remembrances with knives and guns—too many wars and too many wounds. But, as always—I somehow manage to survive.

The Next morning, I awoke to the aroma of coffee and sizzling bacon. I slipped into a well-worn terry cloth robe and sheepskin slippers and staggered into the kitchen to find Maria cheerfully engrossed in preparing breakfast at the old gas cook stove. She was wearing snug blue jeans and her long raven hair swayed freely as she worked.

Sneaking up behind her, I gave her a nice goose on her firm behind and she squealed and looked at me affectionately.

"You go away today, Mr. Patrick? I will pray for you,"

she said while making the sign of the cross over her heart.

"Thank you, Maria. You always pray for me."

"*Si*. And you always come back, so keep doing that."

I couldn't argue with that logic.

After two cups of coffee and a hearty breakfast of bacon, eggs, potatoes, and homemade biscuits, I felt like a new man. I took a long hot shower and shaved, then climbed into some well-used Khaki pants and a comfortable pair of tan Sperry Topsiders. A light blue tee shirt and my old leather Navy flight jacket completed my normal business suit.

It was a beautiful day, so I decided to take the convertible. I asked Maria where Lukban was and she informed me he was over at the garage. My house sits atop a sheer escarpment of rock-ribbed peaks. To get to the garage one must descend a stairway carved into the face of a boulder down to a floating bridge. The bridge traverses the water to a boathouse sitting at the water's edge adjacent to the three-car garage. Like the house, the garage is made from rocks with heavy-duty metal-skinned doors that open electronically.

I walked across the bridge to discover that Lukban had just finished washing my white '68 Deville. Although he's been with me for over fifteen years, I'll never know how he reads my mind.

"How did you know I'd want the Cad?"

His Filipino eyes squinted but his judicious laugh provided no answer. I eased into the driver's seat and fired up the engine. While it was warming up I unlatched the top and pushed the button. The ragtop rolled smoothly into its boot. I turned off the engine and climbed out. Lukban and I stood there admiring the automobile. I could tell it was his favorite. I'd have to give it to him someday.

"Raymond, I've got to go to Mexico. A week or more I'd guess. I need you to pack me something appropriate?"

Smiling, He leaned over and opened the glove box, and punched the trunk release button. When it opened, there were my travel bags already packed. I shook my head in awe. Glory was bouncing around anxiously in anticipation of the possibility of going with me.

"Did you pack both hunting and fishing clothes?" He nodded.

"Lightweight clothes?" He nodded. "Camera and film?" Another nod. "Bullets?" I'd tried to trap him—but he wasn't buying.

He laughed. "No bullets ... No guns in Mexico."

"I placed my arm around his shoulder and hugged him.

"I don't know how you read my mind—but I'm glad you do, old friend."

He looked up at me sternly. "You be careful, old friend."

We walked back over to the house and soon I was ready to go. I said goodbye to Lukban and gave Maria her traditional goodbye hug. I kneeled and gave Glory a long last hug, whispering my fond goodbye and telling her to be a good girl. She licked my face appropriately and begged me to go, still hoping. Her pleading eyes and wagging tail were hard to take, but business beckoned.

Lukban escorted me to the garage. As I backed out he pushed the button to open the electronic security gate and watched me away. I took the one-lane blacktop to the security gate, hidden from the main road by several huge boulders. Once past the gate, a one-lane dirt road jumps onto highway 18, which winds around the lake.

CHAPTER 2 - DRIVING TO SAN DIEGO

It was a great day. The sun played cat and mouse through the big trees stabbing the air with shafts of bright sunlight. The atmosphere was moody and the dark green hues of the pines arched skyward above me as I passed through Snow Valley.

I drove easily, letting the big engine purr like a contented tiger. It's the only vehicle I own that I hadn't gotten as a present so it was special to me. I'd personally paid a little under six thousand dollars for the spanking new beauty a few months ago, mostly because the 472 cubes were bigger with more torque than any other American V-8. I'd made sure it had every available option including all-white leather, which had been my pick from the 147 optional upholstery choices.

I'd bought the Cad because I had this feeling that American automobile manufacturers were heading for a fall. Each year our cars had been getting bigger with manufacturers trying to outdo each other with size and power. Detroit had learned over the years that bigger cars bring bigger prices and since General Motors set the standard—big iron had been in.

However, in the last couple of years, thanks to Senator Abraham Ribacoff and his buddies Ralph Nadar and Bobby Kennedy, big iron had big trouble. It started when politicians discovered that cars were killing some 50,000 Americans a year. That's when the head of the National Highway Traffic Safety Agency called the automobile "The nation's number one health hazard."

When Bobby Kennedy nailed the Chairman of General Motors on television and tricked him into admitting that GM's profit last year had been 1.7 billion dollars, but that they had only spent 1 million dollars on traffic safety—the shift hit the fan belt—and the bells in Detroit began to toll. Inflatable air bags were only one out of the 208 requirements of the National Highway Traffic Safety Act. Like a bulldog, when the government gets its teeth into something, they seldom let go. I didn't suppose they would ever stop now.

I passed through Running Springs and started the slow winding descent to the bottom. The macadam spiraled down through the verdant mountains with the sun slipping in and out behind puffy gray clouds. The sky was electric—a sort of aquamarine tinged with gray like it was threatening to rain.

From the height, I could see a brown soot layer covering the Riverside/San Bernardino area and extending out over the Pomona Valley. LA makes the crap and the winds of fate blow it away from LA and into the natural trapping basin northeast of the city. Like the fat cats have a contract with nature to deliver their smog to the poor people living in the less expensive suburbs.

As I descended, my ears began to pop and the temperature rose. By the time I got to San Bernardino, the craggy rock outcroppings had disappeared and the two-lane had become a freeway. The air was summertime sticky and instead of breathing the clear mountain air, I was now coating my lungs with LA smog.

I rolled effortlessly along and began to smell the unmistakable odor of fire. The traffic slowed and became bumper-to-bumper along Highway 10. After thirty minutes of playing stop and go, we crept by a huge brush fire blazing away.

The rubberneckers were getting their money's worth. It was so close I could feel the heat. The ashes and cinders fell like rain from large rolling clouds of smoke. I realized that most of what I had thought was smog was smoke from the fire and my rain clouds had been mere apparitions. It was merely a typical day on the Los Angeles freeways.

I'd had enough. I'd intended to take 10 into LA and then turn south and head down the coastline. But I'd already used up my quota of big-city patience for the day. As soon as I could, I swung east on 395 and headed for Riverside.

This time I was lucky and the traffic was light. After a while, I grew bored and turned on the radio. Aretha Franklin was pouring her heart out with her latest called 'A Chain of Fools'. I turned the music up and let the Caddy do its thing. By the time I hit 91 and swung south toward the coast, the Temptations had me on 'Cloud Nine'

The ride was pleasant and time passed quickly. I felt like a fat cat. I had great wheels, bitching music, and a new job. What more could a dude want? I took 91 until it ended in Costa Mesa and then snaked down Newport Boulevard toward the beach, leaving all traces of LA traffic congestion and smog behind.

A little over three hours from the time I left home, I was on the Pacific Coast Highway watching the blue waves of the Pacific breaking over the white sandy beaches. I rolled past the construction mess called Fashion Island and on through the picturesque Jewel of the Pacific known as Corona Del Mar. From there to Laguna the postcard-perfect road runs scenically through grassy pastureland where equestrians parade their mounts along the bluffs overlooking the ocean.

Sure enough, the Christ-like white bearded greeter, sans robe, was standing on his corner in Laguna Beach. He waved cheerfully as I drove by. I wondered how he found the time to stand in that one spot day after day, season after season, waving at everyone who passed. 'Wouldn't it be something', I mused, 'if he is The Second Christ and when he dies the world ends?'

The warm sun buttered a perfect day. When the Pacific Coast Highway ended at Dana Point, I had to jump back onto the freeway to skirt Camp Pendleton. There was little evidence of urban development, just the freeway knifing through the rolling grassland.

From there to Oceanside, the wide freeway flows smoothly and the long arm of the law is kind of short. Traffic averages around 75 with many folks driving 85 and 90. I took it easy, setting the cruise control at 69 MPH, knowing I'd never get a speeding ticket there. Cars shot around me like I was parked. After a while, I began to spot the sad matrixes of housing developments blanketing the hillside. Civilization was encroaching fast. I figure in twenty or thirty years the countryside between San Diego and Los Angeles will be one continuous neighborhood.

Here's a little self-exposure. I have this disease, which I call "Raceitus" that forces me to never drive the freeway when I can take a more scenic route. Therefore, at Oceanside, I turned off the I-5 freeway and picked up the old Highway 101 beach road, which stretches from Oceanside to La Jolla and let the big Caddy purr. In Encinitas, known for its six great beaches, I passed by the gardens of Paramahansa Yogananda's Self-Realization Fellowship Temple, a landmark since the 1930s. I considered pulling in at the Swami's Café across the street for a cool drink but thought better of it and went on.

Just outside La Jolla, I came to nostalgia cove and for old time's sake had to pull over. The twinge was deep. I turned off the motor and cranked the music up. The song was appropriate. It was a new Otis Redding and it ripped me well. 'Sitting on the Dock of the Bay'. The rolling breakers and pungent sea air made the memories flood.

There were a dozen surfers, using short little fiberglass turds for surfboards and wearing designer wet suits. I had to give it to them though. They were good, hot-dogging and making those midget boards dart about like wild farts in the wind. I faced disappointment. Time is such a bastard. My old balsa long board would probably give these kids a real laugh. Letting go of old abilities is hard. Although I hadn't been on a board in years, I still belonged to the Wind and Sea Surf Club. We were the first, and a unique group—to say the least.

As I watched the surfers, I remembered watching the hot-dogging Australian Nat Young barely beat out Corky Carol on his small board at the U.S. Championships at Ocean Beach last year, starting the short board revolution. Now Corky had his Mini-Model. I recalled listening to this eccentric dude named Bruce Brown pitch me for money to finish his movie, which turned out to be the hit 'Endless Summer' that had come out a couple of years ago. I remembered Hobie Alter making his mark with fiberglass surfboards—later with Catamarans. Memories. Me? I had gone on to become a problem solver. Who would have thought?

A little before two, I bid adieu to the surfers and headed toward San Diego. The sky was clear and clean and I felt excitement course through my veins in the balmy weather. Perhaps, I'd been on vacation too long and it was time to get back into the game. San Diego was still there and still beautiful. What can you say about a city where every view is postcard perfect? Traffic was light and, in a few minutes, I was rolling into the parking lot of the Half Moon Inn.

I felt slightly apprehensive, but shrugged the feeling off and marched over to the desk. A tall, lithe, natural redhead with sapphire eyes and pouting Marilyn Monroe lips stood behind the desk. Her well-endowed chest rose majestically as she breathed deeply. She smiled seductively at me when I told her I had a room reserved and fed her my name. Her alluring eyes widened slightly as she turned to retrieve my key.

"Here you are, Mr. Race?"

The voice was soft as honey. I immediately knew that I needed her. I think she knew it too. Her expression said perhaps. I had time for one quick flirt.

"My friends call me, Pat."

She laughed. It was husky like I knew it would be. I was peering back over my shoulder at her as I walked out and damn near hit the doorway frame.

The room was a typical forty-dollar-a-day job radiating discriminating taste and an expense account budget. It had a deep pile of coral carpets and a playground bed with magic fingers. I turned the air conditioner off, called room service, and ordered a fifth of Seagram's and some ice.

A two-dollar tip and five minutes later I was stretched out on the bed enjoying a drink and fantasizing about nailing the redhead when I dozed off. My internal alarm clock woke me just before five. I washed my face, combed my hair, and was sitting there sipping a drink and listening to my stomach growl when the knock came.

It was time to meet my prospective employer.

CHAPTER 3 – MEDIUM RARE

I opened the door and we studied each other for a few seconds. We both nodded and he walked in, carefully closing the door behind him. He was middle-aged and short, about five-nine, with salt and pepper short-cropped hair and carrying a righteous paunch that is more often than not a sign of soft living. But, I didn't read him that way because he carried himself too well—even though slightly on edge. I made him at two hundred-fifteen pounds. His intense cobalt eyes studied me like a hungry lion, staring down a limping antelope, belying his soft appearance. He was wearing a lightweight two-piece dark brown suit. A slightly worn spot on his coat and the bulge told me he was packing shoulder heat. I pegged him as a throwback to the cloak-and-dagger days of the early fifties.

He looked at me inquisitively. "Race?"

I nodded. He smiled, but the smile-lines didn't reach his eyes so I knew it was only a polite gesture.

"I'm Smith."

I wondered why he'd chosen such a generic name. His name was no more Smith than mine is Race, but it helps in the association so I went along with the game. My Race identity had been established by the CIA a long time ago and so well—that rather than undo it and reclaim my original moniker—I'd kept it. I'd become that typical unmarried guy with no family, who lived at the Oakwood Apartments, Unit 33C on Sherman Way in Van Nuys. That's an isolated end unit with lots of privacy and to make it hard for any neighbors to spy on me. It's set up with timers that make the lights go on and off at appropriate times as someone lives there. My fingerprints, driver's license, social security number, and all other documents verify my identity. I have a small saving and a checking account at the BOA in Van Nuys and my bills are paid on time by check. My infrequent mail is delivered to a post office box. Anyone investigating would find out that I am employed as a private investment counselor for several wealthy individuals, who collectively have so many people working for them that they don't even know who I am. If anyone checked my apartment, they'd find it to be clean and well-furnished, regularly stocked with fresh food and clothing.

They'd even find dirty clothes in the hamper. What they wouldn't discover, however, would be the well-hidden, silent motion detection cameras that would record their every move. As he stood there giving me the once over, I wondered if Smith perhaps knew my real name.

The thin zippered portfolio tucked under his arm was a nice effect. He helped himself to a chair and I sat on the edge of the bed, realizing my stomach was growling for some food.

"Have you been waiting long?"

"Not long."

There seemed to be no point in elaborating and he seemed satisfied with my brevity.

His Richard Widmark eyes sparkled with experience—the kind that only comes from seeing the darker sides of life. He glanced about the room and finding nothing out of the ordinary allowed himself to ease back slightly in the chair. He looked directly into my eyes.

"I hear you take an occasional risk?"

More code. He was taking no chances.

"I sometimes dance with the devil when the stars are right."

I sized him up. He didn't look government.

"How do you know Raymond Benadiaz?"

"Through mutual acquaintances."

"Are you with the Company?"

He grinned and replied, "Nope."

So, he wasn't CIA. Then whom did he represent?

"Are you Fed?"

His half-hearted grin made me suspicious.

"I embody certain individuals who, for reasons. I cannot divulge, choose to remain anonymous."

Not FBI or CIA. It was my turn to grin.

"Before we proceed, suppose you show me some identification ... Mr. Smith."

It was becoming a grinning contest.

His face got somber and serious.

"Nope. You care to show me any?"

We both laughed. I borrowed a line from the Duke.

"Well ... I guess you'll do!"

"Good. Now that we understand one another, let me explain what this is all about."

"I was pretty sure you'd tell me sooner or later. In the meantime, this salt air makes me hungry! Let's go get something to eat and you can fill me in over a steak. Your treat!"

His eyebrows raised and he nodded his head, so I knew I'd pushed his hot button. "Why not ... I can always eat."

His stomach verified that. I told him to make himself a drink and excuse me as I made a brief visit to the john. While in there, I pulled and wet a hair and stuck it in an inconspicuous place on my small shaving kit bag. I wanted to know if my stuff would be tossed while we were out. I had no particular reason—just force of habit. I like to get the rules down. You don't survive in my game without being careful.

While I was busy in the bathroom, he'd found my whisky and poured himself a short one in a plastic glass, dropping in a couple of cubes from the ice bucket. As I walked back into the room, he was stirring it with his finger. He was certainly not a graduate of the knife and fork academy.

He tossed the drink down quickly. Before we exited the room, he calmly tucked the portfolio out of sight in the small of his back under his coat into the waistband of his trousers. If it made him uncomfortable, he never showed it. We leisurely strolled the three blocks along Shelter Island Drive to the Chart House, which, as any local could tell you, had a justly deserved reputation for serving the best steaks in San Diego.

We climbed a flight of stairs to the second-floor entrance and were seated by a limp-wristed *maitre'd* in a comfortable booth overlooking the Shelter Island Yacht Harbor. It was a perfect day for sailboats. Everywhere I looked, canvas billowed gently in the warm Santa Ana breeze. The fishing boats were just returning from their day's outing. Seagulls brazenly circled like Indians around a covered wagon in the hopes of scavenging up a free meal of offal or unused bait.

Sound carries well over water and the marina was filled with the never-ending clatter of sailboat halyards slapping against masts, water lapping against creaking hulls, ropes rubbing on cleats, automatic bilge pumps doing their thing, and countless other noises. While we waited, we sat listening to the harbor symphony.

He followed my lead and we both ordered medium-rare New York cuts with extra garlic mushrooms and baked potatoes. He suggested, dry martinis to pass the time until the steaks arrived. I had hoped to lubricate his tongue some with alcohol, but I quickly deduced that I was barking up the wrong tree. He downed three martinis before they brought out the food and was still judge-sober and pumping me with small talk.

He stated, "I understand you were with the Company."

I knew he was referring to the spy school in Langley, Virginia.

"Yeah, I was recruited out of the Naval Investigative Service."

He knew how to fish. "You spent time at the Farm then?"

I could see where he was headed so I went ahead and gave him a brief background.

"I was born a Navy brat in Key West. My father was a Submarine Commander. He went down in number two and his posthumous Medal of Honor got me into the Academy. I graduated in '53 and became a SEAL just in time to wrap up Korea. I became an Intelligence Officer and later joined the NIS. I grew frustrated with marching and saluting during the Cold War and let myself be recruited by the CIA. I became disenchanted after a couple of bad assignments and resigned in '63. Then I tried the LAPD for two years."

"How'd you like being a cop?"

"It was full-time boring. Neighborhood monitoring and departmental tactics just weren't my bag. The fun badges are only in movies. Most real cops are merely underpaid citation issuers."

He squinted his eyes. "You moved around a lot."

I didn't know if he was just jerking my chain or not.

"Moved around? Yeah, but not in the way you think. I kept my options open and took them. People like you keep hiring me for risky tasks that require someone ... like me ... with the skills, training, experience, and stones for dangerous missions. So, sure, I have moved around a lot ... to dodge more than my share of bullets and fire-breathing dragons."

"But a man with such knowledge and bravado as yours likes the action, don't you?"

"Yeh, I guess. Like a vampire, I need an occasional dose of lifeblood."

I realized it was my tongue that was getting lubricated, so I backed off.

He'd found out what he wanted to know, so we lapsed into silence. The charbroiled steaks were excellent and we ate enthusiastically, making idle conversation. He knew how to eat. He handled his knife as well as Errol Flynn brandished a sword. When he'd finished it looked like he had sacrificed a virgin on his plate.

We laughed our way through dinner. He was an amiable son of a gun, and I couldn't help but like him. He was pro enough not to mention any more business during the meal. Once we heard a shot from across the street and he had his hand under his coat before he realized it was only a signal from the Marlin Club that one of the boats had returned with Marlin aboard. He bulged his eyes intentionally at me and chuckled at his faux pas.

Afterward, as we strolled back to the motel, at his request, we intentionally crossed the street to pass by the sidewalk scales where the lucky Marlin fishermen hauled their catches up to be weighed and admired by the crowed. The scales are located next to the sidewalk so that passersby could gather to see the catches being weighed and souvenir photographs were taken.

There were three nice-sized Marlin hanging as we walked by and I could feel the excitement in the air as Bermuda-shorted tourists milled about taking pictures and admiring the shiny blue game fish. We paused for a moment and I noticed that he seemed to enjoy watching the crowd rather than the fish. I was impressed.

Once we were back in the room, Smith got right down to business. He pulled out the portfolio which had remained tucked in his waistband the entire time and withdrew a manila folder while I poured us each a drink.

I sat down on the bed next to him and the briefing began.

"Okay, here's the pitch."

As calm as could be, he flopped a package of brand-new twenty-dollar bills on the bed.

"It involves these."

I whistled my appreciation softly but resisted the impulse to grab the money.

"We think they're being made in Baja some place. Someone has been laundering this stuff into the country so rapidly and in such large numbers during the last few months that we can't even make a close estimate of the dollar amount."

I calmly picked up the packet and thumbed it while he continued.

In the old days, the pirates could just melt down their plundered gold and silver coins. Nowadays it is all paper juggling with banks. Chasing hundreds of cash deposits through international banking systems is like swatting files with a rolled-up newspaper at the city dump.

Nowadays, once money is in the system, funds can be laundered through various intermediary banks using interlocking deposits and loans. Of course, all banks want to improve their deposit base, so it is easy to find someone to turn their head to. Naturally, they'd deny it if they were caught, and it would be hell to prove.

I tossed the package back on the bed.

"How can I be of help to you? You want me to stop someone from doing their laundry?"

"Not exactly. Here's the kicker. Although you could spend them at any bank—these bills are kind of counterfeit."

I glanced up from the money and looked into his eyes. "What? How do greenies get to be 'kind of counterfeit?"

"Oh, this is real money all right—printed with American twenty dollar plates—using the proper paper and ink formulas. We conservatively estimate that close to two hundred million dollars have been laundered in just the last three months."

My ears perked. I swallowed hard and looked appropriately amazed while he continued.

"I know that sounds like a lot of money, but in terms of our economy, it isn't. In fact, up to now it may have even done some good, but eventually, someone will let the cat out of the bag. You know how bad cat poop smells.

At that point, every country in the world will panic, leaving nobody to pick up the very expensive tab."

"So, you're saying ... it is counterfeit, but it isn't?"

Frustrated, he grumbled, "Right! It is and it isn't. The money is being printed with real plates. The people doing the printing also have the proper materials and supervisory assistance necessary to print all the twenty-dollar bills they want. How much do you know about how our money is printed?"

"That's not my strong suit. I thought the T-boys handled the funny money business."

He squinted. "In the country—yes. But they prefer to avoid international scandals, and this could turn out to be a doozy if it gets out."

"Sounds complicated ... and that whoever tosses in some detergent might get their shirt tail in a wringer ... if these almost counterfeiters are prevented from having their laundry day."

CHAPTER 4 - MAKING MONEY

He squinted to look serious.

"No not really. It is not that big of a problem. We don't require any brain surgery—merely some extermination. However, I'll fill you in the best I can anyway."

He took a long slow pull off his drink and continued.

"First, perhaps I ought to say that it is difficult to explain exactly what money is—because the idea of money itself is paradoxical. It is just paper, that's been churned out by some authoritative entity as a symbol of value.

All U.S. paper money is the same size, which is 6.125" wide by 2.625" tall. The primary difference between a one-dollar bill and a hundred-dollar bill is what is printed on the paper. Everyone knows that a small piece of old scrunched up, badly worn, often folded, paper with any amount printed on it is in itself worth little or nothing. Its only true value is the solidness of the organization behind it."

I made a terse comment, "Yes, I understand the concept of paper money and that's its worth depends on the national entity guaranteeing it."

His continuous diatribe began to bore me.

"It costs about a penny to make each paper bill, regardless of its denomination. The average bill only lasts a year to eighteen months before it wears out, so it takes continual printing just to keep the supply going. Bills are printed from engraved steel plates. The engraving process is the work of several expert engravers who give it the wealth of fine detail that counterfeiters cannot duplicate, whereas photocopying and acid etching usually produce the plates for counterfeit bills.

The finished design is cut into a flat piece of steel, or die, which is subsequently heated with potassium cyanide to harden it. Once hardened, the dies are pressed into steel cylinders or master rolls. The master rolls can then be used to transfer the design onto as many other softer steel plates as desired."

"That's interesting," I stated, hiding my lack of enthusiasm. "What's it all mean?"

"It means that a trusted senior official, with sixteen years of respectable service in the U.S. Bureau of Engraving and Printing Department, has quietly waltzed away with a master twenty dollar cylinder."

"Even so, wouldn't the special paper prevent someone from making passable money?"

He nodded his head.

"Good question, but the answer is ... no. The paper used for our currency is based on a formula, made from cotton and linen rags obtainable from many sources in the United States, as well as other countries such as England, France, Belgium, and Scotland. If one will pay the price, it is not all that difficult to get an all-rag bond made with approximately twenty-five percent linen and seventy-five percent cotton.

Any sophisticated paper mill could produce it with a little guidance. In this case, we think it is being made in Baja somewhere."

He paused to catch his breath and continued.

"The cloth is boiled until it turns into a mush-like pulp which is then beaten and chopped. Small red and blue threads are added to give the paper its distinguishing internal characteristics. The pulp is then rolled into sheets of paper and the bills are printed with green ink on one press run and black ink on another."

I admitted that his knowledge and description of all this was quite thorough.

"I thought the ink was impossible to duplicate."

"That's what the government would like everyone to think. They've been running that bluff for years. The truth is it's not hard to duplicate if one knows the formulas—-"

"And the missing trusted official knows the—-"

"You got it. One Friday evening, at the end of his regular shift, Line Chief Miguel Gonzales left as usual. Despite the closed-circuit camera monitoring and tightly supervised twenty-four-hour guards, he managed to smuggle stuff out.

On Monday, when he didn't return to work, it was discovered that crucial items were missing, including a twenty-master roller, and of course, the seals, numbering device, and facsimile stamps. More important, Gonzales also took with him the knowledge to make all the money he wants. Losing the hardware was bad enough, but the knowledge—-"

"Sounds like someone left the barn door open?"

"Yeah. They shut the barn door, but the horse had already escaped."

"And you want me to make sure he ends up in the glue factory?"

"In a manner of speaking, yes ... you could say that! People must have confidence in their currency. The injection of all of that unaccounted-for money is a distortion of reality that cannot be tolerated. If it isn't stopped, it might screw things up so badly, it kicks the United States off the Gold Standard. God only knows what would happen then. Most likely, if there was no accounting for it, politicians would be printing money as fast as they could spend it."

I chuckled, "Hell, they already do that! So, tell me again why the Treasury Department isn't handling this? Such a matter is their business."

"Oh, they have been quietly trying—but since Gonzales is a citizen of the U.S. and we can't prove he is in Baja—the Mexican government refuses to cooperate, much less allow our agents to stomp around in their county looking for him. The reality is—too many rules. They are far too visible and thus far, totally ineffective. One of them has vanished, and we suspect the worst. With Mexico being our largest trading partner, we must continue to maintain our good relationship with them. That's where you come in."

I pulled his chain. "I'm not sure I want to work for the Secret Service."

"Are you kidding me?" They don't even know I'm here. You are not going to be working for any government agency."

"I see. Then I'm beginning to get the picture. Sounds like a private sanction that could get messy, complicated, and perhaps bloody. I know if I was sacking up a hundred million a month, I'd look down on someone trying to put me out of business."

He didn't hesitate. "We are willing to negotiate your fee."

"You'd better. So, talk to me."

"How does this sound? We'll pay you a flat twenty-five thousand in advance, plus another buck and a quarter if you manage to succeed."

He was talking good numbers, but too low for what I'd risk.

"First off, I always succeed. Second, I'd be risking my neck and that number isn't going to be high enough. So, try again."

"I have been told you are the best. However, I'm prepared to give you a bailout option."

"How's that?"

"You bird dog them... and you can pick up another fifty thou ... and let me handle it from there. It will be your choice."

"Let's get this straight. I flush them, and if I don't like the game, I show you the nest and I'm clean... for 75K U.S.?"

"It's good for me if it's good for you."

I was hooked, but not reeled in, so I played with him. "I'll need to charge a little more if I almost die."

He didn't even flinch. "We can work something out if that happens."

He was still singing in tune so I ran my final chorus by him. "How about a good performance present? I always get a bonus, based on the success of the mission."

His grin was back. "I've heard that you like to be surprised with a gift. You do this job right and I'll get you a present that will make your brains fall out."

I stuck out my hand, but then quickly removed it.

"How do I know you have the dough. If I perform and you welch on our deal, you're my next target."

He grinned and replied as he offered his hand.

"I'm a man of my word with a backer that has the money for your fees. Besides ... I don't want to become your target or anyone else's, so I won't welch on what 's been agreed upon."

We shook on it. His grip was warm and rock hard. I could see the tension leaving his face. Without asking, he splashed three more fingers of whiskey and pumped a slug into his hollow leg.

"I'm glad you're on board. Now, let me tell you a little more about money."

"Proceed at will. I'm all wallet."

"I won't bore you with all that bald eagle and olive branch crap, or all the ways that thirteen appears on each bill. Bills are printed on an ordinary two-color rotary press and once printed, the treasury seal, serial numbers, and signatures are then printed all at once on each bill's face, thirty-two at a crack.

Finally, the Federal Reserve district seal is overprinted on each one. They are then cut and banded into packages of one hundred notes each and wrapped for delivery into bricks, each containing forty bands of one hundred, or four thousand bills. One brick of the twenties would face out at 800 thou. A hundred and twenty-five bricks come to a hundred million smackers."

These were big numbers. I was impressed.

"What about the serial numbers? How do they get around that?"

"No two bills ever have the same serial number thanks to a complex numbering system that allows for printing over 62 billion bills without duplicating a number. Our pseudo-counterfeiters are duplicating actual bill numbers. And, to spot one, you would have to somehow get your hands on both bills at the same time which is tantamount to matching up two snowflakes."

"Sounds like a big problem. But why don't they just change the serial numbering sequence?"

"They have. But Gonzalez just matches it or goes back a few years. It is complicated and nearly impossible to monitor number sequences when someone doesn't play fair. The average citizen wouldn't believe the problems governments have had over the years with counterfeiting epidemics.

During the American Revolutionary War, the British Government almost won by creating unlimited amounts of bogus Continental currency. And, it is estimated that during the Civil War, about a third of the Confederate money in circulation was counterfeit.

Some of our railroads were built with it. In 1930 a hundred grand in phony hundreds turned out to be the product of the Russian Government and we know that the Nazis made billions of dollars in funny money. When the allied armies smashed them, they were printing American and British currency right alongside their "buzz bombs".

"Yeah, I get the picture."

Smith rolled his eyes.

"And this time it is even more serious because the money isn't all that funny."

"You mean there is no way of detecting these twenties then?"

He shook his head.

"That's the sum of it. On most counterfeit money the details are blurred and obscured. It's often printed on watermarked paper and there are usually minor flaws in the portrait, especially around the eyes. The lines are broken, serial numbers crooked—scrollwork, seals, and the other designs are not sharp and clear. I'm afraid these bills are mint perfect."

He picked up the packet of twenties; tossing it into the air and snatching it back in talon fingers like an eagle grabbing its prey in flight. He shook it under my nose.

"This stuff spends anywhere."

I looked up at him calmly. "Which means...?"

"We want the dragon's head."

I took a deep breath and said, "Let me get this straight. Do you want me to skip down to Baja, and scour a few million square miles of sand and cactus for this Mexican, John Smith? Then, when I find him, I'm to whack off his gourd. Is that right?"

Smith laughed. "If you think you can."

I nodded my head and faked a yawn. "Sounds reasonable to me. Can I count on any help from you if I happen to step in a pile of it?"

He snarled. "Never heard of you."

I snarled him back. "I figured as much, yet ... I'd prefer it that way."

He handed me a 5 X 7 photograph.

"Here's a picture of Miguel Gonzales."

The photo was of a neatly dressed well-built Mexican in his late fifties or early sixties. He appeared to be happy and healthy with a thick thatch of white hair and clear brown eyes framed by laugh lines and gold-rimmed glasses. As I studied the picture Smith narrated.

"It may not be of much help because he hasn't been seen for some time. However, these photographs should be of some assistance."

He handed me several grainy 5 X 7 color pictures. Judging from the background, they appeared to be taken in an airport and some of the details were lost due to a blowup.

"These are recent telephoto shots of the only known mules. The girl is the carrier and the black is her guide dog protector. They were carrying bricks when these shots were taken. Unfortunately, we lost them before they could be taken into custody."

I studied the picture of the girl. She was tall and young, in her mid-twenties with a sensuous body that had nicer curves than Mulholland Drive. Her pouting lips were painted a bright cherry red, the color that sets men on fire. Shoulder-length champagne hair softly framed a delicate face and sea-blue eyes beckoned me even from the picture. She was the kind that could make a man's soul itch.

Smith continued to brief me, "She is going by the name of Mickey Carey and has been spotted in the San Felipe area. It shouldn't be too hard for you to find her there."

I reluctantly laid her photo aside and studied the next one. It was of a muscle-bound black giant. He was every protagonist's nightmare, a perfect adversary, completely bald, park-bear mean-looking with a 'don't mess with me' expression that I tended to believe was real.

"She calls her accomplice, Tate. We don't know anything about him, but I'd bet he's banging her. Their ID searches have turned up nothing. As best we can tell, neither of them has a criminal record, driver's license, or social security number. They simply do not exist at all. All we have is these pictures and their traveling names, which are probably as phony as the money they were carrying. We want you to make contact with them. Find them and you will find the source of these."

He pitched the packet of twenties onto the bed.

"Remember, neither the government of the United States nor Mexico will know you are on this. I'll expect you to keep it that way."

I didn't like the way that sounded. "Just so I'll feel better, you are somehow representing our uncle, aren't you?"

He gave me a blank stare as a warning shot and remained non-committal.

"As I said before, I represent certain concerned citizens..."

I finished it for him. "Who wishes to remain anonymous."

"That's the job. Are you in?"

"How could I turn down such an opportunity?"

"Good."

"So, tell me more about these mules."

"We only know that they are couriers. They were making a Las Vegas drop last month to a subversive organization when we lost them, right after these photos were taken. They have probably made other drops as well.

I took a shot. "By Subversive, do you mean 'Mafia'?"

"I never said that."

"Naturally."

"Although we're not certain, we've got a pretty good idea that the money is being printed somewhere in Baja. Perhaps near San Felipe, since that's where this girl has been seen. Unfortunately, the operative who spotted her has since disappeared. You're to do whatever you feel is necessary to achieve the desired objective.

Smith had one more for the road. Before leaving he told me that if I got snookered, or ran into a blind alley I should come back to the Half Moon Inn, check in under my name and wait for further instructions.

That was it. No emergency phone number. No infiltrated contacts. No help at all. It could turn out to be a real pisser. Like a good scout, I walked Smith out to his car. What a man drives is often a good insight into his character. But, of all things, he was getting around in a baby blue VW beetle. How could I read that?

He sat in the bug with its little motor chugging and looked up at me wistfully.

He quipped, "They also tell me you're lucky."

"I try to be."

He put the car in gear and gave me a parting shot as he drove away.

"Good. You're going to need it!"

CHAPTER 5 – THE HANGER

It was nearing sunset and I had decided to wait until the next day before getting started. Lustful thoughts of the redhead from the lobby kept dancing through my mind. But, when I went in search of her, I was disappointed to discover that she had already gone off duty. Somewhat dejected, I went back to my room and had a lonely drink, telling myself that it wasn't meant to be, but there would be another time.

Before a mission, life seems to become more precious and even the simplest pleasures are magnified. I needed the emotional fix of being around ordinary people with ordinary problems. Being in the game had given me insights. Some were good and some bad. Along the way, I developed an attitude. I'd chased that guy in the black robe around and he had taken a few swipes at me with his scythe, which had made me more cautious and given me a genuine appreciation for how good it felt not to be chased.

The walls of the room imprisoned my mind so I slithered into my bathing suit and headed for the pool wearing the hotel provided robe. I dropped the robe into a poolside lounge chair and dove into the deep end.

The water was velvety soft like melted butter. In my business, failure to keep one's body in top shape is a significant handicap. So, I tested my endurance by swimming twenty-five vigorous nonstop laps of the Olympic-size pool. Afterward, I stood wheezing and gasping in the shallow end waiting for my breathing to return to normal. It took some time. For the first time, I was going on a mission without being in the best of shape, but it was too late to try to get it back in one night. Was age catching up with me, or was I merely a victim of the easy life of Cub Island? I'd have to remember to pace myself on this one.

There was an orange blossom tang in the air, and the leaves of the well-landscaped trees danced excitedly in the disquieting sweet Santa Ana. High buttermilk clouds striated the sky with all the shades of roses, framing a large golden-autumn sun. I swam until long after it was gone. The winds lay down and the night tingled with electricity. Somewhere in the darkness, a siren wailed.

I went inside and got ready for a night on the town. I needed to embrace the earthly mundane and felt compelled to submerge myself into the everyday world, knowing I would soon find myself once again in that fantasy world where danger lurks around every corner and reality becomes the dream.

I took a quick shower and stood in front of a wall-length mirror drying my sun-freckled body. Although the recent swim said otherwise, I looked to be in good shape, standing a shade over six-two and balancing the scales at one ninety. I peered at my slightly bloodshot eyeballs and the pale brown eyes that looked back seemed impersonal and vacant. I didn't know myself.

It was time to lubricate the anxieties. My nerves were dancing on the edge because of the impending task. I didn't feel like taking a car, so the 'town' for that evening consisted of four joints in the Shelter Island area. I wound up drinking way too much Chivas Regal scotch and shooting pool with some locals in a beer bar called the B & W. By the closing time I had consumed sufficient adult beverages to make it an uncomfortable stagger back to the Half Moon. It is easy to note afterward that there is nothing worse than too much alcohol.

I lay across the bed with my head pounding and my body screaming for repentance. My stomach kept trying to get back into my mouth so I finally acknowledged the inevitable and crawled into the bathroom and stuck a finger down my throat to rid myself of the poison. After driving the porcelain bus for a while, I dragged myself back into the bedroom where I fell across the bed and passed out.

The next morning I awoke to discover that alcohol fairies had taken their revenge by crapping in my mouth and leaving a jackhammer headache chipping away at the inside of my skull. So much for anxiety.

I stumbled into the bathroom and made the 'never again' promise to the poor slob that lived in the mirror. I brushed away the fairy fluff and took a long hot shower that restored me to a semblance of life. My stomach was as empty as a hot air balloon so I downed the free continental breakfast that came with my room, consisting of a raspberry pastry, a small airline-style container of orange juice, and coffee. It was all I could handle.

When my hands no longer trembled and the jackhammer beat had subsided, I knew I would live. I placed a phone call to Switzerland. As Smith had promised, the 25 large had already been deposited into my account. It was a go. I called my friend Curly Wyatt at the airport and told him I was coming.

I was feeling almost normal by the time I got rolling. I put the ragtop down and let the California sunshine work its cure. It was one of those typically beautiful days as I headed for H22, my hangar at Lindberg Field.

San Diego is one of the few cities in the world where the airport is located right in the downtown area. One of the big thrills for newcomers is getting trapped at a red light on Harbor Boulevard where landing planes come in so low over the road that they blow the dust off your car and melt the wax in your eardrums. It's a hell of a fright the first time, but after a while, San Diegans get used to the big birds buzzing overhead. One of these days one of them won't make it and they'll relocate the airport out by El Cajon someplace. For the time being, however, it was most convenient.

Before proceeding to my hanger, I stopped for a cup of Joe and a brief chat with Curly, the Field Security Officer. He was a retired Naval pilot and naturally bald as a cue ball. We'd been classmates at the Academy and friends ever since. He was not only a good friend but also a valuable contact because he watched my hangar toys better than any guard dog. I wanted to make sure there had been no problems since my last visit.

His Irish blue eyes brightened as I walked into his office.

"Hi Curly, how're they hanging?"

"Snug and tight," was his standard answer. He poured us a couple of mugs of coffee and propped his feet up on his desk.

"So, what have you been up to, Pat? I haven't seen you in a while."

"Not much, Curly—just low profiling it. I've got something in the works now."

"Everything is spot on and ready to go. Just let me know if you need anything else. More spook stuff, huh?"

"You know me. Anything for a buck."

He patted his paunch. "Better you than me."

"Somebody has to do it."

"I suppose so."

We batted the breeze for a few more minutes until it was time for me to hit the road. I turned my empty mug upside down and hung it over his foot.

"I've gotta split, Curly. Business calls."

He never liked to see me go.

"I've got to scout a San Diego State game tonight. I can get you a ticket if you want to come."

"Thanks anyway, but I can't. Who are you scouting for?"

"No big deal. A buddy of mine just signed as an assistant coach under Larry Costello."

"Bucs, huh?"

"Yeah. Got any recommendations?"

I thought a moment. "I like that Alcindor kid at UCLA."

Curly made a face. "Nah! He's too skinny. Not enough endurance for the pros."

"If you say so. I'd check him out though. I'll catch you later."

He smiled. "Okay, Pat. Alcindor, huh?"

I gave him a thumbs-up as I left.

I unlocked the lockbox and punched in the code on the electronic burglar alarm. The big hangar door slid open effortlessly. I eased the Caddy in and shut the door behind me. My toys all appeared to be okay, including the Sky wagon, which looked ready to hit the blue.

Don't get me wrong. I don't fly myself. I have always been uncomfortable in small aircraft. This stems from an accident that happened on a mission when I was a SEAL, but that's another story. In any case, my dislike for planes hadn't stopped a grateful client—the leader of a small African country—from presenting me with a gift of one plus a lifetime rental contract on my hangar.

Although I'd only been up in it twice, it's a sweet bird, a Cessna Model P2068 six-passenger Super Sky wagon.

The kind the Tactical Air Command Special Air Warfare Center uses for light strike missions. It is a single-engine monoplane with a streamlined body and tricycle landing gear. I slid open the large double cargo door on the starboard side and poked my head into the plane to admire it.

Every time I see it I feel guilty, but what the heck? I'd earned it if saving a few thousand lives counts for anything. Fortunately, my hanger was large enough for the plane, an office, a bathroom, and all my gear including numerous weapons, two boats, a motorcycle, and three other vehicles. Right now I was interested in the tan CJ5 Jeep parked in the corner.

It's the long-wheelbase civilian model equipped with several modifications, including bulletproof window glass and a custom-made bulletproof squared-back hardtop. For power, it had a reliable little Buick V6 that required no shifting because of its full-time four-wheel drive and automatic transmission. It is a highly efficient and ruggedly dependable workhorse that had originally been ordered by a wealthy South American dictator who feared for his life. Unfortunately, he had been assassinated before its completion. I had been called in after the fact to avenge his death. The grateful family gave me the jeep.

I'd only used it a few times and this seemed like a good opportunity to give it a workout since it had been modified to operate in both desert and jungle environments. It had been designed to withstand sustained operation in either extremely dusty or wet conditions due to unique features, such as the special raised loop exhaust system with a closed pack muffler and sealed ignition. I removed the dust cover and got behind the wheel to survey the interior. It still smelled new.

I fingered a catch and slid the door panel back revealing a built-in hidden door cavity. Mounted inside is a well-concealed 'Nellie', or sawed-off 12-gauge shotgun, and two boxes of shells. I looked at the weapon and debated taking it or not. Firearms are strictly prohibited in Mexico except for certain properly registered weapons. They aren't on the good guy list, even if you are hunting creeps. Taking the weapon could create a big problem if it were discovered. On the other hand, not taking it could present a bigger problem if it were needed. I considered it and rationalized that risks are part of my job. Nellie was coming.

I began packing and within a half hour, I was ready to go. The jeep was loaded with fishing gear, two sleeping bags, binoculars, cameras, and assorted camping equipment. I took a few weapons including Nellie, a long thin Rapala filleting knife, a two-bladed Buck pocketknife, and a 12-gauge signal flare kit. The flare gun makes a pretty nice deterrent and customs officials would think nothing of it. In a crunch, it could also fire a 12-gauge shell with a little modification.

Although I have some pretty exotic weaponry, I've learned not to carry anything that will nail the lid on my coffin if I get caught in the enemy's camp. Taking a lot of sophisticated equipment on a surreptitious mission is tantamount to waving a red flag and any old Toreador knows that if you screw around with a bull long enough, you will eventually get gored. It's not like I am a virgin. I've been horned a few times, so I don't wave flags.

I remembered something an old soldier had told me after my first CIA mission. I was getting stitched up in a hospital from a knife wound.

He asked me if it hurt and I told him, "Hell yes!"

"Good," he'd replied. "You will remember it better that way. Each scar makes you more careful, and by so doing—extends your longevity."

I'm pretty careful nowadays.

I didn't know why, but I felt more apprehensive than usual about this job. Perhaps, it was just Smith. He was a tight-ass pro but I didn't know a thing about him. However, he knew one of my CIA contacts well enough to track me down. He'd come after me on a high recommendation and freelancers can't be too choosey about their jobs, especially in my pay bracket. Like it or not, I was hooked.

I make a final check of the paperwork. I had the appropriate maps and my pictures of the bad guys. I also had my California driver's license, auto registration for the jeep, and medical vaccination certificate showing I'd had all the required immunizations. Although I had a passport, I still intended to stop in TJ for a Mexican tourist card, automobile insurance, and fishing license, and to exchange some money. If there was anything I'd learned about travel in Mexico, it was to cover your behind with paperwork. I figured my best approach to this job was to be a chameleon, a rich *turista* doing his thing.

An hour later, looking every bit at the tourist, I headed out under the clear blue sky for the nearby sin city of Tijuana, better known as 'TJ'. I took it easy and familiarized myself with the vehicle, cruising peacefully at fifty, and enjoying the drive. In thirty minutes, I was at the border.

I had elected to go through Tijuana and over the mountains into Mexico rather than take the slightly faster and more comfortable journey down the stateside highway to Calexico and Mexicali. Like a giant ant colony, the Tijuana border crossing is the busiest in the world with hundreds of thousands of visitors entering and leaving Mexico daily.

CHAPTER 6 – RIO HARDY

Even though it was midweek and the slack period, there was a half-mile lineup of cars. I relaxed and crept along with traffic until I came to the huge multi-lane crossing. The border guards on the American side glanced at me and waved me through. It is not until you are leaving Mexico that they worry about you. I eased across the border and up to the pot-bellied Mexican checkpoint guard who barely glanced at me.

"Where are you going, *señor*?"

"Caliente!"

"*Buena.* Good luck, Sport."

As I drove by him, I wondered how many times a day he wished Americans good luck as they went to the race track to lose their money. The roads had been completely re-paved since I had last been across the border and I was impressed by their modern appearance. My astonishment ended abruptly several blocks later along with the smooth roads as I drove onto the bumpy gravel road leading into the downtown area of Tijuana. It was like driving a motocross. The narrow road was an abortion of asphalt chunks, potholes, and demolition derby drivers.

Everywhere I looked was abandoned cars rusting along the roadside. I passed the plethora of Mexican auto body and upholstery shops, where for under a hundred bucks, one could get their automobile completely redone. The yards of the tin-roofed shanty shacks were each a mini-junkyard filled with scattered debris and treasured junk collections valuable only in the imaginations of the inhabitants. For some inexplicable reason, Mexicans love to foul the air by burning old tires and the noxious odor of burning rubber created a unique aroma exclusive to TJ.

I drove carefully through squadrons of barefoot brown-bodied children running alongside the jeep, jabbering away at me and hoping for a handout. I turned left on Revolution Avenue and, as usual, khaki cops were on every corner. T-town was jumping. The streets were full of color. Pimps and hucksters selling their 'seesters' to the *gringos*. Working gals slinked from one cantina to another. Freelance cabbies gathered in small groups bragging to each other and quaffing longneck *cerveza* while waiting for their next fare.

I was tooling along carefully, trying not to create a wake when I heard a loud whistle blow. I stopped immediately and an over-the-hill khaki-clad cop with a badge and an old .38 strapped on his hip came strolling over scratching about three days' growth on his unshaven chin. It seems I had run a stop sign, which he had been leaning on. It was tacked up out of sight on a building where no one could see it. I played the game a few minutes and showed him my *licencia* and registration with a Jackson slipped between. I doubted he could read, but he gave me an understanding grin and adroitly slipped the bill into his pocket. Then he handed me back my papers and waved me on my way.

There are thousands of khaki cops in Mexico, but few of them are actually on anybody's payroll. To be a cop in Mexico, one needs only a few bucks to buy a badge, a set of khakis, and a handgun. After that, it is all a matter of guts. They live off of the *mordida*, or bribe, taking a bite whenever and wherever they find it. The most common, of course, is some form of a minor infraction, which can be anything they can dream up.

La Mordidas are the lifeblood of any kind of authority—a way for the underpaid to make whatever deal they can. It's difficult for an American to understand the concept, but in Mexico, bribes are considered more like tips, a bit of inducement to oil the skids, and get something done. It is the grease that lubricates the gears of Mexican society. The country is full to the brim with bureaucracy and the only way to deal with it is to go with the flow.

One of the biggest problems stems from the bizarre legal system, which, believe it or not, is based on the French Napoleonic code presuming a person is guilty until they are proven innocent. There is no such thing as a trial by jury. If you are accused, they assume that you probably are guilty. When trouble arises, such as a traffic accident, everyone who is a party is rounded up and locked away until the matter has been resolved. Most matters are resolved with *pesos* or dollars. The more dollars one has, the more innocent they are.

TJ always seems to have a new Mayor and new cleanup campaign, but it never works. As I got closer to the center of town, the squalor became more obvious. T-town would always be T-town. I jockeyed along in the madcap traffic, fighting the Kamikaze cab drivers and stinking diesel buses over the cobblestone and chug holes of the endurance course they call a street.

In a few minutes, I was at the *migracion* office trying to go with the flow. Two hours later I had accomplished what should have been done in ten minutes. After two more stops to buy Mexican automobile insurance and exchange some dollars for *pesos*, I was finally headed for San Felipe. I was already hot, thirsty, and sick of the country. Border towns do that to me.

Along the roadsides, Mexicans sat contentedly in the warm sun. Sitting in the sun is a national pass time. I believe that there is some genetic trait in the Mexican DNA structure that mandates each of them to sit in the sun for at least three hours a day. They do it so well. After a few minutes, I pulled off into a reasonably clean-looking cafe called the *Solitario Bracero*. An overworked migrant farm worker on a faded sign beckoned weary travelers. The Bracero Program was started because of the manpower shortage during the war to provide migrant manual labor for American farmers and stop the 'open border' policy. It had worked well from 1942 until 1964 providing over four and a half million Mexican Farm Laborers to work in the United States. Most of them sent their earnings home to support their families. Many of them obtained Green Cards and became citizens. Those that didn't buy new tools or vehicles, returned home with pride and dignity. When Cesar Chavez and his labor unions got into the act and tried to organize the farm workers, it pretty much spelled the end of the program. It is simply another example of how the meddling of Government Big Brothers can create more problems than they resolve. Now the poor and unemployed are forced to sneak across the border in search of work. God only knows what will happen if things continue to deteriorate in Mexico and they all decide to come someday.

The buzz of conversation stopped immediately when I walked through the swinging doors, but after the locals had analyzed me they went back to their beers and conversation. A plus-sized big-breasted senorita with sparkling eyes wearing a bright red float dress waddled over. She gave me a greeting smile. "*Que quiere usted*".

I smiled back. During the last five years, I'd spent many hours improving my Spanish with Lukban's wife, Maria. I gave the waitress a *buenos dias* and ordered a Tecate with lime.

I asked her how the food was and she shrugged. I supposed that to her, food was food. I ordered a *Carne Asada* steak with trimmings. A few minutes later, I was wolfing it down along with beans, rice, and flour tortillas. It was surprisingly good. I washed it down with two more beers and dropped a hundred *peso* note on the counter. She started to get me the change, but I waved her off. She was ecstatic and gave me a complete twirl of her dress to show it.

I had decided to head south to Ensenada and drive across the mountains on BC 16 rather than take the better road over to Mexicali and down. As usual, traffic was heavy, but my belly was full and I was in no particular hurry to get to San Felipe. If you want to challenge your driving skills sometime, try a Mexican country road.

I had just started the climb up into the mountains when I found myself behind a big diesel bus. Its foul-smelling fumes smothered me in a black cloud of obnoxious cheap diesel. I followed the thing at thirty miles an hour for about twenty minutes and then, in desperation, I took a chance and zipped around it on a curve.

I almost forced a pickup truck full of screaming Mexican field workers off the road, but I made it—only to wind up between the bus and a huge diesel truck, which was equally as bad. The insane truck driver and the stark raving mad bus driver began to play a sort of 'scare the hell out of the American *Viajero* game'. I wished I had taken the safer route.

All along the two-lane highway little white crosses had been erected on stone piles along the roadside. Each one represented some poor slob that had bit the bullet there. I imagined that they had tried to pass one of the trucks and gone sailing over a cliff. There were crosses every fifty yards or so. I stayed in line and tensed up each time the bus came screaming up behind me and the truck slowed down.

We climbed slowly up the mountain range and the temperature began to drop. The bus driver continued tailgating me and was having a great time amusing his passengers with his driving skill. We finally came to a long downhill grade and the truck driver poured on the coal so I wouldn't be able to pass him. I stomped the pedal to the metal and glanced in the rearview mirror.

I was horrified to see the bus zooming up behind me like a huge steamroller. The little V-6 just didn't have enough guts. I waited until the bus was about ten feet away and jerked on the headlight switch. The bus driver saw the red lights come on in the back of the jeep and I heard the squeal of his brakes as he skidded on the road behind me. I kept the gas pedal to the floorboard and zoomed around the truck at eighty miles an hour, giving him a sincere wave of my middle finger as I passed. The road ahead was clear. I chuckled to myself, feeling good about my small victory.

The air at the top was twenty degrees cooler than it had been in the valley. I knew that it would be forty degrees warmer where I was heading, so I enjoyed the coolness while it lasted. The view was spectacular and no artist could ever capture the panorama accurately—as far as the eye can see the Baja chersonese stretches, gigantic rock mountains moving off toward the horizon, and the arid deserts that had once been the ocean bottom laying at the base of these ice age behemoths.

Baja is a strange place, unlike anywhere else on Earth. It is a peninsula that varies in width from a hundred and fifty miles to a narrow point of only about thirty miles. To the west, it is bounded by the Pacific Ocean, and to the east, by the Gulf of California. Extending southward some 800 miles from where it joins Arizona and California, Baja is twice the length of Florida and a hundred miles longer than Italy. It is an incredible land of tumbled mountains, desert plains, and barren sea-swept shores.

Even though there are large agricultural areas and numerous small towns and ranches, it is mostly thousands of acres of empty wilderness. It's not that man hasn't tried to conquer Baja. It has been scratched and probed for centuries by those seeking to plunder its riches. Scattered across the peninsula are ruined missions, abandoned mines, wrecked machinery, crumbling adobe walls, and bleached bones. For some reason, a barren desolate landscape always conjures up images of gold and treasures. Baja had been plundered all right but had kept its treasures hidden.

A mountain range forms a spine from the northern border extending to the tip, or Cabo San Lucas where Baja ends in a mass of sea-sculpted rocks. The sierras, or mountains, are a continuation of the same range system that extends through the United States to the Aleutian Islands. Baja is mostly desert with some areas only seeing rainfall every five or six years. Throughout Baja, there are strange biological pockets where hardy species of plant life survive by adapting to the harsh environment.

The winding drive down the mountains lasted almost an hour. I descended carefully through the high escarpments, deep canyons, and boulder-strewn highlands. Eventually, the stratified rock began to give way to sandy mesas. Finally, I could see the delta region of northeastern Baja, a 500-square-mile expanse of silt and salt. It is almost completely barren. As I approached the desert floor, the stifling heat hit me in the face like a hair dryer in the hottest setting. I started to perspire heavily.

I was nearing the Laguna Salida, or salt lake area where the Colorado River peters out to become a narrow bone dry plain. It is a harsh and dangerous place where a fierce sun beats down upon the earth, sucking out all moisture and leaving only the parched desert. The air shimmered with rising heat lifting off the desert floor. I imagined that looking down at the Sierra de Los Cucapas was like being in a space capsule. The lonely landscape stretched out as far as the eye could see. Mirages of golden cities and billowing sails danced in the distant infinity. I could see the cones of several dust devils fitfully whirling and whistling across the vast landscape.

When I hit Highway 5 which runs from Mexicali to San Felipe, I turned south toward San Felipe and poured the coals into it. The posted speed limit on the isolated highway is one hundred kilometers, but the Mexicans drive as fast as their cars will go. The desert had been recently kissed by the rain. It was wearing carpets of purple sand verbena, patches of white primrose, and other desert wildflowers. Despite the color, the heat was still unbearable and the desert wind scorched my lungs. Although I still had a quarter tank of fuel, driving in such a remote country made me decide to fill up the first chance I got. When I saw a gasoline sign, I pulled in.

I climbed out of the jeep to stretch my legs. A young, shirtless Mexican attendant came strolling out to help me. The gasoline tank was one of those with a glass top where you could see the fuel. I felt empathy for my jeep as I watched the boy's hand pump the yellowish debris-laden petrol. A group of barefoot bright-eyed children gathered to watch the big event. I sealed American/Mexican relations by giving them a handful of *pesos* and telling them to have a *refresca*. They *mucho gracias* me gratefully. I went into the small store and bought a lukewarm six-pack of Tecaté beer. Then, I hit the road again.

I debated briefly about driving into San Felipe. I decided it would be better to arrive in the daytime and two beers later saw a sign that said 'Campo Rio Hardy'. It looked inviting, so I pulled off. The camp is one of many fishing resorts along the Colorado tributaries in the main part of the delta country. It sits alongside a large stream where willows and mesquites line the banks. There was small yellow primrose in bloom everywhere. The water appeared to have a reddish tint, almost the color of rust.

I bumped down a gravel road for a quarter mile and came to the camp. It consisted of about ten cabins and a lounge and store area all lined up adjacent to the water. The proprietor, a short pudgy jovial Mexican about fifty years old, was pleased to have me. For ten American dollars, I was provided with the farthest cabin on the right, adjacent to the river some 100 yards south of the main lounge.

I parked the jeep in the back and unloaded some gear for appearance's sake. My *cabaña* consisted of a small kitchen, a bath with a self-draining red-tile floor, and a leaking showerhead sticking out of the wall at head height. There was also a small living room area. It was third-world crude—constructed of adobe bricks—and although roughly made—clean and well kept. A cobblestone patio overlooked the river, which was almost half a mile wide in the area of the camp. Like everything in Mexico, the slow-moving water took it nice and easy.

It was getting into the evening. The air had turned a little cooler and was becoming more bearable. I walked up to the lounge and in Spanish ordered a bottle of their best tequila, tonic water, and a lime. The leather-skinned wiry old man behind the aged copper bar gave me a strange look through the thick cataracts of dark brown eyes. But, he saw the American greenback clear enough and climbed off his stool and snaked it smoothly from my hand, assuring me he'd bring my order right over to my cabin.

I went back to my patio and sat in an old metal lounge chair gazing out at the peaceful water only a few feet away. The old man arrived twenty minutes later with my order. I noticed that he had brought a large bucket of ice, which I had neglected to ask for, and two glasses on a tray. I took the hint and he graciously accepted an invitation to join me for a drink. I fixed us a couple, mixing the tequila fifty-fifty with the tonic water over the ice and squeezing in a slice of lime. I handed him one and we sipped at the drinks, which he declared very good.

His name was Carlos and he spoke his version of uniquely bent English that I found amusing. The time and place were serene and picturesque.

Various waterfowl entertained us with aerial displays and an occasional fish leaped up to snatch a bug out of the evening air. The sun slowly burned itself out and the Tequila warmed my insides. Within the twilight, a million unseen frogs started their nightly serenade and a billion crickets joined in. Without any obscuring city light interference, the uncountable twinkling stars of the Milky Way sparkled brightly above us stretching across the blanket of inky black sky.

Carlos began to reminisce about old times and I was content to listen to him talk. He told stories of dove hunting and huge catfish caught in his river. He spoke longingly of the lovely *senoritas* at the whorehouse in nearby *Cinco Siete*. Finally, with the bottle almost empty, Carlos began to wind down. From his yawns, I suspected it was past his normal bedtime. Sure enough, in a few minutes, he excused himself and said that he had to leave. He asked if I wanted anything else and I told him no, wondering if he had a working girl available. After he left, I sat for another hour soaking up life. The place reeked with contentment and I promised myself that one day I would spend some real time just sitting on this very same patio and doing nothing. The fire in my belly grew stronger and when the Tequila was all gone I went inside.

The room was still hot and sticky, so I propped open the door to let out the heat. I crawled into the bed and slipped between cool clean linen sheets that had been made soft by time and hand washing. They had been dried outside on a clothesline and smelled of fresh air and sunshine. I tossed and turned for a while and then drifted off to a sound and undisturbed sleep on the lumpy old bed.

I awoke to crowing roosters and breakfast aromas. I was soon up and devouring a breakfast, *el desayuno*, of *jamon con huevos* on the covered patio of the camp restaurant overlooking the water. After the ham and eggs, I took a quick swim in the muddy water followed by a lukewarm shower, which was as cold as the tap would allow.

The morning sun was already warm and I knew the day would be a scorcher. I packed my gear and made ready to depart. Carlos was nowhere in sight. I supposed he was sleeping in. I felt a little sad about leaving without seeing him, but then I'd already made up my mind to come back. I paid the manager, giving him a five-dollar tip. He shook my hand profusely, wishing me a good journey and begging me to come back, which I earnestly promised to do.

CHAPTER 7 – A SIX BAR TOWN

I armed myself with a cold six-pack of San Miguel for the road and hit the blacktop. The smooth two-lane to San Felipe was easy to drive. Scattered ranches and farmhouses dotted the roadside where determined people somehow created existence from the hostile terrain. The warm morning sun quickly became hot and unbearable. My shirt stuck to the seat and it felt like I was driving through a sauna. When I'd lean forward to pull it loose, for a brief instant the hot air blasting through the open window would cool me down, but the moment I'd lean back it would glue itself to my back again.

I could have turned on the air conditioner, but it felt good to sweat it out. And, sweat it out I did. It seemed as if the beer was oozing out through the pores of my skin as fast as I poured it down my throat. I passed through an area of barren buff-colored sand dunes where the road begins to wind about twenty miles through the painted mountains, or Sierra Pinta, a fantasia of vivid colors and weird shapes. Once out of the mountains, there was another short expanse of desert terrain with the delta area to the left and the foothills of the great Sierra de Juarez to the west.

Finally, I began descending from the rugged range of volcanic hills and peaks onto the sloping plain that tapers down to San Felipe. I had timed it perfectly and was just finishing off the last of the six-pack when I arrived at the outskirts of San Felipe. Not all the beer had escaped through evaporation, so my first stop was a little turn out with some privacy where I hosed down a thirsty-looking Mesquite tree.

I drove around town for a while getting the lay of the land. It was not exactly a one-horse town, but perhaps, a *seis-cantena* town would more accurately describe it. I'd arrived at *siesta* time when the dusty Spanish village was somnolent and quiet. The ramshackle buildings, by American standards, left a lot to be desired. The streets were sandy and it was as hot as the Devil's breath, making me long for a snow cone, or at least a cold brew of some sort.

It was well known that the money influx came almost entirely from the tourists and the fabulous sport fishing in the Gulf of California. The town itself rests peacefully in the neck of a picturesque crescent-shaped bay at the end of the warm blue waters of the Gulf. The bay is framed on the west by a jagged range of copper-colored volcanic mountains that protect it from the prevailing northeast winds in winter. Unfortunately, they also block it from the cooling summer winds, which cause suffocating heat when it is hot, and it almost always is.

It was a dusty tourist trap with sufficient stores to support the fluctuating population. The main drag was several blocks long—a dusty sand road containing numerous "we speak English" joints that were mostly sports fishing chartering businesses. The dirt streets were filled with an assortment of shops. The vendors were friendly and the price was negotiable. Mariachi bands suddenly materialized whenever a group gathered and disappeared back into the Cantinas as soon as the crowd thinned.

Everywhere I looked open-air boutiques were selling their arrays of silver trinkets, baskets, air-brushed paintings, leather goods, Mexican pottery, and probably even some baubles, bangles, and beads. Mexican merchants are highly creative and the many colorful facades created a fiesta atmosphere. There were also several open-air food stands with meats, fish, fruit, and other food displayed or hanging out in the open. The flies were doing well.

If they had a car at all, the small local population owned old post-junkyard automobiles, so it wasn't difficult to differentiate the tourists from the citizens. The citizens were going about their business oblivious to the *gringo* invaders. The women wore full skirts and blouses or the traditional cotton pullovers called *huipils*. The men wore white pullover shirts and sandals with white pants or jeans. Most of them had bandanas around their neck and wore wide-brimmed floppy straw hats.

It was mid-day and *Siesta* time. As is the custom, the already sleepy town was about to come to a complete stop. The mixed mongrel dogs were already slowing down and competing amongst themselves for the best shady spots under cars and porches. Out of sheer necessity, due to the stifling heat, the town would hibernate until three or four in the afternoon. The streets were dead and even the wind had stopped. The palms and India trees soared like sentinels in the glaring sunlight watching over the silent town. The smooth waters of the bay were the color of slate and stretched like a giant grey mirror off into the distant horizon.

However, I knew the Cantinas would still be going as long as the *turistas* had *dinero*. I eased the jeep into a space in front of the busiest-looking bar in

town called the '*Azul Sombrero*'. I went in to get out of the sun and survey the
possibilities. Sure as heck there was a huge blue sombrero hanging between
the stuffed marlin and roosterfish behind the bar. The joint would have been
perfect for any John Wayne movie bar scene. I stood there just inside the door
letting my eyes get accustomed to the darkened interior. The place had that
distinctive odor of stale beer, urine, and vomit. The buzz of conversation had
stopped and all eyes were on me. I felt like I'd just ridden off the range and
was the stranger in town.

Several *putas* were perched around the bar. I knew they were prostitutes
because, quite simply, upstanding Spanish women do not go into Cantinas.
If one is a lady, they do not, under any circumstance, allow themselves to
be seen unescorted in a Cantina. All women who enter do so with the
understanding that they are *putas*. Besides, these gals wore more war paint
than Indians. Their cheap perfume competed with the many other odors.

I stood there until my eyes adjusted to the dim interior. Then I walked
over and slid onto an empty stool at the bar. The conversation hum started
up again and a group of costumed *mariachis* began playing a lively Spanish
number before a table of three young, obnoxious American couples who had
been there quite a while. They were shooting tequila and their table was full
of empty shot glasses. They were loud in typical American fashion but, of
course, the Mexicans would be patient as long as their money held out.

A pock-faced bartender, who probably spoke English as well as I did,
eventually came over to take my order. He put his hands on the bar in front
of me.

"*Algo de beder*"?

I had understood him but gave him back a badly pronounced *no
comprende*. He gave me a blank look and asked what I wanted to drink in
English. I acted relieved and asked for the coldest *Cerveza* he had. He slid
open the lid on the old cooler and pulled out a Carta Blanca. He popped
the top and sat it in front of me scooping up the fifty-peso note I'd laid
on the bar. He hadn't offered a glass so I pulled down on the bottle. It
was surprisingly cold and tasted good. A moment later he plunked down
forty-two pesos in change and smiled when I slid five back for a tip.

I had given a lot of thought to whether or not I should use Spanish, and
had decided to keep that card under the table for the time being. In my line of

work, it is more advantageous to know what the other person is saying than it is to be able to communicate. This is particularly true when they don't know you know what they are saying. I was just another American clod. A *gringo*. Nothing difficult about that.

I hadn't noticed him and was a bit surprised to spot a *policiana* in a sweat-stained khaki suit seated three stools down from me. He was looking right at me and smiled and nodded politely.

"*Buenas tardes, amigo*".

I gave him a grin and replied in English.

"How are you doing, *amigo*? Can I buy you a drink?"

The language barrier was erased as he switched to English. "*Si señor!* A Cervesa would be most gracious."

He moved over onto the stool next to me and I bought him a beer. We made small talk and I judged him to be genuine. I figured that he could be an effective ally and made an effort to befriend him. It wasn't difficult, as he seemed to be gregarious in the best Mexican tradition. He was with the San Felipe Police and his name was, Jesus Gonzales (another Gonzales). J is pronounced like an H in Mexico and he had pronounced it 'hay soose'.

He was polite, middle-aged, about 5'8", and stoutly built with a clipped mustache and a laugh line wrinkled face. His stomach looked to be rock hard and I had to give him credit for being in such good shape doing a job that makes it easy to get fat.

I shrewdly worked him and three beers later, all of which I'd bought, we became good friends. He'd even offered his protection and told me that if I got into trouble, I could contact him at the *Estacion de Policia*. I thanked him and assured him I would remember if I should run into some unforeseen difficulty.

After the third drink, he moved off saying that he had to attend to some very important business, like going home. I bid him a cheerful goodbye and continued nursing my third beer while I considered my options. There were two ways I could play it. I could remain passive and spend a few days hoping to spot the girl or the Black, or I could start asking questions.

Of course, when one sticks their neck out by asking questions, there is always the possibility that someone will chop it off for them. I'll admit it. One of my biggest faults is jumping in too quickly. I told myself to be patient, but after a few hours and a few more beers, I once again realized that I wasn't cut out to sit on the fence like a vulture waiting for its prey to die. I've always been more like the eagle that impatiently goes ahead and kills something. So, I began my inquiries.

I considered trying to buy the information I wanted, but this often results in churning muddy waters prematurely. I had decided to keep the black out of it and concentrate on finding the girl. I already tipped the bartender enough to claim him as a dependent. He was as friendly as a moose in heat. I showed him the girl's picture and asked if he'd seen her.

I low-profiled it and storied him. She was a friend's sister who had recently disappeared in Mexicali. The friend knew I was going fishing in San Felipe and I'd promised him to ask around. I played it hokey straight. I think he bought my line, but he hadn't seen her. I let the subject drop as if it weren't important.

I spend the next several hours casually repeating my story and quietly showing her photograph around. One *puta* thought she might have seen her, but had no idea of her whereabouts. I was on the trail. I decided to stay in the bar as long as it seemed comfortable, rationalizing that I would be better off not circulating.

The beer was starting to get to me and I knew I had to back off. An attractive *puta* who said her name was Carmen draped herself on me. She was a good prop, so I bought her several drinks while we chatted. She made it obvious that she was hot for my body. I'd had that dance before, so I put her off, saying that I had some things to do, but would see her some other time. She finally gave up and stalked away in a quasi-huff.

CHAPTER 8 – WATCHING THE BIG ONE

There was no more to be accomplished by staying, so I left the bar feeling vaguely apprehensive, nothing tangible, just a feeling that I was overlooking something. I said the heck with it to myself and let it pass. I began making a circuit of the other bars in town. I was in my fourth Cantina and had switched too slowly sipping rum and Coke when I spotted the Black.

I etched his photograph in my mind and there was no doubt about it. It was Tate, square jaw and a face like a robot. He had walked in alone and now stood at the opposite end of the bar staring through me with a glazed look as if I weren't there, but I knew he saw me well. His eyes had the intensity of a rebellious slave about to kill his master. He was wearing khaki pants and a white tee shirt pulled tight over bowling ball biceps. His washboard abs rippled through it like furrows of a freshly plowed field. 'I had him' I thought to myself—and a lock on *mucho dinero* . All I had to do was follow him and not blow it—it was a piece of cake.

I stood there slightly amazed it had been so easy. He was a big hunk. He towered two and three feet over the heads of the *putas* who stayed away from him like he was emitting some really bad odiferous vibes. I considered making contact with him but it seemed dumb. So, I just sat and watched him surreptitiously watching me.

When you've had the experiences I've had, you could look most men in the eye and instinctively tell where they stood. Most of the ones I've stared down were afraid. Some were merely bewildered or crazy. He was neither. Tate seemed slightly nervous but confident and unafraid—I figured from knowing he could send most men to oblivion without much effort. So, I played his game. The more we didn't look at each other, the more like a caged leopard he became, and in twenty minutes he'd downed four shooters and two beers. They didn't seem to faze him.

I repositioned myself to study him in the bar mirror and watched him carefully, always averting my eyes when he looked my way. The bout was on and we both seem to know it. It was impossible not to let him see me watching him, but even harder to seem natural in not seeing him.

He reminded me of a cobra considering a strike, but not quite sure if it was close enough to drive the venom home. There was a great mystery behind those dark eyes for sure. Finally, he'd had enough and he turned and bolted through the swinging bar doors. I was there on their second swing and paused inside to watch him kick over a big cherry-red, full-. dress Fat-Boy Harley

Without glancing back, he roared off down the dirt street on the Hog, and by the time I skipped over to the jeep he was two blocks away. I let the motor idle and when I got going, he was out of sight heading southwest. I wasn't worried. He was laying down a dust trail a blind man could follow. Either he didn't care, or he wanted me to follow him. I gave it 50-50 either way. Besides, there was only one unpaved road leading in that direction. I kept a safe distance and slowly climbed the ridge that runs around the peninsula overlooking San Felipe Bay. The dust cloud was like a rainbow with my pot of gold at its end. I felt exhilarated.

After a while, he turned off onto a rough-cut road that led down to a tourist motel called the 'Suntower Lodge'. It was just above the beach across the bay from San Felipe. I was way behind him, but I took no chances and drove past the turnoff for about a mile before making a U-turn and heading back. The four-wheel drive was getting a workout. I stopped the jeep half a mile from where Tate had turned and parked it off the side of the road.

I got out and trudged over the sandy road toward the Lodge. Siesta time was over, but I hadn't gone far when I began to question what the hell I was doing— since it was still oven hot and I had far too much to drink to be wandering around afoot. The *curve* began to flow out of every pore I had. The searing heat baked my brain and the sun cauterized it. After a while, I picked up a swarm of Kamikaze gnats and swallowed them the entire thirty minutes it took to negotiate the half-mile. By the time I got there, I'd collected enough sand in my boots to build a beach. By then I realized how stupid I'd been.

I studied the peaceful seascape below. Gulls floated above the water in circular spirals, searching for their supper. Several large brown pelicans, so graceful in the air, awkwardly waddled along the deserted beach. Black cormorants sat on the rocks drying out their wings in the afternoon sun.

Frigate birds sailed effortlessly overhead with their long-forked tails and graceful wings spread wide as they rode the wind currents.

It was a beautiful scene, but there was nothing more to do—so after a few minutes, I turned around and trudged back to the jeep. By the time I had plodded my way back, my feet felt like I had just marched across Death Valley. I dumped about a pound of sand and several red ants from each boot and stared in horror at the white bubbles, which had risen on my feet.

I knew that I had made a mistake by leaving the jeep and I was upset at my blunder. This was serious stuff and mistakes like this could punch my ticket to Nevrland. I shook as much sand as I could get out of my socks and slipped them back on, followed by my shoes, which suddenly seemed too small for my swollen feet. I sat there watching the sun go down. It was a great vantage point and the sun did an incredible plunge into the water. Soon the air grew cooler and life began to move about. I was totally dehydrated and badly in need of a cold one. Having properly chastised myself and resolved to be more careful, I decided to make a move.

I drove slowly past the Suntower Lodge, which peacefully rested in the same place it had always been—having not gone anyplace since I had last seen it. Back in town I parked in front of a place called the *El Lobo* Restaurant and went in to eat. The best I could do was some very spicy Chili Colorado that left me wondering about the history of the meat. I ignored the thought and wolfed it down, soothing the fiery taste by gulping three cold bottles of Tecaté as I gradually regained my senses.

It was late dusk as I drove back to the Suntower to register. The place consisted of a long row of about fifteen cabins on a knoll adjacent to and overlooking the beach almost directly across the bay from San Felipe. A blue neon sign above it spelled out Suntower in English only with the 'S' not illuminated, making it appear to read 'untower'. Behind the blue sign, the fading sunset spent its last neon rays. In front of the cabins, there was an office and a restaurant with a hand-painted sign in English that read Casita Inn.

Behind the office and restaurant, there was a large open patio and a fully screened-in game room area. Decorative white wrought iron fencing surrounded a small kidney-shaped swimming pool where several tourists lounged under orange and yellow umbrellas sipping drinks and enjoying the twilight coolness. I parked in front of the office and went in. A short, heavy-set Mexican sat behind a Formica counter with his eyes glued to a small black and white television set. I knew better than to rush matters, so I stood there watching TV with him and waiting for him to take mercy on me.

The news was on. I got a lump in my throat when the Mexican announcer said all searches had been called off for the nuclear submarine Scorpion lost on May 29th and the crew had been declared officially dead. I knew a couple of guys on that boat and could imagine how it must have been when the hull imploded. It made me want to hit something, but all I could do was stand there and try to choke off the emotion. A few tears slid down my cheek anyway.

That was followed by an explanation of how President Johnson had assured everyone that the United States would make no further moves to de-escalate the Vietnamese war until the North Vietnamese made a serious effort toward peace. Lyndon's picture was in the background and I could tell from the tone of his voice that the announcer wasn't buying what he was selling. Neither did I.

A commercial came on and the clerk managed to tear himself away from the TV long enough to sign me up for a 150 pesos per night suite overlooking the bay. I faked wiping off some sweat and forced a fake grin as, to calm myself down about the sub going down, I signed the registration card P. Race of Skinnerback, South Dakota. He never even glanced at the signature and didn't care what I wrote or who I was. I paid him twelve dollars American and let him get back to the TV.

The room was small with requisite red hollow tile flooring and the mandatory lumpy bed. Two chairs and a small end table made up the rest of the furnishings. There was a small toilet/shower area but no closet, just several coat hooks screwed into the wall. I walked over and opened the dust-covered blind to look at the ocean. The window was already open and there was no screen. I started to shut the window but saw that it had no lock so I just closed the blind.

The water called so I got into my bathing suit and went out to answer it. It was a saltwater pool, slightly cooler than the air and all mine. I swam for about half an hour, ignoring a table of four poolside drinkers. After the strokes, I took a long shower to wash off the salt and dressed in some old sneakers, a white T-shirt, and a well-worn pair of dungarees.

I started walking over to the Casita Inn for a beer, but my heart wasn't in it since I was still bummed out. I hadn't seen anything of the girl or Tate, but the Hog remained parked in front of a cabin about four down from mine and didn't appear to be going anywhere. I wasn't tired so I strolled past the swimming pool area. The two poolside couples were still drinking, giggling, and slapping mosquitoes in the darkness. As I passed their table, I detected the strong sweet aroma of pot wafting in the evening air. The mosquitoes must have been dying happy.

CHAPTER 9 – SLIDING PUCKS

Out of curiosity, I decided to check out the game room. It was an area that had formerly been a covered patio, now enclosed by a four-foot-high cement block wall with screens the rest of the way up. I squeaked open the wooden screen door and stepped inside. At one end stood a well-used pool table with faded green felt. A ping-pong table was folded up against another wall. Then I spotted the shuffleboard. Standing there like a lost child from another era. I couldn't resist it. It was the long thin board. Not the kind with side bumpers.

There is something almost orgiastic about sliding a small silver puck over a well-waxed board. I walked over to admire it. It was a beauty, All-American, and looked to be in fairly good shape. I dropped a quarter in the money slot and some music notes beeped as the scoreboard came to life and the machine readied itself to play. The scoreboard and shuffleboard lights came on. I spied a can of powered wax sitting on the windowsill and sprinkled the board down.

The pucks were red and blue. I picked one up and it was cold to the touch. I slid it back and forth against the right edge and let it go. It traveled smoothly along the board, barely dropping over the end. It wouldn't take me long to get the touch. I took another puck and made ready to slide it. Just before I let it go the floor behind me creaked and my puck hit the gutter halfway down.

The hair on my neck stood up. My sixth sense normally sets off an alarm when someone comes up from behind. This time I hadn't heard a thing until the floor creaked. The love affair with the board had momentarily distracted me. I was telling myself to play it cool when I heard a deep, resonant male voice.

"I see you play. Care to slide some?"

Without turning around, I answered. "I've been known to."

I turned slowly to look up into two very dark pupils floating in a sea of white eyeballs. It was Tate, still wearing his khaki pants and a white tee. He still had that same expressionless face and his huge biceps. How had he gotten through that screen door without me hearing him? I gave him my best stupid *gringo* look.

"But it's been quite a while."

"Yessh, for me too," he replied. "Hey, I saw you in the bar, care for a for more cold Coronas? I've got some in my room."

"I never turn down a cold beer. Sounds good," I answered, thinking that I'd rather be lucky than good anytime.

He gave me a weak smile. "Sweet! I'll be back in two shakes." As the screen door squeaked shut behind him, I stood there in amazement. Was this real? How had he gotten behind me without me hearing him? I was slipping and I didn't like it. He was like some voodoo priest—a ghost that could walk through walls. Or was I getting too old for the job?

There are lots of rules for staying alive in this business and I'd broken several of them already. There are only so many chances. While he was gone, my mind raced through possible scenarios. The more I thought about it, the more I rationalized that everything was working out pretty well.

I'd found my quarry. Now, I just had to make sure it wasn't me who got snared. This time I heard footsteps and the screen door creaked loudly. He had a small Styrofoam cooler filled with crushed ice and Corona beer. Still, I had this feeling—but the wheels were already in motion and it was too late to jump off the train.

He pulled out a couple of bottles, popped the tops off with an opener tied with a string to the cooler, and held one out for me. "Name's Tate," he said in a deep low-pitched voice as he handed me the beer.

I took the *Cervesa* with my left and stuck out my right hand. "Pat Race".

Quick as a cobra he grabbed my hand in a vice-like grip and pumped it several times. I squeezed back, but he'd easily gotten the best part of it.

I retrieved my hand and asked, "Wanna practice first?"

He shook his head slowly. "Don't believe in it. How 'bout you?"

I called his bluff. "I'm good!"

"All right. Blue goes first." He picked up a red puck in one hand and a blue in the other and placing both hands behind his back switched them back and forth a couple of times and then offered them to me with his palms down and the pucks covered. I tapped his right hand. It was blue.

I collected the blue pucks and leaned over the board with a serious look of concentration. I did three or four sliding arm cocks and let the puck slide. It hung tantalizingly for a second over the end and fell off the board. Without saying a word, he moved in to shoot. I made a point of getting out of his way quickly, and he noticed. I thought I detected a slight grin as I scrambled out of his line of fire, but he kept his outward emotions well-checked as we played.

After we had slid all the pucks, we walked to the other end of the board to tally the score. He had bested me slightly, which is what I intended. The art of being a good hustler is being able to balance yourself on that thin edge between winning and losing. To do so, you must be better than your opponent, but not let them know that you can beat them if necessary.

When both parties are hustling, it becomes impossible to determine the real winner until the final game, the one with all the money on it. That's the only one that counts. All the rest are just sparring contests for feeling out the opponent. We sparred. He was good. Within a few minutes, we dialed the board in. He played seriously and was really into the game. I made small talk as we played.

"I'm here for the fishing. How about you?" I slid a puck down for a hanger.

He glanced up at me with his expressionless face.

"So, you're a sportsman?"

With a deft flick, he smashed my hanger hard and left his spinning in its place.

I wasn't sure if that was an innuendo, an inquiry, or just sarcasm.

"I just like fishing."

My next puck stopped three inches in front of his hanger, effectively blocking it for him. He leaned over the board.

"Yeah? And what exactly are you fishing for?" He laid a double block. I was nor oblivious as to his inuendo.

"Nothing particular ... just whatever's biting."

I sailed a smasher down to clear the board but knocked mine off instead. His hanger was still there. It was his score. We started toward the other end of the board.

"What about you?" I asked. "Are you a sportsman?"

He clicked on the points and remarked. "I'm going fishing on the El Bonita Wednesday morning. You're welcome to come?"

It was an invitation to the prom, but I mustn't be too eager. "Really? Going after Marlin, are you?"

"Nope. Tuna."

I played my cards close to the vest. "Thanks, it's an enticing invite. I'll think about it. Okay?"

He shrugged. "Sure, *No problemo*."

I'd wanted romance and instead, he acted like he could have cared less. Had he been about to cozy up? Had I blown it with coyness? I wasn't sure what to expect from him, but that wasn't it.

He reminded me of a black panther. His stealth and ebony gracefulness made me uneasy. He was cold as an iceberg, but with the personality of a polar bear. My vibes said not to screw around with him, so I didn't. I let him win the first game and most of them after that.

However, one can't play shuffleboard without some conversation, and by the time he was out of beer and we were both out of quarters, I knew a hell of a lot more about him than I did when we started.

He had let it slip that he was from San Francisco and here with a friend, whom I assumed was the girl, Mickey. They had been here several weeks and were going fishing on the El Bonita the day after tomorrow.

When he'd brought up the fishing trip the second time, I took advantage of the opportunity and accepted his previous invitation.

"Alright Tate, I will take you up on that tuna run. I'll be happy to chip in for the boat rental."

A slow smile spread across his face. It was the first time he'd shown me his teeth. They were all there and white as snow.

"Nah! It's on me. We leave about six."

I felt the spit curdle in my mouth. I was in. Or was I?

It was a little after nine when I left him there alone still sliding the pucks. As I walked through the door, I heard a loud smash as he violently slid one of the pucks down the board. I tried not to let my flinch show and didn't look back. It could just as well have been my brain exploding. Once I got outside, it made me shiver. I trusted him about as far as I could throw him, and I wasn't sure if I could throw him at all.

I was glad to get back to my room. I locked the door, and then remembered that the window had no lock. I set my small alarm for 5:30 a.m. and crawled apprehensively into the sack, expecting to toss and turn through a long wakeful night, but incredibly enough I soon drifted off to sleep. Then the familiar old evil images came to dance in my head again. It was a long night.

CHAPTER 10 – SAN FELIPE SHUFFLE

The peace of wakefulness returned when I awoke, turned the alarm off, and got ready for the day. Dawn was just breaking as I strolled out onto the patio. Nothing is as inspiring as the birth of a new day. The motel was surrounded by coral sea and peach desert and offered a grandstand seat for watching the splendid event. Lasers of fiery sunlight shot through the mountain passes from the east, creating a golden crown that blazed on the sun-capped distant peaks in the pale blue sky.

A choir of roosters trumpeted their awakening as the sleepy town came alive. Life gets an early start in Mexico and lights already burned in most of the small shacks as coffee pots gurgled and eggs sizzled. The pungent offshore was light and cool and carried its unique salty tang. It was going to be a great day.

The bay had on its best dress. A few old wooden shrimp boats bobbed on their anchors, masts swaying gently in the early morning breeze. A squadron of black brants swooped along in a vee-shaped line just above the water. Pelicans and gulls maneuvered gracefully over the water shopping for breakfast sardines. The wind-swept beach was a community of birds. The sand was sprinkled with small snowy plovers darting back and forth above the tide line. Graceful avocets choreographed their ballet to the waves while godwits searched enthusiastically through the seaweed that had come ashore on the last tide. It was breakfast time in San Felipe.

An hour later I'd enjoyed *tres huevos con tocino con patata* in the *Casita* Restaurant and was on my last piece of bacon and third cup of strong black coffee when Mickey Carey walked in. She lived up to her photograph. She wore little makeup and her soft blonde hair was done up in a braid that made a cute ponytail. Very feminine, but she was not what you would call petite. I made her 5'9" and about 130. She had deep-set azure eyes with a luminous quality, like the sun reflecting off the sea. She carried herself proudly and the good worm-bleached-out denim jeans snuggled neatly to a well-curved rump. An oversized red and a blue checked flannel shirt tied at the waist accentuated the well-mounded package beneath.

I was perched on one of four stools. There were only three tables in the small *café*. She was alone and I was the only other customer. It would have been socially permissible for her to sit by me. However, she chose a table by the window and sat alone, ignoring my presence. Finally, when she let me make eye contact, I visually pressed her, as if mentally undressing her. It seemed to make her uncomfortable because she glanced away immediately. From then on, I was invisible. As I was considering another approach, Tate walked in. Without speaking he gave me a brief acknowledgment nod and sat down across from her.

She had already ordered and told him so. I could hear their conversation easily. She said she arrived only a few minutes before from a place that sounded like Mighty-Goso. The pot-smoking couples came in for breakfast and, due to their chatter and the rattle of dishes, it became difficult to hear the conversation between Mickey and Tate. Yet, I heard her say she too hadn't gotten much sleep. After breakfast, they left and I lingered over one more cup of coffee.

I strolled over to the office where the check-in guy was still glued to his TV. For all I I knew, he had been there all night. I stood patiently waiting for him to notice me. As usual, the Kennedys were in the news. There had been no evidence of conspiracy in Robert Kennedy's death, and Senator Edward Kennedy, being his opportunistic self, was calling for an unconditional halt to the bombing in Viet Nam. Not to be outdone, President Johnson was criticizing the Warsaw Pact Invasion and things were heating up for the big Democratic conversation-starting next week in Chicago.

I banged the keys down on the Formica counter and the clerk turned around with obvious irritation to see who was there. A fifty-peso tip cheered him up considerably as I paid for a week in advance. I asked him how the fishing had been and his brain was overloaded.

"I do not know, Señor. You will have to go into the town. That is where you can find out."

"*Muchas gracias!*" I said sarcastically.

I needed a quick shower before heading for town. The water was naturally hot since there was no hot water hookup. I had to let it run a while before it was cool enough to shower in. On the way out I noticed Tate boastfully posing on the edge of the pool in zebra-striped bikini trunks.

With the morning sun glistening over his body, he looked like a bronzed ebony statue of some Greek god. Sweat gleamed on the muscles and sinews of his brute-like physique. He acted like he didn't see me, which was fine with me.

I spent the morning looking at fishing gear and strolling around the dusty town. The sane part of me felt like grabbing the money and turning the matter back to Smith. I just couldn't bring myself to do it though. Was it curiosity or some perverted death wish? Perhaps, it had been too easy and I felt like I hadn't earned it. Was my conscience involved? I had no clue.

Shortly after I'd gone freelance, a master player had told me that if my conscience ever started bothering me, it was time to get out. I'd had a rough one and had been forced to eliminate some citizens who hadn't been all that respectable.

"In the final count," he had said, "screw your conscience, the only important thing is to stay alive."

He had been killed a few months later. Was it time to walk away?

Problem is, the job is not all that easy to walk away from. The clubs won't let you. You either did your thirty behind a badge for some three-initialed organization, or you put the badge away and got out there amongst them. I'd given the CIA a good ride, but it just couldn't turn my head enough for the spook business.

The intelligence disasters of the last decade couldn't be written off as 'going with the territory'. The professionals pointed at the press for being negative or the liberals for being soft, but it didn't wash. It's hard to forgive and forget blunders when the rules are flouted and the books cooked.

I should know. I'd grown up in the business. My father, a Naval Commander, had been killed in WW II and his posthumous Medal of Honor assured my acceptance at Annapolis. I became an officer and gentleman in '52 and the SEALs made a killer out of me just in time for Korea. Later I did my first spook work for NIS. I would have probably done my military thirty if the CIA hadn't lured me away from Naval Intelligence.

I gave it a fair shot, but it is a hard trade. We had more moles than a Texas golf course. Bureaucracy is vulnerable to parasitic attack by any unfriendly willing to bend the rules; and the rules say you've got to have positive evidence and physical proof before you can act—just knowing wasn't enough. It seemed like everything was designed to protect the guilty. Screw the innocent—they didn't need protection.

It's hard to work with a paper bag over your head. I'd given it my best shot—but I didn't do well on a need-to-know basis. I mean—how many hot stoves does one have to sit on before they are cooked? Guys like Allen Dulles should never be put in charge of anything, much less the CIA. Being one of the principals, I'd gotten stuck in '61 on the Bay of Pigs and it went down hard. The '*coup de gras*' came on a bad November day in Dallas in '63 when the dream died. I'd been that guy on the grassy knoll with the rifle who disappeared. But I had been trying to protect JFK, and not take him out. The shock of what went down was so overwhelming that I froze for an instant—one that I could never get back. Then the cover-up and denials began. It hadn't been my choice to go mute, but it was that or else. And believe me, the 'else' wasn't too swell an option. But that's another story.

I had to pass the day somehow, so I shopped until *siesta* time and loaded up the jeep with some appropriate new fishing gear and a few trinkets before heading for the Blue Sombrero where I had met the policeman Jesus. Sure enough, he was camped out on the same stool. He recognized me immediately and signaled the scar-faced bartender to bring us two beers. Before the drinks had been on me, but this time we took turns buying. We chatted amiably for the next few hours until he had to go.

CHAPTER 11 – THE NIGHT SHIFT

By that evening, I had become a 'regular' and was having a good time talking with everyone. Even the scar-faced bartender broke down and let me tequila him up. Soon the local *senoritas* arrived for their night shift and I found myself buying drinks for Carmen, the one who had made a play for me the night before.

She was a trooper and laughed at all the appropriate times. Her brown deer eyes sparkled in merriment when she looked at me. She knew exactly when to bat her fake eyelashes and her shoulder-length long black hair was enticingly tossed at all the right times. She had just enough huskiness in her voice to melt a man's heart and an endearing deep-throated laugh that made me want to grab hold and hug her tightly. She was a skilled courtesan and knew how to make a man feel like a king—a master craftswoman in the world's oldest profession in a country where the job is commonplace and accepted—not looked down on or outlawed by a Judeo-Christian society, such as in the United States.

Every Mexican town of any size has an established and legalized *La Zona Roja* or 'red light district' where anything goes. They are frequently referred to as 'Boy's Town' and each cathouse is fronted by a *Cantina* where the booze flows freely, *Mariachis* entertain and the girls meet their customers. There are no particular closing hours, and the *Cantinas* stay open as long as there is someone to buy. Especially on Friday and Saturday nights when poor but horny men, mostly *campasinas*, or farm workers from the surrounding courtside, descend to dance their buns off and get their horns scraped. They swill *mescal*—inexpensive rotgut agave cactus liquor similar to tequila. I have heard it claimed that the pure stuff is nearly as potent as nitroglycerin and will supposedly explode when flung off the fingertips into the air—although I had personally never experienced such a phenomenon.

This legalization by the government allows the *politico* to keep an eye on things, and more importantly, get their cut, rather than driving that good business underground. It's naive for a government to think legislation can keep consenting adults from participating in the world's oldest pastime. Mexico has the right idea. The girls are licensed and examined regularly for health and cleanliness by government officials—VD is kept to a reasonable minimum and the politicians tactfully collect their percentage.

Unfortunately, San Felipe wasn't quite large enough to support its own Boy's Town, so it had adapted a border town ethic and allowed each *Cantina* to do its own thing. In this case, the girls floated around, plying the tourist trade wherever they found it, as well as any locals with the price of a ride. They were paid with small plastic markers for every drink bought for them at the different joints. These markers were spent like money and any local merchant would gladly accept one in payment.

Carmen who seemed to be the queen of the *Cantina* liked the cut of my jib and staked a claim on me. The other *putas* left us alone, casting daggers of envy at her for monopolizing the wealthy *gringo*. I was flattered but knew better than to let my junior partner become involved to the extent of getting in the way of the mission. But, on the other hand, she was charming and witty, with mischievous eyes that interested me. I soon found myself submitting to her beguiling *Latino* way. She was in her mid-twenties and stood a feisty five-foot-four. She wore a pleated knee-length flowered skirt and a white gauze peasant blouse pulled low to accentuate the satin cleavage between enticing-looking breasts. She was a little on the heavy side, but the curves were in all the right places. Her exotic Spanish eyes kept saying: "I dare you".

I dared. In a tourist area, nothing makes friends faster than loose money. I played *Americano,* spending money like there was no tomorrow. I soon had more friends than a politician. I danced off and on with Carmen and by nine o'clock I'd had all her leg brushing I could stand. I realized she wasn't exactly my business, but she was in the pleasure business and my business would keep her. Her flirtatious eyes held me captive, and she had a fire raging that I wanted to put out. It only took one suggestive invitation from her for me to go home with her. She lived several blocks away and we strolled hand in hand along the dusty streets almost to the edge of town.

It would have been considered a slum shack in the USA, but here it was a home. I took inventory as she lit a lantern with a big kitchen match. The three clean rooms were well organized. They consisted of a small kitchen, a bathroom with a shower and toilet, and a combination bedroom and living room.

At her request, I bought a large bottle of white wine from the bartender. She chipped chunks of ice into fruit jars from a larger piece in her icebox. The ice cracked and snapped as she poured the wine. It was good and I stood there sipping away while she kneeled over a faded rose-colored couch and patiently adjusted an old Emerson radio. She fiddled it until he turned in on what sounded like a soft-voiced Mexican crooner. She said he was Julio Iglesias and that he was famous in Mexico, but I'd never heard of him.

The kerosene lamp provided the only light and flickered softly dancing shadows around the room. I was somewhat surprised that she never once mentioned money. Instead, she appeared to genuinely like me. When she had the mood dialed in, she came into my arms. We kissed deeply, her hot tongue probing and stabbing my mouth. Like a missile countdown, the desire stirred deep within my loins. We held a tight embrace and began a slow sensual dance while she rotated her hips against me.

The old wooden floor creaked with each movement and the radio continued to play soft Mexican tunes. She was a voluptuous, teasing woman and I could feel sensuousness radiating from within her firm body. We tantalized each other until the wine was gone and the passions could be restrained no longer. She moaned with elation when I picked her up and carried her to the bed.

The sex was raw. She was completely uninhibited and hot-blooded in the way that all men want. I was the rock and she was the volcano. She was tumultuous, bringing me to a fervent eruption and making the lava flow. We writhed until the bed was drenched and we were fully spent. It was great!

I awoke with a start at a quarter to three in the morning to the loud ringing of her Big Ben alarm clock, which I'd wisely set before crashing. It was a terrible time to be getting up, but I'd committed to the fishing trip. My head pounded and sharp needles jabbed at my foggy brain. I managed to struggle into my clothes and drink a glass of cool water. Carmen lay watching me for a while but was sound asleep when I left. She had never hinted for, much less asked for any type of compensation. I debated leaving her some money but didn't know how she would react and thought better of it. There would be time later.

It was a weird night with strong winds scudding dark rain clouds across the sky. I was a little late and had to hurry down the deserted street to the jeep. I accidentally kicked an empty Coke can that I hadn't seen stirring several sleeping dogs into fits of fierce barking. It woke me up well and I hustled on down the street.

The dark clouds played hide and seek with a full moon producing disquieting moments of darkness and then sudden bursts of moonlight. Buildings and trees stood out like evil spirits lurking in the blackness. The swaying trees reminded me of ghastly dead bodies swaying in the breeze. It was a place of dreams and fairy tales, vaguely perceived and unreal. I didn't see a living soul and I reached the jeep with just enough time to climb into some fishing clothes and grab my gear. I was particularly proud of the new 8-foot flexible tip boat rod with a stainless-steel star-drag Penn reel loaded with 400 feet of 20-pound test monofilament, a rig I thought would surely impress any suspicious eyes.

I hurried to meet the boat. There were no piers because of the crazy twenty-foot tides. It meant that no large boat could get close to the beach. Therefore, I had to traverse the sand about five hundred yards to where a small row boat would shuttle us out to the larger fishing boat. I could see several flashlights dancing around near the water's edge and I knew it was the right place. I was one of the last people to arrive and almost missed my ride out to the larger fishing boat. The young Mexican in charge on the beach didn't ask any questions as I handed him my gear and jumped on board the small rowboat.

Over the years the Gulf of California has had lots of different names. It has been called the *Mar Rojo* or Red Sea, the *Mar Rojo de Cortez*, the *Mar Colorado*, and the Vermillion Sea. Prevailing sea currents sweep an endless parade of fish from the south coastal shelf into the world's largest natural fish trap, including the life-supporting plankton or algae that gives the water its red color. Plankton notwithstanding, the water is normally crystal clear, and in most situations, once away from the beach, one can see at least fifty feet down with no difficulty.

Incredibly enough, even though there are some 2,000 miles of coastline and over 2,000 species of fish, very little commercial fishing is done in the Gulf. The Port of San Felipe de Jesus is one of the few exceptions and several commercial fishing boats were operating there. It is the homeport for a small shrimp fleet and it is only when the shrimp are not running that the boats are used for charter fishing, which is how, I assumed, Tate had managed to sign up the *El Bonita*.

I hadn't spotted Tate or the girl. There were five of us in the rowboat, plus two Mexican crewmen along with our assortment of rods, reels, and fishing gear. The boat sat low in the water with the surging tide slapping against its sides as the boatmen struggled with the oars. I could hear the diesel engines of the shrimper idling and see the grey exhaust layer lying on the water. The odor reminded me of a Greyhound Bus Station early in the morning. We arrived at the larger boat in one of those moments of darkness when the moon was completely obscured.

The old wooden hull loomed out of the darkness and the exhaust fog gave it the illusion of a ghostly Flying Dutchman. We came alongside and smacked up against it in the darkness. The diesel engines were chugging away and a single light dimly glowed in the cockpit cabin. I was getting onto a boat with some people who would kill me without batting an eye if they found me out. It was a risk I had to take.

CHAPTER 12 – HOOKUP

I couldn't see a damn thing. A crewman helped me on board and as I started edging forward along the rail, I bumped into something hard and solid. I caught a flash of white teeth in the darkness and knew it was Tate. I played klutz.

"Excuse me! I haven't quite woke up yet. I'm sorry."

Tate continued smiling, although I wondered if that was sincere or a ruse to throw me off.

"Well, you made it. Welcome aboard."

As I stood beside him, letting my eyes adapt to the darkness, I tried to picture the girl climbing into the rack with him. Somehow it didn't play. As the horizon moved up and down, I began to wish that I was still wrapped in Carmen's arms. We rocked to and fro in the gentle sea and the wine began creeping up on me. I stood there telling myself over and over again that seasickness is all in my mind, but soon the diesel odor and rolling had me in a noxious limbo. I knew it was only a matter of time before the dam broke.

It was embarrassing as hell. Me, a former Navy SEAL being seasick. There is absolutely no other illness like it. I'd been there before and knew there was no stopping it once gravity gives up control and the tickle bites the throat. Take it from an expert—anyone who tells you they never get seasick has never really been at sea. I kept swallowing as long as I could, and when I could no longer fight it, leaned over the rail and heaved my guts out. I looked pathetically at Tate who seemed to be enjoying my predicament.

He was having far too much fun.

Sarcastically, he said, "I preferred you didn't start chumming until we reach the fishing spot."

I gave him a 'don't mess with me glare' but he parried it away, with an antagonistic grin on his face.

One of the crew noticed my predicament and came back to offer me some Dramamine. I refused, telling him that I'd had too much to drink last night. He seemed to understand and, in a few minutes, without me asking, brought me an ice-cold Tecaté. His 'hair-of-the-dog' remedy went down well. The boat was steaming at full throttle and making about 12 knots. By the time I'd quaffed three beers and gotten my sea legs, the sky had started to lighten up in the east. I began to feel like I might live.

The other passengers appeared to be well-to-do Mexicans on vacation. I was pretty sure that Mickey, Tate, and I were the only Americans on board. Everybody else seemed to know one another. They were coolly polite, avoiding me for the most part. They looked at each other as if they all shared some big secret. But, when I'm on a mission, people always look that way to me. Since I didn't feel all that hot anyway, that was all right with me.

We were looking for scaled treasure hiding somewhere in the Sea of Cortez. To the west, I could see powder sand stretches of beach. The bait well was filled with sardines and mullet caught by young boys casting nets into the surf. Beside it sat a barrel full of bloody fish offal for chumming. The waters around us were teeming with life and I was confident we'd find action.

We could have been out for Wahoo, Marlin, or Dorado, but it was tuna we sought. The boat weaved and turned, covering as much territory as possible, with the captain studying his fish finder and looking for working sea birds or other phenomena that would mean fish. It was a time for waiting.

We ran at cruising speed with the crew searching the water for clues. A red glow suffused the sky in the east, and the rain clouds, which had been threatening, somehow mysteriously disappeared. The quietness slowly came to life as the ever-present seagulls began their vigilant convoy awaiting the start of the chumming, which their gluttonous minds knew would soon begin. Brown Pelicans soared like sailplanes above us—occasionally dive-bombing into the water to snatch breakfast.

We were looking for Albacore, a hard-hitting, fast-running tuna ranging from twenty to forty pounds. A feeling of excitement began to manifest and I got a second wind as the dawn unfolded. Then, without warning the ocean became alive. At first, there was a riffle of silver on the water and the air suddenly became filled with excited birds. The 'boil' meant that schools of small fish were being chased to the surface by larger fish below. It was party time for the birds as they plunged headfirst into the water.

We headed for the action and within a few minutes were surrounded by wheeling and fluttering birds. The throttles were pulled back and the chumming started. It was an exciting spectacle as everywhere around us crying, fighting birds dived and battled each other for a snack. Everyone scrambled to get lines baited and into the water.

Mickey was standing coyly next to Tate who was baiting her hook. After she was in the water, he moved a step away towards the stern. It was time to test their relationship. I baited up and dangled my line in front of me, slowly working my way toward them as if I were looking for a good spot to fish. She smiled as I got next to her and dropped my bait into the water. I noticed Tate glaring at me curiously as he spooled out his line. I wanted to see his reaction when I approached Mickey and I did, but it was confusing at best.

I smiled at her.

"My name is Patrick Race! I'm sorry I never got yours."

She returned my smile.

"I don't believe we've been introduced. I'm Mickey Carey and this is my dear friend Tate." She pronounced it Tite.

"We've met," I added quickly. "He invited me on this trip." I eased behind the girl toward him, keeping my rod on one side of her while sticking out a hand for him to shake.

Acknowledging him was a good move. He smiled and waved off the handshake.

His eyes widened perceptibly and he gave me a little verbal jab.

"Feeling better now, are you?"

The ice had been broken.

"Oh yeah. I okay and think I'll make it now."

The boat wallowed as one of the crewmen threw nets of live bait over the side to attract the game fish, spreading them evenly around the boat and stirring the seagulls into a frenzied excitement. They grabbed the bait when they could before it got under far enough to swim for it. Mickey turned toward me.

She said, "Have you fished for Albies before, Mr. Race?"

"Pat," I said. "Yes, I've been out several times from San Diego and Long Beach, but never down here. How about you?"

"It's my first trip. We hear it is wonderful, except that it seems to be more work than sport."

The 'we' had to mean she and Tate. She began to talk about how much fun the ocean was. She kept glancing nervously at Tate who stood alongside her in somber silence.

Just then someone hollered, "hook up" and the fun was on.

There is nothing as exciting as a tuna boat when the fish are running. My bait was swimming away slowly as I spooled out the monofilament. I played out about forty feet of line and my free-running anchovy was moving excellently.

Without warning the line straightened and began to zip off the reel. I gave him about twenty feet and yanked the pole back hard to set the hook. The line snapped tight as the striking albacore strained against it. He began a frenzied struggle to get away and the line slowly peeled out. I let him take it for a few minutes, tightened the drag by feel to the proper amount, and began to ease him in. I pumped it slowly, not wanting to part the line, or pull the hook out of his mouth. In a few minutes, I had him within fifteen feet of the boat and I could see color as he churned madly about in the translucent water.

About then, Tate let out a grunt, as he set the hook on a strike of his own. My line was tending aft and I had to pass over two other fishermen to get clear. The fish ran completely around one of their lines and the fisherman unhappily cut it, allowing me to boat my fish. I thanked him and brought the fish close aboard yelling for the gaff.

A crewman came running with the gaff as my fish leaped and splashed about in the water below the boat. Someone had already boated a fish up forward and it flapped noisily around on the deck adding more excitement to the already hysterical situation. Mickey too got a strike and she let out an ear-piercing scream as the line tore off her reel. Her drag was too loose and I told her so. She thumbed it a little tighter, but the line was still going out.

My fish was a beauty and I had him tired and alongside—ready for the gaff. The crewman swiped at him but missed and the terrorized fish exerted unbelievable strength into one last desperate chance at survival. It dove deep, reeling off ten more feet of line. My arms ached and my knees quivered from the strain of the battle, but I horsed him to the surface again. This time the gaff man snagged him on the first try.

He yanked him up and aboard. It was a beauty and I estimated it to be about a thirty-pounder. Its silver-blue body glittered in the morning sun as it flopped around on the deck. The crewman rushed away to help somebody else boat a fish. All around me people were fighting and struggling to get their fish alongside. The man who had cut his line for me had re-strung it and gave me a nasty look as he scrambled for the side to get in the water again.

I dropped my catch into my tagged burlap bag and lowered it into the fish tank. I stored my pole into the pole rack alongside the cabin and went over to help Mickey. By the time I'd adjusted her drag properly, she must have had out two hundred yards of line. She looked at me with big blue eyes and smiled bravely as she cranked away. The fish was giving her a tough fight and I knew she had her work cut out. It could take hours, but I didn't interfere.

All over the boat, people were screaming and yelling. Tate was engrossed in his hookup, so I continued to stand by her. She seemed to welcome my attention. By the time she'd gotten her fish alongside, some thirty minutes later, Tate was into his third hookup. Several times I'd eased up behind her, putting my arms around her as if to help with her rod. The contact hadn't seemed to bother her, yet it bothered me. Each time she leaned back into me with her soft round rump, it was as if she was trying to arouse me. I had to keep backing off.

These were strong signals, and the game was afoot. I only wished that I knew the rules. Tate and the other passengers seemed to ignore us, so I told myself not to worry about it and to enjoy the sport, whatever it was. I stepped right up and put my arms around her as the gaffer snagged her fish and we laughingly hauled it aboard. It had swallowed the hook. There was just a small amount of leader sticking out of its mouth. I used some needle-nosed pliers and managed to bite my thumb good digging her hook out. I put the fish into her sack and dropped it into the bait tank.

Tate was already boating his third tuna. It was a huge Yellowfin that had been running with the albacore. It had to weigh at least sixty pounds. He had struggled with it and as his dark determined eyes met mine briefly, I felt a chill tear through me. He lifted his hundred-pound bag of fish with his left hand as if it were nothing and lowered it into the bait tank.

I suppressed the feeling of inferiority and went back to help Mickey. After we got her line back in the water, I left her there, went below. and got three cold beers from the boat ice chest. I walked over to Tate and waved one in his face. He glared at me but took it. I tried to butter him.

"That was a hell of a fish you just pulled in."

"It Sho wuz!"

By his attitude, I could tell I had now been moved onto his shit list.

I took the other two cans and strolled over to Mickey who had another hookup. I sat hers down and opened mine, drinking half of it in one huge gulp. The beer was good and as I sipped the rest of it, I watched Mickey fight her fish. It was a small one and only took her fifteen minutes to bring it alongside. Once again, I helped her take the fish off the line and put it in her sack. She was perspiring heavily and wisps of hair clung to her forehead.

Exhausted, she remarked, "I've had it for a while. I'm going below to wash up. I'll bring you back another beer."

She went below and I relaxed in the morning sun. As quickly as it had come, the school of tuna disappeared. Things quieted down except for an occasional Bonita or barracuda hook-up. Tate had moodily moved up to the bow of the boat to fish by himself by the time Mickey came up looking sexy and refreshed.

I stayed as close as she would let me and we spent the next hour lounging in the sun and being friendly. I gave her my usual rich boy cover story and she seemed to buy it. She told me that she was from San Francisco and was merely vacationing in San Felipe. She implied that she was more or less roughing it down here and said that she loved the local folks ... natives as she called them. By the time ten o'clock rolled around, we were both talking about food. As if reading our minds, one of the crewmen came around with a huge platter of hot scrambled egg sandwiches on fresh white bread and cups of steaming hot strong Mexican coffee in white Styrofoam cups.

I took a cup of Joe, two of the sandwiches, and was slightly embarrassed when Mickey only took one. I wolfed mine down and when the crewmen came by a second time, snagged one more. She had not mentioned Tate during the entire conversation and I decided to bring him up as we sipped at the coffee.

"Do you always travel with Tate?"

She didn't appear to be embarrassed.

She replied, "Yes, he's, my friend. I don't sleep with him though if that's what your thinking."

Her face was untroubled, as though she were used to defending her honor.

I faked a blush and said, "I'm sorry. I didn't mean to butt into your personal affairs."

She smiled and leaned against my shoulder. At that moment Tate glanced at us from up near the bow and suddenly broke into an inexplicable grin that left me puzzled. I wondered what the hell he was smiling at. By 11 a.m. there was darkness gathering to the far south. A little later I heard that the captain had received a radio report about a storm brewing in the south. Santa Ana conditions were stirring, forcing warm air northward toward cooling masses pressing down from the north. Because of that, and since we had already boated enough fish, the skipper decided to start back a little early.

The return trip was long and uneventful except for a large school of dolphins we encountered. They played in our bow wake, leaping and jumping, heading north, the same way we were—perhaps to stay ahead of the weather front. We got back to port at *siesta* time. While we waited for a small boat to ferry us in, I hinted to Mickey that I would like to buy them dinner, emphasizing the 'them' so that she would know I wouldn't mind if Tate came along. She thought about it.

She turned her head finally said, "I've a much better idea. There is a dinner party tonight where they'll be serving the fish we caught today. I do hope you'll come?"

"Sounds like fun. Are you sure I won't be in the way."

"No, and besides, you caught one of the fish. I'll take it and have it prepared for you if you'd like."

I considered that, but figured Tate would get suspicious if I gave up such a prize so easily.

"Thanks, but you have enough to do as it is."

She assured me the invitation was legit and that I was welcome. We agreed on the time and to meet at the Suntower Motel, where we were both staying. The small boat came and picked up Tate, Mickey, and me along with two Mexicans. We rode back to the beach in silence.

We trudged across the sand to the road, Tate nonchalantly carrying their two bags full of tuna. It seemed like my fish iweighed a ton by the time we'd reached the road.

We paused briefly at the roadside and I thanked Tate for the trip. He shrugged and grunted without saying anything. He then tossed the smelly fish sacks over his shoulder and marched off down the road toward the lodge, leaving Mickey and me standing there alone. She started to follow him and them, as if on impulse. Before doing so, she quickly turned and kissed me on the cheek.

"See you tonight, Pat."

I stood watching her cute ass jiggle as she walked away. She was a sweet distraction and a complete enigma.

CHAPTER 13 – A FISH FOR JESUS

My fish was already starting to wreak. It was the last thing I wanted to be toting around. I'd considered giving it to Tate, but I thought that might have been too obvious. The streets were deserted and I had lugged the damn thing to the jeep wondering what to do with it when I heard a horn honk. It was the *policiana* Jesus waving eagerly to me. One man's garbage is another man's treasure, so I motioned him over. He wheeled the beat-up old police car about in the middle of the street, sending sand and dust everywhere, and pulled alongside the jeep.

He gave me a big smile and made a drinking sign with his hand, holding an invisible glass, to his mouth. *"Bueno, amigo.* You want to go get *muy borracho?"*

"Good afternoon, Jesus. I'd love to go get drunk with you, but I can't right now. How'd you like an albacore?"

"Si! You do not want it?"

"I enjoyed the sport of catching it, but not the idea of dressing or and cooking it. You take it, my friend. Then you can buy me a beer the next time I see you."

To him, it was Christmas come early. He happily loaded the tuna, sack, and all, into his trunk and headed home for a *siesta.* I was relieved that the fish would be of some use to somebody. Those that think fishing trips are relaxing, never made a tuna run. I badly needed a long cool shower and some zees. I drove back to the motel and barely had enough energy left to take a shower before I fell across the bed.

My *siesta* ended as the sun was going down. I had a dull throbbing headache and was hungry enough to eat a horse. On top of that, I had to rush like mad to get ready by the time I'd agreed to meet Mickey for the party. I wanted to keep my klutzy tourist image so I slipped into a vulgar green and red luau shirt with semi-clad hula girls all over it and a pair of bright yellow pants. Americans on vacation in Mexico don't shave, so I left the whiskers. I stood there checking out my image in the mirror. I looked every bit the part of a wild American tourist all set for a Luau.

As best as I could tell, my room had not been tossed yet. I started to leave but changed my mind. I had found my quarry and was going into the dragon's lair. It was no time for taking unnecessary chances. I dug out the case photographs and burned them over the toilet, flushing the ashes. I took most of my money and all personal documents including my California driver's license, travel permits, etc., and hid them in the Nellie compartment of my jeep.

The only thing I had on me was a roll of several hundred dollars containing both Mexican and U.S. money. It satisfied me that I removed evidence that might incriminate me. A new Lincoln Continental was parked in front of number eight. I walked over and knocked on the door.

Mickey's voice from behind the door, "Come in."

I opened the door., and there she sat on the edge of the bed wearing a sexy off-white mini skirt. I stood in the open doorway admiring her legs and trying to decide if I should enter or not. I didn't see Tate, so I quietly shut the door behind me.

I was shocked by her radiance. She stood and came toward me, looking up into my eyes and smiling sweetly. It seemed like the thing to do, so I put my arms around her and kissed her gently. She pressed her lithe body firmly against me, kissing me back with an intensity I couldn't quite understand.

I eased her away gently.

I asked, "Am I dressed alright?"

She laughed. "It depends what you're dressed for?"

"Well, I didn't know what kind of an occasion it was."

"That's some outfit. I'd say you look ready to party."

"That's me, the party animal."

I let her take me by the hand and lead me out the door.

Acting coy, I commented, "I hope they have good food. I'm starving!"

She batted her eyelashes and tossed me a flirtatious glance.

"Your appetite will be appeased, I promise you."

I understood her suggestive innuendo. She smiled like a Cheshire cat.

"We've got to go now, or we'll be late."

The Lincoln looked as if it had just come off the showroom floor. I helped her into the driver's seat, and then climbed into the passenger's side. The car smelled new. It started immediately and the hum of the air conditioner was the only noise I could hear. She turned on the radio and a Mexican news report was rambling on about the hurricane heading for Acapulco and about how 200,000 thousand troops from five Warsaw pact nations had just invaded Czechoslovakia under the cover of darkness. She grimaced and turned the dial until some Mexican music came on.

"That's better. I hope you don't mind if we have to drive a , Pat."

"No, I fine, as long as there's nourishment and drink at the end of the journey."

I relaxed and watched her deftly handle the big car. We were both quiet for a few awkward moments.

Finally, I said, "Where is your friend Tate?"

"He is already gone. He took them the fish and is meeting us there." She had turned toward Mexicali and I didn't have the faintest idea where we were going. The ocean was behind us with scattered farms and the desert on the sides. It was dusk and a splendid sunset melted away with the day. She was a good driver and the ride was pleasant.

After about twenty minutes, she slowed down and turned left onto a single-lane dirt road. There was a gate across the road and a barbed wire fence ran down the roadside in both directions. A carved wooden sign hanging from crossed timbers read 'Rancho Mitigoso'. I stared to get out to open the gate but Mickey put her hand on my shoulder to restrain me.

A Mexican wearing a khaki uniform appeared from out of nowhere to open the gate. He had a sidearm and appeared to have sprung out of some nearby bushes. I couldn't believe an armed guard would be stationed at the entrance to a lonely farm road. Then I spotted the small shack hidden just off the road. Neat!

I felt leery but kept my mouth shut. We drove down the bumpy sand and gravel road, which made a gradual climb up over a mountain almost directly in front of us. I wondered who would live in a place like this as we bounced along for a couple of miles crossing over the ridge of the mountain and headed for another much bigger mountain slightly to our left.

It was almost dark as I glanced back toward the highway, but I could see nothing except the silhouette of the mountain we had just crossed. The place was invisible from the road. Although there was still plenty of light, Mickey turned on the headlights. Once she had to swerve to avoid a brush rabbit that darted in front of us. After a few minutes, we approached the gate of a ten-foot-high chain link fence with spiraling strands of barbed wire at the top.

She wheeled right up to it and I started to ask her if I should get out and open it when the gate mysteriously swung open by itself. As we drove through, I saw a small camera mounted on a cement pedestal by the roadside. It looked like I'd struck pay dirt because someone didn't want unexpected company. I swallowed hard as I looked at the chain link snaking over the rolling hills into the horizon. No one would get in here easily, 'or out' a tiny voice echoed in my head.

We were now on a paved blacktop that wound through a long gorge to end up at a mission-style single-story Spanish-themed adobe ranch house. Contented cows and horses milled about on the hillsides. There were several mini-villas clustered around some well-landscaped pathways. Several other outbuildings were scattered about what looked to be a large working cattle ranch. There were about twenty cars parked off to one side, in a large blacktopped area. A circular drive took us to the main entrance where a parking attendant in a white jacket opened the door for us.

Off to the right was a pond with lily pads where a platoon of ducks and a few geese paddled quietly near the water's edge. I could see there were secluded gardens, tile-framed fountains, and a sparkling pool. Giant Mexican fan palms swayed in the breeze. The grounds were manicured with lush tropical foliage. Winding cobblestone walkways lined with Indian Laurel and Jacaranda meandered through the gardens. Tiny white lights were strung in the branches of silver-white Palo Blanco Acacias or Lysiloma Grandida trees for illumination.

Lights blazed inside the house. It was like I had stepped out of time and place. It was the last thing I'd expected to see there in the middle of nowhere. As we walked up the red tile walkway to the entrance, I thought to myself that someone needed lots of money to maintain such a hangout.

I faintly heard angry dogs barking somewhere in the darkness, but as we approached, they were drowned out by the sound of cheerful Mexican music emanating from inside. Two large formally attired greeters attentively manned the entrance. One of them nodded to Mickey in recognition as we passed under a small portico and into a huge room where a few dozen formally attired guests stood around amiably chatting as white-coated servants scurried about with trays of drinks and snacks. The décor was over-the-top luxurious with lots of space and hefty posh furniture. The place was brimmed with hand-painted Mexican tiles throughout and walls were adorned with expensive-looking oil paintings of cattle, horses, toreadors, and various Mexican war heroes.

It looked like the party was just getting started. It was a semi-formal affair with men in expensive suits and women in evening dresses. Most of those present were Latinos, although there were a few Anglos and Asians, sporting plenty of diamonds and gold. Somehow, it wasn't my idea of what the local aristocracy should look like. For someone who had wanted to blend in, I couldn't have been more eye-catching. Decked out in my classic hula outfit I was as inconspicuous as a one-eyed loud-mouthed drunken nun raising hell in a cathouse.

Mostly, the middle class in Mexico is sparse, with the populous consisting of the haves and have-nots. The vast majority of the people falling into the latter persuasion. This place belonged to the haves ... the two percent that sucks the cream off the top of the country, in the best Latin American tradition. They were mostly the descendent of the *Mestizos*—a mixture of the pure high-class Spanish and the indigenous races. I saw no *Morenos* ... the overwhelming majority of the population. They are second-class citizens called Afro-mestizos who are people of mixed African, Guerrero, and indigenous descent—considered to be of the lower cast and unworthy of positions of power.

I felt singularly out of place as we entered the large room where people milled about. It's hard to do Shakespeare wearing a clown suit so I put on my best stupid face and let Mickey take the lead. Oblivious to their sardonic stares, she trolled us right through the thick of things and into another large room where a group of *mariachis* played and couples danced on a red-tiled dance floor.

I noticed a tall, light-skinned unusually gaunt Mexican with a pencil-thin mustache studying us intently and I found myself being pulled toward him by Mickey as if a powerful magnet was attracting her. I braced for the introduction.

He stood about six-six, but couldn't have weighed more than a hundred and thirty pounds. He had dark thick black slicked-down hair that glimmered in the lights. His face was sad with a long thin nose that hooked down over the well-trimmed mustache hovering above thin bluish lips slightly upturned at the corners. He had a noticeable dark mole high on his left cheek and sunken cheeks with a dimple on his chin. His dark eyes were narrow with tiny pupils and crow's feet wrinkles. I thought to myself that some quirk of nature had stretched its imagination. He was anything but a stereotypical Mexican. Mickey introduced us.

"Pat Race I'd like you to meet, *Señor* Tiente Solorio. People call him El Sol."

He gave Mickey a sour look of disdain as we shook. I surmised that she wasn't privileged enough to use his nickname. El Sol's bony hand was limp fish cold like a dead mackerel and his high-pitched voice was slightly nasal. I immediately didn't like him. He gave us a haughty brush-off.

"Excuse me, I must attend to other guests."

As he stalked off, Mickey looked at me for a reaction. I shrugged my shoulders.

"So that's the 'Sun' huh? I got news for you. To me, he's not all that bright."

"Well, in any case, he owns this ranch," she said.

A tray of champagne drinks floated by over the head of a waiter and I snagged two of them. I handed one to Mickey and we clinked our glasses together.

After a few minutes, we wandered into another room where a twenty-foot banquet table was buffeted out with just about every kind of food imaginable. My stomach did flip-flops. Mickey and I looked at each other and nodded our heads in agreement as we headed for the grub.

We worked our way down the table. My eyes were as hungry as my stomach, so I piled my two plates high with a mixture of everything. Mickey took a small piece of baked fish, some beets, and a lot of salad mumbling something about watching her waistline. I commented that her waistline looked pretty damned good to me, but that mine would have to watch out for itself. We found an empty corner table and sat by ourselves eating in silence.

CHAPTER 14 – THE NUTTY TRUTH OF IT

We were almost finished eating when I spotted Tate heading our way. He cut an impressive figure—wearing a blue lightweight single button suit and easing through the crowd towering above everyone. He knifed along like a dolphin parting water as they gave way for him. There was no way the suit could mask his rippling muscles, which made him about the most imposing badass I'd ever seen. He glided over to Mickey's side of the table and with a blasé nod to me, leaned down and whispered in her ear—then stalked off without so much as a word to me.

Whatever he'd said shocked her, for her face went ashen. I looked at her curiously.

"Is there a problem?"

She shrugged and moaned, "Tate's just over-protective."

"I hope he doesn't overprotect you enough to use some of those muscles he's packing around."

She grimaced and said,. "I wouldn't worry if I were you."

I started to remind her that she wasn't me, but let it pass. There was a slow song playing, and having satisfied the inner man, I asked her to dance. We strolled out onto the dance floor and she came into my arms easily. She was light on her feet and rubbed against me provocatively for a couple of slow tunes. Then a fast one began and we started to work up a sweat. Before long, she fanned her face with her hand and suggested a walk around the grounds to cool off. I was ready to get out of the place myself and readily agreed.

We took a hallway leading through the house and came out into a tropical garden area. She placed her small hand in mine and led me as we strolled past willow trees with low-hanging branches that brushed gently against us. A slight breeze made the atmosphere delightful. At the end of the path, we came to a wooden bridge that crossed over a small man-made stream, which I surmised ran over to the pond. Lights under the bridge illuminated the slow-moving water below where multicolored coy swam lazily about, occasionally nipping a bug off the top. The only thing that disturbed the tranquil setting was the sound of dogs barking somewhere in the distance.

In the pale light, Mickey's face was lovely and it seemed natural as she came gently into my arms. Our lips met in a sweet kiss and the desire was obvious. Without saying a word, she led me across the walk toward a group of six small cabins overlooking the valley. Each had a path leading to it and as we strolled along. I figured we were heading for one of them. She started humming a song that I couldn't quite catch and soon we came to the last cabin. Sure enough, she walked up the path to the door.

We went inside and she flicked on the lights. The place was nicely decorated and divided into three rooms. The kitchen was on the right and immediately adjacent to it was the combination living room and bedroom. Next to the kitchen, and in the far corner, was the bathroom. There was a large king-sized bed in the far corner of the main room against the wall. I scooped Mickey up in my arms and carried her to it, kissing her on the way. I laid her down gently and cradled her in my arms.

She pushed me away.

"I don't want to ruin my dress. Take your clothes off while I slip into something else."

She danced across the room turning off the lights and leaving me on the edge of the bed in near darkness. As she disappeared into the bathroom, I stood up and began to yank off my clothes, thinking what a lucky bastard I was. I was about to get lucky ... for the second time in two days ... and all here in my enemy's camp.

I could hear fabrics rustling as she undressed and I stripped eagerly. In a minute I was buck-naked. Patrick Junior was into the arousal and stood at full attention, impatiently waiting for her to come out. I turned the bedspread down, flopped bare-assed onto the bed, and pulled a sheet over me. In a moment I heard the bathroom door open. I peered through the darkness as she giggled and slowly stuck out one lovely white leg. I felt like running over and biting it, but it was her party.

She came out slowly, wearing a thin, transparent nightgown that faintly outlined her figure, even in the darkness. I opened the sheet and she slipped seductively onto the bed. I could smell the freshness of her as she melted into my arms. I kissed her gently and rolled halfway over the top of her. She struggled away from me trying to tell me something, but I kissed her into silence. Finally, she broke away gasping.

"Pat!" she said.

"Yes, darling."

"I just wanted to ask you something."

I kissed her on the forehead and said, "Yes Mickey, go ahead."

She said very calmly and matter-of-factly, "Someone said you were showing my picture around and asking for me at the Cantina?"

I've had many shocking moments in my rocky life, but never one as totally rattling as this one. I'd skillfully chosen that exact moment to lower my right hand while she was talking. She attempted to twist away to avoid my probe, but it was too late.

My hand passed her small firm breasts and at that exact moment made contact with her little hot button. Only it wasn't a hot button. It was a joystick, complete with a small, but definite erector set. I was dumbstruck. My brain exploded and the top of my head started tingling with blood rushing to quench the fire. I was instantly thrown into an infuriating rage. Thoughts of murder flashed through my mind. I shook my head and something rattled about inside it. I started to laugh.

What had she said? I knew I had to immediately do something violent, but what? Somehow, call it instinct, I felt the hairs on the back of my neck stand up and by the look in her eyes, I knew someone was behind me. I tried to turn over, but Mickey had my left arm pinned under her head. Damn it! I mean … his, head. I shoved Mickey away and rolled over onto my back. As I was struggling to come to my senses, I detected motion above me and intuitively yanked my head to the side, moving just in time to see something flashing downward at my face.

I jerked to the right and felt a sudden thud against the side of my head and a pain in my left ear. Through the darkness, I could make out the smiling teeth of Tate glaring down at me. I could feel his hot breath on my face. He had pinned me to the pillow. Mickey squealed and struggled out from under us to roll off the bed.

I instinctively grabbed Tate's right arm with both hands trying to push it away, but he just made a confident deep-throated chortle and slowly raised it. He held it above my head and I could see that he clutched an ice pick, which was dripping my blood. He was starting to transfer the ice pick to his left hand to pierce my other ear, or my brain when the adrenaline surged through my body with a message:

'Kill this big bastard or die!'

In a split-second instant, I let go of his right arm with my right hand and jacked it back into the pillow to get as much driving room as possible. Then, screaming at the top of my lungs I summoned everything I had to smash upwards with the palm of my open right hand. I didn't have to think about where to strike because the hand automatically sought its target. Instantaneously, my blow landed just below the bridge of his nose.

I felt the bone give under the force and there was a crunching sound as his nose broke and the Volmer cartilage shot back up into his brain. He jerked backward in pain, dropping the ice pick on my chest and grabbing at his face. He fell to the floor and I leaped off the bed and kicked him in the ribs with all my strength. It was a wasted effort because he only had a few seconds of life left in him.

I fumbled around in the darkness and found the light switch, flicking it on. Tate lay on the floor gurgling. Mickey stood transfixed staring down at Tate's motionless body in absolute terror. I walked over to Mickey, grabbed his/her nightgown, and yanked it with all my might, sending him/her flying across the room minus nighty. He/she spun like a top and bounced off the wall.

Blood was pouring from my left ear and I dabbed at it with the nightgown. I stood there looking at Mickey's skinny, well-shaped, but undoubtedly male part between his/her legs. He/she averted his/her eyes and stared at the floor. I shook my head in disbelief and went into the bathroom and turned on the lights. There was a hole through the shell of my ear. I washed the wound in cold water and dried it with a bath towel hanging there. I reeled off a handful of toilet paper and pressed it into my ear.

I went back into the main room and started to dress. Mickey cowered in a corner like a frightened animal. While I dressed, I thought of kicking him/her in the balls but reasoned that it wouldn't do any good. I finished dressing and started to leave when something made me turn around, walk over and I kicked him/her in the balls. It did me some good, but not enough. He/she lay on the floor curled in a knot, whimpering. I shook my head sadly and walked outside, one hand pressing the wad of toilet paper into my ear.

One of the primary requirements for my job is the ability to read a situation quickly. Longevity is directly proportional to doing so. I'd been told that my survival instinct made me one of the best. Now, I was being allowed to prove it. In the brief moment I had to evaluate the situation, I considered the options and concluded that there were none.

Before me, there were at least five unflinching gunmen. I didn't fight because they had their weapons pointed directly at me, so I had no chance of overcoming them. I offered no resistance as two of them moved up behind me.

I heard the sound before I felt it as my head collided with an asteroid. It tasted like a mouth full of copper pennies. The sensation overpowered all emotion and my brain became a supernova that shot me through reality into the blinding abyss of time and space. It felt almost peaceful as I collapsed. The last thing I remembered was the eerie sound of dogs barking and the smell of freshly cut green grass.

CHAPTER 15 – RATS

The nightmares were of fiery hells that blazed eternally until at last the pain brought back the world of reality. One minute I was being sexually overwhelmed by a huge black beast on a bed of hot coals and the next I was laying in the dark with something eating my head. At first, I thought I had merely jumped into another nightmare and I lay there for a moment listening and feeling the thing gnawing away at my ear. It didn't seem to hurt me any more or less, and some part of me made an analytical evaluation of the situation. After a while, I decided it was an animal.

I wasn't sure if my hands were tied or even if I still had them, but as the edges of a slow panic began to creep into my dull brain, I knew that very shortly I would find out. I tried a finger first and when I was able to move it, I tried all of the fingers and then slowly, very deliberately, I began to raise my hand toward my head until I felt the soft fury of something that was eating my ear. I grabbed it with what strength I could muster, pulled it away from me, and threw it with all my might. It smashed against a wall across the room. It squealed and I could hear other ... rats scurrying away.

I decided I wasn't dead, although parts of me felt like it. My left ear throbbed in pulsating cycles of pain. I lay there in a daze on the edge of the hard wooden cot. Somehow, for the life of me ... I couldn't move. My return to consciousness aroused someone's curiosity because the darkness was shattered by a flashlight beam that stabbed me in the face through a small barred window from within the door. The pain from the light was enough to make me cringe. I lay there trying to catch my breath and listening to footsteps clicking slowly away.

After a while, I managed to sit up. I tried to get my bearings, but I was confused. My cell was dark and stank of putrid odors I didn't want to identify. The only illumination was an eerie faint yellow light coming through the small barred window of the door. It cast pale shadows around the six-by-ten-foot room. There were solid walls on all four sides, except the heavy, solid metal door, which had a small peep window with bars to look through, and a small door on the bottom, no doubt to slide stuff into the cell.

The concrete walls were damp and the decaying timbers rotted and spotted with fungi. Huge rats and spiders roamed freely about eating each other and anything else they could find. The furniture consisted of a small wooden cot with no mattress or covers. My money, watches, shoes, and other personal effects had been removed. The personal accouterments inventory was two plastic bowls by the door. I eased off the couch and onto my hands and knees. I slowly crawled over to the two bowls and chased the busy rats away. One bowl was full of a liquid, which appeared to be water. Several bugs were floating around in it, and the other contained some gunky-looking dark stuff.

My throat was parched. It felt like they'd emptied a vacuum cleaner bag in it. I fished the bugs out of the water and cupped my hands and took a small sip. It was warm but good. I first sniffed and then struck a finger in the bowl of grog and pulled out a lump of something. I brought it up to my nose. Someone had a hell of a sense of humor. I reasoned was boiled prunes. It went down sweet and smooth. I told myself I wouldn't eat them all, but I couldn't help it. It was like trying to stretch a bag of M&M's. I'd soon eaten the whole bowl knowing I would inevitably get the turkey trots. I lay there in agony for what seemed like uncountable hours. Much later, when two more bowls of prunes and water came, I left the prunes for the rats.

It was not my idea of a fun place to be. I was afraid to go to sleep and afraid not to. My incarceration became a world unto itself, with no day or night. Time had no meaning and existence seemed only an illusion. After a while, more prunes and water arrived and the bowls began to stack up. I ate some more of the prunes and started marking time by the number of new bowls. I had six empty bowls when I woke up and puked prunes on my hula shirt. I didn't even care at that point. At eight bowls, a pitter became footsteps, followed by the loud rattling of a key in the lock and the thunder of the door clanging open.

There were three men. Two stayed outside and clanged the door shut behind a small man in a white coat who stepped into my cell. He approached me and began swabbing my ear with an astringent that burned like hell.

He was a neatly dressed forty-something Mexican and wore expensive looking gold-rimmed glasses and nice shoes. Unlike me, he smelled clean. I spoke to him softly in English.

"Are you a Doctor?"

He ignored me but continued dobbing at my ear. I was talking to myself. I took another road.

"Will I live?" I mumbled softly.

He ignored my words with the same silence.

"Screw you then. Get out of here!" I screamed.

He stopped dabbing to look at me.

"Are you going to talk to me or what?"

He spoke in perfect English.

"Your ear is infected, but you'll live. I've given you an antibiotic."

My numb mind asked, "Great, but where am I?"

"You are here."

"Where is here?"

"Here is where you are."

I wasn't up to him. He had his whole brain and mine seemed numb, dumb, and mostly gone. In a few minutes, he left, and except for the ear job I wasn't any better off. Getting myself into this fix was a mess I couldn't remedy. Why hadn't I just taken the Smith's money and hightailed it? I'll never know. I'd often admitted to myself, one of my biggest problems was not being willed to let go.

It wasn't the first time I'd stepped in it, but n my stubbornness, I wasn't writing my obituary yet. In my business, the only time you are counted out is when you are down and under. I was barely vertical, but I wasn't under. I called the bluff and lost the hand, but as long as I was still breathing ... the game was still playing out. In the long run, after you've done your best, the only thing you can do is try and hope that your best is good enough.

Time passed slowly. I collected four more bowls. Standing at the barred window, I could watch the guards walk along and look into each cell. I could see more cells across the hall and they all seemed to be identical to mine, but I couldn't tell how many or the number of guards there were. I got more prunes and water in bowls. The water helped, but I soon developed a total revulsion for the prunes. Each time I smelled them, my bowels would revolt. I relieved myself in a corner and the despicable rats cleaned it up.

I began to doze on and off and in my delusion was roller-skating across a shiny floor with a beautiful girl when someone shook me back to reality. I opened my eyes and a guard was standing over me.

"How do you feel, señor?" he said in Spanish. "You to come with us now."

I shook my head and mumbled, "*No comprende.*"

He jerked me to my feet. Even as weak as I was, I thought I could have taken him out easily, but there were two other guards at the door ... and had no idea how many were beyond that. In my sea of trouble, I just hoped the devil didn't come by in his speedboat. My legs and balance were wobbly and my bare feet felt numb to the hard coldness of the concrete floor.

Soon I was walking down the hall, with a guard on each side and one to the front and back. I felt like a lonely piece of baloney in a sandwich. We walked down a passageway to where another guard sat reading a Mexican newspaper. He keyed open a large wooden door and we took another long narrow hall that disappeared to the left in a gentle curve. The passage was about five feet wide and had concrete floors and walls. It looked like we were in some underground structure. There were doors on both sides and we walked until we came to an elevator.

One of my escorts pushed the "up" button and in a few seconds the door of the elevator opened and we got in. There were five buttons numbered two through five and one at the bottom labeled 'B'. One of the guards punched the number five and the elevator went up slowly. It opened onto a much nicer-looking corridor with a tiled floor and painted concrete walls running off from the elevator in both directions. We exited and walked left to the end of the hall. One of the guards pushed a button on the door and a small Mexican in a white steward's jacket opened it up.

We entered a large room that took my breath away. The floor was carpeted in a deep white pile that my toes buried deep into with a comfort I liked. The room was about thirty feet long by twenty feet wide. The furniture was ultra-plush and there were two sofas and three easy chairs all in the same brown leather. There was a wall-length bar, assorted cocktail tables, and at the far end in the corner, a cherry wood, kidney-shaped desk.

Behind the desk sat, my tall skinny Mexican friend, El Sol. He smirked and was smiling at me. The guards marched me over to the desk and stepped back, leaving me standing before him like a spent slave or a truant schoolboy.

He remained seated and I considered diving across the desk and wringing his scrawny neck. He was smoking a small plastic-tipped cigar and blew a stream of blue-gray smoke at me as he spoke in Spanish.

"Mr. Race, you look like shit, but I presume you feel better?"

I let my eyes widen at my name, but acted like the rest was Greek to me. I looked away. There was a small plate glass window in the wall adjacent to his desk and I took several steps toward it and was amazed when no one stopped me. The view was spectacular. The window was recessed like it had been built into a cave, and bushes were growing around the edges. Down below, a mile or more away I could see the ranch house. We were inside the mountain. El Sol's voice tried to bring me out of my trance.

"I am talking to you," he said in Spanish.

I still didn't hear him. He turned to the head guard.

"Does he speak any Spanish?"

The guard told him that he didn't think so. It was working. Solorio switched to English.

"Mr. Race?"

I cocked my head haughtily, and looked at him.

"This is some view."

He stood and walked over to me. Before I could anticipate it, he'd swung his long skinny arm and smacked me in my sore ear with a closed fist. It wasn't all that hard but the blow sent rockets of pain searing through my head. Through a great effort of will I managed to remain standing, but I'm sure there were tears gathering in my eyes. He was pleased with my reaction. My ears were ringing and I could feel a trickle of blood running down my neck.

"I don't like people who turn their back to me, Mr. Race."

I growled and looked savagely into his eyes. He evidently didn't like what he saw for he retreated behind his desk. The guards looked at each other in amusement as Solorio sat down and didn't say anything for a few seconds. I turned around again to look out the window.

It was all English from there.

"Mr. Race, would you care to have something to drink?"

By the placating tone, I knew he was probing. I nodded my head.

"How about a cold beer?"

He pushed an intercom button on his desk.

"*Un Cerveza, por favor.*"

I tested my leash. Glancing casually around, I walked over and dropped into one of the stuffed leather chairs. All eyes were upon me, but no one stopped me. I was moving about on my own and controlling the situation.

Son of a bitch, I thought. He wasn't a pro. He was just a criminal. Pros didn't play head games. They'd slit your throat and take your pulse before they left. A criminal will tie you up so you can escape testifying against him later. So, he wasn't a pro. He was only a criminal that hadn't been caught yet. The CIA were pros; the KGB and MOSSAD ... all of them ... pros. Pros are only interested in the truth. They don't buy the bullshit. A pro is a pro all the time, and not just on occasion. El Sol thought he was one, but I reasoned I'd wise him up later.

A white-coat-wearing servant came in and went to a bar at the far end of the room. In a moment he handed me an opened can of cold Bud. I took a long hard pull and punctuated it with a belch.

"Now then, perhaps we can talk," said Solorio.

He got up and walked over to sit in a chair next to mine. He had a whiney slightly nasal voice.

"I think perhaps you recall our first meeting. I'm Tiente Ruiz Solorio and you are drinking my *Cerveza.*"

I gave him a faint smile and snorted, "And I've been incarcerated in your shithole eating your damn prunes, so yes, I know your sort of hospitality well."

"He blew me some smoke and sneered.

"Ah yes. You are Mickey's friend. The type that likes boy girls."

I glared at him, wondering how sensitive his hot button was. I decided to test it.

"Did you ever hear the expression, go shit in your flat hat?"

The blood rose on his face. He bit his tongue and swallowed hard. I could see he was on the edge, but in control enough to force his silence.

"Mr. Race, would you care to have something to eat?"

"If it's more prunes, no thank you, but I could use a little more suitable sustenance."

He nodded to the steward.

"Bring him what he wants."

I thought a second and said, "meat and potatoes, and anything solid."

The guards cracked up. They were all in on the prune fest. El Sol giggled nervously. He told the servant in Spanish to go and get me something 'solid' to eat. The servant left the room. He snickered. I supposed it was some Mexican inner-circle joke about giving Montezuma his revenge.

While I waited for my dinner, El Sol sat and played with his mustache, not saying a thing, but snickering from time to time. I could tell he had an overwhelming need to talk but was deliberately concealing this truth from me. We sat looking at each other. Finally, he ran out of patience.

He snickered, "Our custody chambers do leave something to be desired. But then, one can't expect all the comforts of home when being detained against their will, can one?" Another snicker.

"What the hell are you getting off on?" I asked.

"Ah ha! A talking mood. The question is, Mr. Race, what do you want from us? You've certainly been going out of your way to seek out the er... friendship of a certain employee of mine, namely Mr. Carey. You have caused no amount of unnecessary embarrassment and now you have even permanently discharged another loyal employee, Mr. Tate. Now the question is, Mr. Race, what are you doing chasing after my people?"

"For Christ's sake, Solorio ... I just got the hots for her. How the hell was I supposed to know she was a he?"

He grinned at this as if he were enjoying some private joke. "Yes, Señorita Carey does have her ways."

I nodded my head. "Yeah, he makes a nice broad, but why did big Tate pierce my ear? I didn't do anything to him?"

He looked at me and tweaked his mustache some more as if trying to decide how much to tell me.

"It is indeed unfortunate that you found it necessary to, er... eliminate Mr. Tate. However, he was beginning to create more than his allotted share of problems. He was acting on his own when he attempted to kill you, Mr. Race, so I harbor no grudge against you for disposing of him."

Was this a ray of light? He was a cool bastard. He'd gotten onto me easily, but I could understand how. I'd begun exposing myself when I opted to start showing the girl's picture around. If you're looking for someone and they're not looking for you, sticking your head up is a sure way to get someone to take a shot at it. Had it worked too well?

CHAPTER 16 – TRUTHFUL LIES

I assumed he was trying to ascertain how much I knew. If he'd thought I was harmless, he would have probably already disposed of me. Even though he was only a criminal, he was an evil son of a bitch. Yet, he was letting me deal, so I picked the game, choosing blind man's bluff.

"I didn't kill Tate deliberately. He was going to kill me and I think I got in a lucky blow or something."

He grinned sardonically as if he didn't believe a word I had just said.

"Mr. Race, you deliberately—for reasons presently unknown to me set out to find Señorita Carey, and when you did, you deliberately ingratiated yourself. You asked numerous people in San Felipe for information regarding her, and then you tried to get intimate with her. I want to know why? I want to know who sent you here and for what? You will tell us, Mr. Race. You will tell us now ... or you will tell us later, but we will get the information with or without your cooperation!"

There it was then. His horse was out of the barn. I sat there in the chair looking at him and I knew that he meant exactly what he had just said. But, why was he speaking of himself in the plural sense? I knew it wasn't because he had a mouse in his pocket. I decided to toy with him.

"Okay! After I get something decent to eat. I don't like to sell out on an empty stomach."

I struck a vein. He stood up and nodded to someone behind me, then walked back to his desk, sat down, and lit up another one of his small plastic-tipped cigars. We sat looking at each other while we waited for them to bring my food. Two guards stood obediently by the door casting furtive glances at me.

Time passed very slowly. The silence in the room became heavy with El Sol bearing the full weight. I noticed little beads of perspiration forming on his forehead, and the guards were impatiently shifting from foot to foot. After what seemed like an hour, but in reality, was only a few minutes, a steward arrived carrying a tray of ham and cheese sandwiches and some cold potato salad. There was also a metal pitcher of cold milk.

I took my time eating and chewing the food well while deciding how I was going to play it. I reasoned that I could tell him just about anything he wanted to know and it wouldn't hurt anyone. I tactfully plowed my way through three of the sandwiches and drank half the milk in the pitcher.

El Sol watched me eat, seemingly with fascination. He had the tenacity of a waiting vulture. By the time I finished, he decided to change his approach to become Mr. Nice guy.

He said, "I do envy your appetite. I certainly wish I could eat like that. Unfortunately, I have been cursed by fate with this body and it's not possible."

I replied skeptically, "Stay in your damn downstairs hotel room for a few nights and you'll work up an appetite."

He acted like he hadn't heard me. "I suppose we might as well get on with it."

I licked my fingers and acted aloof and disinterested.

"Suits me. Where do I start?"

He came over and sat in the chair beside me again.

He stated, "How about starting with what you are doing here in Baja and why were you looking for Señorita Carey?"

"Well, you may not believe this, but I honestly thought that he was a she. This guy I met in Mexicali gave me a picture of Mickey and told me she was missing. He said there was a big reward for finding her."

He seemed skeptical and asked, "What guy?"

I took my time as if trying to work up my courage to sell out. He wasn't a pro so I knew he wouldn't kill me immediately. That would come much later ... after the torture. After he'd had his fun. So, I jacked him good. They had me anyway and no matter how I danced there was no way Solorio would ever let me foxtrot out of here alive. At some point, I would be faced with a situation where I would have to escape or die. I fully realized that if I were going to ever get out of there, it would be as a consequence of my action and not his mercy.

I needed to buy time.

"You see, I had no reason not to believe that Mickey was a girl and I was told that she had last been seen around San Felipe. This guy was offering a five-thousand-dollar reward. I mean ... I was coming down here anyway. Why not ask around?"

"That's a nice story, but a fabricated one. Don't play games with me, Mr. Race."

"Of course not!" No, I swear it's the truth.

"Enough cat and mouse ... or in your case ... rats. Exactly whom do you work for?"

Noting that he wasn't buying what I was selling, I made an admittance.

"It's complicated. Let me explain. It all started in Mexicali in a bar last Tuesday. I was having a drink and started talking to this guy named, Smith. When he found out that I was coming down here on a fishing trip, he offered me a reward to find out about his missing girlfriend. He said her name was Alice."

"And whom does this Mr. Smith work for?" El Sol was getting impatient.

"He said he was a plumber, but I don't know. I'd never seen or met him before."

He scowled. "And how were you supposed to get the money, if you found the girl?"

"He gave me the number to call, written on the back of a coaster from the bar... unfortunately... somewhere along the line I lost it."

He glared at me and shook his head from side to side. "That is pure bullshit, and we both know it!"

I told my story over and over again, amplifying and modifying it as needed. I put in enough bullshit to start a fertilizer factory.

I let him break me down slowly, talking incessantly and telling him anything he wanted to hear and everything under the sun except the truth. I was trying to convince him that I was one of those amoral types who would sell his mother to save his neck. The problem was that he refused to believe I had told him everything because I hadn't told him anything.

Could I be a dumb klutz after all? I suspected he wasn't sure and that's all I could hope. It bought me time. He sat there smoking and tweaking his mustache, listening and interrupting me occasionally to ask questions I couldn't answer.

I rambled until he seemed to be growing bored.

"Can I have a shower and some fresh clothes? I've been honest with you and I don't see any reason why you should mistrust me. I can't cause you any more trouble and I could even be useful to you."

He grinned and said, "Yes, I think you may be very useful to me."

He rose and said to the two guards, "Take this *tonto gringo* back to his cell."

The guards yanked me to my feet. As they led me out, I glanced over my shoulder at Solorio who was picking up the telephone. Who he was reporting to? The guards took me back to my cell and threw me in with the rats. At the moment, things were going pretty well.

Now that my belly was full and the cards were all on the table, I felt a little better. All I had to do was find a way out. It might be easier said than done. I was sitting in the darkness still plotting my escape a few hours later when they came for me again. This time I was taken down the hall into a room that looked like a Mexican version of a five-dollar-per-day hospital suite in a third-world country.

The same man in the white coast was waiting for me. The guards wrestled me down to the floor and bound my arms and legs with tape. Then they strapped me onto an operating table. I knew this time he wasn't going to take care of my ear. I watched him prepare something ... until the moment I was blindfolded. Then, a few minutes later, I heard several people arrive. I lay there as helpless as a newborn babe. I struggled a little, but it was hopeless. Soon I felt the sting of a needle in my right arm and heard El Sol's voice.

"Happy dreams, Mr. Race."

I tried to mentally resist, but soon slipped away as the drugs won over my nervous system and consciousness took wing. I seem to recall hearing someone mentioning peyote and sodium thiopental and other drugs I couldn't understand before it all went black. Feelings of madness and depression invaded my being and I rode with it, letting thought submerge into the dark subconscious, wondering if there would be a tomorrow, and wondering if I cared.

CHAPTER 17 – TRIPPING

I drifted on clouds of crystallized wind that blew me through porous steel walls, which solidified around me as I passed through. Gaseous solutions filled with disembodied heads swirled around like meteorites, colliding to shatter into symmetrical monstrosities that peered at me with disfigured eyes. I convulsed and coiled my body into intricate honeycombs that slid down cold steel burrows into dark caverns and recesses of the mind where evil lurked and laughed.

The journey was shockingly real. I couldn't navigate because directions didn't exist and I couldn't die because there was no such thing as death, only an endless succession of experiences. When I could scream no more, and beg no more, and my eyes had been plucked out by fire-breathing rats, existence ended and I passed into eternity through the perpetual kaleidoscope.

I was in hell. Demons danced and fires raged. It was a cacophony of screaming souls. I could hear demons speaking in grunts and squeals and smell their evilness about me. At last, they left me alone. It was peacefully cool, and I realized hell wasn't supposed to be cool. One of the demons stuck his snout right in my face and grunted, emitting a foul odor that scorched my lungs. My dream then ended.

It was not a pretty sight. I stared bleary-eyed at a fat hog through half-closed eyelids. Then I saw others. Some wallowed in the mud. Others scratched crusty backs against the board fence. Was I one of them? Could I have died and been reincarnated as a pig? Life couldn't be that ironic.

I tried to sit up, but couldn't. I opened my eyes wide to find the demons still there. They had thrown me into a pigpen. I was nude and my body was covered with slime and mud. My initial impulse was to struggle—try to escape. Common sense said otherwise. I was weak and helpless. My hands were now cuffed behind my back and when I tried to move my feet, I discovered that they were still taped together.

It was almost dark. The air was cool and I slowly realizd I was what appeared to be a pigpen with about ten or twelve good-sized hogs snorting and nuzzling about me. As if this were not enough, I could hear the anguishing noise of many dogs. They growled and barked continuously, like the Hell hounds of the Baskerville gathered in one place. They sounded as if they were experiencing great agony. I shared the same emotional state.

The hogs were surprisingly tame and for the most part simply ignored my presence in their pen. Maybe I smelled too foul for even the likes of them. I propped my head up on a pile of mud and pig poop in order to survey my surroundings. It was a typical pigsty about fifteen feet square with a sheltered section at one end and feeding troughs running across the front. Two guards stood chattering as they observed my reactions to my filthy environs. The barking seemed to be emanating from a barn that I reasoned was about a quarter of the way between the pigsty and the ranch house. The incessant noise grated on my nerves. In this entire scenario, there had to be insane minds involved.

I could see the mountain in the background and about five hundred yards away portions of the ranch house were visible. About a quarter of the way to the Ranch was a building that looked like a barn with a large circular structure that I couldn't discern behind it.

The air began to turn cool as the sun went down. The slightest breeze sent shivers of goosebumps up and down my nude body. I certainly was in a hell of a fix, but at least I was still alive. The constant howling and barking of dogs were proof of that.

My blood circulation was restricted, and when I tried to move my legs it was hopeless. The best I could do was to flex my knees and wiggle my toes. The guards watched my antics with amused looks on their faces. Under the present circumstances, any escape seemed impossible. I began to think I wouldn't survive the night in this pigsty. I was practically freezing already. I asked the guards several times in English if I could have a blanket, but they ignored my pleas and seemed to enjoy my suffering. I considered spewing obscenities in Spanish, but then thought perhaps it was wiser to refrain from antagonizing them more. Besides, my Española might be the only card I had left, and I wasn't going to play it until I had to.

The guards laughed and joked with each other in Spanish. I could make out bits and pieces of their conversation. Once, I heard one of them say something akin to me being the fat one's entertainment. I shivered in desperation and frustration as I sidled up next to a big sow. Incredibly, she seemed to accept my company. Her body heat kept me warm and possibly saved my bacon ... through the night at least.

I lay on my back and snuggled up to the sow as I stared up at the crystal-clear night sky. After a while, the drugs kicked in again and I began to hallucinate. I began to feel like I was God and that the stars were actually below me. I lost myself in the spectacle of their majesty among the dark veil. They shimmered and danced and the Milky Way became a gossamer shroud of silvery grains of time reflecting across the inky blackness below me ... in a murky lake of nothingness. They were as far away as reality and as close as shutting my eyes. My body quivered as I fitfully drifted into the merciful unconsciousness of slumberland throughout the remainder of the night.

When I awoke the next morning, my body-buddy hog had gone and I felt nearly frozen to death. There was a dark sky above and a cold wind blowing through the pigpen. I tried to roll over only to discover that my hands and legs were numb. One of the Mexican guards was smoking a cigarette. Even though I don't indulge, the smoke was enticing.

Finally, when I was sure I could stand it no longer, pinkness began creeping into the ink. I lay in the dawn chill until something started the dogs to barking again. Shortly thereafter, a young Mexican boy came out with two buckets of slop for the hogs and poured them into the feeding troughs.

I considered trying to eat some of it, but the way the hogs fought for it I didn't stand a chance. Besides, I couldn't move anyway. My lips were dry and beginning to crack, so I begged the guards.

"*Por favor*, Could I please have some water? *Agua*?"

They laughed. One of them said, "*Agua, si*!" Then he unzipped his pants and urinated on me while I lay there helpless. The warm pee splattering over my face was disgusting, but its warmth actually felt good. I hoped that one day I'd get a chance to adequately thank him. If indeed I ever again get another day.

I watched the sun move slowly across the sky, cursing myself again for not taking the money and running. As the sun did its bright hydrogen act upon the air, it got hotter by the minute. Guessed that around 10:00 a.m., I was competing with the hogs for a cool spot. The sun baked the mud and it gave off a foul odor that scorched my lungs. Even the Mexican guards had moved off about twenty yards. Everything was blistering hot and after almost freezing ... now I was simmering like a steak on the grill. Just before I turned into bar-b-cue, they came for me.

There were four of them. They cut away the tape binding my legs and lifted me to my feet. My legs would not support me, so they had to physically drag me. I wreaked like a skunk and felt like a sack of rotten potatoes as they dragged me toward the barn. The nearer we got, the louder the barking became. As we drew closer, I could see that the building behind the barn was some type of a small arena. Then we were in the barn where the barking dogs created sound shock waves that ripped the mind. I couldn't help but take a deep breath of the cooler air. It was flavored with that rank manure and molted straw aroma found exclusively in barns.

Night came again, and I couldn't make out the details at first. The barking made my ears ring and it was hard to think. As my eyes slowly adjusted, I saw wire cages stacked around holding the dogs. There were about two-dozen very large mutts. It was easy to tell they hadn't been nicely treated because they were growlingly angry and mean-looking. They were damn scary pets—mongrelized mixtures of wolf-like German Shepherds, Pit Bulls, Rottweilers, Doberman Pincers, and various unidentifiable breeds. They watched with glazed and hungry eyes as I was manhandled about and strung up like a dead cow with my cuffed hands looped above my head over a swinging suspended hook secured to a four-by-four cross beam.

Then the guards sprayed me down with cold water from a hose turned on to its maximum pressure. The heavy spurt stung my body as it knocked off the mud and pig excrement. When I was rid of the stench and grime, the guards left me hanging there alone. By standing on my toes, I could relieve some of the pressure, but in my weakened condition I didn't have the strength to support myself. I allowed my body to collapse, putting all the strain on my arms. It had all been too much. I have discovered that when I get tired enough, it's best to simply let go. So, I did. I closed my eyes and let the bliss of unconsciousness again wrap me in its arms once more.

CHAPTER 18 – HANGING AROUND

When I came around again, my arms felt like they were being ripped out of the sockets. I quickly rose on my toes. I could feel the toes popping in both feet as I strained to relieve the pressure on my arms. I sure as hell couldn't take much of this.

I surveyed my situation. The dogs were all in individual cages. They were doped or rabid, judging by the saliva that dripped continually from their mouths. They stared nervously from their small wire cages like new zoo animals. Occasionally, something would set one off and they would all break into fits of barking that reverberated through my spine. It was the cruelty of the worst kind. The barn was unbearably hot. I hung there for what seemed an eternity or two. Then I began to hear cars arriving outside, but for some reason, I wasn't sure I wanted to find out why.

Just before I was going to give up my ghost and die, I heard voices approaching the barn. One of the big double doors swung open and there stood a group of people looking at me. Despite my dire situation, they were all very jovial.

El Sol was leading the pack. With him were three well-dressed Mexican men and one woman. I put the men in their mid-twenties. They all wore expensive Fedora straw hats and had oily, slick black hair, tailored three-hundred dollar raw silk suits, and buck-fifty Italian shoes. The class was erased by the *Puchuco* tattoos on their hands and penetrating eyes full of arrogance. They looked like the type that picked their teeth with a stiletto.

However, it was the woman who filled up the eye. She was huge, perhaps 250 and tall, a shade under six feet. She was lost somewhere in her fat forties or fifties and had a face that matched her grossness. Her oversized lips were a garish bright red with off-putting reddish-orange hair and hideous inch-and-a-half long nails painted gold like Cleopatra claws. She wore a bilious purple and rose-colored floral sack dress that had to have been turned out by some psychotic tent maker.

She was carrying a glass of champagne and wearing more gold and diamonds than Sammy Davis Jr. on his best day. She'd probably been semi-attractive when she was fourteen, but now her bloated face begged for mercy. She had bags under both eyes and thick dark brows that looked like she had been using tar for mascara. In short, she was fat and f'd up beyond belief. She smiled at me lasciviously with greedy eyes that traveled over my nude body like she was looking at an expensive fur coat she was about to try on. Despite my agony, the mere sight of her sent shivers up my spine.

As Solorio led the group over in front of me, the dogs stirred into a new frenzy of barking. He stood casually examining me while waiting for the dogs to quiet down a bit so he could talk. When he was finally able, he chatted amiably in Spanish speaking directly to the woman as if I were not there.

"Here's our American Toreador, Señora Gonzales. He's been hanging around all day."

Everyone laughed but me.

"He's held up remarkably well, despite our harsh treatment. He's good. Even Dr. Ruiz's truth serum couldn't' break him. He wouldn't reveal to us his employer. No doubt it's some government agency. Perhaps, the same one as the other *gringo*. He knows about our printing business, but it doesn't matter for soon we won't have to worry about him."

She licked her big lips and lumbered over to where I was hanging. I considered spitting at her but restrained my anger. The men followed her like she was the lead fish in a tank and knew where the food was.

She stood before me sipping from the glass in her left hand, eyeballing me like I was a warm cookie. My eyes were glued to hers and she dipped her pudgy fingers in the champagne and brought them up to my mouth. She pushed a sweaty palm up against my lips and all I could see were gold and fat fingers. The champagne tasted salty and the gold felt cold. There was at least one ring on each finger and I assayed the hand out well into six figures. She slowly slid her hand downward and when she passed nipple city I knew she was going to travel south of my border.

Sure enough, she grabbed both of my testicles in her right hand, lightly juggling them as she smiled. She slowly lifted the champagne glass with her left hand and took a sip while making a vice grip with her right hand. Her eyes sparkled as she squeezed away. It felt like my entire body was on fire and I did the only sensible thing. I passed out.

When I awoke, they were gone but the dogs were insanely barking and pawing at their cages. I hung there watching the dogs and trying to tell myself that I'd been in worse situations. Offhand, I couldn't think of any. Something was gnawing at my brain and I couldn't dig it out. I was trying to remember something Solorio had said that I had thought was important.

Then a vision of the fat woman licking her big greedy lips floated across my mind and I remembered—he had called her Señora Gonzales. I had found my quarry. Then I remembered he had referred to me as an American Toreador. Some men came in and began to move some of the dog cages over near a sliding door that looked like it led out to the arena.

I kept on hearing people's noises. Sounds of laughter and conversation filtered in from the area of the arena. A crowd gathered out there as if waiting for the entertainment to begin and I had this horrible feeling that I was to be it. My gut squeezed into a knot and I tried to tell myself that this wasn't happening to me, but it was. Pretty soon the guards came and took me down. They released the handcuffs yet my hands and feet were numb, so I fell to the floor. They let me lay there for several minutes while waiting for my circulation to return and then they began kicking me until I got to my feet.

CHAPTER 19 – AN UNHAPPY TOREADOR

When I was able to stand on my own, they opened the sliding door and shoved me into a large round drainage pipe. My legs didn't want to work at first. I could see light at the end. It was obvious they wanted me to go through it, and having no other alternative I stumbled into the stygian darkness of the musty tunnel, my eyes straining to adjust.

My heart pounded as I plunged toward the opening. I took my time, taking slow deep breaths and trying to regain some strength. The stale air smelled of manure and blood. I lurched along, trying to come to my senses. When I reached the end, I stepped out into bright sunlight and was completely blinded by the glare after being in the darkness. As my eyes slowly came back into focus, I could see I had entered a small pit-like area where three or four dozen people sat high in grandstands anxiously watching me.

The stadium had a hard-packed sandy floor and solid wooden walls about ten feet high. There was no other exit except the tunnel through which I'd entered. It suddenly dawned on me that it was a small coliseum for fighting—or more likely—they'd created an extra large dog-fighting pit. It was barbaric and it seemed I was to be the Christian being fed to the lions.

A burst of applause reminded me of my nudity. How could they enjoy such vileness together? I remember thinking that El Sol must have some all-powerful control to be able to expose that many people without fear of being outed. The collective evil was almost beyond comprehension. They could have at least given me underwear to die in. Feeling ridiculous and embarrassed, I did the first thing that came to mind. I shot them the finger and took a bow. The applause grew louder.

El Sol sat next to Gonzales. They looked quite content. I started walking toward them when a noise from the tunnel caught my attention. A hefty dark brown German Shepard came charging straight at me. The hair on the back of my neck bristled. In a brief instant, I had to evaluate the situation before the dog reached me, I could see froth bubbling out around its fanged-back teeth. No doubt it was rabid. That's all the time I had because the dog was in the air.

Using more instinct than reason, my weakened body kicked my legs backward and I dropped face-first flat to the ground. The dog sailed by over my head, striking me with its rear legs, and tumbling. An adrenalin rush made me somehow find the strength to rise to my feet before it righted itself. I started to advance toward it, hoping to take it by surprise. I was way too slow. It growled and fanged its teeth.

While I tried to decide if I should attack the dog, it stood there snarling deep in its throat and looking at me pathetically. It appeared to be as confused as I was, and for a brief instant, I thought perhaps it wouldn't attack again. Then instinct took over and it started circling me slowly, its head shook, causing slobber to sling from its jaws. It hunched into an attack position, so I knew it would soon spring.

A myriad of thoughts flashed frantically through my mind. I reasoned that guard dogs are taught to go for the throat and I wondered if this animal had once been a guard dog. Despite its rapid rage, would that training remain locked in its fevered mind? It kept its head low and began to circle faster. I turned slowly, keeping my face toward it. The vile witnessing audience was deathly quiet. I thought to myself how I'd like to get the audience two or three at a time in the arena with me. That would have been entertaining.

Suddenly, the Shepherd sprang again, leaping high in the air, fanged teeth searching for my throat. This time I was ready, and I fell away backward grabbing for its legs with my hands as it got even with me. Luckily, I somehow got hold of the right foreleg.

Continuing my backward fall, I jerked its leg downward with all my strength as it sailed over my head. I first felt and then heard a resounding snap just before I released it to fly through the air over my head and land on the hot dirt and manure of the arena. I rolled quickly to my feet ready for another attack, but the dog was helpless. It pawed the earth a bit and then lay there with the bone sticking through the skin of its broken leg, biting its tail and rump, making dark red blood flow over the ground.

By now, my eyes adapted to the brightness and I could see my despicable spectators. In a brief moment, I recognized some of them. They were the same people who had been at the party and some of them had been on the fishing trip. A few were laughing at my victory, but some of them looked gloomy. Gonzales looked at me as though she was disappointed. Had this been ancient Rome, I knew her thumb would be turned down. My mind raced as I searched for a possible way out. In addition to the ten-foot-high wooden wall, I could see armed guards posted all around the area and there was no other visible way out ... except the tunnel.

I was looking toward it when I heard Solorio's whiney voice cry out in Spanish. "*Dos perro!*"

A lump of fear materialized in my throat and I staggered over against the wall of the arena just outside the tunnel and waited. Two frenzied animals came running out, one right behind the other, not even aware of my presence. The fools calling the shots didn't realize what to expect from the dogs. I looked over at Solorio and Gonzales. She smiled and said something to him, which caused him to frantically motion for them to speed things up by making rapid circles in the air with his hand.

He yelled out. "*Tres mas!*" that meant three more.

Great! Now there would be five dogs in the ring with me. The first two dogs ended up practically in the center of the ring viciously fighting each other. A huge wolf-looking mutt charged right past me and ran toward the two fighting dogs. Another dog—a massive Doberman type—came trotting out slowly, thick gooey slobber dripping from its mouth. It froze just outside the tunnel its attention directed at the three fighting animals. Then it sensed my presence behind it and started to turn its head toward me.

I couldn't wait any longer. I grabbed it from behind in a death lock to break its neck when I heard a soft padding sound behind me and felt something bite into the calf of my left leg. I continued squeezing the dog in my arms, but the Pit Bull chomping at my leg managed to get enough of a hold to pull me over onto the ground.

I squeezed with my right arm, using all my strength and letting go with my left hand to reach down and grab the Pit Bull. This proved to be a dumb move because it quickly got hold of one finger and bit down. I could feel its teeth sink in, striking the bone. I tried to pull it up to me, but the dog in my right arm was wiggling loose and I had to ignore the other one. I somehow got my finger free and wrapped both arms around the dog in my arms crushing it against me with all my might.

The Pit Bull wasn't getting enough action because it began to work its way up, obviously going for my testicles. I felt something snap in the

Doberman in my arms and I started to let go, but it was still conscious and I had to continue holding it with my right arm. By now the Pit Bull had moved up and was preparing to attack my manhood.

I continued squeezing the dog in my right arm while I used my left hand to fend off the Pit Bull momentarily by slapping at it. It opened its mouth wide to snap down and without thinking I instinctively rolled toward it, jamming my left hand into its open mouth, ramming it as far down its throat as I could. It crunched down without much effect. The Doberman in my right arm began coughing and making gurgling noises. I shoved my left arm even further down the throat of the Pit Bull and it too started to cough.

My mouth was full of sand, blood, and hair. My brain screamed at my rational mind to just get away and let instinct handle it, fight the animal with the animal. My mind called a bluff and abandoned me completely. The reason was gone and the animal was in control. I rammed my left arm in and grabbed hold of something that felt like guts. The dog convulsed and vomited on my arm.

I lay there with my death grip. I could feel the hot sand burning my bare skin, and over the murmuring crowd, I could hear my own heart pounding like a sledgehammer. I slowly released the Doberman. It was finally still. The Pit Bull impaled on my left arm still showed some signs of life, so I grabbed it by the ear with my right hand and rammed my left arm as far as I could down its throat. Its eyes bulged as it gurgled and sputtered blood around my arm. It had tried to clamp down and my arm was stuck. I rolled over to get a better position and slowly pulled with all my strength until my arm came out with a slippery, sickening pop.

I glanced at the audience. Everyone sat transfixed, as though frozen in time. The only sound that could be heard was snarling and growling that the three fighting dogs were making. I tried to struggle to my feet, but they wouldn't support me and I fell to the dirt, catching myself with both forearms. My lungs ached with pain that I had never felt before and then I heard El Sol's squeaky voice cry out in English from his corner of hell.

"Send out more dogs!"

I somehow found the strength to stand up. I tried wiping the blood from my eyes and saw my mangled fingers. The sight made me furious and I brought my bleeding hand up to the top of my head like a salute and swung it out flinging blood at the audience.

I shouted as loudly as I could, *"Ye estoy hasta aqui!"* An often-used Spanish saying meaning ... I've had it up to here!

I started staggering toward the tunnel—the only way out. The audience stared at me in wide-eyed disbelief. I glared up at them through blood-red eyes.

I thought to myself, "You dirty bastards! I'll live if it kills me!"

I bolted directly into the tunnel to meet the mad dogs running out to kill me. Somehow, I managed to muster a surge of energy, which gave me the strength to let out a long primal scream as we charged each other. "Aaaiieeeeaaahhh!"

The tunnel amplified the sound and when we met in the middle I was wailing like a banshee from hell. I guess I spooked them as much as they scared me for they seemed as confused as I was. I somehow managed to run right through them in the dark. My heart almost exploded as we passed each other. Perhaps, there was a chance after all. I summoned everything thing I had in running toward the closing tunnel gate ahead.

CHAPTER 20 – THE ESCAPE

I twisted in mid-air and leaped the last six feet to hit the sliding door with my shoulder and all of what was left of me. The boards splintered in all directions, most of them falling with the door across the two astounded guards who had been knocked to the floor. Using my momentum, I rolled over toward the nearest guard and snatched the 45 automatic from his holster before he even realized what happened. I cracked him on the skull with the gun butt so hard it sounded like a sledgehammer hitting a railroad spike. He was down and out.

I quickly jacked the chamber back and flipped off the safety, pointing it toward the other guard who was still groggy but was now struggling to his feet. I stuck the gun right in his face, and he started to put up his hands, but changed his mind and reached for his weapon. That was all the justification I needed. I pulled the trigger and shot him point blank in the face, splattering blood everywhere. The deafening gunshot set my ears on fire with a loud ringing that momentarily vetoed rational thought.

I frantically searched around as the dust began to settle. I couldn't believe it. I was alive. I jumped to my feet and started moving toward the double barn doors, but I could hear excited voices and footsteps approaching fast. There were two handles on the doors and I quickly drew them together and grabbed a shovel I spotted leaning against the wall. I jammed it in between the two handles; temporarily locking the door from the inside, although I knew it couldn't hold for long.

The gunshot set the remaining caged dogs barking and howling loudly. Then I realized that part of the ringing in my ears was coming from them. As I stood there, watching them hysterically biting and pawing at their cages, I had a brilliant idea. I ran over to the cages and began to throw open all the latches while leaving the doors closed.

Once I had unlocked them all, I started flinging the doors open before the dogs could react. I leaped onto the ladder going up to the hayloft. The freed animals began jumping out of their cages and were sizing one another up, as if unsure what to attack first. I lay there panting on the loft floor.

Then I heard someone yell out in Spanish, "Break the damned door down, you idiots!"

I crawled over to the edge of the hayloft and peered over just in time to see the door fly open and three Mexican guards came racing into the barn. When they saw what was waiting for them, they turned and fled with the dogs snapping viciously at their heels. A few seconds later all hell broke loose. The air was full of screams as the savage canines found their way into the spectator's stands.

I caught a glimpse of Gonzales sprinting for the ranch house with one of the animals snapping at her portly ass. I tried to laugh, but it hurt too much. I hobbled over to the hayloft window, which faced away from the fighting area and house in the direction of the pigsty. There was a rusty pulley with a rope hanging on it that reached within eight feet of the ground and I swung out and began lowering myself until my arms gave out and I dropped the rest of the way landing on my feeble legs, which collapsed like rubber.

My ankles hurt like hell from the fall and my shoulder was throbbing where I had hit the door, but I managed to hobble over to the nearest cover. It was a sage and cactus thicket, which led down the valley away from the mountain. Only then did I realize that I had left the gun laying in the hayloft. A costly mistake, but it was too late now. So without weapons or clothes, I started into the scorching heat of the day. The blazing hot sand seared my feet as I stumbled along.

I staggered forward until I could run ... and ran until I was totally out of breath. Fortunately, it had been downhill and I managed to get a half-mile or so away before I could go no further due to the stabbing pain in my hands, arm, and sides. I paused to listen for anyone following me. There was a furious cloud of dust on the road leading out to the highway made by cars streaming away from the ranch. I could hear an occasional shot, which I assumed to be one of the dogs going down. I sat down on an uncomfortable rock in the shade of a fifteen-foot-tall ocotillo and took a quick inventory.

I had assorted cuts, punctures, bruises, a mangled and broken finger, no clothes, no gun, no food or water, only a half-assed idea of where I was—and to top it off—I was no doubt now infected with rabies. I'd certainly been in better situations in my life. I consoled myself with the fact that I was still kicking—at least until rabies set in—and even this unpleasant scenario was more hope than I'd imagined a few minutes ago.

I figured the temperature was hovering in the low hundred and something when I started moving again. I didn't have time to rest. Death was chasing me and when the only thing standing between you and death is you, it somehow lessens the hopelessness of exhaustion.

I tried to recall everything I knew about rabies. I knew it to be a highly infectious disease, carried in the saliva of the affected animal. I wasn't sure what the incubation period was, but I reasoned that it would come on rapidly and knew I only had a short time to get help or die.

If I didn't, I knew I would start to become depressed about everything and eventually go into convulsions and probably try to kill myself. I also knew that one of the biggest dangers of the disease is the hysteria it causes following a bite. Telling yourself to be calm, and doing it are two different things. I had to get back in control somehow. I tried to remember what I had once learned in the desert survival course I'd taken with the Navy SEALS at Twenty-nine Palms years ago.

Practically every plant, tree, or shrub that grows in the desert has some purpose. It may be a friend or a killer, but it has some use, like the giant Cardons all about me. Their pear-like fruit is inedible, but their white flowers secrete a sweet sap much like honey. I plucked off several flowers and sucked at them, the sweetness giving me a slight, satisfying surge. But, it wasn't just the sustenance of food I was after.

My priority had to be a protective coating for my skin. Using a large rock like a hammer in both hands, I knocked a small limb off a Cardon and placed it on a larger flat rock. Then, using my hammer rock, I began pulverizing it. Once I crushed it up I began smearing the sticky substance all over my body. It felt good on my skin. I coated my feet good and then sprinkled them with loose sand, which stuck in the goop creating a thin protective coating against the burning sand. It made walking almost bearable.

A short time later, I came across a Jojoba plant, which has sweet-smelling berries that to me taste a lot like almonds. I gathered a handful and munched at them for energy as I hot-footed it along. I desperately needed to do something for my tender feet, which were being fried by the hot sand despite their sand coating. I searched desperately for an old six-pack cover or some other garbage, but apparently, tourists hadn't yet frequented this part of the world.

A bigger problem soon presented itself for I had come to the edge of life. Before me, as far as my eyes could see, lay countless miles of rolling sand dunes and death. The area was so harsh that even cacti couldn't survive there. The sun was at its height now and its intense heat was already taking its toll. The easy thing to do would have been to find some precious shade—lay on the ground and die.

I was sure that they would send someone out after me—if only to make certain that I was dead. Heading out into the desert was certain death. I considered trying to make the road, but a nude, bloody, rabid Caucasian would have little chance of hitchhiking down a Mexican road. It also occurred to me that they would have men on the road, just in case I tried a foolish stunt like that.

I walked out into the desert a few steps. The scorching sand burned my feet and the blazing sun seared my skin. I knew that I couldn't survive an hour out there, and I resigned myself to the fact that I had to make my stand where I was. But how? An unlikely plan began to creep into my brain. It was all I had so I went with it. I backtracked a bit to where I'd passed a large mesquite tree and carefully ripped a big branch down. I began dragging it behind me as I traversed the edge of the desert making my way toward the east and civilization.

I made sure that an occasional footprint was outside the path of the limb as I weaved back and forth, occasionally falling in the sand as a dying man might have done. Then I spotted a rock outcropping consisting of several large garage-sized boulders and several smaller ones nestled in a heavy thicket of Mesquite and Cholla cactus.

It was time to set the stage. I was some two hundred yards away from the rocks so I turned and staggered out into the desert dragging my branch behind me. I intentionally laid out a slalom stagger over two sand dunes but could go no farther because the scalding sand was unbearable to my blistered feet.

Being very careful, I reversed my path and began walking backward, using the branch to make sure that no footprints pointed back towards the boulders. I was sweating heavily and my feet were in agony. When I reached the edge of the dunes, I turned around and saw that I had been somewhat successful in making it look as though I had stumbled out into the desert trying to cover my tracks behind me.

I used the branch to sweep away my tracks to the rock area and then stripped the smaller branches away until I had one rather crooked limb. I selected a large boulder that looked as if it would conceal me from the ground. Next, I found a half dozen softball-sized rocks. One by one I tossed the rocks and the branch up on top of the twelve-foot-high boulder.

Once I managed to get them to stay up there, I had to climb it. It was boiling to the touch, but using the last bit of my strength, I managed to drag myself up on top of it. I felt like an egg in a frying pan lying spread eagle on top of the huge boulder in the mad dog sun.

I used one of the rocks to fashion the branch, pounding the end of it into as good of a point as I could. When I was done with my makeshift spear, I lay as motionless as possible. Every movement placed some new portion of my bare skin into contact with the hot rock. I kept recalling another time when an old warrior had once told me that if you sold your soul to the Devil, you had no right to complain about the heat ... something I found to be quite ironic and highly appropriate in my situation.

After a while, my eyelids became too heavy to keep open and I fell into an exhausted trance. Something snapped me alert and I rolled slightly, burning my skin and almost falling off the boulder. I cursed silently for mentally drifting and wondered if they had come by already or not. By the sun's position, I decided that I hadn't been out for more than a few minutes at most. I could feel my pulse in the fingers and arm of my mangled left hand and arm pounding like hell. My shoulder throbbed and I ached all over. My legs were cramping up from being in one position for so long.

I began to daydream. More time passed and I found that I could barely move the fingers of my left hand, which had swollen up like a water-filled rubber glove. It had been at least two hours I thought—perhaps three—since I'd escaped and I was beginning to wonder if they were going to come after me. The sun beat down mercilessly. Now and then I could hear the sound of gunfire coming from the area of the ranch house. I took pleasure in thinking of all the trouble I must have caused. Then I heard them!

CHAPTER 21 – ROCK WHACKED

Nature protects her animal children by allowing them a warning of creatures stalking them. A hunter or anyone else who has ever spent any time at all in Mother Nature's domain will tell you that it is almost impossible to sneak up on someone hiding. I should know. I've tried it.

My stalkers were not hunters. They sounded more like a troop of rowdy Boy Scouts. Now and then, I would hear the snap of a broken twig, a silent muffled curse, or the sound of someone slapping at an insect. I clung silently to my hot rock and tried to keep my breathing as shallow as possible.

I waited tensely as they drew nearer. Then I saw them. There were three, all khaki uniformed Mexican guards. My heart sank when I saw that one of the men held the leash of a German Shepherd. I knew the dog's incredible sense of smell was thousands of times better than the ability of its human counterpart. Even though the dog wasn't a bloodhound, it was evident it had my scent. It would sniff at the ground and then look around as if to see if the guard noticed it also, not realizing that the handler couldn't smell the distinct odor. Each man carried a shotgun slung casually across their arms as if they were rabbit hunting. I suppose they figured that I would not be any more difficult to trap and kill than a rabbit. They took their time scanning the woods with one guard on each side of the dog handler.

I caught glimpses of them as they moved toward me. They were hot on my trail and I breathed a sigh of relief when I saw them pass about fifty yards to the west of where I was hiding. I peeked over the edge as they got even with my rock. The dog stopped and its ears stood up. As far as it was concerned there might as well have been a red-painted stripe two feet wide leading straight up to where I was hiding. It looked right at me and I thought I was a dead man. The dog knew I was there all right. Its problem was how to communicate that message to the lard-ass bastard at the end of its chain. The handler was in charge though and gave the leash a hard yank dragging the animal onward. The dog turned and looked up at him, then shook his head as if to say "what the hell" and trotted on. I thought that I would rather have the brains of that animal than those of its master any day. The dog continued to glance back in my direction, but the Mexicans ignored it, obviously following the visual trail I'd laid out.

They were soon out of sight, but I could hear them telling each other to be quiet and slapping at insects. When I heard their laughter, I realized that they had come to the dunes and spotted my tracks leading out into the barren sand. I was about to climb down when I heard them returning. What was up?

This time there were only two of them and the guy with the dog was absent. I assumed they had left him waiting by the edge of the dunes while they went back to make their report. They were blabbing away and going to pass right under me. I considered leaping down on them from my rock, but I told myself that I would probably miss and break my damned neck.

I chose my stick and one of my best rocks, knowing I had to go after them fast. I waited until they had passed by and climbed down as quickly and quietly as I could.

I dropped to the ground and discovered that I could hardly move my feet at first. I gathered myself onto my legs to then quickly get the circulation back into them. I then went quietly after them. Only a real fool would take a rock and a stick to a gunfight, but I intended for these primitive weapons to be my equalizers, intending to avoid their guns. They were laughing and talking about the crazy gringo, the mad dogs, and about how one of them almost got El Sol. Because I wasn't wearing any boots to squeak, or clothes to rustle, I got to within ten feet of them and was just about to charge when the one on the right heard something that alerted him and looked casually over his left shoulder. His eyes grew wide with terror and he started to open his mouth to yell, but by then it was too late.

I rushed them like a charging rhino and was only two steps away when I released the rock in my right hand with as hard a throw as possible. It smashed him right in the face making a sound like a watermelon being hit with a sledgehammer. He went out quickly and didn't even have time to scream before he fell. The other guard started turning a fraction of a second later. He tried to avoid my spear and started bringing up his shotgun to blow my brains out. He'd only raised it a few inches when I drove the stick into his gut and we both went sailing several feet, smashing into the ground with me on top. My makeshift spear protruded from his stomach and, as I pushed it to the side of my body, the shotgun fell across his chest. I grabbed the barrel with one hand and the stock with the other, jamming it up under his windpipe and pressing down.

He put his hands on the gun and tried to push me away. When he realized that was impossible, he began clawing desperately at my hands and then tried in vain to pull the spear out. He attempted to scream, but only a muffled sound escaped his lips. I kept pressing down with all my strength. His eyes stared into mine and I watched death come to claim him as a victim. It takes longer to strangle someone than most people imagine. The long seconds seemed like an eternity while he continued struggling.

Finally, his strength abandoned him and he relaxed, succumbing to the inevitable. I kept pressing down. Cyanosis set in quickly and his face started turning blue. His eyes bulged and rolled up into his head just before he passed out. Everything became silent and still except my pounding heart and rapid breathing. I collapsed across his inert body waiting for reality to return. In a few moments, I checked both their pulses. They were in their next life. It had been a while since I'd looked into death's eyes from so close.

I lay there panting while watching a large red ant crawl across my arm. After the ant had crossed and I was sure my heart wouldn't burst, I sat up. I sized up the two and decided that the one I had smashed with the rock was larger and nearly my size. I flipped him over, but when I saw his face, or what was left of it, and how bloody the mess was, I decided to use the smaller guard's shirt. I began stripping them. To protect my feet I put on both pairs of socks. When I got them down to their underwear, I remembered how I had felt back in the arena, so I left them both wearing their skivvies.

Getting dressed was a slow process. My swollen left-hand complicated matters. When I tried to shove it through the long shirtsleeve, pain shot up my arm like I'd stuck it in a fire. Somehow, I managed and in a few minutes, I was wearing the shirt, jacket, and hat of the smaller man and the pants and shoes of the other. The well-worn shoes were too tight to tie, but by leaving the laces loose I managed. Anything was better than punishing my feet any further.

I dragged the two bodies behind a large rock and scooped sand over them. By the time I'd finished, my clothes were drenched in sweat. I took inventory. Weapon wise I was in pretty good shape. I had two shotguns and a standard-issued U.S. Military forty-five caliber automatic. I checked the clip and noted it only contained five slugs instead of the maximum seven. I rammed the clip back into the gun and stuck it into the waistband of my pants. I was a little disgusted at finding a U.S. military weapon being used by these creeps, but I remembered that the Mexicans legitimately purchase most of their weapons from the United States.

I checked one shotgun and was startled to find that it wasn't even loaded. The guard would have felt stupid if he had managed to pull the trigger. I cleaned out the jacket pockets and found eight twelve-gauge shells. I loaded the shotgun and put the rest in my jacket. Not wanting to lug it around, I buried the other shotgun. I started walking back toward the ranch house but kept worrying about the guard with the dog. He could mess me up either by going back to the ranch or walking out into the desert to find the end of my trail.

It wasn't what I wanted to do, but it had to be done, so I turned around and started back for him. I moved slowly, inching my way toward the place I hoped he would be waiting, stopping every few minutes to listen. I made slow but steady progress. I came up to the south of where I thought he would be to use the soft sand to muffle my footsteps. When I was about a hundred yards away, I spotted him sitting in the shade of a mesquite tree, staring out at the desert.

He had cruelly secured the leash of the dog to a small Cardon some ten feet away in the hot desert sun. If it struggled, it would become entangled in the cactus. It was obediently lying there as it watched me make my approach. When it growled, I'd have to shoot. The guard was whittling on a twig with a pocketknife. His shotgun lay beside him on the ground. I had the forty-five cocked with the safety off.

As I got closer, my worries diminished. When I was fifteen yards away, I thumbed the hammer shut and then quietly stuck it back into my waistband. When I was laying on the rock previously, the dog had tried to warn him of my presence but had only suffered for it. As if teaching its master a lesson, this time it just watched me with ears pointing upward. While I eased up behind him, the Mexican casually whittled away. I was within five feet with the shotgun cocked and trained on him.

I snarled and said, "*Bueno, amigo!*"

He stopped whittling and looked up at me like he'd just been hit with a hard-driven golf ball on his forehead. He slowly closed the knife while the dog placidly took in the situation with unconcerned eyes. He began to tremble and his dark brown complexion turned ashen with fear. As I pointed the shotgun at his head, I recognized him as the one who had urinated on me while I was in the pigsty.

I smiled and thought, "Thank you, God."

He tried to smile but his trembling lips only managed to part enough so that I could see his teeth chatter. I slowly reached in and unsnapped the chain from his forty-five and eased it out of the holster. I picked up his shotgun and carried all the guns about fifteen feet away and dropped them on the ground.

I turned around and he was just getting to his feet. He realized that I was giving him a chance, but he wasn't all that happy about it, even though he was about my size. We looked into each other's eyes and I started slowly toward him. When I was five feet away he flicked open his knife again and the blade glittered in the sun. I continued toward him and he stood as motionless as a wax statue with the knife pointed at me, his eyes glued to mine.

Very few people are capable knife fighters, and he didn't look to be one. When I was within striking distance, I tested him by blinking my eyes quickly and he jumped backward, proving he was an amateur. I smiled and feinted with my right hand. As I'd anticipated, he swung wildly at it, stabbing in the air as if he were sticking a stationary target. I brought my left arm down across his right wrist in a hard slashing blow that met his upward swing, knocking him forward to the ground. As he fell, I kicked his right shoulder with the point of my right boot, throwing him over on his back. The knife flew out of his hand.

He started to scream and tried to stand at the same time, but as he got to his knees, I kicked him in his Adam's apple, snapping his head back and cutting off the scream. I slashed him across the eyes with an open karate chop that broke his nose and knocked him over onto his back leaving his legs buckled back under his body. I could have toyed with him more but didn't feel like playing games. I jumped high into the air and landed with all my weight and both feet on his right leg. It made a loud cracking sound as it broke. He went out cold.

Our brief commotion had started the dog barking. It had been straining at its leash, but now that the action appeared to be over it stood there watching me. Its tongue hung out of its mouth and I could hear its rapid panting over my heartbeat. I wiped the perspiration off my forehead. Then, avoiding the dog completely, I grabbed the guard by his broken leg and dragged him back under the tree he'd been leaning against. Taking my time, I stripped off all his clothes and used his belt to make a loop around the ankle of his broken leg. There was a good-sized limb on the mesquite tree about six feet off the ground. I propped him against the tree and looped his belt around it, hoisting him into the air upside down.

It took all my strength, but I managed to hold him up while I wrapped the belt around the limb and knotted it securely, leaving him hanging suspended a foot off the ground. His unconscious body began clonic spasms and jerked violently as it felt the pain of his broken leg. He was bleeding from the nose and had a large blue welt forming where I had kicked him in the neck. A piece of bone was sticking out of his leg. He looked fine to me.

His shoes were two sizes larger than the ones I had on, so I put on his socks over the other two pairs and eased my feet into his high-top work boots. My feet quivered in appreciation. I put on his shirt and quickly buried the rest of his clothes in the sand. I had hoped he would come to while I was urinating on him, but he didn't. I zipped up and started to leave, but the dog's whining cry made me turn around. It sat staring at me with big brown eyes and I walked over to where it was tied up. I kneeled and held my hand out cautiously to let him sniff it. As my hand got within six inches of the dog's mouth, it snapped viciously at me and I yanked back just in time to avoid the jaws.

In an angry reflex, without thinking, I smashed the dog in the mouth with the butt of the shotgun. It fell to the ground and began writhing about, blood flowing out of its mouth where its teeth had been. Then I realized it had probably attacked me only because it smelled the odor of rabid dogs. I knew it would die if left in the sun and I felt sorry for it. I unsnapped the leash and dragged the wounded animal into the shade over by the guard, securing the leash tightly around the Mexican's throat, and walked away. I stopped after a few yards and looked back. The dog had stood up and was licking the Mexican's face with a bloody tongue. The revenge hadn't felt all that good.

CHAPTER 22 – MAKING A BREAK

My gas tank was running near empty and my feet hurt like hell so I took it slow and careful, stopping every few minutes to rest and listen. In an hour, I was concealed in a thicket about two hundred yards from the ranch house watching the guards making their rounds. It was late afternoon and I decided to wait until dark before making my move. I studied the guard situation closely and believed I spotted them all.

There were four cars, a pickup truck and Tate's Harley parked in the front drive. As best I could tell, there were about five armed guards posted at intervals around the ranch. The closest one to me was by the main entrance of the house. He would occasionally disappear inside for a few minutes and then come back out to stand in the doorway.

The arena and barn were on my left, about midway between my hiding place and the ranch. There was brush cover up to the arena, but from there to the ranch it was all open ground. I'd have to cross the open area either running and firing or walking and waving. I did not detect any guards stationed near the arena, so I was reasonably certain I could make it that far unobserved.

I lay quietly until just after sundown when four more guards headed into the woods with flashlights some two hundred yards to the east of where I was hiding. They were going out to check on the three who had gone after me. It would take them at least an hour to find the dead guards and the one hanging from the tree. The sun was sinking fast and I knew it would be pitch dark in another half hour, so my luck was holding up in that respect.

As soon as the group going into the woods was out of sight, I began crawling toward the barn keeping the shotgun handy. It took me about twenty minutes to crawl the fifty yards. I remembered the Stalking Games we played in SEAL Training. Each situation varied, and we learned to blend in with the landscape and become invisible. The closer we got to the subject, the slower we moved. Initially, we'd stalk smoothly and quickly from cover to cover, becoming stealthier as we drew closer to the target. At short distances, our movement became painstakingly careful as we snaked low and slow over the ground.

With the sun down, and concealed in twilight shadows, I stood behind the barn, mentally preparing myself for what I had to do. It was time. In my condition, I certainly wasn't up to a mad dash, so I casually sauntered out from my hiding place and started walking slowly toward the house. I tried my best not to limp and kept my eyes on the guard standing in the doorway. When I was twenty-five yards away he looked at me through the darkness and I raised my hand and waved at him, mumbling something low and intangible in Spanish. He waved back. I kept walking.

I strolled nonchalantly up alongside the nearest black Lincoln sedan while the guard in the doorway scratched his chin and looked at me. I stuck my head into the open window and almost shouted with glee when I saw the keys dangling from the ignition. I thumbed back both hammers and laid the gun across the top of the car, slipping my finger through the trigger guard. While I did this with my right I used my swollen left hand to open the door. The pain was excruciating. That was as far as I got.

The guard on the porch shouted and started to aim his rifle at me. I squeezed the trigger and the shotgun jumped backward in my hand. He was framed in the doorway and my shot caught him right in the chest, propelling him backward into the ranch house. I tossed the shotgun on the seat and leaped into the Lincoln, slamming the door and pumping the gas pedal at the same them. I prayed for it to start on the first go and it did.

By the time the engine was running, another guard came storming around the side of the house. He ran right up to the passenger window, so I lifted the shotgun with my right hand and pulled the trigger. The deafening explosion and concussion momentarily numbed my mind. I stared at the hole in the window where the guard's head had been. Glass was falling all around and my ears rang like I was inside of a huge tolling bell. It took me a few seconds before I could see and think well enough to put the car into gear.

I snapped out of my trance and dropped the empty gun, jamming the gas pedal to the floor. The big motor roared to life and I grabbed the wheel with both hands and left a trail of burnt rubber and flying gravel behind me as I skidded away from the ranch house. I fought to stay on the road, but the big car kept sliding from side to side until I realized I had to ease up on the gas pedal to keep control.

I thought I heard the sound of gunfire coming from behind, but couldn't be sure because my ears were still ringing. I wasn't about to stop to find out. By then I was going seventy over a road that was designed for twenty-five miles an hour. The Lincoln bounced, swerved, and skidded all over the road. With a lot of luck, I managed to keep it at least half on the road all of the time.

I slowed and hit the chain link gate doing thirty. It sprung open and I poured the juice into it over the mountain. I reasoned that if I could reach the main road I only had two choices. I could head for Mexicali, which is what they would think I'd do because it had the sanctuary of the American border. Or I could head toward San Felipe, which was a dead end. But first, I had to get past the guard or guards at the entrance of the main gate. I knew they would be waiting for me.

I had the headlights on bright and about a half mile from the gate, I could see two guards standing in the middle of the road. They were both pointing rifles at me. I saw a flame leap from one of their weapons. The windshield shattered. I instinctively threw my right arm up to protect my face as the inside of the car was filled with small shards of flying safety glass. I punched the gas pedal down harder and scrunched down like a low rider on Sunset Boulevard as I headed straight at them.

My only chance was to make them think I was a madman. I began blinking my headlights from bright to dim as fast as I could. About that time, the car hit a gully and bounced up into the air like a stone skipping across water. I kept seeing the flames spit out of their weapons and hearing the shots smack into the car. When I was fifty yards away, I turned the lights off. All of a sudden, their easy target was gone.

I was heading for them fast. I stomped the accelerator to the floor and pulled the light switch. The glare suddenly engulfed them again. By then, I was less than fifty feet away. I twisted the wheel as sharply as it would go to the left and hit the brakes, putting the car into a slide. They tried to react, but by then it was too late. They both tried desperately to scramble out of the way. I caught one of them with the right rear fender and sent him flying into the fence. The Lincoln had completely reversed itself, but momentum continued to carry it toward the highway.

It smashed through the gate in reverse with boards splintering and barbed wire scraping across the top. As it slid to a stop, I slammed the car into park and jumped out, emptying the forty-five through the dust at the other fleeing guard. I heard a loud cry and saw him drop. I glanced around. The guard I'd struck with the car was gift-wrapped in barbwire and totally out of it.

I looked back toward the mountain and could just see the faint glow of headlights approaching the ridge. Using the empty forty-five like a hammer, I broke out both taillights, got back into the car, and turned the lights off. I slammed the car into reverse, backing it onto the road with the front pointed toward San Felipe. I punched it and drove as fast as I dared, straining my eyes to see into the darkness. The front end wobbled like crazy and shards of glass blasted me through the broken windshield. I used all of the roads and when I rounded several curves, flicked the lights back on and accelerated to eighty miles an hour.

I began to feel shock setting in. The road was hypnotizing and I knew I was fading fast. The warm wind blasted me through the open windshield and I kept shaking my head to clear my mind. I turned on the radio and put the volume up as loud as it would go. The car was instantly filled by the loudest rendition of "Rancho Grande" anyone ever heard. I'd hoped the noise would keep me awake, but it only irritated me, so after a few seconds, I turned it off.

The pavement weaved and danced in front of me. I had to slow down to sixty to keep the car under control. I felt fatigued as it was creeping up on me until I was driving in a semi-conscious stupor, unaware of anything but the swaying blacktop. The wobbling front end set up a vibration that felt good, although the power steering made handling the big car effortlessly. I could feel myself letting go. My lethargy ended when I felt the car sail into space. I consigned my dilapidated body to the gods of fate and the world spun around. Then oblivion closed in and everything was quiet except for the sound of metal expanding and air hissing out of a tire.

CHAPTER 23 – ROADKILL

I was in a deep sleep when I felt something warm on my cheek. I cracked my eyelids to discover the face of a small brown angel touching me. I started to shut my eyes again when I realized that the angel was a young Mexican boy. I tried to sit up but there was a steering wheel in the way and I remembered that I had been in a wreck. The boy's eyes were wide and scared.

He spoke to me in Spanish. "Are you okay, *Señor*?"

I replied in Spanish. "I think so. Who are you?"

He pointed and said, "My name is Juan. I live there. I heard the crash and rode my bicycle here to see what has happened and I found you here."

"Do you speak English?" I asked.

"*Si*. I mean... yes... *un poco* ... some."

I sat up, noting that the steering wheel was pushed back two feet farther than it should have been and that the Lincoln was at a steep angle. With his help, I crawled out and stood in waist-deep roadside weeds testing my various parts to see if they all still worked. One of the headlights still burned brightly and I quickly turned it off. I looked back up toward the road and whistled when I saw that I was a good fifty yards from it. The top was smashed down and it looked like it had rolled several times.

The boy watched solemnly as if waiting for me to tell him what to do. I studied the angle of the car and realized that I had gone off the road, over a gully into a field of weeds. I looked at the boy.

"Juan, will you help me? I'll pay you."

"Yes, *Señor* ... no pay is not necessary."

"Thanks! Then help me cover up the car so that it can't be seen from the road. I don't want anyone to know I've wrecked it."

He nodded his head indicating that he would help me, so we started pulling weeds and piling them on the Lincoln. The boy saw what I was doing and had an inspiration.

"Wait *Señor*, I know something better."

He started walking out into the field and, having no idea what he had in mind, I staggered after him. He stopped about fifty yards away at an excavation with steps leading down into the ground. Across the top was a large, faded tarpaulin covering the hole.

"This is my *querencia*."

I wasn't familiar with the word and I told him so.

"It's my special secret place," he explained. "We can use this to cover the car up."

We drug the tarpaulin back and began pulling it over the Lincoln. Just as we were finishing, lights came speeding down the road from the direction of the ranch. I grabbed the boy and jumped behind the cover, hoping that they wouldn't see the skid marks or anything else that would indicate I'd gone off the road. Two cars sped by and the boy looked up at me with questioning eyes. I put my hand on his dark hair and ruffled it.

"Okay, Juan. Do you think your bicycle will hold two of us?"

He nodded his head and we started wading through the grass toward the highway. When we climbed up onto the road, I looked back at the Lincoln and was pleased to see that it was completely hidden from view. Since I hadn't braked at all, there were no skid marks or other signs to show where I'd left the road except for the crushed grass where it had rolled to a stop. I reasoned that by morning it would have returned to near enough normal to pass any but the closest search.

With some difficulty, I managed to sit the small boy on the handlebars of the fenderless bicycle, which delighted him to no end. Despite my aching hand, arm, and sore body, using the last of my strength, at his direction I peddled the hundred yards or so down the road and into the yard of his house. It was a small shack with adobe walls and a tin roof. A large hungry looking white mongrel dog, which reminded me of the ghost of a wolf, started barking ferociously as we approached.

He was, no doubt, unaccustomed to visitors—much less someone with all sorts of dog odors clinging to them—like me. I'd had enough dog problems to last a lifetime, but I knew what had to be done. I dropped to my knees and lowered my head, extending my swollen left fist for it to sample. The dog whiffed me over and only because Juan kept assuring it I was all right, reluctantly decided to let me intrude on its territory.

I followed Juan into his humble home. The floor was hard-packed dirt, but it was clean dirt, and there is a difference. A single kerosene lantern provided the only illumination. Juan's parents and half dozen brothers and sisters immediately surrounded us as he began to give them a somewhat garbled account of what had happened. The father kept glancing back and forth from Juan to me, nervously looking at my wounds and bruises, many of which had not been caused by any car accident. I stood there patiently while Juan jabbered away in Spanish, explaining what he thought had happened, including the cars chasing me.

I let him wind down. When he was through, I looked at the father.

"*Señor*, please ... I must speak with you alone. I have something important to tell you."

The father looked at his short stocky wife for approval and only after she nodded her okay did he start outside.

He commanded softly, "Okay, you children stay in here."

We stepped out into the night air. He stood about 5'6" and couldn't have weighed more than 120. His wrinkled skin was dark from basking countless hours in the harsh sun. His clothing was worn and tattered, and he wore sandals over bare, dirty feet. He looked hungry and tired. In his strata of Mexican society, it is the custom for men to discuss important matters among themselves. I looked at this small, frightened man staring up at me ... a wounded, wild-eyed gringo. I needed to climb into his heart quickly.

"*Señor*, my name is Patricio." I stuck out my hand and mustered the biggest smile I could. He looked up at me and I could see the tension leaving his wrinkled leather face. He smiled, exposing the few teeth that remained in his mouth. He would never have had the money for dental care. Like millions of others, he and his family took whatever came their way, surviving from day to day, life to death, never once complaining about the crappy cards life had dealt them.

The world is full of these decent quiet people. They spend most of their time and energy scratching for enough food to continue their meager existence. He had every right to feel like he had been screwed by the fickle finger of fate, but he didn't. Instead, he grabbed my extended smooth soft hand between his heavily calloused hard ones and pumped it up and down.

He stated, "I am Rolando Aguilar."

He was, after all, a gentleman, and Mexican custom said it was impolite to turn away a stranger in need. Lots of folks think they want a simple life.

Few of them have the will to live it very long. This man had known no other. Using my best Spanish, I presented him with my version of the accident, simply explaining that I was running away from criminals. I asked him if he would go into town and contact the policeman named Jesus Gonzales and tell him that his friend Pat, the American policeman, was hurt and needed help. His eyes widened when I used the word policeman about myself.

"Please inform Jesus that I said to bring one thousand pesos, which I'll give to you. Please, you nor he should tell anyone else about me or where I am. Will you do this ... *por favor?*"

I figured the thousand pesos, which, was under a hundred dollars American, would be as much or more than he would make in a year. He would have done the favor without the money. But, the *mordida* would not be refused. I had his commitment. He reassured me in his best English, which might have been funny under other circumstances.

"*Si, Señor! I go mucho pronto!*"

He looked at me and as if realizing for the first time how bad off I was,

He called to his wife, "Juanita, come quickly."

Juanita came out and he spoke in rapid-fire Spanish.

"This man needs our help. I have to go into town. Take care of him and do what he asks of you."

She stood there quietly looking at me. She started to ask him a question but he was already on the family bicycle and peddling the many miles to San Felipe.

I walked back inside and collapsed on a faded worn-out couch with springs poking through. It reminded me of the hundreds of junked couches that line Colorado Boulevard each New Year's Day after the Rose Parade. Here, it was their best piece of furniture.

All of the children gathered around me. One of them had fetched a bucket of cool water and a clean rag. They watched intently while their mother dabbed at my wounds. I sank back into the couch and watched the dark brown eyes wince each time she touched a sore spot. Her touch was gentle as a deer's kiss and try as I would, I could not stay awake. I drifted off thinking about my mother.

CHAPTER 24 – THE COMING OF JESUS

"*Madre de Dios*! What has happened to this man?"

I opened my eyes to find Jesus staring down at me with concern. I looked up at him and mustered a faint grin. He shook his head from side to side. I forced myself to sit up on the couch despite the pain screaming at me to take it easy.

"What has happened, *amigo*?" asked Jesus.

I shook my head and low words gurgled from my lip. I spoke in English.

"I'll tell you later. Did you bring the thousand pesos?"

I could detect apprehension in his eyes. Here was another man who had no reason to trust me, but custom required him to do so. He handed me a rumpled thousand-peso note and I could tell by the way he handled it that he considered it most valuable. I took the bill and immediately handed it to Señor Aguilar. He accepted it shyly, his face breaking into a huge wide grin. "*Gracias. Mucho gracias, Señor.*"

"*De nada*, I replied. "You are most welcome."

I tried to stand, but my legs were on strike and I collapsed back into the couch. I looked up pathetically at Jesus.

I murmured, "And thank you, Jesus." Then I asked, "Give me a hand, will you?"

Immediately he extended his hand to me, and Señor Aguilar, seeing the situation, grabbed me gently by my left arm. They helped me to my feet and I half staggered and was half carried outside where they piled me into the front passenger seat of the police car in which Jesus arrived.

I rolled the window down and Jesus leaned in as I quickly explained the wrecked car and asked him to tell the family to say nothing about it and not to go near it. I asked him to tell them that someone would come for it after a few days. I listened as Jesus accurately relayed the message. The boy Juan came up to the car and put a small brown hand on my right arm and patted it. I reached out and ruffled his hair. He smiled, but I couldn't help but notice as we drove away that there were tears in his eyes. I knew I'd never forget him or his compassionate parents.

I waved at the boy but didn't say a word as we drove off. Going along in silence, My mind struggled to stay conscious. Jesus was being patient while I decided what to tell him. He rolled up his window halfway and dug a pack of cigarettes out of his shirt pocket. He offered me one and against my better judgment I accepted it. It was a Mexican cigarette. He flicked the cover open on a silver-cased BIC lighter and I let him light my cigarette. The flames licked my face in the wind, and when I took a puff it was so strong I coughed.

Jesus laughed and lit his own. He took a deep drag and looked at me, shaking his head. I was having trouble staying awake. My head was spinning, so I flipped the cigarette out the window and closed my eyes. The open window blasted me in the face with warm air vibrating my skin like air bubbles in a Jacuzzi. I relaxed for just a moment and faded away.

When I slowly came to, I was still in the car with the motor off and Jesus sitting beside me. I glanced out the window and noticed that we were parked off the road in some kind of pull-off. I could hear the sound of crickets and I felt something cold on my face. I turned to look and Jesus was touching my cheek with a cold bottle of beer. I sat up and pain fired up inside my head.

"How long have I been out?"

"Almost two hours, my friend. I let you sleep for a while. Now it is time to talk."

He was right. He handed me the cold beer and I took a long pull. Taking my time, I explained in Spanish what happened to me without telling him why I was in San Felipe. My rudimentary Spanish didn't seem to bother him, but as soon as I mentioned Rancho Mitigoso, his face paled noticeably. I had just struck a nerve.

"*Ah.., Vida Loca, La Casa de El Diablo*! Everyone knows it is the house of the devil."

I briefly told him what had happened, including my toreador experience with the dogs. I kept it as simple as possible, not telling him that Mickey was a he/she, or mentioning the real purpose behind my visit. He sat quietly smoking and shaking his head from time to time, muttering silent curses under his breath. Each time I mentioned the ranch, I could see that he was truly nervous and anxious about the place.

He didn't seem quite as sure anymore. He had to know that if he helped me, he would risk becoming involved with Solorio himself. He hadn't asked me whom I worked for and I didn't offer any explanations. He knew I was on a hot trail and I assumed he figured I was some sort of policeman, which is the way I preferred it. I told him that I wanted to make certain that El Sol's men didn't find me for a few days and that the family who helped me mustn't know who I was or tell anyone about me.

I promised to keep him and his family out of it if he would help me. When I finished my story, Jesus looked at me in the darkness.

After a few seconds, he said, "I'll help you, my friend. I'm sure the Aguilar family will not tell anyone about you, Pat. I can promise you that. What do you want me to do?"

"I've got to rest someplace and heal a bit until I can make plans. I must see a doctor, and I was hoping I might stay at your place."

"Certainly you can stay with me, but with all my children perhaps you wouldn't..."

I shrugged and asked, "How many do you have?"

"Seven, but one of them is..."

"Never mind, Jesus," I stated. "We'll think of someplace else. How about Carmen? Do you think she would put up with me?"

"That's a good idea. She lives by herself and no one would ever think of checking for you there."

CHAPTER 25 – CAT & MOUSE

We arrived at her house at about ten PM to find her gone. Jesus left me on the creaky front porch sitting in a rusty old glider that had at one time been painted yellow. I listened to crickets and night birds while he went off to find her. I sat there trying to organize my thoughts. Something kept nipping away at the back of my brain. I couldn't quite bring it to the surface.

I was distracted by a striped grey tiger cat that jumped down from a nearby fence onto the tin roof cover of Carmen's butane tank. The cat held the limp body of a mouse between its teeth as it trotted across the corrugated tin roof. It paused at the edge looking at me and swinging the mouse in the air as if seeking my praise.

Then, it sat back on its haunches and blinked luminous jungle eyes through the darkness of the empty night. I supposed it truly enjoyed its life of sleeping all day and prowling all night. It lay down on the roof and dangling its head over the edge, dropped the mouse to the ground.

I watched with fascination while the half-dead mouse made a staggering run for the safety of nearby weeds. The cat laid its ears back flat against its head and poised on the roof. Then, in a surge of motion, it leaped out into space landing on top of the mouse. I suddenly felt a strong kinship with that mouse. If I'd had the strength, I'd have chased the cat down and freed the mouse ... but I didn't."

My eyelids grew heavy and the last thing I remember was telling myself that I would just close them for a few seconds to rest.

When I woke, a tall, thin neatly dressed Mexican wearing a white short-sleeved shirt was leaning over me holding a cold stethoscope against my chest. I startled him by trying to sit up quickly. He placed a firm hand on my chest and pushed me back down onto the bed.

I looked around and recognized the inside of Carmen's bedroom. She stood at the foot of the bed with red eyes and it was obvious she had been crying. Jesus wasn't in sight. There seemed to be something very important I had to do, but I couldn't remember what it was. Carmen was looking at me with great concern and I looked meekly at her and smiled. I started to say something to her and I remembered what I had to tell the doctor.

"Doc," I said in Spanish, "I've been attacked by rabid dogs and I may have rabies!"

"Yes, I've been told that," he said in a deep resonant voice. "We've had a lot of that lately. I'll be back with the serum in fifteen minutes."

He got up to leave and paused in the doorway.

"From the looks of you, it must have been quite a battle."

"Yeah, but you should have seen what I did to the dogs."

The doctor grinned and walked out the door. I stuck out my good hand to Carmen and she took it, kissing it gently. "You've had me worried sick."

I felt my stomach stir restlessly and realized I was hungry. "Carmen, I'm very hungry. Do you have anything to eat?"

She looked at me, and a big smile spread across her face. She stuck a small pink tongue out through perfect white teeth and wrinkled her nose at me.

"You crazy *Americano*. You come here *efermo* and all you can think about is food. *Bueno*, Carmen's restaurant will take care of you *pronto*."

"*Muy bein, gracias!*"

"*Secre mucho*," she replied and winked at me.

She hurried into the kitchen muttering a string of Spanish oaths. I lay back and fought with my eyelids while I listened to the sound of pots and pans rattling around. A lantern flickered on a small table next to the bed. I enjoyed the odor of crude petroleum as I watched the rising heat waves shimmer up through the smoke-stained glass chimney and disappear into the air. I tried to go over the strange circumstances that led to my capture, but my brain was on holiday so I gave up on concentrating and turned my attention back to the dancing flame in the coal oil lantern.

In a few minutes, Carmen was back with a pot of strong hot coffee, two old chipped blue mugs, a plate of soft scrambled eggs, fried Mexican chorizo sausage with potatoes, and some warm tortillas. She set a small breadboard in my lap putting the plate of hot food on it. She poured two cups of coffee and sat in a chair next to the bed and watched me eat. The aromas of the food blotted out all other thoughts and I anxiously set about devouring it. Carmen watched me with a peculiar look of amusement on her face.

When I finished, she took the empty plate away then came back and sat on the side of the bed. She leaned down, pressing her full breasts against me, and kissed me hungrily on the lips. She drew back and started to say something, but a loud knock at the door interrupted her. Without hesitation, she got up to go see who it was. I wondered what the hell I would do if it were El Sol's men at the door. She cracked the door open cautiously. Then smiled.

"It is the *medico. Adelante.*"

The doctor was all business. "I've brought the serum. This is not a pleasant thing."

"Believe me Doc, I'll take care of all your expenses. At the moment, I don't have any money with me but..."

"Do not worry. Your friend, Jesus, has taken care of it. He made it clear that no one is to know where you are, or how I have treated you. I understand that and will cause you no problems, *Señor* Race."

I'd read him wrong. I stuck out my good right hand.

Then I said, "I'm Pat, a pleasure to meet you."

He shook my hand and said, "My name is Arturro de Aguirre Renalto. Just call me, Doc."

We shook hands and he promptly began ministering to me. After a few minutes, I could stand it no longer.

"Okay, Doc! What's the poop?"

" Poop? *No esta aqui!*"

"I mean, what's my prognosis? Am I going to live, or what?"

He stopped digging in his medical bag and looked at me. "*Probablemente*, but you have danced hard with *el diablo*,

Americano! You must take rabies treatments, which is no small thing. You will not know for a good while if you have the disease for sometimes it takes up to a year for incubation.

"A year?"

"Do not worry. Someone bitten all over, as you have been, should know within 20 to 90 days. The closer to the brain the bite is, the shorter the incubation period."

I hoped he wasn't trying to cheer me up.

"Okay, so thanks, Doc. If I do get rabies, what are my chances?"

He looked at me sternly. "*Señor* Pat, there is no cure for rabies. If you get the disease ... you will surely die."

I swallowed hard and winced at the statement.

"I've heard that it's not a nice way to go."

"You heard right. The hydrophobia, or thirst for water, is accompanied by terror and spasms at the very sight of it. The virus enters the nerves and eats its way through the nervous system until it reaches the brain. It is a form of encephalitis. The victim may be thirsty and longing for a drink, but if water is brought before him, he will recoil and have spasms of the throat. This fear progresses until the very mention or thought of water causes convulsions."

"Well, at the moment, I'm not a bit thirsty."

He was somber and not at all amused.

"Hydrophobia does not occur until the disease is developed. By then, the patient will experience wild episodes of excitement, followed by moments of complete sanity. There will be periods of salivating and sweating, the same way a typical rabid dog reacts to the disease. In the end, the victim lapses into a coma and dies."

"Is that all? I assure you, if I sense myself coming down with such symptoms, I will take my life before it gets that bad."

"*I comprende!* Besides the rabid infections, you also have a broken finger, which judging from the swelling on your left hand, will cause you a great deal more pain. You are seriously sunburned all over your body in addition to having numerous puncture wounds. There is a big dark bruise on your right shoulder. Your feet are badly blistered, and there is a strong chance the wound in your left ear is infected. You are covered with numerous cuts, contusions, and abrasions. It's a miracle that you aren't still in a state of shock caused by your wounds and near complete exhaustion."

"Yeah, well ... how soon do you think I can get back on my feet?"

He looked at me, smirked and shook his head.

"First off, it is critical that we get you started on the rabies inoculations and immunoglobulin immediately. You will need to take large amounts of the vaccine. I'm afraid it is going to be quite painful."

While I was contemplating my physical dilemma, he got ready to give me the first injection. After hearing this conversation, Carmen stood at the end of the bed eyeing me as if I had just arrived from Mars. Within a few seconds, the doctor readied the huge syringe with a yellowish liquid in it. The plunger was drawn back and he pressed it lightly, pissing a tiny jet stream across the room through an unbelievably long needle.

My eyes registered horror, as I stared in awe at the monstrous needle.

"I'm going to give you an inoculation in the anterior abdominal wall. The dosages call for 0.5 milligrams of serum per kilogram of body weight, which in your case, is about a half pint.

My body involuntarily spasmed and for a moment thought briefly of running. Then I realized I'd do well to even stand. I then reasoned, about what would happen if I didn't get the shot, so I resigned myself to the fact that I would have to take it.

"Go ahead, Doc ... Shoot away. I must tell you in all fairness that I'd rather take it on sugar cubes."

He leaned over and pulled away the sheet, exposing my bare stomach. Intense stress racked my already painful body, and I pushed my head back into the pillow as hard as I could. I would have passed out, but I was too nervous and the adrenalin I had left in me surged. I felt a sharp stinging pain as the needle broke the skin. As he slowly injected the serum it felt like ice and fire descending into my stomach. I noticed that Carmen had to turn her eyes away. The liquid in the syringe slowly disappeared and my guts began to feel the coolness of the liquid of life invasion.

"That was the first inoculation," he said.

He slowly pulled the needle out of my stomach and taped a piece of cotton over the puncture hole.

"You will have to take twenty-one more using the same duck embryo serum—one each day and you must not miss a single day. After that, you'll need a booster at ten days and another at twenty days. If you make it that far, you may live."

My stomach pulled itself into a very tight knot.

"Whoa! I sighed, my voice weak. That's pretty serious stuff."

It does not come any more seriously. I am going to clean the puncture wounds with a solution of nitric acid using a metal probe and leave them open to heal by themselves. It will hurt some."

"I hope not as much as that drill bit you just sank into my guts."

I waved for Carmen to come over. She came and sat down on one side of the bed as the doctor worked from the other. She took my right hand in hers and clutched it tightly. I watched her eyes until he had finished, wincing occasionally when he would hit a particularly sensitive spot. After about thirty minutes, I felt the jab of another needle in my left arm,

He looked up he said, "For infection."

I nodded and went back to watching Carmen. In ten minutes he was finished. He gathered up his gear and handed me a small bottle of pills. "Take two of these every four hours. They will help ease the pain. Do you want me to give you something to make you sleep?"

I garbled a silly laugh, "Yeah, a large hammer and a swift blow on my noggin"

He smiled. "I'll come in the morning to see how you are doing."

After he had gone, Carmen took my head in her lap and rocked me back and forth until I fell asleep. It didn't take long.

CHAPTER 26 – ROAD TO KILL

In the dream, I was riding Pegasus across a field of green grass. He galloped powerfully over the smooth turf, barely touching the ground, his feathered wings keeping us light as a bird. Then, he stopped and I flew over his head through the air, uselessly flapping my arms. I couldn't fly, so I sailed down toward the high fence that pointed skyward below me and landed on one of the fence posts. I slid down with it sticking through my stomach and out my back. Pegasus came up and started licking my face with his pink sandpaper tongue.

I wouldn't die. Each time, just before death, I would come fading back into the scene riding across the field astride the magnificent white flying horse to impale myself on the fence post again and again. My subconscious brain finally decided it couldn't take any more. So, I awoke. I opened my eyes. I was lying beside Carmen in her bed. She was sleeping peacefully and had a soft purring cat-like snore. I sat there in the dark, perspiring and listening to the tick-tock of her Big Ben alarm clock. It was 3 AM.

I slowly struggled to my feet and popped down two of my pills, swilling them down with some of the cold coffee left beside the bed. I staggered across the room and out onto the front porch. It was a humid night with offshore breezes stirring. In the darkness, a distant flash of heat lightening illuminated the horizon. A storm was coming.

I had Patrick Jr. in my hand and had just introduced him to the evening air when I heard the porch creak as Carmen stepped out. When she saw what I was doing, she laughed and came up behind me gently wrapping her arms around my arms and chest. She let me lean back into her soft breasts until I finished.

"You're crazy, Pat. You know I have an indoor bathroom. Why did you come out here?"

"I don't know. I suppose it's just the call of the wild."

Together we walked arm in arm back to bed and she climbed in beside me. Her body generated heat like a furnace. I snuggled up against her for warmth. Her skin felt soft as silk and I was soon asleep again. I awoke to the sound of a car motor backfiring. At first, I thought it was a gunshot and tried to sit up. I hurt from head to foot, so I lay back down. It was daylight and Carmen was still peacefully asleep beside me. I watched her while I thought about what I had to do. Suddenly, I heard a creaking from the front porch and my heart leaped up into my throat. The screen door slowly opened and Jesus came tiptoeing into the room.

I shut my eyes, leaving only tiny slits through which I could watch him. He slipped quietly over to the bed and looked down at us. I would have been frightened except for the huge grin on his face. He slid his nightstick out of its holder. I could stand it no longer, so I peeked to see what he was doing. When I looked up at him, he put a finger to his lips and drew back the baton, then quickly smacked Carmen across the ass with it. She shrieked and leaped out of bed muttering a string of choice Spanish obscenities at him. I smirked at Jesus who was laughing uncontrollably.

"What for you sleep, you lazy woman when you should be fixing breakfast for the hungry men?"

Carmen waved him a middle finger Mexican bird.

She shouted, "*Bessa ma coola!*"

Jesus flopped down on the bed and looked at me sternly. "How are you feeling, *amigo*?"

"I'm still breathing, and might live if I had some coffee." Carmen trotted off obediently to fix it. She clunked the

pots and pans about in the kitchen.

I said to Jesus, "I owe you my life and then some. One day I'll repay you."

He smiled and stated, "Do not worry, my friend. Would you mind telling me once again in the light of this new day just what happened?"

I patiently explained once more how I had managed to get myself captured at the ranch. He looked stunned when I told him about the mad dogs and how I escaped into the woods. He just sat there nodding his head and staring at me intently as I explained how I had managed to steal the Lincoln and wreck it. I didn't say who I was working for because I wanted him to continue thinking I was an American official of some sort. I spoke for about five minutes, quickly going over everything I wanted him to know

Then I said, "Now you see why it is so important for no one to find out."

Jesus sat quietly rubbing the stubble on his chin for a few minutes.

"What do you want me to do now, Pat?"

I patted him gently on the knee.

"Nothing, just buy me some time. You might make sure the car's well hidden. Don't do anything to arouse suspicion, for they'll be hunting for me."

He stood up and said, "Okay. No one will find you here. I have to go attend to some matters. But first, I want to tell you something about the place you spoke of. Rancho Mitigoso belongs to Teresa Gonzales who is a distant cousin of mine. She *mucho accomodado en mucho importancea mujer.*" She's not a woman to be messed with.

When he told me that Teresa Gonzales was his very rich and important cousin, my heart skipped a beat. Then, I remembered that in Mexico practically everybody was everybody else's cousin. He sensed my concern.

"Don't worry my friend. I hate that evil bitch and she does not even know I exist. She is a pig. Now, I must go take care of business."

By the look in his eyes, I knew that he meant it. He patted me on the shoulder and left without saying another word. Carmen had been standing in the kitchen doorway quietly listening to our conversation. Her face was flushed with a strange look that I couldn't read. As Jesus drove away, I had this unpleasant feeling that I was making a mistake by letting him go. If I was, I sure as hell couldn't do anything about it at this point.

In a few minutes, Carmen was handing me a glass of water for my pills and a steaming hot cup of back coffee. I got the medicine down, but the coffee was too hot to drink, so I cradled it in my hands and inhaled the strong aroma. It helped clear my foggy mind a little. Carmen excused herself and left to go shopping. By the time I'd downed the coffee, she returned with some sweet Mexican pastries. I nibbled at one while worrying about Jesus.

I was sitting up in bed testing my various sore muscles when Doctor Renalto walked in. He looked at me sitting there.

He asked, "Amigo, do I perhaps take you off the critical list?'

"I sure hope so, Doc."

"Had any craving for *agua*?"

"Only to take a hot bath."

He chuckled, but then his expression got serious.

"Yes, that's a good idea. I am alarmed, for it does seem like an epidemic is spreading. Rabid dogs have bitten three others up north. I have to go treat them after I am through with you."

He didn't appear to notice my uncontrollable smirk but set right to work cleaning the wound on my ear. Next, he examined my left hand.

"I think we shall have to put a splint on this finger."

I pulled my hand back.

"I'd prefer to wait. Can't you just tape it? A splint would only hinder me if I have to... to ... do any work."

"It is your finger." He shrugged and started dabbing away at my ear. As he treated my wounds, an idea began to form in the back of my head.

When the doctor pulled out the syringe to give me another rabies shot, Carmen, who had been quietly watching came forward.

She said, "I have to go out. I'll be back in a few minutes." I waved goodbye to her as she went out the door.

As he held the big needle above me, I took a chance.

"When are you going out to Rancho Mitigoso, Doc?"

He squinted his eyes at me.

"How did you know I was going there?"

I had no idea what Jesus had told him about me.

"Dose all conversations between us have Doctor-Patient confidentiality?"

"If you wish."

"I do. When are you leaving?"

"In about an hour. What do you have in mind?"

"I just might want to go with you."

He didn't say anything but gave me a disapproving look as he squirted a small test stream from the syringe. This time the pain was even greater because I expected it. It felt like he was shoving an ice pick into my belly. When he'd finished and began to put his equipment back into the bag, he took my arm.

"It must be some strange business you are in. You can come along if you want. But in your condition, I warn you. It is a dangerous place."

I've been told that already. If I go, it will be in the trunk of your car. You would have to smuggle me through the gate and then I'd get out before we get to the ranch."

He scratched his head and nodded slowly. He knew how serious I was.

"I think you are crazy, but I could do that if it is that important and you are compelled to do such a foolish thing. Now, I have to go back to my office to get my medical supplies. Tell Carmen to let me know if you decide to go."

"Fine, Doc. Please be certain you don't let anyone know that you are treating me, especially people from the ranch. If they find out, they'll probably kill us both."

He grimaced and pursed his lips, exhausting a big breath of air. Then he turned his palms up in mock surrender, nodded his understanding, picked up his bag, and disappeared out the door.

After he left, I tried to conceive a plan, but every idea seemed full of holes. It would be a rough go anyway I played it. My instinct told me to run, but I wanted to see what was under that mountain. Still very sore from all my wounds and the rabies injection, I lay back against the pillow and wondered how I could get back inside. I had no idea it was going to be so easy.

CHAPTER 27 – BETRAYAL

Soon Carmen returned with enough food to feed an army. She'd also brought me three American magazines, a deck of playing cards, a razor, a toothbrush, shaving cream, and a quart of tequila. It looked like she was ready for me to move in permanently. I motioned for her to come over and she did, sitting next to me on the bed. I reached for her and she came to me, her mouth meeting mine tenderly.

"Carmen, when this is all over, will you go away with me for a long time?" She smiled and slowly nodded her head.

She filled two fruit jar glasses about halfway with bourbon and then went into the kitchen to get some ice. In a moment she came back and handed me one. Her eyes sparkled and we clinked the glasses together.

I made a toast, "*Salud y pesetas, y amor el tiempo la gustoda.*"

It meant, here's to health, money, love, and the time in which to enjoy them! We drank. We laughed. I taught her how to play Montana Red Dog and she lost about a thousand dollars worth of matches to me before noon. Out of consideration for my recent physical condition, I'd already ruled out the possibility of getting Doctor Renalto involved in the risk and decided not to go with him after all. I was also beginning to worry about Jesus and hoped nothing had happened to him.

When I mentioned this to Carmen, she explained that he had been up all night and had most likely gone home to get some sleep. I doubted he'd do that, but I was immobile and there was nothing I could do.

We had a late lunch and then went out to sit on her front porch while she talked about her life. I felt myself becoming attracted by her innocent and playful ways. She was completely uninhibited and untouched by modern civilization. Her man was her man and whatever he did was the right thing to do. As we sat, drank, and enjoyed the warm sun, I felt content and wished things were different—that I could spend the rest of my life with her nestled in my arms. She kissed my broken finger and then my lips with a tenderness that you can only find in such a girl.

After a while, the sun got to be too much so we went inside, took off all our clothes, and got into bed. We kissed and cuddled and held each other. I fell asleep, contentment conquering the reality of the world.

The creaking floor woke me again. This time I wasn't so lucky. Everything was deathly quiet and without opening my eyes, I knew there was something evil in the room. Carmen was cradled in my arms. I'd never be able to free myself to fight effectively in my posture or condition.

So, I just asked, "Should I get some clothes on?"

"You can get dressed!"

It was a man's voice. I opened my eyes and gently put my hand over Carmen's mouth so she wouldn't scream. She struggled briefly until she realized I was the one holding her. I let her sit up slowly while I eased off the side of the bed. There were four men and I knew from the fedoras two of them wore and the looks of them that they were El Sol's.

"Get dressed, *gringo*. Make one foolish move and we'll kill the girl."

I looked at the one who spoke. He was in charge and was calm and skinny, about 5'5" with a heavily pockmarked face and dark unwavering eyes that said he'd been around the block a few times. He was nothing at all like the innocent guards I'd encountered back at the ranch.

The six-inch thirty-eight caliber Smith & Wesson with a silencer on it declared to me that he was the alpha. The one who caught my eye next came close to me. He was a heavyset, dark-complexioned enforcer type with slicked-down black hair and eyes that darted about nervously. He wore a cute little ponytail hairdo and was waving a very nervous thirty-eight with a silencer in my face. I could smell onions on his breath and figured if I weren't so weak, I could take him out easily. But mister pockmarked face stayed well back—far enough to prevent me from attempting anything that would get me killed.

I began to dress slowly and released Carmen, whose face reflected her fear for me and herself.

"Easy boys, I won't cause you any trouble. Just leave the girl alone. She knows nothing of this."

"We won't hurt the girl," said pockmarked face.

After I was dressed, I held still while onion breath sidled up behind me with a third thug, and they stuffed a rag into my mouth. Then onion breath taped it shut with silver duct tape wrapping it around my head. He then taped my hands behind me. They jerked me to my feet and we started for the door.

Carmen had not said a word the entire time. Her eyes were big as saucers and I was praying that she had enough sense to keep her mouth shut. As we started for the door, I turned my head to look at her. She was scared stiff and sat in the middle of the bed nervously pulling the covers up around her naked body. There was a small flash and I heard a very soft 'pfft' from onion breath's gun and saw a faint tug in the covers Carmen was holding.

I shrugged off the two that were holding me and kicked the shooter in the groin as hard as I could. He fell to the floor with a feral scream. The pockmarked face to my right turned quickly and shot him between the eyes. He stopped screaming. Had I been fully functioning I would have made a better accounting. But, I was barely functioning. I turned toward the man who had shot him and he was smiling, as if he'd just played a winning hand. I nodded and tried to thank him but it came out all garbled and someone hit me in the head. 'Not again!' I thought as the room started spinning. I tried to check on Carmen and caught a glimpse of spreading redness in front of the blanket and her limp arm dangling over the side of the bed. Then something else tapped me on the back of the head and abruptly everything went peacefully silent.

They were holding auditions for the National Drum and Bugle Corps in my brain when I again became conscious. Besides the splitting headache, my hands were cramping from the tape. I was in the back seat of a car between the two men who had taken me from Carmen's. The one on my right had a gun tucked into my ribs. We were bouncing down the road toward the ranch and I had an unpleasant thought that it might go off accidentally. As I sat there between them, I started thinking of Carmen and involuntary tears began rolling down my cheeks. I learned long ago that grief is that sad gift we leave our loved ones at the end of life's journey. My heart hurt like hell.

I kept asking myself why they had shot her. Then it dawned on me that they had intended all along to not leave any witnesses. That meant that onion breath had been a sacrificial pawn—someone the cops could blame her death on, leaving me completely out of the picture. It all made sense. Evil makes its own rules.

We drove on past the ranch house in silence and turned left onto a small narrow dirt road that wound through an arroyo toward the mountain. It finally branched off to the right and ran up to the base of the mountain. We pulled up before a solid rock face and the driver honked his horn twice.

Just like in Ali Baba and the Forty Thieves, the wall slid back to reveal a tunnel leading into the mountain. I began to realize what a hell of a big place it was as we drove inside. A uniformed guard was standing at the entrance and he closed the camouflaged entrance after we had passed through. We proceeded down a long, dimly lit tunnel. Wooden shoring lined the sides, giving the tunnel the appearance of a mine.

I saw no other people along the way. We entered a large cement-floored garage and storeroom area. In the center was a structure with a loading dock sticking out from the back of it. Equipment and crates were piled up around the dock and one side of it served as the parking area.

Several cars were parked next to the wall, including four identical black Lincoln Continentals, one yellow Ford truck, and my jeep, which was parked alongside a police car at the far end. Did this mean that they had Jesus, or was he just visiting? They led me past the loading platform to a single elevator that I knew would surely take me up to El Sol.

I recognized it as soon as we stepped in. One of the guards pushed number five and we rode up in silence. When we arrived, we traversed the long corridor leading to Solorio's office. We stopped in front of his door and one of my guards reached out and knocked politely. From within, came the unmistakable falsetto of El Sol's irritating voice, "Come in!"

CHAPTER 28 – MAKING FRIENDS

I was strong-armed into the room with a guard on each side like a recalcitrant child being forced to stand in front of the feared principal's desk. El Sol sat smugly behind his cherry wood kidney-shaped des. He wore an all-knowing look on his face like that of a happy bulldog trying to sell a vicious glare. Gonzales was tightly wedged into one of the large leather chairs. She wore what seemed about 25 pounds of gold jewelry and a self-satisfied smirk, licking her upper lip like a fat lizard that had just polished off a juicy fly.

Mickey was wearing a light blue mini-skirt. She/he sat demurely in a straight-back chair with his shapely legs crossed in what would be an eye-catching manner to someone who didn't know how the wind blew. She/he tried to look me in the eye, but didn't have the staying power and had to lower her/his eyes to the thick carpet.

I felt like an overripe banana as I stood there waiting to get peeled again. Solorio puffed on a little cigar.

"Race, you've caused us a great deal of inconvenience. I do not regret that we shall now be forced to dispose of you in a manner even more unpleasant than before."

I called him a rotten sonofabitch, but my curses were unintelligible because my mouth was still taped shut. He was curious.

He told the guards, "Remove the tape."

A guard cut the tape around my head with a pocketknife and ripped it off, pulling out a bunch of whiskers and hair at the same time. It hurt like hell. I took a deep breath.

"Solorio, how did a weak-spined asshole like you get to have so much power and influence over these vermin of yours?"

My wisecrack reached him and he began rambling on about how he was going to make me suffer more than I could imagine as he nervously tugged at his mustache. Gonzales hung on his every word, obviously enjoying my predicament. She licked her lips again, reminding me of that cat playing with its mouse. I was going down for the third time and didn't much like the way it felt.

Mickey continued staring at the carpet and nervously wringing her/his hands. Was I mistaken, or was Mickey expressing subconscious compassion? I badly needed someone in my corner, and any ray of hope had to be explored. I had to escape by any means possible. If Mickey were the weak link in their chain, then I'd have to find a way to get to her/him. I stood there in a daze, only half listening to El Sol ramble as my mind raced through the possibilities.

I wasn't too surprised. I'd seen the police car parked below. Did they have Jesus or was he on the payroll too? Was this going to be the last chapter in his and my life? I had the questions but not the answers. I decided to ask.

"Where is Jesus?"

Gonzales could no longer sit passively and spoke directly to me for the first time.

"You don't worry about him, Cowboy. You will soon join him. We may even let you die holding his hand. My cousin will love your company. You made a big mistake coming here alone."

I tried a smirk of my own. "How do you know I came alone?"

Her eyes twinkled. "You're alone. That's why you're here again."

I started to say something but hesitated. You couldn't argue with her logic. Besides, there was no point in pissing her off any further since it was her and Solario calling the shots.

Mickey stood and walked slowly up to me, stopping with his perky breasts pressed into my chest. She/he looked up at me and made a girlish fist. Then, taking deliberate aim, punched me daintily right on my nose.

"That's for Tate."

It was his show. It smarted like hell. But all I could do was grimace and grin as a trickle of my warm copper-tasting blood ran down my mouth. It must have looked funnier than it felt because both Gonzales and El Sol broke into hysterical laughter. Mickey stepped back and rubbed her/his knuckles.

Gonzales was almost orgiastic. She was laughing so hard tears were running down her cheeks. She motioned for one of the guards to help her up. With some effort, he tugged her up out of the chair and she waddled over to stand in front of me. Locking her tear-filled brown eyes onto mine to catch my reaction, she ran two fingertips through my blood drip and pressed them daintily against her fat pink tongue like she was taking communion. Then she took a big hard pinch of my right cheek and squeezed so hard it almost made tears come into my eyes. Then she slapped me three hard ones on the cheek with an open palm. I could feel the coldness of the gold dangling from her various rings and bracelets slamming against my face. She grinned sadistically.

She snarled and said, "*Felino,*" calling me a big pussycat.

I knew the type. Most sadists keep their innermost emotions locked away deep inside, but here was one that wanted to share her perversions. She liked it up close and uncomfortable. She was the very definition of bad. She was the wicked stepmother, the evil witch, and the insane queen rolled into one ... and to top it off ... she seemed to like me.

I shortened our brief love affair.

"I hope you get rabies from my blood."

Her eyes grew instantly big and angry. She'd had enough. "Take him to see his friend," she said in Spanish.

As they led me away, I glanced back at Mickey who was still rubbing her/his fist and noticed that pockmarked face stayed behind to make his report. I wondered if he would merely have to explain or if he could brag about the deaths of Carmen and his missing sidekick.

We did the elevator trek and I was led down the familiar halls to the cellblock area and thrown into a room with Jesus. It seemed familiar. I recognized it as being the same room where I'd been drugged. There were several shelves, a medical table, and five chairs, two with restraining straps. There was also a rather obvious one-way mirror on one wall.

Ordinarily, such a tactic might mean that I was in with a plant, but not this time. I was sure of that as soon as I looked at him. I had to turn away at first because I was unable to stand the sight. He was nude and strapped into a torture chair with tightly wound silver duct tape cutting into his chest. He looked like he'd been the training dummy at a fencing school. He'd been burned with cigarettes or hot irons. Tiny nicks and slashes oozed coagulated blood all over his body. Three fingers were missing from his left hand and it looked as if the wounds had been cauterized because thick black blood coated the stubs. He was still alive, but only barely. Someone knew just how much he or she could push it without killing him and I knew that such knowledge only comes with experience.

No, he wasn't a plant. He was sporty. I knew they would be watching us, so I played my part. There wasn't much I could do for him since my hands were still taped behind my back. I knelt in front of him and spoke his name softly. When he realized who it was, he raised his head. His voice was weak and strained.

"*Hola,* a*migo.*"

His mind hovered close to the edge. He squinted his eyes just once. Upon seeing me, he relaxed and let it go. His head slowly tilted to where his chin was resting on his chest. He was out of it. As I looked at his brutally mutilated body a burst of saliva in my mouth tasted of bile and vomit and a hot rush of anger tingled through my body.

I had little doubt that the room was bugged. They didn't need to keep either of us alive. This was strictly for fun. Jesus' chest rose and fell regularly and after a while, I decided that he wasn't quite as bad off as I'd originally thought. It was merely confirmation of my theory that they weren't in any hurry.

It was a long slow show. I sat motionless for about an hour trying to figure out how to pull off a miracle until Jesus started moaning. I stood over him and in a few minutes, he came to. He fluttered his eyes open and looked up at me.

His first words were, "I didn't tell them ... *nada*."

I reassured him, "I know you didn't. How are you doing?"

"I think they almost killed me."

They had. It had been a stupid question. I decided to tweak their ears.

"Don't worry. Everything will be all right. Before they captured me, I sent a report to my people. They'll come for us as soon as they get it."

Jesus smiled painfully at the thought.

"*Bueno*! When did you send it?"

It was a perfect response.

"Last night. It's in code. When my people get it, they'll come in here blasting every one of these bastatrds.

He seemed relieved, so I kept on.

"We already knew about their operation. We've just been waiting for the right time. Even if they kill us, their organization will still be destroyed, and they'll pay for our deaths with their blood."

He'd passed out again as I was talking, but I continued, hoping our captors heard and smelled my fertilizer.

I knew they had when a short time later three guards removed me from the room with Jesus and took me back to my old cell. I asked politely and one of them took mercy on me, cutting the tape off my hands. I thanked him and said I was very grateful. I lay on the cot thinking. The swelling in my left hand had slowly gone down. I could move all but the third finger, which hurt like hell. My pierced ear continually throbbed. The pain kept me awake.

Was this the end of my rope? Had Lady Luck decided to abandon one of her favorite children? My thoughts skittered. 'Walking the Floor Over You' kept running through my mind even though I wasn't walking the floor. I couldn't remember if it was Hank Thompson, Hank Snow, or Hank Williams that had sung it. But, I was sure it was one of the Hanks.

Finally, what I guessed to be around midnight, three guards came for me. This time they handcuffed my hands behind my back, and then we made the now familiar trek to the elevator and up to El Sol's office. He was alone. I almost laughed when I saw the Baja California mail sacks lying on the floor of his office. He gave me a sarcastic smile.

"Would you be interested in picking out the letter you wrote, Race? Perhaps, that gesture would serve to convince me to be lenient."

I laughed until one of the guards tapped me on the back of the head with his gun. I turned around and glared at him, considering attacking him with my feet, but Solorio intervened.

"Come now, Race. You should reconsider. If you refuse," he shook his head sadly.

Sarcastically, I grumbled, "It's nice you're all choked up about my welfare."

He wasn't giving up. He licked his lips.

"You can only die once, but once can take a long, long time here. *Comprende?*"

"I'm sure your charming courtesan will enlighten me."

He smirked contemptuously and said. "You may be sure of that."

"Then you find the damn letter. How do you know I mailed it? Perhaps, I passed it along to a courier, or used a microdot, a tape recording, or maybe a damn carrier pigeon?"

He was furious. He glared at the guards, kicking a pile of mail into the air and scattering it across his office floor.

"Take him away," he screeched.

He then waved his arms around in the air at the piles of mail. He instructed a guard, "Burn all this."

CHAPTER 29 – THE NIGHT VISITOR

I sat in the darkness pleased with my small victory over El Sol. The handcuffs had been removed, but I wasn't going anywhere. There was a guard in a chair right outside my cell. Time passes slowly when you've nothing better to do than kick rats away. Then I heard a familiar falsetto voice at my cell door.

"Pat, can you hear me?" Of all people, it was Mickey. I walked over and peered through the small window at her/him. The guard was gone and she/he was alone.

I couldn't help being sarcastic.

"How're they hanging, Mickey?"

Mickey wasn't in a playful mood.

"We must talk quickly. The guard is in the bathroom. I have a proposal for you to consider."

I wasn't buying this new Mickey.

"So, what's on your effeminate mind?"

"I need your help."

I snarled, "Hey! I'm the one in this rat cage. How can I help you?"

Mickey pressed her/his face against the bars, just inches from mine.

She whispered. "I think they're going to kill me and I want to break out of here. I need you to help me escape. If you agree, I'll help you escape also. Are you interested?"

"Naw, just let me die! Of course, I'm interested, or is this just more of yours and Solario's twisted games?"

"No more games. Just listen. I'm going to go in about an hour. I'll come for you then. Be ready. I can't talk anymore now. Can I trust you?"

"More so, can I trust you?"

"Touche! Okay then. See you in an hour. Be ready."

Was Lady Luck still in my corner? I'd always said I'd rather be lucky than good. My mind was racing. The possibilities were incalculable. I passed on trying to figure it out. It was the longest hour I'd ever spent. Time had no meaning. You can only count so many 'one thousand ands' before your brain melts and fuzz sets in.

At last, I heard footsteps approaching.

I heard Mickey say in Spanish, "Wake up, Carlos. Señor Solorio wants to see Race."

A sleepy voice said, "At this hour? Does he know what time it is?"

Mickey said, "Would you like to go up and tell him?"

I heard Carlos grumble, but get up out of his chair and he must have pulled out his handgun. Then he handed it to Mickey.

"Take my gun. I'll get him. You keep him covered while I put the handcuffs on."

I could hear the sound of the door opening and their footsteps coming down the hall. A key turned in my cell door and it opened. Carlos shined a flashlight right in my face.

"Get up! El Sol wants to see you."

He stood there holding the flashlight in one hand and the handcuffs in the other. He put the flashlight under his armpit and held the cuffs out for me.

"Turn around".

This guy hadn't seen enough movies. I could see Mickey's profile erotically outlined against the light of the doorway. She/he was holding the only gun. I took a pace toward them, making like I was going to turn around when Mickey made her/his move. She/he quickly stepped up behind the guard and tapped him on the head with the gun butt. She/he didn't hit him near hard enough to do any serious damage. The startled guard dropped the flashlight and put his hand to his head and turned to look at Mickey. By the time he'd got his look, I'd monkey-punched him in the temple so hard that both his feet left the floor.

Mickey cringed as the guard's head smacked down against the cement floor.

She murmured so as not to attract others, "Christ! I think you killed him."

"I hope so", I said rubbing my throbbing hand. "Are there any other guards out there?"

"Not right now. The other one at the entrance is on his break, but he'll be back in about half an hour. We need to move fast to get out of here alive."

"Wait a minute." I assertively took the guard's gun out of Mickey's hand and cracked the downed guard another good lick on the head. It sounded like I'd hit a home run in a baseball game. "That's how you do it."

Mickey sighed softly. "You sure don't take any chances, do you?"

"A little insurance. You've seen the movies. They always revive and come after you—no sense letting that happen." Mickey shivered and shrugged her/his shoulders.

"So, what the hell do we do next?" I asked.

"Follow me."

Mickey strolled off down the corridor and I followed, half expecting to be shot at any second.

We took the corridor to the elevator and it to the second floor. We had seen no one up to now. It was Mickey's lead. She/he took us into a small office where she/he pulled a small brown suitcase from beneath the desk. I didn't need three guesses to know its contents were green.

"That's your 'running away from home' kit, I assume."

I snatched the suitcase out of his hands and laid it on top of the desk popping it open. It was full of new twenty-dollar bills.

My eyebrows raised at Her/his treasure,

"How much is in there?"

"About three hundred thousand."

"Nice little fund. You sure it's enough?"
Mickey looked at me seriously.

"The water's too hot for me around here. Gonzales is getting ready to dump me, so I'm beating her to the punch."

I had lots of questions but it wasn't the time or place to ask them.

"That's okay by me."

As we started to leave, I noticed a schematic thumb-tacked to the wall near the door. It was a map of the place, so I ripped it down, folded it up, and stuck it in my pants pocket.

"How do we get out of here?"

Mickey peeked out into the passageway and then motioned for me to follow. We made it to the elevator and he punched the bottom button.

"There is a guard posted down here. He'll probably be asleep. If necessary, I'll distract him and you take care of him any way you can. Don't shoot him because we also have to get past two more guards at the entrance."

We got in the elevator and rode down in silence. Mickey stepped out cautiously and motioned for me to follow. Sure enough, the guard was sleeping in a chair. We tiptoed up to him. I took the gun barrel in my right hand and lifted his hat with my left. He opened his eyes just as I swung down. There was a solid thump and he shut his eyes again. I pushed his hat back down and looked at Mickey.

"Is That okay?"

She/he shivered. "You're a good thumper."

"You'll never know."

"I hope not,"

I paused momentarily, considering taking my jeep, but decided it would have been too obvious.

Mickey said, "We had better hurry."

I followed her lead ... thinking it was useless for me imagining this feminine person as a male. She started walking quickly toward the cars. We climbed into a new Lincoln with Mickey driving and me squatting down out of sight in the back seat. We drove slowly along the tunnel.

Mickey spoke softly, "I think we can get out of here with no trouble, but be ready in case they won't open the gate."

"I understand. You say the word 'night' if you need help and I'll come up blasting."

We proceeded through the tunnel for a few minutes.

Then Mickey said softly, "Here goes nothing." I heard the click as she stabbed the switch to dim the lights. She slowed to a stop. I made myself as small as I could get, the thirty-eight cocked in my right hand.

I heard a man's voice say, "*Buenas noches, señorita..*"

"Mickey answered. "*Como esta usted?*"

The guard replied in English. "Where are you going?"

"I am going down to the ranch."

"Señor El Sol said you were not to leave."

"I know, but I must go to the ranch."

"*Uno momento.*"

"Good night!"

I rose to see a guard walking toward a small guard shack. I eased open the back door and he turned around to see what the noise was. When he saw me, his face blanched. He reached for his gun, but the leather strap caused him to fumble the half-second it took me to reach him. I moved fast aiming for the temple, but he instinctively turned his head and I smashed him in the face with the gun butt. His face splattered and blood gushed. He reeled toward me and I caught him and clipped him in the back of the head with the gun again, as hard as I could, lowering him to the floor.

Wiping blood off my hands onto his shirt, I glanced at Mickey.

"Where's the other one?"

"I'm not sure, he's supposed to be here."

I took the guard's gun out of the holster and stuffed it into my waistband. There were two buttons on a small panel and I pushed one of them. Nothing happened so I pushed the other one and the door started sliding open. I walked back to the car and got into the back seat. Mickey put the car in gear.

"See why I needed your help," she stated.

I pointed, "Yeah! Now Go! The road beckons."

CHAPTER 30 – INTO THE NIGHT

We drove slowly toward the ranch. I remembered my previous escape and didn't want any more flying glass so I reached across Mickey and hit the buttons to roll down all the windows.

"How many guards are at the ranch?"

"I've no idea. At this time of the night, probably one or two I suppose. They'll try to stop us. As you heard, I'm not supposed to leave the mine."

"Mine?"

"Yes, mine. I'll explain once we're out of here. I hope we can get past the ranch."

"We will. Drive normal. If they try to halt you, stop the car and wait for them to come over. Don't cut the motor off or get out of the car for any reason. Make them come to us. Tell me how many of them are coming. When they're about ten feet away give me the same good night signal. Remember, we have a surprise on our side."

As we neared the ranch, Mickey clued me.

"Two of them are waiting by the road. Should I stop?"

"Yes. Just do as I said."

Mickey slowed the car to a stop.

She said urgently, "Two of them, one on each side, coming up fast. Good night!"

One of the guards stupidly stuck his head in the left front window. I pointed my gun at him and pulled the trigger. He had just opened his mouth to speak when his world exploded. The bullet caught him right in the teeth. He flew back away from the car making an awful inhuman sound.

I rose waving the gun about wildly and looked out the window. The other guard was not a fighter and was bolting for the safety of the house. My mind raced. If we sped off—I knew he'd turn and fire. He was a natural coward. Such types make good hostages and since I had already crashed the main gate once, I knew we needed another way out. Perhaps, he would do.

Even though I knew all hell would soon break loose, I jumped out of the car and with all my reserved strength bounded after him. I caught him in six leaps and brought him down with a flying tackle. We rolled over and I came up on top with my gun stuck in his open mouth. He was paralyzed with fear. I snatched the gun out of his hand and stuffed it too into my waistband. I then got him on his feet and guided him to the car.

Mickey kept revving the engine and I thought for an instant she was going to speed away, but she waited until I'd shoved my prisoner into the back seat and climbed in after him. The shot had sold the farm. Another guard came running around the corner of the house and I popped off a quick shot at him. It changed his mind and he dove to the ground.

I yelled at Mickey, "Get us the hell out of here."

She tromped on the gas, spewing rocks and gravel behind us as we sped away in a hail of bullets. Lights were coming on back at the ranch house and I knew we'd soon have El Sol's whole army after us.

I spoke to my prisoner in rapid Spanish.

"How many guards are at the main gate now?"

Mickey interrupted. "There are two."

"Are you positive?"

As if her confirmation was worth something, my prisoner verified it.

"She is right. There are two guards at the gate."

We bounced along at seventy miles an hour, coming up fast on the chain link fence gate. I noticed that it had been fixed, so I told Mickey to slow down. She slowed to forty and knocked it down again. Just for the hell of it, I put a bullet into the TV camera as we passed. Now we were on the sand and dirt road leaving a huge dust cloud behind us as Mickey deftly fingered the power steering over the ruts.

I had hold of the guard by the front of his shirt and judging from the wetness of his pants and the odor, I was sure he'd never get a hero badge. I twisted his shirt around my hand like a tourniquet and shoved my fist up into his Adam's apple, lifting him off the seat. I stuck my face close to his and got eyeball to eyeball.

"You want to live, *Hombre*?"

His face said it better than his mouth.

"*Si! Si!*"

"Then do what I say and you will."

A glimmer of hope spread across his contorted face.

"*Si amigo.*"

I didn't see any lights behind us, but I knew they were coming.

I told Mickey, "Stop about fifty yards from the gate and we'll see how persuasive our friend here can be."

I tightened his tourniquet as much as I could and his face screwed up like a woman giving birth. I gave it to him slowly... again in Spanish.

"When we get to the main gate we are going to stop and you will get out. You tell them I will kill all of you if they resist. You tell them to give you their guns and you bring them to me and then all of you can walk away. Either you all live, or you all die. It is your choice. Have you got it?"

He nodded that he did, so I made him repeat it to be sure. Then I explained it to Mickey in English to be sure she understood.

We made the twenty-minute drive in less than ten and about a hundred yards before we got to the gate Mickey hit the brakes. The big Lincoln slid all over the road and came to a stop about fifty yards from the closed gate. Both guards had their weapons out and aimed at us from behind the guard shack.

I opened the door and let my prisoner out. He started toward the gate guards frantically waving his open hands over his head and shouting at them to listen to him. One shined a light in his face as he approached. Mickey was right on the edge.

"What if they don't do it?"

"Then I'll kill them. Just sit tight."

The three argued for a brief moment and his argument must have been pretty persuasive because the two armed sentries gave my representative their guns. Like a faithful dog, he started back toward us with them. The other two stood in the middle of the road with their hands over their heads. It was a typical Mexican surrender. No wonder the country had so many revolutions.

I kept my gun on him and ordered him to hand them to me in the back seat. I was getting to have quite an armory. I saw lights on the road now. I pointed my gun in the direction of Mexicali and yelled at my three prisoners.

"You all start running down that road and don't look back."

They looked at each other for an instant and realizing that what I said was good advice, started hot-footing it toward Mexicali.

I swung open the barbed wire and wood gate to let Mickey drive through. The lights were only a mile or so away, heading toward us fast. I grabbed Mickey's chin and made her look into my eyes.

"Listen well, missy, if you want to live. Wait until I tell you and then drive, at no more than fifty miles an hour toward San Felipe. When you've gone exactly two miles, turn around and drive back here. If I'm standing in the road, pick me up. If not, keep on going, and good luck."

Mickey nodded her head that she understood. I grabbed the two rifles and three pistols from the back seat and slammed the door. I laid them on the ground inside the gate and closed it securely. Mickey gunned the motor impatiently but waited for me to tell her when to leave.

I picked up the weapons and ran over to the left side of the road and jumped into a gully of knee-high weeds. The lights were closing fast and were now only about a mile away. I was sure that they would see Mickey's lights heading toward San Felipe so I yelled.

"All right, Mickey. Leave your lights on and get going."

I didn't have to tell her twice as she sped off toward San Felipe.

Now it would be just me vs. the bad guys.

I said to myself, "Race, you'd better make this work."

I did a quick weapons check, taking the safeties off and making sure they were all loaded. I pressed myself deeply into the weeds, already feeling insects crawl over my body as I watched the lights approach. There were three cars. The first one stopped ten feet from the gate and flicked its lights off and on, but nothing happened. The driver stuck his head out the window and yelled back at the car behind him in Spanish,

"The bastards are gone. I saw lights headed for San Felipe. Shall I open the gate?"

The driver of the second car stuck his head out the window.

He yelled, "No, you stupid son of a bitch. We'll wait until Solorio hires another gatekeeper."

An excited guard jumped out of the passenger seat of the first car and ran over to the gate. He swung it open and started to get back into the car so it could drive out. The other two cars pulled in tight behind him. I spotted three men in the first car and two in the second. Thus far, I had no idea how many were in the third.

I took slow and careful aim with the rifle at the driver of the first car and just as the man who opened the gate got back in, I fired. The bullet smacked the driver of the first car in the head and he slumped forward over the wheel.

I swung the gun to the right a little and took out the gate opener. Swinging a little more to the right, I took out the back seat man.

I continued swinging the rifle smoothly to the right until I was lined up with the driver of the second car who was no more than ten feet away. He was looking directly at me and attempting to balance his gun on the windowsill. Before he could get it aimed, I shot him in the left eye. The other man in the second car had his gun out and was crawling over the driver's body to aim at me. I shot several times into the car and he fell back into the seat.

By then, the third car was backing away as fast as it could. I squeezed off quick rounds at it until the rifle was empty. I dropped it and grabbed my backup. I pointed it back at the first car, but nothing moved. Then I heard a click and knew someone was opening a door. I aimed at where I thought he was and waited. The interior light came on and as the door swung open, I started firing rapidly into the car. I heard a scream and someone fall to the ground and rolled down into the gully on the other side of the road.

The third car was still backing away like mad. I emptied the second rifle into it. After a dozen shots, the car swerved backward, crashing into the ditch alongside the road a hundred yards away. I picked up a handgun and squeezed six more shots into it, but there didn't appear to be any need. I lay there panting like a racehorse. By the time the dust settled, I was reasonably calm. It was time to check my work.

All of the men in the first two cars were dead. I pushed the driver aside and got into the first car and backed it across the road, blocking the left half of the road as completely as possible. Then I jumped into the second car, placing it across the other side of the road. It would be hard to get around them. I threw the weapons and ignition keys into the field except for one handgun, which I stuffed into my waistband.

I decided I had time for a quick pocket check and found what I was looking for on the first body, a book of matches. I carefully shot three bullets into the gas tank of each car. There were lights coming toward me from San Felipe and also coming from the ranch. I hoped that the lights coming from San Felipe were Mickey's.

Gasoline began running out onto the ground from both cars. I walked out into the middle of the road and waited. The car coming down the road swerved and slid to a stop alongside me. It was Mickey. I ran back across the road and folding one of the matches over, lit it, turning the flame to ignite the whole book and when it flared, I tossed it into the nearest puddle of gas

It leaped toward the tank as I raced for the car. Mickey saw what I was up to and swung the left back door open. I drove in and she punched it before I had time to shut the door. We'd only gone a few feet before the explosion. The shock wave lifted us a little but Mickey kept the big car under control.

I sighed with relief and slumped back into the seat. In a few seconds, there was another explosion as the other car blew. "It'll be a while before they get around that mess. Let's head for the good ole US of A."

Mickey let out an ear-damaging rebel yell as we sped by the fleeing guards. The windows were still open and the fresh air blasting across my face felt good. I climbed over into the front passenger seat. I still had my luck.

CHAPTER 31 – MICKEY'S STORY

Mickey held it steady at eighty-five and we sailed along smoothly. It took a few miles before I calmed down enough to even think sensibly. Mickey was still frazzled, glancing back and forth nervously from the road to the rearview mirror. Her voice cracked when she spoke.

"Do you think we'll have any more trouble? I mean, do you think they will try for us in Mexicali?"

I saw no point in lying to her.

"I don't know, Mickey. You know more about El Sol than I do. Suppose you tell me just what the hell you do know about all this."

She shuddered.

"This wind blast is too much. May I close the window?"

I nodded. After she'd shut the windows, Mickey turned on the air conditioning. She'd stalled long enough and knew it was time to talk.

"If I tell you everything I know. Where does that leave me?"

"You'll stand a hell of a lot taller in my book for one thing."

"All right, I guess I might as well. I've sold out anyway and it might help you ... whatever it is you're trying to do. You will let me keep the money won't you, Pat? I want to go to Switzerland and I need this money. You can guess why."

I knew what she meant, but I was curious to see how her mind worked.

"Tell me about it."

She glanced at me to see if I was serious and I guess decided I was. She started telling me her story, pausing from time to time to collect her thoughts.

"It started in my teens. People thought I was just gay for a long time... but that didn't work for me. I was too restless. No matter how hard I tried to ignore it... I felt like I was a woman trapped in a man's body. Many people... including my parents thought it was disgusting. I fought it and fought it, but eventually, I came to realize that I just had to deal with it. At 23, I ran away to San Francisco where I met other transgender people like me. I went to counseling... and... and saw lots of psychiatrists and other doctors. But the feelings never went away... I eventually discovered that there were hormones available to help change my male body to a more feminine appearance. There is a gender-change operation that will transform me more wholly into a woman. That's what I want... and... and... why I need the money."

"All right, Mickey. I believe you and I have to say, you are pretty brave. It takes a lot of courage to do what you are doing. If we get away, the money's yours. I think you've earned it!"

Mickey blushed at my compliment and gripped the wheel tightly.

"I'm glad you understand. It's not that I don't trust you, Pat, but you did kick me awfully hard in a still sensitive place."

"At the time, you needed it."

"I suppose, but it still hurt."

"Good! Not as much as my ear I'll bet."

Mickey winced. "yeah, I'm sorry Tate did that."

"So is Tate. Why'd he try to whack me?"

"I don't know anything about it. He had a key to my cabin. I think El Sol ordered him to kill you."

"But in bed? With you? Surely, you didn't think..."

"I wasn't sure. You'd be surprised. A lot of men..."

"Bullshit! Quit blabbering and tell me what you know."

"Okay! You don't have to get mad. I'll explain everything. Do you know about the money?"

"Let's say I do to save time."

"Do you know they print it in the mine?"

"Why do you call it a mine?"

"It is an old abandoned gold mine left over from the seventeen hundreds. I've heard there were... or are... lots of them in Baja. El Sol told me it was originally an old Indian mine... I guess gold was precious to the Indians and they had mined it for years. Unfortunately for them, it was more precious to the conquering Spaniards who plundered all the Indian gold they could find."

She exhaled a big breath of air.

"There were rich veins of gold all through Baja, so the Spaniards began using the Yaquis as slave labor to mine the gold. Once the Indians realized what was going on, they began hiding their mines from the Spaniards. This was one of them and it was cunningly closed to prevent anyone from ever finding it."

I got the picture of El Sol's greed.

"But, Solorio did."

"Not exactly. What I was told is that the mine remained hidden, until it was acquired in the nineteen-thirties by a couple of Mexican ranchers. The partners bought the ranch for cattle ... until they discovered the abandoned mine. Supposedly, they secretly mined it for several years, digging into the mountain and successfully taking out millions in gold without ever letting the government find out. The vein petered out in the forties. Señora Gonzales' husband ... or at least I heard it was her husband ... bought it in fifty-two and it was a working cattle ranch until El Sol came into the picture a few years ago. What I was told is that Gonzales' husband mysteriously disappeared and El Sol built it up to accommodate the printing operation. I think it is jointly owned by Gonzales and Solorio, but there are some others involved."

Mickey paused, thinking carefully about what she was about to say next.

"You see, El Sol found us ...Tate and me ... on a recruiting trip about a year ago in San Francisco. I met Tate several years before in San Francisco. He was an In-The-Closet-Gay and we got along well. He was my ... my ... protectorate, but never a lover. We were just living together, along with some other free spirits in Haight Ashbury trying to attract as little attention as possible. We were broke, hungry, and growing tired of the hippie lifestyle. I guess we were easy pickings. So, when El Sol offered us a chance to earn some big money, we both signed on right away not fully realizing what we'd have to do, or the inevitable consequences."

"So, what did you have to do?"

"Almost nothing. It was the easiest job I've ever had. All we had to do was deliver packages by car across the borders at Mexicali, Yuma, or one of the many other crossings. We never had a bit of trouble. I'm sure the border crossing guards were bribed because we were given certain times and places to take the packages across. Several times I accompanied a shipment to Las Vegas by plane. We knew we were smuggling money all the time but began to get suspicious about the whole deal when El Sol kept paying us off in new twenties."

"But, you still liked the job?"

"Why not? We got to travel and had plenty of money. It was a real trip. Tate blew it about as fast as El Sol gave it to us. He must have spent fifty thousand dollars in the last year alone. Solorio didn't care until I started rat-holing it. They were just beginning to trust us and let us in on a few things, until last month when El Sol discovered that we had put fifty-six thousand into a ranch in New Zealand. He had a shit-hissy fit and that's when he started putting the squeeze on us."

"The squeeze?"

"Yeah, we were on a sort of probation, and our luck went bad and ... and ... we er ... got busted at an airport. We managed to get away, but ever since then we've been in the doghouse and Tate would have done just about anything to get us back in El Sol's good graces. We were on a sort of leave of absence and trying to figure out how to get out completely when you came along. I thought at first you were a plant that El Sol put on us, but when you fell for the party routine, I realized you were after something else. I still don't know what you do ... or who you are working for."

"Never mind that, go on with your story."

Mickey shuddered her shoulders.

"Gonzalez is the real monster. I think the dogs were her idea. She likes to watch them fight. They hold dogfights from time to time and invite lots of ... what they call... *importante jefe* ... to the ranch to see them. I've never wanted to watch or even been invited. I don't think they infect all the dogs with rabies, but the rumor is that they do ... and that the dogs are running wild outside the ranch. It's strictly to keep the workers from trying to leave. It works well."

She paused a moment to seemingly remember Tate.

"We thought we would get back in El Sol's good graces ... so we ... uh ... brought you to the party that night. That's when Tate tried to do it ... only you ... you ... killed him instead."

Her eyes misted over and she drove on as if hypnotized. I found myself feeling sorry for her and wondered if my instincts were right. Only time would tell.

"So, good sport Tate was ordered to kill me."

"I guess so, but I wasn't in on it. Oddly enough, Tate hated violence."

I found that hard to believe.

"Seriously? Are we talking about the same person?"

Mickey smiled. "I'll tell you something about Tate that will make you feel better."

"If you insist."

"He was born in Detroit and reared in the streets. At the age of eleven, a rival gang severed both of his testicles. He over-compensated by using steroids to build up everything else. He was anything ... but a stud."

I laughed despite trying to suppress it. "So, you didn't want them and he didn't have them. No wonder you two made a good pair."

"Well, that's history now." She patted her suitcase. "I just want to get out of the country with this."

"Is that your savings?"

She looked at me. "Not really. I stole it."

I was glad she was being honest about it.

"Good for you."

She was silent for a moment.

"After you killed Tate, El Sol was furious with me and had me taken to the mine to keep an eye on me. It was my prison. I was trapped there and trying to figure out how to escape. I managed to get the money in the suitcase and hide it. When I saw you today, I knew you might be able to help me get away."

"Is that why you punched me in the nose."

"Yeah! That was just for show. I'm sorry."

She looked at me beseeching forgiveness.

I wasn't giving it.

"Yeah, well ... go on."

"I don't know exactly how the money is made, except they print it on the fourth level in a huge room restricted to almost everybody. Everybody has to sign a log when they go in and uh ... they have a guard tower with machine guns observing everyone. The room is guarded twenty-four hours a day and I've only seen it once when El Sol was giving a tour. There's a huge vault at one end of the room that only El Sol and Gonzales can enter. I've never seen the inside, bu I figure they keep the money there until it is sent out."

"Where does it go from there?"

"I don't know where it all ends up, but a lot goes to Las Vegas, Chicago, and Miami. At least, that's where I've taken it."

"What's the relationship between Solorio and Gonzales?"

"I'm not sure. As I understand it, her husband was very wealthy. He bought the ranch years ago, but no one ever sees him ... just her. Somebody told me it was called Rancho Gonzales until Solorio appeared on the scene, but I've never seen Señor Gonzales."

"What does "Mitigoso' mean?"

"I haven't any idea. I don't even know if El Sol works for Gonzales, or if it is the other way around. Several times in the last year though, a strange group of men visited the mine for what seemed to be some kind of inspection. They appeared to be very important people. They're supposed to come again next Tuesday evening, and that's another reason I wanted to get out. I think those men are the ones behind it all."

"You say they are coming Tuesday? How do you know this?"

"Quite by accident. I heard El Sol talking to Gonzales and he was saying something ... uh ... something about the visitors next Tuesday evening. They got quiet when they saw me, but it was too late. I don't think they know I heard them though."

"What do these guys do when they come to the mine?"

"Mostly they just walk around and look at things. They could be either counting the money or giving instructions. I have never been introduced to any of them, and not that I would ever want to be."

"Why's that?"

"They are pretty rude and make me uncomfortable."

I didn't press her but waited for her to continue on her own.

"Let's see... I've already explained that the money is printed on the fourth level, which is the largest area. The presses run pretty much all the time, except when they're broke down, which is often from what I've heard."

"How many presses are there?"

"Damn! I don't know. I was only in there one time. It's full of printing equipment. Things like, you know ... rollers ... cutting machines, and all kinds of technical stuff that I don't know anything about. I have no idea how much money is printed each day, but it's a lot. Once it is all cut and packaged, I think it is stored in the huge vault."

She slapped her fingers to her cheek. "Oh yeah ... there's a back entrance."

"A back entrance?"

"There's another way into the mine from the other side. A rough sandy road leads up to the mountain. That's how they bring in the supplies."

I took out the map and turned on the dome light. I studied it while Mickey caught his breath. The map showed the back entrance all right, but no road outside the mountain.

"Are you sure about that back road?"

"Oh, yeah, I'm sure. I've heard it's very rough, but I've never actually seen it myself. I have heard drivers bitching about it though."

"How often do supplies come in?"

"From what I know it is usually on Tuesdays unless there is a special run for something badly needed. It is always just one truck at a time.

"Do they use Mexican drivers?"

"Yeah, I think so."

I thought about it for a moment. "How many people would you say are involved in the whole operation?"

She considered my question.

"Maybe about... about... two hundred."

I whistled softly. "Whew! That many, huh."

"There must be at least that many at the mine and ranch alone ... not counting the ones in the field. There's a small community built into that mountain. There are ranch workers, guards, cooks, housekeepers, mechanics, press operators, and countless others necessary to run it all. The common laborers... er... housekeeping people and warehouse workers and such... are all lower-class peasantry that El Sol culls out of Mexico. As an added precaution, the only employees permitted to leave the premises regularly are us, couriers, and certain trusted guards."

I was astounded.

"You mean the workers never leave?"

"Right! They make them sign a contract. Everyone has to live within the confines. Some of the guards are not even allowed to leave alone. They use a buddy system so that there is always one watching the other. But the workers remain there at all times. They have colored televisions, games, an exercise area, and all the comforts of home. I don't suppose most of them ever dreamed they would have it so good. He's even worked out a private plan where they leave their earnings in a sort of ... community investment fund and accumulate interest on it. When they insist, and few ever do, he pays them off in cash ... Mexican money."

"In other words, they're prisoners."

"I've heard El Sol say in jest that they have long-term, non-cancelable contracts. At first, everyone thought he was a saint. By now, most of them have a few thousand dollars saved up and they'd just as soon leave. However, that's proved to be easier said than done. Solorio won't let anyone go. He keeps extending their contracts ... or at least he calls them contracts ... under which they sign on for another year at a good increase in pay. The poor fools keep getting in deeper and deeper."

She shook her head in disgust.

"Several have insisted on leaving and if they couldn't be talked out of it, Solorio eventually relented. I've noticed, however, that whenever anyone leaves, they are accompanied by some inner-circle-guards. I'm pretty sure they never get out of the gate. I think they may be taken out and shot. Most of the workers have resigned themselves to the fact that they are there for the duration, so prisoners are likely an accurate assumption. Supposedly, El Sol has worked out arrangements for everyone to go to Brazil when it is over, but I don't think many of them believe him anymore."

"So you think many of them would leave if they could?"

"There's little doubt, so far as I can tell. They're sitting on a powder keg and they know it."

"Yet, they allow themselves to be held captive. What morons."

"I imagine it is the first time most of them ever experienced any convenience like Solorio provides. Even in confinement, they have practically every luxury they could want. There are excellent living quarters and recreation areas. El Sol has gone so far as to import female compañeras for single men. Once, they even had a wedding in the mine. El Sol rigged it so that one of the female workers and a printer could get married. Originally, he was like a father to the people, but lately, some rumors and vibes seem like an undercurrent of rebellion. Perhaps, it's only my imagination."

"I doubt it. Don't families ever check up on the employees?"

"Maybe they would if they could, but no one knows where they are. It's pretty clever. The workers are recruited in out-of-the-way places. I guess they make a big deal out of their fake contracts with lawyers making promises and lots of supporting paperwork and such. Once the workers sign up, they are secretly transported to the mine in the back of enclosed trucks so they don't even know where they are, nor do their relatives. He only selects from the destitute and when he waves visions of the "promised land" under their noses they eagerly sign up. He claims that if it were not for him, most of them would already have died of starvation or disease anyway."

"Were you and Tate allowed to freely come and go?"

"Yes! The couriers have to be treated differently. They are more aware of the situation. As I said, both Tate and I were pretty destitute when El Sol found us. I suppose in some ways like most of the others. There's no reason to leave as long as you don't get in over your head ... as Tate and I did."

"I think I now understand what the dogs are for."

Mickey shuddered again as she bit softly into her lip.

"You got it! They are the hobby of that fanatical fat ass Gonzales, or as the workers quietly refer to her *'fanatico gordo asno Gonzales'*. They're not used so much to keep people out, but rather to prevent the workers from evasion. They maintain a few rabid dogs at all times, passing the virus from one animal to the next before they die. The barking never stops and everybody knows about them. The rumor Gonzales spread is that the entire perimeter is protected by rabid dogs, but I think it is only a few wild dogs that they feed someplace out there in the desert and allow to run free."

"You have to admit, that's some effective hobby and cheap operative security."

"I've heard Gonzales brag that no one has ever escaped."

"Except us. I hope that chaps his and her ass."

She beamed and laughed, "Yeah me too ... except us."

CHAPTER 32 – CROSSING OVER

Mickey finally relaxed, apparently glad to be getting it all off her fabulous fem chest. I noticed that her knuckles were still white from gripping the steering wheel so tightly. She inhaled deeply and her face had a noticeable flush even in the dimness of the car. Despite my reasons to be hostile toward her, I found myself condescendingly sympathizing with her. She seemed to have talked herself out and I sat in private contemplation berating myself for almost letting the dragon devour me.

I was upset about leaving Jesus behind but rationalized that there was no way I could have brought him out with us. Thoughts of Carmen and her warm body kept flitting into my mind. Mickey read my mood and put it on the radio. A Mexican crooner was singing *O Jos Verdes*, or Green Eyes. Even though her eyes were russet brown, the song reminded me of Carmen as I stared out the window into the night. Soon we could see the lights of Mexicali.

Coming into any Mexican city can give one the impression that all the Mexican people ever do is walk. The roadsides are always full. Thousands of men, women, and children sauntered along the dusty roadsides like vagabond Gypsies. Most of them wore sandals made from tires and carried heavy bundles on their heads.

The Lincoln's air stream left a cloud of dust behind us covering the walkers, but most of them were impervious to the rich gringos in the big automobile that sped by. We were from another world they could only dream about.

It was late Saturday night and most of them were heading away from the city toward their small shacks built out of scrap wood, cardboard, and a few pieces of scrap tin. Inside the shacks, they would flop on a flea and tick-ridden mattress made of straw with three or four others and wait for the warmth of the morning sun. Then, they could begin another excursion down the dusty road toward the prosperity of the big city of Mexicali. There they would shine shoes, sell flowers, or simply stand on the corner and beg, hoping that someone would give them a few *pesos* to purchase *tortillas*. The unlucky ones would go hungry. The young girls might sell their bodies. At least, they'd have a room of their own, and maybe even a television and air conditioner. I wondered how many of them would have liked to go to the mine and work for El Sol. I supposed that they all would.

Now and then, one of the poor manages to get enough education to crawl out of the low-class gutter the government corruption keeps them in. Once they do, they never forget where they came from and they work hard, always wanting more, willing to work fifteen-hour days. Then, after three-quarters of a lifetime of struggle, they end up with the same benefits and privileges that even the poorest Americans are born with. No wonder they're streaming across the border in waves. I wondered how the United States would cope with it if someday they all decide to go there. Of late, it seems as though they all do.

Yes, I thought as I looked out the window, almost all of them would walk to hell and back for the chance to work for El Sol.

Mickey's voice brought me from my trance. "We'll be at the border soon."

"You want me to drive across or do you think you can handle it?"

"You forget ... that's what Solorio hired me for."

We were in the bustling neon and sweat-drenched downtown area of Mexicali. The cobblestone streets were filled with those colorful slobs called *turistas*. We were approaching the border and I began to worry about getting across. We hadn't discussed it.

"I suppose we had better work out some sort of stratagem for crossing the border. Let's leave the suitcase with the money in the back seat where it is. It will look less suspicious that way and at least they'll think we are stupid smugglers if they catch us. Do you have any idea how to get us across? It's more in your line of work than mine."

"I don't know if you noticed, but the plates on this car are California. So, how's this? I'm your wife and we've been vacationing in Mexicali all day. We came down from Los Angeles just this morning."

She had me. I hadn't noticed.

"You are dressed like a woman and you look like a woman, but you've got more balls than a tennis instructor."

"If that's a compliment thanks. If not ... then kiss 'em."

She snarled and then let it drop.

"All right then. If they do decide to search us, there's nothing in the world we can do except possibly buy our way across."

"Yeah, or let them lock us up and hope that somebody besides El Sol bails us out in ten or twenty years."

"The suitcase is full of clothes if he asks and that's all. We have no veggies, fruits, or nuts in the car."

"Except for my present company, of course."

Mickey laughed but growled.

"Just stay cool. These border guards can smell fear like a dog."

I flashed on the mad dogs. Mickey gripped the wheel tightly as if bracing himself for the acting job.

"Don't forget, Pat. I'm pretty good at concealing things."

I couldn't help but smile. "Yeah. I know."

Mexicali and Calexico are but one town—sliced through the middle by the border—hence the two names. The border crossing is centered in the downtown area and a drunk can stagger from a bar on the American side to a *Cantina* on the Mexican side in a few minutes.

The border crossing consists of a reticulation of lanes branching off a two-lane street so that there normally isn't more than a five-minute wait. We were near the threshold of the border entrance and I could see that traffic was reasonably light. Mickey smoothly guided the car into one of the lanes. A uniformed highway patrolman stood between the lanes as a vanguard to the real border guard. He glanced casually at us as we rolled by.

A weary-looking bald American wearing the dark blue uniform of the border patrol stood watching us drive up to the gate with cold impersonal eyes. We rolled alongside him and Mickey pushed the button to lower the window on her side. The guard looked right at me and flicked his flashlight on my face as if recognizing my picture on a post office wall. A lump of fear rose in my throat and I felt like a condemned man on his way to the gas chamber. I kept my bad ear turned away and my mangled finger out of sight.

"Good evening," said the guard.

Mickey leaned out toward him and said in a very feminine, controlled voice, "Good evening, sir."

"How are you mam?" the guard asked Mickey.

"Just peachy," Mickey said in a cheerful voice. "And you, sir?"

The guard looked straight at me.

I opened my mouth to speak and managed to blurt out something that sounded like "I'm fine".

The unregistered gun in my waste band was worth a ton of prison time all by itself if they happened to find it. Mickey sensed my apprehension and reached over and laid her hand on my cheek softly.

"He's all right, Officer. I'm afraid my husband has had a little too much to drink. It has been a long day."

Mickey had won him over. The guard grinned like a Baptist minister at collection time as he winked at Mickey. He glanced briefly in the back seat at Mickey as he put a flirtatious hand on her arm,

"Do you have anything to declare?"

"I declare that I had better get my husband home before he passes out."

"No fruits or vegetables?" He still had his hand on Mickey's arm.

"He left the limes from his many Margaritas in the club, other than that … no, none at all."

He stuck his head into the car a little farther.

"Where have you been?"

Mickey smiled demurely. "Just in Mexicali for the day."

"Okay folks, take it easy, and get you and your mister home safe. Come back again."

He winked at Mickey again and patted her on the arm before she drove off.

Mickey chuckled softly and pulled the car into the United States.

As we drove away she said, "Not if I can help it, big boy. Nervy son of a bitch, huh? Flirting with your wife under your very nose."

"Not in this lifetime! How about pulling in at the first gas station? I need to check my drawers."

Mickey chortled. "What do you say we stop for a cup of coffee someplace?"

"Suits me. I could use something to clear my head."

CHAPTER 33 – PASSING FOR NORMAL

We drove quietly for a few minutes and the giddiness subsided. Mickey spotted an Oscar's Drive-In.

"Will this do?"

I had no objections so we pulled in and took the last place on the left. Mickey left the lights on but turned the motor off while we sat in the car and waited for a waitress. A large, economy-sized, big-butted brunette came wiggling over. She leaned in on Mickey's side of the car, and in a deep voice asked,

"What'd y'all like t'night?"

The excitement of escaping made Mickey capricious.

"A cheeseburger without onions, small fries, and a Coke," she said in her most masculine voice.

She then looked at me. "How about you, darling?"

I was happy myself, and there was no point in breaking the mood. Using my best falsetto, I ordered two cheeseburgers, two large fries, and two jumbo chocolate malts. The Amazon waitress stuck the pencil back behind her ear and wiggled away to tell her contemporaries about the weirdoes down at the end. Mickey was positively glowing.

I felt the call of Mother Nature.

"Can I trust you not to leave me here if I go to the head?"

"Take the money with you if you don't trust me?"

"I never argue with a good idea."

I grabbed the suitcase off the back seat and headed for the John. Our waitress was watching and I noticed her pointing me out to one of the other curb hops standing inside their glassed-in enclosure. The bathrooms were to the left side of the entrance and I opened the door and went in. I whipped a paper ass-gasket from the machine and placed it on the toilet, sat down, and was just beginning to get comfortable when Mickey flung open the door to my stall.

"Shh..." he hissed, frantically pointing outside. "There's a car out front—El Sol's men! They just drove up. Probably been following us since the border."

"Calm down. Did they see you?"

"Shoot! I think so."

"I was trying to..."

Mother Nature would just have to wait. I grabbed a wad of toilet paper and did a quick swipe and yanked my pants up. "Did they see you come in here?"

"Yes. And so did the waitresses. We don't have long."

"Then let's get the hell out of here." I grabbed the suitcase and eased open the door. The enemy was not in sight. I dashed out taking my pistol out and flicking the safety off as I ran. Mickey followed close behind practically stepping on my heels. We turned the corner. The back of the place was dark and looked deserted so I headed that way.

Mickey almost fell as she skidded in some grease on the cement, but I caught her. Her eyes were wide with fright and she looked helplessly at me for guidance. I spotted a cherry red Shelby Mustang convertible parked near the end of the building in the shadows. The top was down, and inside a teenage couple was busy exploring each other.

It was the Mustang or the large open field to the northeast of us. After my desert trek, I didn't feel like any more Daniel Boone stuff, so I chose the car. I grabbed Mickey's hand and led her toward the Mustang.

"There's our ride. We've got to use the kids. Just follow my lead."

I realized I had absolutely no identification since all my possessions had been left in the jeep.

I whispered to Mickey, "Do you have a wallet?"

"Yes, but..."

"No buts! Give it here." She fumbled around for a second or two and pulled out a pink patent leather wallet. I opened it up and there was a California driver's license with a picture of her in drag. That's one thing about California. If you could pass the test, and had the money, they'd give you a driver's license in any name and with whatever information you provided.

I looked pathetically at Mickey.

"Come on and keep your mouth shut."

We ran up to the car. The kids in the car didn't hear or see us because they both had their eyes shut and it was easy to see that they were about to get down to the meat of things. I tapped the boy on the shoulder. I had to tap him three times before he realized someone was there. The couple pulled apart with a popping sound and looked up at us with frightened faces.

"We're in trouble and need your help." I flipped open Mickey's wallet for a split second and waved it rapidly in front of the boy's face. "We are FBI agents and there are some hoods around the front that want to kill us. Will you help us get away?"

The girl started shaking. I handed her my gun. She grabbed it by the barrel.

"Look, hold this on us if you are worried. We have to get out of here now. They could come after us any second. This suitcase here is full of money we took from their hideout. I opened the suitcase so they could see inside. I peeled off a stack of twenties from the top of one of the packets. "This is for helping us get away."

The girl said, "Maybe you should call the fuzz," and she handed the gun to her boyfriend.

"Shut up, Cindy. You saw his identification."

He gave the gun back to me.

"Get in the back, sir. Of course, we'll help you and you don't have to pay us either."

I shoved Mickey into the small back seat and then jumped in after her.

I gave the suitcase to the girl and said, "Put this on the floor between your legs, and if anything happens to us, take it to the nearest police station and tell them Agent Tucker sent you. They'll understand."

The girl got into the play. "Geez... it's just like James Bond and all. Don't worry! We'll get you out! Won't we Frankie?"

He fired the engine and the big 428 roared to life, sounding like it was ready for the racetrack.

Frankie laid his arm across the back of the front seat. "Where to, Agent Tucker?"

"Just drive away slow and natural like with your arm around Cindy. Head toward San Diego."

"Check!" He eased the car into gear and backed up. Then, exactly as I'd instructed, drove around to the front and out into the street. I was crushing Mickey down as we pulled away. Once we'd cleared the lot I stuck my head up quickly to peek over the seat. There were six people in front of the men's room including four Mexican enforcers, our waitress, and another guy who looked like the restaurant manager. It was an impasse as if none of them could decide what to do.

Frankie knew what to do. This was his backyard. He made a couple of quick turns, took a short cut and we were headed toward San Diego. The powerful Shelby throbbed along at seventy. Mickey's blonde hair billowed out behind her in the breeze and Cindy sat in the front seat beaming at us in admiration.

I figured I'd play the hand we were dealt, so I asked the obvious question.

"What are the chances of your taking us into San Diego, Frankie?"

"Oh, I'll do ... Can I do it, Cindy?"

"Well, I don't ... What will your parents think?"

Frankie and Cindy looked at each other. I could tell that Frankie was a guy who would make the most of a given situation.

"Hell, we'll stay out all night if we have to."

I closed him immediately.

"Okay, but listen! We have to pay you a hundred dollars each. Regulations you know. We have to!"

Frankie smiled and gunned the car up to ninety.

"Don't worry, Agent Tucker! I'll get you there!"

I had to calm him down.

"Okay, but please slow down. We don't want you to get a speeding ticket."

He slowed back to seventy.

"Would you like me to stop and put the top up?

He looked back at Mickey. She was a fast learner. She raised his arms into the wind and smiled.

"Oh no! The air feels good. Before escaping, we were locked up in their hideout for two weeks."

Cindy had her neck glued over the seat as she watched us intently.

"Should I turn on the radio?"

Mickey answered her. "Sure. We got kind of out of the swing being locked up that way."

She turned it on and adjusted the volume to just under the ear-drum-shattering threshold. Some cat named Jimmy Hendricks was making a guitar bleed. I wasn't sure if this was what the kids called 'heavy metal' or not, but as far as I was concerned, this guy couldn't carry Les Paul's lunch. Frankie cranked the volume up even higher to where it made my brain throb. I started to complain and realized it was better than conversation. We drove along like that for about thirty minutes until the radio station began to fade away and Cindy turned it off. It was a mercy killing.

Frankie had to gas up, so we pulled into a roadside Enco station. Nature was again calling me desperately. As insurance, I took the money case from Cindy and went to the toilet. Mickey and Cindy had mysteriously become pals and disappeared into the ladies' room together.

They were still gone when I got back. The attendant pumped our gas and I helped Frankie put the top up. I noticed the gas cost almost 60 cents a gallon, so I handed Frankie one of the new twenties. It spent fine and Frankie insisted on giving me back the change. The 'girls' took a long time and just before I started to go in after them, they came out chattering away. If the girl had any clue as to Mickey's below-waist equipment, she didn't show it.

Soon we were back on the road. The air began to grow colder as we approached the mountain passes and I was glad we had put the top down. As we elevated up into the mountains, Mickey elaborately explained to them how we had been trapped, escaped, and fortunately met them.

She told such an excruciatingly-interesting story that I found myself listening along. The kids swallowed it eagerly and I didn't interrupt. Mickey seemed to be enjoying herself and after she finished telling them about the harrowing experiences, she coyly snuggled up against me.

She said, "And, when we turn in the money and close out the case, we're going to get married!"

I could have slugged her, but it was a perfectly happy ending as far as Frankie and Cindy were concerned. They also snuggled up in the front seat, I suppose fantasizing about someday becoming secret agents themselves. After a while, I drifted off into a tranquil half-sleep, opening my eyes now and then to make sure that the world was still there.

The mountain fragrances swallowed us as we weaved upward past the tall birch and oak trees. Then we hit the high, cold altitudes. Frankie handled the car like a one-armed racecar driver, but when we topped the pass and started down the winding cutbacks, he had to use both hands on the wheel, which sort of cramped his style.

After a while, we were passing through the small mountain community of Alpine, which claims to have the most ideal climate in the world. Mickey was asleep and Frank and Cindy nuzzled against each other innocuously. I could see the lights of El Cajon and knew that we were almost there. It was nearly 5:00 a.m. and the sky was starting to show pink in the east when we rolled past the luxurious hotel strip built over the beautiful pasture land of Mission Valley. We were in San Diego.

Following my direction, Frankie swung onto Highway 395 cloverleaf which dumps into the downtown area. I had him drive us right up in front of the Court House, in the center of the downtown area. I wanted to make certain that Frank and Cindy had no idea where Mickey and I ended up.

I had to shake Mickey out of a sound sleep. She climbed groggily out of the car and stood there yawning and stretching on the sidewalk, looking like a cheap concubine who had just finished a Shriner's convention. I carefully took the ten twenties I had removed from the suitcase and handed them to Frankie.

"You have to accept this transportation reward. One more thing..."
Frankie gamely took the money and tucked it into his shirt pocket.
" Sure, anything."
I tried to look serious.
"You two must keep this as quiet as possible. We don't want the bad guys to find out you helped us and come after you."

Frankie and Cindy looked at each other tensely and quickly agreed. I shook hands with Frankie, wished them both good luck, and watched him burn rubber down Broadway. I hoped they went home instead of taking a little vacation with the money I had given them.

Mickey stood shivering in the cold morning air patiently waiting for me to tell her what to do.

"Are you all right?"

She shrugged and quipped, "Am I all right? To be perfectly honest, this girdle is killing me. My bra has chafed my left tit raw, and my panties stink. These heels have crippled my feet permanently, and my hair is a mess. My mascara and eye shadow are ruined, one of my false eyelashes is loose, and my nails look like I've been picking cotton. Other than that, I'm just peachy!"

I laughed and stated, "Yeah, I have a new respect for women. I suppose we might as well walk up to the Grant and get a couple of rooms. It's too late to do anything else tonight."

We started trudging several blocks to the hotel. I once started to take her arm, but caught myself and walked along briskly with her plodding beside me. It somewhat confused me to imagine myself thinking of him as a woman. A group of morning-after marines made some nasty remarks about me and the good-looking broad. One snarl from me quickly silenced them.

I told Mickey I needed some walking around money. so we ducked behind a Buster Brown shoe store island window display for a little privacy while I made a quick five hundred dollar withdrawal in crisp twenties from the suitcase. Mickey watched closely but didn't say a word. I didn't feel like arguing with her and she knew it. A passing black and white cruised slowly by and two young cops gave us the once over before deciding there were bigger fish to be caught, so they moved on.

It was time to crash, and I wanted some sane time to myself before checking into the Half Moon Inn. The Grant would do just fine. Opened in 1910 with much fanfare, the Grant hotel was the oldest and probably the nicest in town. It had 285 rooms and 60 suites, most with two poster beds, Victorian chairs, and fireplaces. I was strictly interested in the beds. The clerk eyed us suspiciously but didn't say anything as I told him we needed two rooms and signed in under the name of Pat Michael for a single room.

I didn't know what Mickey had expected, but she didn't say a word as she somewhat indignantly signed in by herself. I bummed a dime from her and bought a San Diego Union from the lobby vending machine. I normally spend an hour each morning with two of my best friends, Mr. Coffee and the Times. When I'm on a job, I seldom have time for the realities of life.

A bellhop tried to grab the small suitcase but got set straight real quick. Mickey clutched it like a drowning man clinging to a life ring. Not to be discouraged, the bellhop took the room keys and escorted us to our rooms anyway, as if we were incapable of finding them on our own. Even though I hadn't so requested, the rooms were adjacent to each other. I slipped the bellhop a dollar tip from the change I had left over, and he ambled away leaving us alone.

As we stood there in the musty-smelling hallway, listening to the elevator descend, Mickey had a slightly confused look on her face as if she didn't quite know how to let go. I did. She had kept her word and as far as I was concerned the party was over.

"Good night, Mickey. If you're still here tomorrow and want my help getting a plane ticket or anything, let me know. If not, good luck."

She looked at me strangely and said, "I'm going to Switzerland, and I am going to have the gender change operation. When I get back ... if I get back, will you still be my friend?"

I don't know why I said it. "What makes you think I'm your friend?"

She looked as if heshe was about to cry.

"Can I ask just one question?"

"Sure! Ask me."

"Who are you really? Whom do you work for?"

I gave her the best answer I could.

"I work ... for myself."

She looked like a dog that had been kicked in the face by its master.

"Oh! Of course, you do."

Sometimes, I am a real son of a bitch. I keyed the lock and opened my door. Mickey was still standing there with a sad look on her face as I stepped into my room and shut the door. It had been a hell of a few days, but thanks to her, Jesus, and a lovely Mexican family, I'd somehow survived.

I stumbled into the bathroom and peered into the mirror at the heavy growth of my beard. The eyes that stared back at me were not sparkling or forgiving—merely vacant and bloodshot.

I climbed out of my clothes and into the bathtub intending to just take a quick shower. I adjusted the spray to a warm flow. It felt good against my bruises and wounds, as I watched the dirt and dried blood run off and spiral down the drain.

It was one of those times when the dirt felt like it was more than skin-deep. I just didn't want to get out of the water. I flipped the levers to turn off the shower and divert the water through the faucet to Jacuzzi hot. I stopped up the tub and lay down, allowing the extremely hot water to fill up to the overflow. I grabbed my newspaper and lay there for a long time, reading and adjusting the water from time to time with my toes.

It was the same old world. In Chicago, Senator Hubert Humphrey was nominated and Ed Muskie of Maine was going to be his Vice President. Ike had been taken off the critical list. The Soviets had launched another COSMOS and we had conducted another underground nuclear test in Nevada. There was a long report on how the Viet Cong had been using women and children as shields when they attacked our troops just a few miles from Saigon. Governor Ronald Reagan grabbed some copy by announcing that the United States' national interests were at stake in Vietnam. I couldn't help but wonder what the hell Reagan knew about Vietnam that the world didn't already know since the whole war was being fought on television.

It was like a small sore that you keep picking at. It gets bigger and bigger until it turns into cancer that eats you up. Everybody knows cancer must be excised or it will eventually devour you. It had turned to cancer and I hoped the prognosis wasn't malignant. So far, the United States had acted like a viral young athlete accustomed to good health, refusing to believe he has been afflicted with a deadly disease.

The biggest problems are the policymakers themselves. Vietnam is a brutal country and I figured that one day we would wake up to realize it. The world is full of such places—Afghanistan, Syria, Pakistan, Iran, Iraq, half of Africa, and countless others. Those places will never change until the superpowers learn to leave them alone to fight their own battles. Most of them would still be fighting each other with sticks and rocks if the affluent hadn't provided them with tanks, bombs, and bullets.

I was glad I'd been left out of it. It wasn't my kind of war. I'd believed for some time that if we didn't quit screwing around over there and get down to business, it would drag on forever. You can't almost fight a war. You either give it all you've got or you don't fight it at all. The soldiers were getting tired and the people back home were getting sick of watching the war play out every night on their televisions. It was a war of political backstabbing and ass-covering, of fake body counts and waiting for your tour to end.

Will we ever get 'compassion fatigue'? Everybody feels for the repressed, but life is a bitch and we can't all be born into affluence. That's just the way the planet works. There will always be the haves and the have-nots, the persecuted and the downtrodden, prisons and repression, starvation and death. Like it or not—that is us. That is humanity!

When I was lobster red and thoroughly waterlogged, I climbed out and wrapped myself in a towel. Still steaming, I pulled the drapes back and opened the window. I stood there breathing in the cool night sea-salted air and wondering if mankind would ever find its soul. Below, on Broadway Street, the sailors ended their night of drinking and carousing. They staggered noisily, mostly in twos and threes, down Broadway toward the waterfront and the sanctuary of awaiting ships.

I stood there like a detached god, observing the night-world end and the day people start to crawl out from hiding places. I watched a homeless drunk stumbling along below. He stopped to take a leak against the building while he finished a cigarette, flipping it away in a spiraling red glow. A dying night wind scooped it up and carried it over to a gutter where a tiny bit of moistness extinguished it. The nocturnal bar-flies and the hustlers had all given up and stole quietly down the lonely streets, mascara ruined and hair mussed, to climb up various creaky stairways in cheap hotels and spend the day sleeping like vampires in their seedy lairs while waiting for another night to arrive.

As sleepy as I was, I still watched the sun show itself. Sunsets seem to take their time, but the sunrise is always in a hurry. They are each a special moment in time. One minute the sun is below the horizon and before you know it the big orange ball has lifted into the sky to start another day.

Down below the newsstand opened morning bundles to see what achievements the world had made while the nation slept. I shut the window halfway and pulled the drapes. It was all I could do to make it to the bed and pull the covers down. I crawled into the soft whiteness teetering on the edge of reality, feeling safe for the first time in a long while. I closed my eyes. Sleep came quickly and took me to that special temporary dimension where nothing is impossible and time doesn't matter.

CHAPTER 34 – THE DAY AFTER

I was snoozing away when the phone rang. I answered it before the second ring. It was the hotel operator reminding me that checkout time was in ten minutes. I begged for an extra hour to check out, which she reluctantly agreed to after I told her some lies.

I splashed some water on my face and tried to call Mickey's room. There was no answer and I knew she had gone. I hoped she made it. Next, I called the Half Moon Inn and made a reservation under my name, saying that I would be arriving in a couple of hours. The clerk seemed to know who I was and immediately told me that I would have the same room as before.

I used the phone book to look up the names of Mexican doctors. Anticipating that some Spanish might be required, I settled on Dr. Francito de Vasquez and dialed the number. I got an answering service and when I'd finally tracked him down he was a she. She sounded competent, so I got her attention by saying that money was no object and my life was at stake. I told her that I was on important business and didn't have time to visit her office. I explained that while I had been on vacation in San Felipe, I had been bitten by a dog suspected of carrying rabies and that I had already had two shots of serum.

I gave her Doctor Renalto's name in San Felipe and asked her to call him and discuss the proper dosages, etc. We discussed the need for confidentiality and her fee, settling at three hundred dollars per outcall treatment, and made an appointment for 4:00 p.m. in room 27 at the Half Moon Inn. She assured me she'd be there on time.

I turned on the television to discover there had been a severe earthquake in Northeastern Iran with twenty-two thousand estimated deaths. Algeria had released the remaining crewmen from the hijacked airliner of July 23, and the polls predicted that Nixon had a lock on the Republican ticket.

Having that out of the way and without looking at the menu, I rang up room service intending to order the biggest breakfast they had. I was curtly informed that breakfast was over since it was almost noon, but that the Grant grill was open.

I slipped on my ragged-looking clothes and stumbled downstairs to the nearly empty old-fashioned Gentlemen's Room and slid into a comfortable booth. The dining area, which appeared to be stuck in times past, had dark paneled walls, very old hunting prints, and formally clad waiters with bow ties. Despite my various wounds, stinking clothes, and appearing to look like a homeless wretch, the hotel room key I conspicuously displayed on the table bought me a light-footed, overly friendly waiter named Ernest to take my order. He was just delivering it when a well-dressed couple came in. Ernest promptly informed them that ladies were not permitted before 3)) p.m. They left in a huff and I began to work on my excellent Monte Cristo sandwich, which came with some kind of tangy berry sauce. I also enjoyed a double side order of my favorite banana bread and an extra large glass of cold milk. I wolfed the food down and polished it off with several cups of some strong dark coffee.

I kept thinking about Smith. I'd taken the money so I was his employee, but as far as I was concerned he'd only rented me. I was my own man. I'd come too close to buying the farm and he'd already gotten his money's worth. I left Ernest a nice tip and got five dollars worth of quarters from the hotel cashier. I decided to call my friend Raymond Benadiaz at the CIA for a quick chat since Smith had name-dropped him as recommending me. I found a pay phone just off Broadway. Perhaps, it was too late to start checking on my employer, but it had been a while since I'd talked to Benadiaz and a call wouldn't hurt.

I'd served my time in the CIA, but I'd grown tired of the low pay and long working hours. The causes seemed to be losing their nobility. After the Dallas Book Depository fiasco, I concluded that a warm bed every evening was more important than a power badge, so I'd pulled the plug. Some didn't take kindly to my early retirement, so I wasn't exactly popular in certain circles. Benadiaz wasn't one of them, however, and it would be good to hear his voice.

It took ten minutes of coin dropping, musical phone fumbling, and being put on hold before I finally got to speak with someone I knew well enough to talk with me. It was Chris Laskey, one of the senior officials who had been a shooter on one of my missions. We'd spend two wild weeks in a South American jungle together. Remind me to tell you about that one sometime. When I'd coded him so he knew it was only a social call, I got right to the point. I explained that I'd tried to reach Benadiaz but kept getting danced around.

Laskey's voice softened. "I hate to be the one to inform you of this, Pat. He went black two months ago."

My heart jumped into my throat. "Damn! Don't tell me that Chris."

"Sorry, Pat."

"Was it a dragon?"

"Yes."

"Anything I can do."

He thanked me but assured me the matter had been taken care of. I asked him if he knew anything about Smith and he said that he'd personally never heard of him. It was a wasted call and I wished I hadn't made it. Benadiaz had been killed in the line of duty. Another good guy sacrificed for the cause. I was more than curious, but I knew digging up any more details would only bring down a pack of troubles. The old flames were just starting to die around the campfire. No sense starting the blaze again. Now, Smith was even more of an enigma.

I strolled down Broadway to the Greyhound Bus Station, slipped down the stairs to the men's room, and dropped a quarter in one of the coin-operated electric razors. I started to knock down the whiskers, considered who might have been using it before me and thought better of it. Instead, for another dime, I bought a cologne splash from the automatic Dispensing Machine. A few minutes later, still unshaven, but smelling good, I was out strutting in the bright Sunday sunshine of downtown San Diego. I didn't look too different from most other street people.

I ambled up Broadway toward the plaza where several bald gown-draped "Hairy" Krishnas, as I called them, were competing with two sidewalk saviors preaching from the small green lawn. Their audience consisted of still-sleeping winos, hung-over sailors, and a few poor folks of the bus-riding class waiting for busses. I watched the circus for a few minutes and then walked down Broadway until I found a locker club open. I bought some passable clothes, a pair of comfortable tennis shoes and some skivvies. I used the dressing room to change and deposited my old wardrobe in the trash.

Back out on Broadway, I spotted a yellow cab parked by the curb. I opened the right front door of the taxi and climbed in.

"Shelter Island!"

The cabby nodded cheerfully at me with slightly bloodshot eyes. I put him in his late forties, a burly man with buzz-cut hair and wearing an old khaki Chief's hat with the gold braid removed. There was a gaudy U.S. Navy tattoo on his right arm. I noticed his name was Crockett from the cabby I.D. tag hanging on the sun visor. Because it was so easy, I pulled his pud.

"Nice day huh, Chief?"

He studied me in the rearview mirror with furrowed brows.

He then went on a tirade. "Where did I serve with you? Now don't tell me. Let me guess. Was it in Frisco or here in Diego? I know! By God! You were on the Hornet. Bos'n Mate, right? Are you still in or what? Hot damn! It's good to see an old shipmate. You know who I ran into the other day that you might know...?"

He went on like that until we got to Shelter Island. The meter read two sixty-five, so I dished him a fiver.

"Keep the change, Chief"

" Thanks, shipmate. What was your name again?"

"Tucker," I said, remembering last night.

"Oh yeah. I remember. Boatswain Tucker, right? I'm Davey Crockett."

"Yeah, I remember, Davey." He grabbed my hand and pumped it up and down. "Take it easy there, Davey. Don't let the lubbers get you."

"Okay, mate. See you later, Friar Tuck."

He drove away babbling to himself. I walked under the big half-moon and into the lobby where the pretty redhead with the husky voice welcomed me like an old friend.

"Helloooo... Mr. Race. We've been expecting you. Booyyy... yoouu look like you lost a battle..."

"I did, but the war isn't over yet."

"Sounds interesting."

"Remind me to tell you about it sometime."

She fluttered butterfly eyelashes over limped blue eyes and leaned across the counter.

"You have a visitor. He's waiting in your room. He said you wouldn't mind."

I melted with annoyance and replied, "You can let anybody you want to wait in my room anytime. Hell, you can even wait in my room. Anytime at all."

She smiled. "You never know..."

"Anytime."

These 'anytimes' were getting serious. It was early afternoon and people were milling around, but I still had to be sure. I slipped the .38 out of my waistband and snuggled it up under my left armpit, outside the coat, which I have found to be an excellent place to get it from if ordered to put up your hands. I eased the key into the lock and opened the door, peeking inside.

Nothing happened, so I stepped into the room, stuck the gun back into my waistband, and tiptoed inside. Smith was lying on the bed fully clothed with his shoes on. I softly shut the door so as not to awaken him. He was peacefully snoring and looked nothing like the dangerous individual I figured him to be. He looked as innocent as a sleeping Rip Van Winkle.

I don't know why I did it. Perhaps it was the subconscious exhilaration of being safe, or perhaps, it was my mischievous nature. I just couldn't resist the impulse. So, taking my time, I cautiously undid his shoelaces and retied them together into a massive lump of granny knots.

Then I quietly opened the curtain flooding the room with light. With the stage ready, I went into the bathroom slamming the door behind me as loud as I could. I heard Smith cry out and leap off the bed. He fell in a crash. I took a nice long and loud wiz before going out to meet him. He was lying on the floor with a gun in his hand. He glowered at me intently as he untied the shoelaces.

"Very damn funny!" he grumbled and sneered.

I didn't laugh because he looked like he might shoot me. I closed the curtain and sat down on the edge of the bed and grinned as much as I dared until he finished. When he was done, he stuck out a hand and I helped him to his feet.

He sat down on the bed with me and checked me over with a stern look on his face.

"Well. Well. Well."

"It's the story of three holes in the ground."

"You look like you came in last in an ass-kicking contest. What have you been doing? Fighting mad dogs?"

I knew he wasn't telepathic and lucky guesses don't count in my business, so I knew he already knew.

"Some, but they weren't mad for long."

"I figured it was you."

"Speaking of which, I have an appointment in a little while with a doctor to get some rabies serum. I'm a little bit late in getting it."

"Sounds like you stepped in a serious pile of fertilizer. Care for a pull while you tell me your story?"

I said I didn't mind if I did, and he poured us a couple of Seagram's VO. The ice in the pitcher had almost melted, so he splashed a little water on top of the russet-colored booze. I took the drink and gulped about half of it. It blazed down my throat and landed nice and warm in my stomach.

Smith looked into my eyes.

"I hear you had an interesting vacation. What the hell went on down there?"

"Sounds to me like you already know."

"Some, but I want to hear your side of it."

I didn't quite trust him, even though I'd taken his money. I spoke slowly and clearly, leaving out anything self-incriminating. I told him about the 'Rancho Mitigoso' and how I'd made a contact with Mickey and Tate. I explained how I'd been forced to kill Tate. He seemed to like that and acted amazed as I elaborated on how I had been jailed, drugged, and forced to deal with mad dogs in front of a lot of strange people. I didn't tell him that Mickey was a trans, or that she'd escaped with the money, nor my involvement with Jesus and Carmen.

His blue eyes never flinched. He was a good card player and I couldn't read his face at all. I thought about taking the map of the mine out of my pocket but for some reason, I didn't. He was patient, not interrupting or hurrying me. Two drinks later, I had finished. I was playing twenty questions with him when there was a knock at the door.

"That'll be my doctor."

Smith stood and commented, "I'll disappear until you're finished."

I knew he needed to make his report.

"Give me an hour."

"I'll give you three."

He pulled a package of twenty dollars bill out of his pocket and handed it to me. "Here is some walking around money. Call it a little bonus."

I tossed the money in a dresser drawer and opened the door. Smith seemed surprised to see the well-dressed distinguished-looking middle-aged Mexican woman. I extended my hand to her.

"Doctor Vasquez?"

She took it and we shook. "Yes. Mr. Race?"

Once Smith departed, I withdrew three hundred from my stash and gave it to her. She got right to work. She'd called Doctor Renalto and needed no explanation on how I had gotten into such a condition. She scanned my black and blue body with professional curiosity for a few minutes and sat about preparing a rabies injection.

When she stuck the long needle deep into me, it felt like there were hot cinders in my belly. Afterward, she worked on the cuts and dog bites. My ear was pretty much scabbed over and she treated it with disinfectant. She decided that one of my leg punctures looked infected so she reopened it and took about a dozen stitches to re-close it. She bandaged it and wrapped it tightly with tape. She wanted to splint my still-swollen finger. But, at my insistence, left it alone.

After she left, I lay on the comfortable bed for a few minutes staring at the white ceiling. The doctor suggested I soak my hand in ice, so I used the ice remaining in the ice bucket and did so. It didn't help a whole lot.

I could hear the sounds of laughter and splashing coming from the swimming pool. The more I thought, the less I wanted to think. So I got up and took a long shower, this time leaving the water as cold as I could get it. By the time I finished the leg bandage had become loose, so I removed it.

I felt cooped up so I dressed and went outside for a limping walk. It was a happy Sunday and the tourists were out in full bloom. A parade of sightseers in cars crept bumper to bumper along Shelter Island Drive. I walked several blocks to the Beach Boy, went in, and had a Barcardi and Coke. The bartender frowned when I gave him a twenty, but a two-dollar tip made him more friendly.

I polished off the drink and ambled across the street to the Chart House and had an exquisite Prime Rib with a delicious Caesar salad. My inner man being satisfied, I bought a fifty-cent cigar at the cash register stand, lit it, and strolled back toward the Half Moon Inn puffing away. I still had an hour or more to spend, so I walked about a half mile to the Municipal Fishing Pier, which protrudes out into the San Diego Bay entrance channel. My cigar was a stub by the time I got there and I stuffed it into the sand cigarette stand at the entrance to the pier.

The Pier was crowded with fishermen. I smiled when I noticed that a few Sunday fishermen were wearing suits and ties. I walked out onto the pier and sat on a bench looking across the harbor. The fishermen were busy pulling in Bonita, Mackerel, and an occasional Halibut.

Across the harbor, lay North Island situated in the middle of San Diego Bay, and the Coronado Silver Strand, which runs down into Mexico. Behind it, to the Southeast, the smoky gray Baja coastline was vaguely visible as far as the eye could see. From this vantage point, it seemed dark and mysterious.

When I got back to my room an hour later, Smith was waiting for me. This time he was awake., and he got right to the point.

"They liked your work, but we'll handle it from here."

Here was my chance to bail out. It was decision time. I knew I'd already made it, but not with my brain—with my gut.

"Who and What is 'we' ... Mr. Smith? Don't be so anxious to turn me out to pasture."

"What? Are you serious? You still want to play?"

My 'tadpole brain' had been overloaded by my 'alligator mouth.' I rubbed several sore spots on my body and snarled.

"Yeah, I think I just might."

He seemed to doubt my convictions.

"I understand how you can feel that way, but we can handle it from here."

I stiffened in my seat and backed him into a corner.

"You think you can go charging in there with the Marines?"

He evaded the question.

"Don't worry about it. The hundred and fifty thousand is already in your account."

I surprised myself by remarking, "Hell, it isn't just the money. It's become personal and I want to finish the job, El Sol, and his malicious empire."

"He grinned and asked, "Are you sure you're still up to it?"

I remembered how Jesus looked when I'd last seen him.

"Yeah! I'm damn well sure!"

Smith confirmed my decision by slowly nodding his head and exhaling a deep breath. His eyes examined my many cuts, bruises, and aching body.

"I do understand your determination for revenge."

I felt the air from his breath blow over me and I knew it was done. That was it. I'd committed, and he didn't argue with me. I couldn't be sure, but I suspected that was what he wanted all along. He rubbed his chin.

"Your problem now is...how do proceed from here?"

"The easiest way would be to fly over and drop an atomic bomb in their lap. That's what they all deserve."

"That would work, but that would cause an international response and be a little excessive."

"Maybe, but no matter. I'll come up with something a little less dramatic."

He grinned. "Something equally effective, I trust."

"Yeah, at least!"

"All right. But, if you fail, we'll do it our way. Our only problem is that our way might stir the media pot too much. You think you have a chance of pulling it off alone?"

"I'll somehow come up with a way."

I hadn't told him about the back entrance through the supply road.

"You're sure you don't need our help with anything?"

I stubbornly replied, "Nope. I'll handle it."

"Don't wait long, for we need this matter resolved as quickly as possible."

I made it clear that I understood the urgency.

"In consideration of that, I'll come up with a plan by tomorrow."

"Pat, I hope you'll understand this, but I want you to know that this comes from the top—not from me."

"Your top ... not mine, but say what you must."

"I can only get you forty-eight hours."

"So, I'm on the clock? Okay, I'll plan for that."

"There's two reasons: One is a hurricane heading that way, and second because some people think they might be getting ready to pull a disappearing act."

"I knew about the storm. I'll work around it. What happens if I'm not out by then?"

"We'll come in blasting and won't be able to pick and choose the good guys from the bad."

"Okay! I *comprende* and understand. Do me a favor though, will you?"

"Sure, if I can ... just ask."

"If I don't come out, I want you to look up the desk broad, the redhead with the husky voice."

"Yes, I know the one you mean."

"Take her out for me and..."

"Say no more. Consider it done."

"Thanks!"

"Even if my wife divorces me for it."

"Your wife? I didn't know you had a Mrs. Smith. Are any little Smiths running around?"

His face got stone serious. "One last thing ... about that phone call to the CIA this morning, to check on me."

Oops! He had me cold on that one. I played it cool.

"Yeah, so what about it?"

"Life can become too short when your nose gets too long."

I looked into his eyes and knew he wasn't kidding.

"And I need to be careful where I stick my snoz ... Gotcha!"

CHAPTER 35 – A NIGHT ON THE TOWN

It was time for a breather. I was tired of tourists and decided to taste a bit of the real city. I peeled two hundred from the package Smith gave me and grabbed a yellow cab parked in the hotel driveway. I had it drop me in front of the Plaza on Broadway. The usual entourage of sailors, marines, gays and other assorted weirdoes strolled, sat, and lay around the plaza. I went into a bar across the street from the plaza to have a drink.

The place was dark and moody and smelled of disinfectant. A motherly type stood just behind the curtained doorway. Without glancing at me, she asked to see my ID card. I gave her a snarl and she looked into my eyes and motioned for me to come on in, realizing that I was long ago over the I.D. Hill. I had two watered-down Chivas Regals on the rocks and left.

By then, the daylight retired and the city put on its nighttime face. A steady stream of cars roared up and down Broadway blowing their horns and looking for company and trouble. Young boot camp liberty seaman apprentices proudly wearing their two stripes staggered about on the heels of any female that happened to walk by. Occasionally a carload of college girls would drive by causing a barrage of 'Hey, baby!' and 'Here we are honey!' from the sailors.

Some of the swabbies wore civilian clothes, but it wasn't difficult to spot them for they all had short hair and that military look. There were numerous bars, all advertising 'THE BEST LOOKING GO-GO GIRLS IN TOWN'. Every one of them also had a 'GO-GO GIRLS WANTED' sign hung in their front window.

Everywhere I looked, sidewalk hucksters were peddling expensive diamond rings at five hundred percent markup, or Gold Leaf Bibles for Mom. They stood around in front of the small half-empty shops with their 'Sign In' books that listed 'All your buddies from back home'. Most were ex-hookers that had gotten tired of selling themselves or military rejects who couldn't hack it in the service.

They had faces like long-lost brothers and they grabbed at the young sailors or marines whom they called Sport, Buddy, Shipmate, or Old Timer.

Their direction was, "Sign the 'Buddy Book' so your friends from back home will see your name when they come, or see if you can find the names of your friends from back home who have already signed."

Once they got control—after the long sales pitch—the farm boy would buy his girl back home a thousand-dollar diamond ring or a gilded gold-leafed Bible for Mom. All it took was a small allotment check for several years. I walked past the hucksters with disgust. One red-eyed dude grabbed me and I turned on him glaring him in the eyes. When he saw my look of disdain, his hand went rigid, but he held onto my sleeve until I pried it loose. I left him dazed and wondered how long it would take him to regain his 'Howdy Partner' composure.

I wandered, enjoying my philosophical scrutiny of the night scene. I decided to go to a movie and checked out the Horton and the Sprekles Theaters. My choices were 'The Lion in Winter' or 'The Graduate'. I didn't know who the Dustin Hoffman kid was, but I needed a few laughs, so I plunked down a buck-fifty in the window and went inside to catch the show. It was a good flick, but I couldn't get my mind off the job ahead. When I staggered out, it was almost nine-thirty. I flagged down a passing yellow cab. The driver slid to the curb and opened his door.

As fate would have it, "it was my 'old shipmate,' Crockett. "Howdy, Davey!" I said as I climbed in beside him.

"Well, I'll be a purple pregnant petrified piss ant! If it ain't Boats Tucker. Where to Boats?"

"The Same place," I stated.

"You got it, Tuck."

He swung around and headed down Harbor Drive, launching into a long narration about some of the guys with whom we'd sailed. I let him ramble, listening to sea stories that he no doubt told so many times he believed them himself. Before we got to Shelter Island, he covered WW II and Korea, liberty in Hong Kong, Sidney, Sasebo, Yoko, Frisco, and countless other places. We finally pulled up in front of the Half Moon.

He turned in his seat to look at me and remarked, "Sure has been good talking with you again, Boats."

I climbed out and smiled at him.

"Yeah, Davey, See you around."

I gave him the usual five-dollar bill and he did the usual fumbling for change until I told him to keep it.

Back in my room, I left a wake-up call for seven and hit the sack. I hadn't realized how tired I was. It wasn't long before the dreams came again.

CHAPTER 36 – THE PLAN

Anyone who's ever been in the club knows that the military lives in a world all its own. It has two faces. There is the one the public sees ... and the real one. The visible one marches and salutes, while the real one covers its rear and goes on liberty. It's a complex bureaucratic machine that no one ever really understands—a universe of cumshaw bartering and backstabbing—where everything is filled out in triplicate, and where things would seldom get done unless the rules were bent instead of blindly followed.

Beneath the surface, the rules are overlooked in exchange for competency. It's a world of favors for favors, controlled by senior sergeants and chiefs. A favor might start at the top but, as the military mind likes to say, shit rolls downhill, so sooner or later it gets down to the senior enlisted who get the missions done.

I'd been transformed from an ordinary naval officer into a member of the Sea Air and Land Team, otherwise known as SEALS at the Naval Special Warfare center just down the bay from San Diego at the SEAL Training Compound in Coronado. The SEALs are the U.S. Navy's principle Special Operations Force. There, I'd drilled tirelessly for six months until the fourteen-mile overland runs and five-mile swims became merely exercise. I learned to sink ships, climb mountains, kill or disperse sentries, abduct the enemy, and motivate myself to carry out a mission no matter what adversity I encountered. As if that weren't enough, I'd also gone through Army Parachute School at Fort Benning, Georgia.

No matter what else ever happens, I would never regret having been a SEAL. I'd be lying if I denied it was a fascinating and significant part of my life. I learned discipline, determination, and survival tactics. I became a super commando capable of carrying out military missions far beyond the abilities of ordinary men, a member of the most ferocious fighting group in the world, and a scuba-suited hit-and-run raider trained for infiltration, demolition, sabotage, and reconnaissance.

Not many of us made it through the training, but those that did share a camaraderie that goes deeper than rules and regulations, request chits, and military formations.

Now, I needed a favor quickly and I knew just who to call. I dialed the SEAL Base at Coronado and asked for Master Chief Petty Officer Red Bottoms. I'd known Red since he'd been second-class gunny in my SEAL unit. I'd saved his life twice and he saved mine once. I knew I didn't have to explain anything to Red—just name the favor and it would be done regardless of the degree of difficulty. He was one of the few people alive who knows my real name.

It didn't take long before I reached him on the phone.

"Hello, Red. How're tricks?"

I didn't need to say who was calling, he recognized my voice.

I heard him snarl, "I'll be a son or a bitch. If it isn't the mysterious... er... (he almost said it, but caught himself in time)... Lieutenant Race? How the hell have you been?"

"Sore, but there's no use complaining, Red. I need a favor."

"I figured that when I heard your voice. Go ahead, just ask."

"I need some plastic."

He was all business.

"as in ... C-4 I'm thinking."

"Right, about four pounds with timers."

"Whew! Sounds like you need a big blow. Anything else?"

"Yeah. I need a free fall chute and reserve."

"Standard military rig or something more fancy."

"Standard. I'm not into fancy."

"Okay, anything else?"

"One more thing ... I need one of your special master keys."

He laughed." You still wear a 34?"

"Maybe, but it's been a while, so you better make it a 36."

"You got it, Pard. When and where?"

"You know the place. H17B, as soon as possible."

"I'll gather, so let's say ... be there at 1400."

"Perfect! See you then."

I made a quick call to Lukban to check on things at the home front. I guess I also needed to hear a friendly voice. Everything was fine except Lukban said he was worried about me. I could detect apprehension in his voice. I told him not to worry and to expect me home in about a week. I knew that Solorio couldn't find my abode because I'd always taken special care to avoid anyone discovering its location.

I put in another call to Doctor Vasquez and made a three PM appointment at my hangar.

There were no cabs out front, so I called for one, specifically asking for my old shipmate. He was on another run, so I hopped in the one that arrived. I had him drop me at Curly Wyatt's office.

As usual, Curly was happy to see me. Without asking, he immediately poured us two cups of coffee.

He told me, "I told my friend about that Alcinder kid."

"Good. He won't be sorry if they draft him."

"So, what are you up to, Pat?"

I knew I only had to ask.

"I need a favor, Curly."

"Sure, I can. What is it?"

"I need you to fly my plane down to Baja this afternoon."

He whistled. "Oooh! You do know there's a bad storm coming?"

"Yeah, I heard about the storm. We'll have to work around it."

He shook his head. And shrugged his shoulders.

"I'm not sure you can. It's a bad one... from the South Pacific. Bouncing off Acapulco right now."

"Maybe we can beat it. I must get to a place about 40 miles northwest of San Felipe, and I've got to go this afternoon."

"Gimme a second."

He picked up the phone and punched a number.

"Hi, Jim. It's Curly. What's the latest on the Baja blow?"

He listened a moment, then placed the phone back on the cradle shaking his head.

"It looks like it's going to be heading straight up the Gulf and it's a big one ... with 90 to 125 mile per hour sustained winds."

I could tell he was serious. I laid a Baja map on his desk and pinpointed the area where the ranch was located.

"This is where I've got to go. It's a life or death matter for certain people."

"Yeah, I figured that was the case."

"It doesn't get any more important, Curly."

He studied the map for a moment and then stood up.

"Give me a few minutes. I want to take a look at this thing myself."

Within five minutes, he was back from the tower and fumbling through satellite pictures and weather reports. After a few minutes, he looked up.

"It'll be a bit of a rough ride, but we've got a short window. If the storm doesn't change course radically, it shouldn't arrive until late tomorrow. So, we might be okay."

"Then, you're thinking we can make it?"

"I'm thinking you're nuts, but yeah, if the storm's course holds, we can."

"Great! I'd like to leave about sixteen hundred. I'll be parachuting out at a certain destination and you can return without ever landing."

"Parachuting? Damn, Pat! You must be dealing with the devil again. You have all the fun. This sounds more interesting every minute. I'll file us a loose flight plan over Baja as if we're meteorologists studying the storm."

"Perfect. I'll brief you on the way. In the meantime, I've got a million things to do before lifting off. You get the plane gassed and ready. Put all the expenses on my bill."

CHAPTER 37 – CHANGING RACES

Curly would handle things from there. I walked over to my hangar and opened one of the big doors, leaving them open for Red as I began checking my gear. He arrived promptly at two o'clock and drove his military jeep right into the hangar. I pushed the button to close the door behind him as I walked over to greet him.

"Thanks, Red. I appreciate this."

We shook hands and he seemed concerned.

"you're still playing dangerous games, Pat. "

"You know me. I never get enough."

He gave me a fake yawn.

"I get bored as hell sitting behind a desk. You need any company?"

"Thanks, but not this time, Red. It's something I've got to do on my own."

He feigned disappointment.

"Oh well. Do you still remember how to use all these toys?"

I grinned at him and let him explain them.

"A little refresher won't hurt."

"Okay. I've brought everything you asked for plus a couple of other items I thought you might need. The plastic explosives will fit into the compartments of these packs which you'll carry strapped in front of you next to your reserve chute in this special vest."

He opened up one of the packages to reveal a buff-colored clay-looking material which I knew was the plastic explosive.

"This is the most recent version in plastic. It has a shattering power many times that of the older more conventional stuff and can be easily molded at temperatures between 25 and 125 degrees Fahrenheit. It has a sensitivity rating much more resistant than TNT and is not affected by moisture. I'm sure you remember, as with all plastics, it does leave poisonous fumes after detonation. It also has a little lower melting point."

We placed the explosive onto a small table.

"I brought you this new electric timer. Its case is small and only weighs thirteen pounds. There is a tester mounted in a timer section of the case that contains a small test lamp and a test switch. Full brilliance indicates sufficient power to achieve the desired detonation.

"The timer is a spring-driven clock mechanism. Similar to all such devices, it can be set for anytime between 15 minutes and five hours. Don't set the timer duration shorter than desired, because the time cannot be increased once it is set. A safety plate prevents the closing of the circuit accidentally and the timer is now set at zero on the clock mechanism. To permit detonation of the charge, the safety plate must be removed after setting the desired time."

I watched and listened to Red intently, even though I'd had extensive training on similar explosives.

"To hook up the timer detonator, all you have to do is connect these two lead wires, set the clock to the desired time and it will close the circuit when the desired time has elapsed. As I said, this is new stuff and I sure wouldn't recommend being in the immediate vicinity when it goes off."

"I've got it. What else have you got here?"

He pulled out a large bulky package.

"One standard twenty-eight-foot backpack-type military parachute with reserve. It has been modified with special vents in the canopy for better control of the toggle lines. Do you still remember how to get into it, Old Timer?"

"I'd better, hadn't I?"

"One of the newer sky diving chutes would be a lot easier ride."

I raised my hands. "Not for me. I don't do it for sport."

He laughed. "I remember. And, we mustn't forget your master key."

"Great. It is set for three minutes, right?"

"You got it."

He lifted a large cardboard box out of the jeep. "I also brought you this survival kit. Take anything you need."

I began pawing through the equipment, keeping some matches in a small tin container, a canteen, salt tablets, a pen flashlight, Coolray Sunglasses, a compact plastic raincoat, a small extendable 60-power telescope with an achromatic lens, and a Gerard diver's watch with altimeter. To Red's dismay, I rejected the flares, grenades, diving knife, .45 automatic, binoculars, stopwatch, two walky-talkies, and fifty feet of one-quarter-inch nylon line.

Once I made my selections, I let Red know that I was in a hurry and he said he didn't mind

"Just get your as home in one piece, and promised me you'll get drunk with me when I get back."

"If and when I do return, you can be sure that we'll tie one on, Red. I promise."

Curly came for the plane as soon as Red left. After he got it out of the hangar I walked over to the nearest pay phone and looked through the yellow pages. It was time to find a beautician. It took me twenty minutes to locate what I was looking for, but my persistence paid off. I fired up the caddy and thirty minutes later, walked into the 'Happy Snipper' beauty parlor in a small shopping center off Rosecrans.

The shop was empty except for the tall guy sitting in a salon chair reading a fashion magazine. His hair was a mop of brown curls that hung several inches below his collar. He was wearing green bell-bottom slacks and a lemon-colored Errol Flynn shirt that matched his well-cared-for face—just the kind you wouldn't want to get marooned with on a desert island. wi

He had to be my man.

"Hi, my name's, Race. I have an appointment with Burgess."

"I'm Burgess," he replied in a shrill voice dripping with sweetness. I stuck out my hand and he took hold with his very warm hand and gave me a slight squeeze.

"From your call, I know exactly what you want. I spent nine years working as a makeup artist for the studios."

I wasn't quite convinced yet.

"It's really important. I need you to make me look Latino ... like a Mexican. Are you sure you can do it?"

He smile and said, "Absolutely! I'm not going to use any cake makeup or powder. You will look like the real thing. Before you arrived, I obtained everything I need from a pharmacist I know. First, we'll soften and cleanse your skin with a cosmetic cream consisting of mineral oil and beeswax, emulsified with water and borax. Then I'll apply a small-particles ochre and sienna-based organic dye containing tetrabromoflourescine—or as we say in the trade—Bromo acid."

I'd heard enough and just wanted him to do it.

"Okay... okay!

When someone asks what time it is, you don't need to explain how a watch is made.

Just hop to it then. Time is of the essence."

I laid $300 in his hand and without saying another word he quickly shut the blinds and put out the closed sign. Then he began to Twitter about, setting up his equipment and paying me no attention. As far as I could perceive, he seemed to know what he was doing. He looked like a mad scientist as he mixed his concoctions. I watched him work in fascination.

In a few minutes, he said, "Strip down to your shorts, please."

I gave him a questioning look and sneered.

"Mr. Race, I'm assuming you don't want to apply the stain to your clothes, do you?"

Suddenly, I became a bit apprehensive.

"How long is it going to take for this stuff to wear off?"

"It varies, but I'd guess about a week."

"What the hell!" I replied.

I had to do it. So I stripped while he watched me with a sheepish grin. He sized me up as if trying to make up his mind about where to start. He dabbed some liquid onto a cloth and began swabbing my body. It was cold and made me shiver. Every time his hands strayed off course, I'd cough and he'd get back to business.

He laughed and said, "Now, don't worry, this won't hurt at all."

I forced a burp. It took him about twenty minutes to get me clean and another twenty to apply the body dye. I thought he was done, but he wasn't.

"Now we'll do your hair."

"What?" I said. It's dark enough isn't it?"

"No way Jose," he snickered. "Trust me. I know haaiirrrr color ... and yours won't pass as Latino. I'm just going to use a harmless synthetic organic extract, which might make it a little stiff, but it won't smell or irritate your scalp, and then your appearance will pass."

He spent another twenty-five minutes on my hair. I chose a full mustache—but passed on the beard. He couldn't understand why I wanted him to leave the five-day-old stubble. But, I insisted and he finally gave in, just shaving the area above my upper lip where he glued on the fake mustache.

By combing my shiny new black hair, he was able to cover up the wound in my ear. He seemed to enjoy himself a lot and by the time he was finished, we were such good friends that he insisted on giving me a free mole. I chose a dark one and had him put it by the corner of my mouth like the actress, Anne Francis'.

Lastly, he slipped the dark pupil contact lenses into place promising me they were long-lasting and that I could wear them for at least a week before I'd have to take them out.

I knew Burgess was dying out of curiosity, but true to his word, he never asked me why I wanted to become Hispanic.

When he'd finished and I was dressed, I pulled out my new sunglasses and put them on. I stood looking at the strange-looking Mexican dude in the mirror. He smiled at me, so I smiled back. It would do.

"You know." Burgess said, "You don't make a half-bad-looking Latino."

I thanked him, gave him an extra $50.00, and got the hell out of there.

On the way back, I stopped at a Mcdonald's and ordered two big Macs with fries and a large Coke, speaking Spanish with the clerk who didn't catch on that I wasn't a Mexican. My disguise seemed to be working fine. I took a booth and ate, wondering if it might be my last meal. I arrived back at the hangar a little after four. Curly had the plane ready to go.

CHAPTER 38 – INTO THE STORM

I spent an hour the next half hour getting my gear ready. I always clean all my weapons before putting them away and knew everything was operational. I dialed in the combination of my gun safe and swung it open. All the weapons were sighted and checked out. They were also unregistered and couldn't be traced. I pulled out one of my favorites, an Ingram M-10 machine pistol. It weighs less than four pounds and is slightly less than ten inches long.

It fires 700 rounds of .45 caliber cartridges per minute, although I've never figured out why since the clip only holds thirty rounds and takes about two seconds to empty. With the silencer in place, it would sound like a BB gun and stop anything moving. Not only does the wire mesh donut silencer muffle the exhaust gas noises, but it also contains the muzzle flash and reduces the recoil. I screwed the silencer into place and checked the weapon over.

For backup, I selected an Israeli .22 caliber pistol also with a silencer. It's great for quiet work up to about fifteen yards and I planned to be looking some people in the eye. There are many different schools of thought about reliability and stopping power when choosing handguns. I like the .22 because it's small, lightweight, easy to conceal, and extremely deadly if the right bullets are used.

While the Ingram .45 caliber bullets could go through an automobile lengthwise, only stopping after it wedged into the engine block, the smaller .22 could still penetrate seven inches of softwood. I'd never found a body harder than that, particularly when using the right ammunition. I always laugh when I see the good guys on the screen behind couches, car fenders, and doorways while someone sprays machine gun fire around them. Such hiding places might work in the movies, but in my job, you would die quickly.

Ordinary .22 caliber bullets make a small hole going in and coming out. The kind I use spread out on impact so they won't pass through the body. They are designed to do all their damage to the first target they strike. There is nothing all that fancy about them. It only takes a drop of mercury in the hollowed-out tip to achieve this. When the bullet exits the gun, the mercury is pressed back into the cavity, but as soon as it strikes a target the mercury vaporizes and explodes.

This type of bullet is even more effective than Dumdum bullets, wherein a hollow tip causes the lead to fragment and split apart upon impact. Of course, such bullets are illegal to use—but for some reason are often used by those intending to shoot their fellow men. You would be surprised how common they are in certain deadly circles. They create a normal entry wound and they usually won't even pass through a body. If they do, the exit hole is big enough to see through.

One of the hardest things to do is to not overpack for a mission. When I first started freelancing, I was like a well-to-do lady packing for a vacation. I found myself needing a U-haul to transport all the tools of the trade that I just couldn't leave home without. I'd eventually learned to take only the bare necessities, especially if I had to carry it all, as I would in this instance.

I opted for ten 30-round clips for the Ingram and a box of Dumdums for the .22. That was enough for a nice little war. I put them in my take pile. I selected a sheathed stainless steel survival-type knife with a honed edge at the top and a six-and-a-half-inch blade. I also chose a scuffed-up pair of comfortable work shoes and my favorite old brown felt hat with a two-inch sweat stain around it. I took a hand compass, a small extendable telescope, a compact combination first aid snakebite kit and my jump helmet.

I couldn't help but admire the huge pile of gear on the workbench. With the equipment I selected and the stuff Red had brought me, it appeared as if I was undertaking a foot crossing of the Sahara.

I was still standing there admiring my tools when Doctor Vasquez arrived. She didn't recognize me and I had to tell her who I was. She gave me an inquisitive look as she glanced nervously around the hanger. But once she realized I was me—she became a pure professional and went about her business. I was amazed she didn't pump me for information—another instance of money overruling curiosity. I told her to skip everything but the rabies shot.

Ignoring my sudden tan she handled me like an everyday patient. I lay down on the couch in my small corner office and she fired my belly up again. I had ordered an extra day's shot. For another hundred dollars, she had it neatly packaged in a small brown zippered medical case with foam rubber cutouts that protected the huge syringe and one day's dosage in a glass medical bottle. She spent a few minutes briefing me on how to administer it properly, scooped up the seven hundred smackers, and left. I sure didn't look forward to sticking that needle in my belly.

It took me fifteen minutes to neatly pack everything into two special carrying packs I'd had sewn together so they could be carried over the shoulders like a newsboy carries his papers. Once the gear was ready, I slipped into a pair of old dirty khakis that I had kept around for just such an occasion. They made my skin crawl, but I knew I'd be glad later. For the jump, I put on some Dingo jump boots with steel toes and reinforced ankle leather. I was ready to go.

It was a quarter to five when Curly pulled the bright red and white Cessna Skywagon up beside the hangar. He'd had perfect timing. He climbed down and walked into the hangar where I was standing. He looked at me strangely and started to turn and walk out. I had to stop him. I shouted.

"Hey! It's me, Curly!"

He quickly looked me over and then realized what I'd done. He walked toward me shaking his head from side to side and whistling.

"Hey, *Señor*, do you have a green card?"

"*Si, Señor!* How do you like my custom paint job?"

He smoothed the invisible hair down on his bald head.

"It is hard to believe that's you under there, Pat."

"It's me alright. I wish it wasn't. Is the plane ready?"

"All set. Are you ready?"

I looked around the hangar to make sure I'd restored everything properly. Then realized that if I didn't make it back, it wouldn't matter anyway. We walked over to the plane. I took a stroll around it while Curly beamed in appreciation of my interest.

"It's still a very sweet bird, Pat."

Curly knew how I felt about small planes.

"Yeah, if you're bird-brained."

He laughed. And said, "We need to get airborne as soon as possible if we want to make it before dark. Are you ready to go?"

"Soon as I get my gear stored."

Curly climbed into the port side pilot's seat and began readying the plane for takeoff. I stowed my gear in the rear of the plane, then closed and locked the hangar door.

Curly revved up the engine as I climbed in beside him.

"I'll take this baby off your hands anytime you want."

I'd heard it before. How great the six-cylinder air-cooled engine was and how one could do just about anything in this 25-foot-long workhorse with the 36-foot wingspan, including aerial photography, dropping supplies, parachuting, or just plain cargo work. It carries eighty-five gallons of gas which gives it a cruising range of over a thousand miles, which is pretty unusual for such a small plane. It will make almost 200 knots with a ceiling of about 15,000 feet.

As we taxied away from the hangar, Curly picked up the radio transmitter of the Cessna 300 Navcom and asked the tower for takeoff instructions. The plane has a complete range of radio and navigation equipment including an Automatic Direction Finder and marker beacon receiver for LORAN fixes. It is equipped with a Cessna 400 autopilot and blind flying instrumentation for night or inclement weather flying.

I couldn't hear what Curly received over his headset, but in a minute or so, we taxied out onto the airstrip. He busied himself talking with the tower and I braced for the takeoff. Curly was all business as he played with the instruments and I left him alone, content to watch him work.

He revved the engine and the plane throbbed as we sat on the runway waiting for instructions. We were given clearance and a runway, with a southwesterly takeoff at 1726 hours. At the given time, Curly gave me a thumbs-up signal and we raced across the pavement lifting off gently toward the large apricot sun hanging over Catalina.

We banked slowly over Point Loma and headed out to sea. The Cabrillo Monument, an old Spanish lighthouse established as a tribute to the Spanish explorer who founded San Diego in the 16th century, stood tall and proud atop the end of Point Loma. I could see the tourist cars parked around the monument and silently wished I were down there with them.

I briefed Curly on our destination and explained that I wanted to make at least one pass over the unfriendly eyes at the ranch. We selected a course that would take us straight out into the pacific, so we would come up on the place from the south. We'd cut across Baja over to the Gulf of California toward Bahia de Los Angeles and fly back up from the other side. I hoped that would give any observers the idea that we'd just come from a fishing trip.

It was a warm afternoon and the sun was hanging low. However, billowy cumulus mushrooms were lining the southwestern horizon and the darker, solid storm front over Baja. The ocean below shimmered in a mosaic of greens and indigos as we flew over the coral reefs. Curly didn't talk and I didn't press him, preferring to use the time to organize my thoughts.

We purred smoothly along at 7,000 feet and I passed the time asking myself questions I couldn't answer and watching our shadow race along on the water beneath us. I noticed several sea birds below us, all migrating to the north. The farther we went, the more the wind buffeted the little plane and the nastier the ride became.

After about an hour or so, we were into some bad weather and the sky above us became grey. I swallowed hard as we started a slow bank toward the Mexican coastline. I decided it was as good a time as any, so I climbed into my parachute rig just in case. I was right. The plane began to bounce and struggle as we neared the Baja coastline. We had to climb to clear the mountain ridge rising majestically from the dirty sand-colored campo beneath us.

I shuddered with each wind draft as I gazed down at the barren deserts and wasteland rolling along the Baja chersonese, remembering what it was like to be afoot in the scorched land below us. We climbed to 12,000 feet and the air keened in raw currents through the tall mountain passes, tossing the small plane about like a butterfly in a windstorm. As we flew high over the promontory, I could see the darkness of the storm out in the open gulf working its way northward.

Had I been flying alone, I would have turned back long ago. A pissy rain began to beat against the windshield. The sky vacillated between clear and dark as we flew under heavy bands. I kept looking at Curly for a signal, but he was busy jockeying the plane. I was tense with a capital 'T' and my knuckles were white from gripping the seat frame. I watched the wings dance up and down and felt like one could snap off at any minute. We'd surge several feet and each time I almost did a Big Mac in my pants. This was going to be one occasion when I'd be glad to jump out of a plane.

We danced in and out of torrential rain. For a few moments, there would be no rain at all and then the cyclonic circulation would deliver us a solid wall of water. Off in the distance, I could see the inky blackness of the storm front. Lightning, like dragon spit, spewed out of darkness, road-mapping the sky in golden veins of fire. The Barometric pressure gauge kept dropping and I needed some reassurance from Curly, so I touched his shoulder.

"Are we going to make it?"

He gave me his all-knowing pilot smile.

"Don't sweat it. This is a piece of cake. We're only at the far outer rim of the big blow. Imagine what the winds are like near the center. How'd you like to try and fly through it?"

I think he was enjoying himself. I swallowed my stomach back down and gave him a faint smile.

"Don't ever let me do this again."

Then we were in the sunlight. It was almost surrealistic. Bright golden shafts of light stabbed down through the clouds, setting the drab mountain passes on fire with explosions of color. The recent rains had dressed the countryside for church. Everywhere I looked were large colorful patches of purple verbena, crimson fields of poppies, white primroses, and yellow Palo Verde trees. Even the rare elephant trees were wearing pink blooms. One moment we were skimming over the painted landscape and tangled mountain ranges of San Borja and Calamajue; and the next, we could see the blue glistening waters of the Gulf of California.

Within minutes, we were over the isolated fishing settlement of Bahia de Los Angeles, a third of the way down the Baja peninsula. No paved roads lead to this isolated Garden of Eden and the only way in or out is by boat or airplane. The small sand runway airfield is pretty crude and only a few true sportsmen and good pilots dare land there.

At this point, the gulf is only seventy miles wide and I could see many islands below us. From our vantage point, the misty blue-grey islands seemed to float on the water. Far out in the gulf, I could see the storm at work. Great thunderheads were piling up on the horizon. A great churning of wind and energy was at work as the typhoon raced our way. Hurricanes feed off the seawater temperature, and the warm waters of Baja appeared to be a magnet pulling it directly into the Gulf of California. The sun glared from behind the cloudbanks, forming a brilliant red and orange path across the gulf and outlining the islands like rims of fire.

At last, we turned north toward San Felipe, which lay approximately forty miles directly ahead of us. Now, the storm was well behind us and I was confident we would make it. Our timing was perfect and it was near dusk as we approached San Felipe. The storm tide was already coming in and landing at the structures closest to the water. Below, we could see people frantically boarding up windows, loading vehicles, and getting ready for the impending onset of the approaching storm.

I thought of Carmen and began looking for her house. Thinking I saw it as we sped over the village, my heart twanged as I remembered her soft, warm body. As we made one final loop over San Felipe and headed toward "Rancho Mitigoso", I began to wonder exactly what we would find there. I tapped Curly's shoulder.

"Can we go down some and stay parallel with the road? That would make it easier for me to spot the place."

He nodded and throttled the plane down to about 150 knots, flying parallel to the highway. The road was full with a steady stream of cars heading away from San Felipe. In a few minutes, I saw a black charred area along the roadside ahead and recognized the road leading to the ranch.

I yelled, "That's it on the left."

He immediately started banking the plane and following the small road leading up and over the mountains.

I told him, "The ranch house will be over the mountain ahead and slightly to the left. Keep her as low as you can without making it look too obvious."

He gave me a thumbs-up sign and started slowly pulling back on the joystick to clear the first small mountain. The plane has a VHF transmitter and an Omni-directional for picking up radar emissions. I turned it on to see if they were using radar or not. I didn't pick up any emission, so we flew directly over the ranch house and banked gently up the mountain containing the mine.

Although I couldn't make them out, several people were milling about between the arena and the ranch house. They looked suspiciously at us as we passed over. I opened the small side window and waved my middle finger at them enthusiastically as we passed them. Two of them waved back, not having the faintest idea of what I had been trying to tell them.

We climbed over the top and then slipped down the other side to the west, racing the shadow of the setting sun below, which was swallowing up the desert in a sweeping blanket of darkness. I spotted the road leading away from the mountain and pointed down at it.

"Parallel the road to the left."

We followed that road for about thirty miles. Even in the near darkness, I could see that it wound through the sandy cactus country and exited onto a small unpaved road that dumped into the main road leading past Rancho San Jose and on into Ensenada. It was almost dark now.

I motioned for Curly to turn back.

I spoke loudly, "I guess I'd better do it."

"Do you want to make another run?" he shouted.

That calmed me down a bit.

"I don't think so. It'll be too dark. Just turn around and get me closer—as close to the road as you can."

"Roger! Will do."

He took a wide turn, flying across another mountain to make it appear as if we weren't overly interested in the place, and then we sneaked in from the south. I began struggling into my jumping packs. Between them and the chute rig, I was bulked to the max. Curly was paralleling the road leading away from the mountain to the south.

"How high do you want to b to deplane?"

"Keep it around 7,000 feet. That should be high enough so as not to appear obvious."

I remembered something a grizzled old sergeant major jumpmaster once said.

He alleged, " It doesn't matter how many jumps you have made, or how good you are, or what your rank is—every time you leap out of an airplane you only get one chance at survival."

The altitude I mentioned meant I must do a thirty-second free fall. Thirty seconds of sheer terror. I'd made 48 jumps in my time in the SEALs, and 14 of them were in combat situations. I'd never once enjoyed it. It wasn't my kind of thrill, but it was a necessary part of the job. Someone once asked me how I could be sure of the number. I wondered how anyone could ever forget it.

The number 49 clicked into my head. Now, it was go-time again. Curly motioned for me to get ready.

"I'll put you south of the road and you should be able to get pretty close to it. The wind is from the southeast at fifteen to twenty-five miles per hour, but there could be higher gusts because of the storm. You will likely have a good drift rate."

I struggled and fastened my jump helmet. Unlike athletic helmets, jump helmets are designed for absorbing energy rather than deflecting it. I know there are lots of crazies who ride motorcycles and jump out of planes without brain buckets. I'm not one of them. I checked my reserve chute, the altimeter, and my watch. I was ready to go. Although the sun was taking its final peek over the horizon at our altitude, the desert below had been swept into complete darkness and was now a lurking abyss.

I almost fainted when I looked up and Curly was standing beside me until I realized he'd put on the automatic pilot.

"Okay, Pat. Are you ready to hit the silk? We're throttled down to one hundred knots and it'll be a little rough stepping out. Good luck and don't land on any cactus!"

I wished he hadn't said that. I gave him a thumbs up and slid the door open blasting the compartment with a roar of chilled air. Curly patted me on the back. I stepped up to the door and with a face that must have looked like death warmed over ... I leaped out into the vast darkness. Sometimes you have to dive into the abyss to find out what it contains.

CHAPTER 39 – SAND

When a man knows he is falling toward the ground, a million thoughts flash through his mind. Mostly, he tries to remember all the right things to do—and that's what I was doing. I talked to myself rapidly, my mind racing ahead of my ability to carry out the commands— assume a stable spread facing the earth. There that's right. Damn—it seems I'm a long way up. Check the altimeter... don't panic now... easy... dark as hell ... concentrate. Fifteen seconds elapsed—I'm now at terminal velocity. Can't see anything below. It's so dark.

I kept reassuring myself that I could handle it. The wind rippled my clothes as I strained to see the ground. I began to imagine landing in a big pile of cacti and had to force my concentration back to my jump: That's it ... twenty-five seconds elapsed ... at 3,500 feet. Tuck a little. Thirty-five seconds now. I'm nearing 1,500 feet. Pull the ripcord now. Twenty-two pounds of pressure on the ripcord release pins from the locking cones—flaps drawing back by the spring opening bands—pilot chute springing back beyond the negative pressure area above my body. Getting a bite of air now. Open you, bastard! The wind got me! Drifting fast! See the ground now. Coming up at me fast.., no I'm coming down fast! Canopy filling with air. Assume an upright position, canopy open. Brace for a shock!

Then, like a yoyo reaching the end of its string, I felt the air shudder and my chest snap back. That was it. I was hanging in the saddle. I'd made it. I glanced at my altimeter. It read 1,000 feet. I smiled and checked the perfect twenty-eight-sided polygon canopy above me. All four sections of each of the twenty-eight gores were billowed with air. I could literally hear the air rushing through the center vent and the window vents of the canopy. Now all I had to do was land safely. In the distance, I saw the running lights of the Skywagon come on as Curly rolled his wings for me.

I began looking for a clear landing zone and searched for the road, but couldn't see it. I was drifting fast. Then I thought I spotted it dead ahead, so I grabbed at the toggle lines that ran up to the suspension lines, and tugged. That vented the chute behind me and thrust me rapidly forward.

I caught my first glimpse of the sand at about two hundred feet. Since I was now dropping at only about eighteen feet per second, I figured I had plenty of time to pick a nice soft landing spot. I began to assume the standard landing position and tried to swing around to face the wind, but a quick gust swung me like a pendulum. Suddenly I saw a huge cactus sticking upward like a mighty phallic symbol pointing right at me.

I immediately forgot all about using the toggle lines and started kicking like mad to avoid the big cactus. I was yelling profanities as I came down right on top of it. I was lucky enough to kick away from it with both feet, shoving my body out and away, but unfortunately, the chute came down over it. I landed hard and started to roll until I felt the harness yank back hard, knocking the wind out of me.

The chute snagged the thirty-foot cactus just tightly enough to prevent me from rolling. I lay on the ground sucking in huge quantities of air and muttering silent oaths as I looked up at the sky and listened to my plane's engine fade away. When my breathing returned to normal, I stood up, slipped out of the harness, and looked at the cactus. My chute sheathed the giant Cardon perfectly like a giant condom.

I landed smack in the middle of a well-populated cactus jungle. I'd jumped at that magic time—just as the curtain of darkness closed. Everywhere I looked the cacti population stood like silent sentinels in the night. I felt like a million eyes were watching me.

Of the more than a hundred varieties of cactus found in Baja, more than half of them are endemic to the area. Like men, cacti come in many shapes and sizes, from small button plants to giants dominating the landscape. Some look like stately trees while others grow as vines, such as the creeping devils that blanket the desert floor with a terrible nest of spines, impenetrable as any barbed wire battlefield. Then, there are the sprawling thick tufted Chollas with millions of barbed spines that severely punish all creatures stupid enough to come into contact with them.

Cactus spines are highly effective protective weapons designed by Mother Nature over millions of years. They range from stiff needle-sized spikes that can puncture a tire to small hair-like glochids that disappear like invisible splinters under the skin. I was in the middle of the dense cactus jungle. The bizarre landscape seemed like a dream of some grotesque world from another universe. It was all around me.

There were towering Yuccas and giant Cordons, which grow up to fifty feet high and are found in no other place in the world except Baja. There were huge freak Ciro trees with their slender tapering tips bent and twisted into arcs and loops and other grotesque shapes like giant psychedelic carrots growing upside down above the ground. There were stands of snakelike Ocotillo with thorn-clad stems and short thick-bodied porcupine barrels. There were Agave Century Plants and the smaller shrub-like Jatrophe, Matacora, and Lombok. There were thorny Mesquite trees and the spiny Pitahaya used by Mexicans for fences.

I checked to see how much damage the giant Cordon had done. The Dingos had absorbed most of the punishment. I told to myself not to panic and to get my priorities in order. I broke out my little flashlight and found a small clearing. Then, sitting on the warm sand, I removed my boots and carefully pulled the spines out of my pants and shins. Then I began trying to dig the spines out of the boots with my knife. They were embedded so deeply that, after a few minutes, I determined it was a futile effort and decided to chuck the Dingos. I dug the work shoes out of the pack and put them on. In the darkness, it took me almost an hour to cut and rip the chute off the cactus. I folded the best of it up and then, out of habit I suppose, I buried the small pieces of the chute, jump boots, and helmet under the sand, saving a couple of strands of the chute lines. It was just after 8:00 p.m. before I finished.

In all my excitement, I forgot about the fake mustache, and in a panic, my hand flew to my upper lip, whereby I was relieved to discover it was still attached. I reasoned that the adhesive used to hold it in place must be very tacky.

My next task was to find that road. I was sure it was still to the south of me. I started walking in that direction. I had to circle a lot of cacti, so I kept checking my small hand compass from time to time to make sure I was heading in the right direction. I knew the desert well—recollecting how during SEAL training we'd run sprints in the dunes—falling and rolling until our sweaty bodies were coated like sugar cookies. Days later. I was still spitting grit out of my mouth, and rubbing it from my eyes and ears. Yes, I knew the desert.

It was like a giant maze of needles. The cactus jungle was practically impenetrable and sometimes I had to trudge a hundred yards just to make fifty feet. It was slow going and I had to stop and empty my shoes several times. A little after 10:00 p.m., I stumbled onto the road. In a state of near exhaustion, I collapsed in the middle of the road and lay there catching my breath while I idly strained the warm sand through my fingers, except for my mangled, sore one.

It took some time before my breathing returned to normal. I sat there in the darkness staring up at the fast-moving cosmic veil of space, I felt small, insignificant, and wondering if someplace up there my fate for the coming day had already been charted. I knew it was going to be a long night. I used the largest piece of what was left of the chute and the lines to fashion a sort of tent borrowing a six-foot cactus for the center pole.

You've got to be alone in the middle of the desert at night to know what it is like. This was the devil's playtime, with a bright werewolf moon sweeping in and out between dark patches of fast-moving storm clouds racing across the sky northward as if being chased by some giant dragon. Behind them, through small patches of clearness, stars twinkled like the many eyes of God peering down upon me.

Most desert creatures hunt and eat at night. They were already on the prowl. The coming storm must have made them uneasy and I was right there on edge with them. The darkness was full of sounds of twigs snapping and the whirring and clicking of kangaroo rats, mice, lizards, and insects scurrying about. I could hear my heartbeat and my labored breathing.

An owl flew close by me in the dark, its beating wings magnified a thousand times louder by my imagination. My mind amplified each sound and I peered vainly into the inky night searching for invisible creatures. Coyotes and wild dogs howled in the distance and I began to fantasize about the mad dogs, which I'd set free roaming about out there. My ears were super sensitive and I imagined all sorts of creatures prowling about. I could almost sense their night eyes watching me from the darkness.

The cacti formed contorted shadows against the faint horizon and all about me their spiny, sharp, silent fingers pointed skyward as if trying to warn of the coming dangers. Around midnight, a rain sequence started coming down hard. I sat under my crude shelter listening to the rain and wind as it began to pound for several hours. Although I didn't know it, the typhoon pivoted and would be delayed coming to this area of the Baja, sparing me that worry ... for the time being. Then, as quickly as it had come, the rain stopped.

The limited food supply consisted of four protein bars, and two bags of nuts, plus I had an apple that Curly gave me. I sipped at the canteen and saved the apple until around four in the morning. I finally ate it to stop my stomach from growling.

It began raining steadily at about 5:00 a.m. but stopped about an hour later, just before dawn, I spotted a large dog prowling around in the twilight. I readied a weapon, but the mongrel never came near me.

With the grayness of daylight, the desert began to grow silent again. The eastern sky metamorphosed from a deep purple rose to white gold. The giant cactus, which had seemed so mysterious, became lifeless as its shadowy darkness waned. The desert seemed alive, and the morning air permeated with the fragrance of the Desert Dahlia and Barrel Cactus flowers.

It had been a hard night, but with the morning came beauty and signs of festivity from the life-giving rain. Moisture still clung to the cacti and overnight the desert seemed to blossom with color. The Ocotillo burst forth with small scarlet flowers. The tops of the cordons and yuccas were crowned with little white blossoms. The Ciros were covered with tiny bright green leaves and practically every plant looked as if they budded forth with unique shades of pink, yellow, or scarlet. It was a rare and beautiful time in the desert, yet the temperature began to rise as soon as the sun cleared the horizon. Fortunately, the sun stayed mostly hidden behind the gray cloud bank. My mouth tasted like gritty cotton and the tepid canteen water didn't help much. But, it was time to get busy. I struggled to my feet, bones creaking and cracking.

I stretched and yawned and decided to say good morning to little Patrick Jr. I picked out a little barrel cactus and stood there watching as the yellow liquid streamed down the grooves. Suddenly, a large diamondback rattler slithered out from under it, shaking his rattles viciously. I hot-footed it away from the cactus, splattering my pants with golden dew as the big rattler, not liking the situation any more than I, snaked off into the desert. I zipped and then began to dig a hole in the sand where I then buried the parachute material, saving the lines. By then I was sweating profusely.

Now, all I could do was pray that the supply truck would come and that I could stop it. I had considered lying down on the road hoping the driver would stop, but negated that idea. I had to block the road somehow so the driver would have to stop and get out. Then I got an idea. I'd dig a trench across the road and he'd have to stop. I took my knife and started scooping the loose sand out of the middle of the road. It was arduous work, but, by 7:30 a.m. I had dug a four-foot wide by two-foot deep furrow all the way across. Once it was big enough, I sculptured it, doing my best to make it look like rain runoff had done it. As an additional precaution, I found a large almost fossilized seven-foot-long Cordon stump and used my parachute lines to drag it into the road positioning it so that it was protruding from the middle of my gully.

I bulldozed all the loose sand to the roadside and stood there sweating and panting like a racehorse that had just finished a race. Then, I stood back and admired my work. Nothing but a tank could get across now without stopping. If my trench didn't do it, I'd have to shoot them, and at this point, I was ready to do anything to carry out my plan. I broke out my little telescope and sat down in the shade of a yucca, sweltering in the humidity and nipping at the canteen. I wished I knew what time to expect that truck but I didn't. My mustache itched like mad and I wondered if the rain had washed away my hair color. I wished I'd brought a little signal mirror, which I could use to check myself over and possibly shine a sun reflection in the driver's eyes. At the moment, I also wished I were home. I wished for a lot of things. In an hour I was jumpy and in two hours I was beginning to wonder if this was such a good idea after all.

The sun kept trying to peek through, but the clouds wouldn't let it. I built and tore down a nice sand castle in the damp sand. I'd resolved that if the truck didn't arrive by two in the afternoon, I would head for the mountain on foot. I figured I was about ten miles away and I hated the thought of hiking that far with backpacks and low-top shoes.

Rain fell off and on several times and when it did I tried to open my mouth to the sky to capture the moisture, but it seemed to take forever to catch enough to swallow. I felt like I was in an easy-bake oven as the sun steamed away the moisture while slowly creeping across the sky above the clouds. The thirsty ground sucked up every bit of the moisture and the sand was already starting to dry out again.

The humidity was stifling and my stomach kept growling and tightening up in knots. I tore into and ingested a protein bar, but it did little to slake my hunger. On the other hand, eating in the desert can be devastating since lots of water is needed to break down the food. I sipped sparingly from my canteen, stretching the precious water. A human body burns off three quarts of water a day and without replenishment heat stroke and dehydration quickly sets in. I was far from dehydrated though, and if I didn't exert myself anymore, I knew I could last the day.

I also knew I could get enough water if it were necessary from the cacti, but moving required effort and perspiration ran freely with the slightest exertion. So I moved as little as possible. I took several salt pills, but if they helped I couldn't tell it. The weather changed every few minutes, alternating between cloudy and wind-blown and hot and stifling. The sultry air was scorching and the wind ferried a harshness that made the throat dry and raspy. At about quarter to one, I noticed some glinted movement in the west. It had to be the supply truck.

CHAPTER 40 – A LITTLE CONVINCING

I began to see it through the scope from about five miles away. It crawled painstakingly over the rough rutted road and I had plenty of time to wait. It seemed like I watched it for an hour, but when I glanced at my watch it had only been fifteen minutes. I moved up the road some twenty yards from my trench, intending to stop the truck with bullets if the trench didn't do the job. I sequestered myself behind a big sand pile and waited, the M-10 clutched tightly in my hand.

I was sweating profusely and my clothes were drenched. I watched the truck through the telescope bounding toward me, leaving a trail of dust and smoke behind. It was an old Dodge stake body, a two-and-three-quarter-ton puddle jumper. I pressed down into the sand, keeping myself hidden from the road. While I was wondering what would happen if the driver didn't see the trench, a huge reddish-brown scorpion crawled leisurely up on my left hand and sat there with its tail cocked over its back, apparently looking right at my face. Had it gone up there by accident, or did it have a purpose?

Adrenaline pumped madly through my system. I recalled a bit of trivia that claimed that ten times more people die from scorpion stings than rattlesnake bites. That fact didn't cheer me. I nervously observed it watch me, as I pondered how the sting would feel, all while the truck was getting closer. Sweat dripped from my face as I lay in this dest sauna. For a moment, I considered smacking the scorpion with the machine pistol in my right hand. I couldn't take my eyes off it as it calmly sat there with its lobster-like pincers resting on my fingers, its venomous tail curled back, and its stinger poised in a striking position.

Then all hell broke loose. I heard squealing brakes and a loud crashing sound. The sudden motion and noise of the truck must have scared the scorpion for suddenly it leaped off my hand and darted for cover. I raised my head just in time to see the rear wheels of the truck bouncing over the trench and up into the air. Somehow, through fantastic luck or driving skill, the driver made it across the trench and managed to keep it on the road. It slid to a stop right by me. I leaped up and raced toward it ... gun in hand. The driver opened the door as I ran up. He started to fall and I caught him as he tumbled helplessly into my arms. I could see a knot the size of a goose egg forming on his forehead.

I quickly checked the truck over. It was a stake bed job with big spiked snow tires that would crawl through anything. There was a green tarpaulin stretched across the back and tied down with ropes. Everything seemed okay.

The driver was still unconscious as I used my parachute lines to tie his hands behind his back and secure his feet together. I propped him into a sitting position and began trying to revive him. My canteen was almost half-empty, but I splashed water on his face. He started moaning and came to with an intently stressed smile revealing several missing teeth. He was a small, skinny Mexican about forty years old with a leathered face that was more grizzled than his years, and the body of one who had worked all their life.

He opened his eyes and spoke in slurred Spanish,

"Mother of Christ! What has happened? Who are you? What are you doing with me?"

I pulled his face close to mine and took a chance, speaking in Spanish

"*Como se llama?*" It meant, what is your name?

"*Paco, jefe.*"

"Okay, Paco. You tell me what I want to know and you'll be all right. What happens when you drive up to the mountain? Who meets you and what do you do? How do you get rid of the supplies? Explain that to me ... quickly!"

I guess my Spanish hadn't been that good and Paco acted suspiciously. It brought a moan of pain from his mouth. Things began to add up in his foggy mind for his eyes suddenly glazed over with determination. My disguise wasn't working. He'd determined my Latino look was phony and began speaking in broken English.

"I tell you nothing *jefe*—El Sol will kill me."

I laid him back onto the sand. He was more afraid of El Sol than me. I'd have to change his mind. I needed to get the truck rolling and I didn't have time to screw around with him. Someone could be watching from the mine with binoculars and I didn't want the dust cloud to stop too long. I had an idea.

I had to impress him fast. I dug out the kit with rabies serum and a syringe. I removed the syringe and stuck the needle through the plastic cover of the bottle, filled the syringe with serum, and pulled it out with a pop. His eyes grew wide as he stared at the huge needle. I maneuvered it so the stream would hit him in the face and squeezed the plunger. A small stream of rabies serum shot onto his face and he squirmed as though it were acid. The liquid trickled down over his mouth, but he was not going to lick it off his lips.

I leaned down close to his face and used my roughest voice.

"Paco, these are bad germs. You know Paco—this stuff is what El Sol uses to cause the dogs to go loco. I'm going to stick this needle into you if you do not tell me what I need to know right now, you'll get rabies. Then, I will leave you out here—tied up—and let you slowly go mad in the heat. This is your only chance to speak."

His mouth was clamped in silence, but his eyes said otherwise. I slowly undid his shirt and exposed his stomach. He had saucer eyes as he intently watched me bring the needle to his belly. I had only shoved it in a little bit when he broke.

"Wait! Wait! I'll talk! I'll tell you everything!"

And talk he did.

"I drive up and honk twice where the road ends. Then they open a hidden door for me and I drive into the tunnel and on through to the parking lot. There some men unload onto the loading dock and they sign for the supplies on the invoice that is in the glove compartment. Then I drive out. Sometimes I eat there first. That's all *señor* ... I swear.."

"Do you have to show any identification?" I asked.

"No. The guards all expect me or whoever delivers. It's easy."

"How many drivers are there?"

"I'm not sure. I don't know them all."

"What's on the truck this time?" I asked.

"Food, beer, toilet paper, stuff like that."

"Anything else I should know?"

"No, *Señor*, I swear on my mother's grave." I knew he was telling the truth.

Now came the hard part. I lay down in the sand alongside him and pulled my shirt up exposing my belly. I opened a small packet containing a wet alcohol pad and rubbed it over my skin and the needle for sterilization. Paco's eyes almost fell out of his head as I carefully inserted the huge needle into my stomach right between two previous punctures and slowly pressed the syringe plunger. I'd given myself shots before, but never anything like this. It was unbearably painful. Somehow, I managed to get the job done. Paco had shut his eyes tightly the minute he saw the yellow liquid start to disappear into my stomach. He wanted no part of my insanity. I didn't blame him.

Having no further use for him. I dragged him to the trench and dropped him into it face up. It provided a little shade to protect him.

"I'm taking the truck. I'll be back for you when I finish my business. I wouldn't advise you to struggle, or yell—you are too far away to be heard—it will only tire you out and it might attract the crazy, rabid dogs loose here in the desert."

He shut his eyes. He could probably wiggle loose in a few hours. I looked at him laying there and thought that if he couldn't and I didn't make it back, at least his grave was already dug.

CHAPTER 41 – FITTING IN

The first thing I did when I got in the truck was to remove my shoes and socks. I dumped all the sand out of my shoes and shook them off the socks. Once that was done, I checked myself over in the oxidized rearview mirror and seemed to still appear Latino, so I reasoned I was good to go.

I figured the truck would be out of alignment but hoped it would still run. I was lucky it hadn't blown a tire. I tried driving it a short distance and though the front end wobbled a bit—it ran okay. After a few miles, when I was well hidden behind a large dune, I stopped. It was time to rig the package.

I dug out the explosives and connected the lead wires from the timer to the detonator charge, which is a long thin metal tube containing an explosive-charged bridge wire and two lead wire connections. The detonation charge is assembled in layers consisting of the time delay charge, a priming charge, and the base charge, which sets off the explosive. I connected the two plastic-covered copper wires to the timer and passed them through the detonator to the priming charge, which is detonated when half an amp of current is passed through the lead wires.

I was sweating copiously and nervous as hell. I had to keep wiping my hands on my trousers. It took me a minute to carefully set the timer for five hours, knowing I could adjust it later if I wanted. Once the explosive package was set, I carefully hid the pack behind the driver's seat. I strapped the knife on my belt and shoved the Ingram under the seat so I could get at it quickly. I laid the .22 on the seat alongside me and checked the rearview mirror.

I was roasting. The truck too was like being in a sauna and had no air conditioning. Because both windows were down I was blasted with fits of the hot desert wind. I visualized my Mexican skin dye melting away and streaking my face in white, but the mirror said otherwise. I ground the granny gear in and popped the clutch. The truck lurched forward and started rolling. I shifted into second and bounced off down the road. That was as much gear as the road would handle and I fought the big steering wheel constantly to keep the rig under control.

It was one of the last of the rough riders. It seemed like I hit every pothole and rock. I almost lost it once when the road veered sharply to avoid a thick stand of Cholas. The forward motion offered no relief from the stifling heat and soon perspiration was oozing out of every pore. It rolled tackily down under my arms and legs. It felt like I had been in the sauna way too long. I was leaking from every pore. In fifteen minutes, I was as drenched as if I had been swimming with my clothes on. The air was ripe with the stench of my body and clothes. I kept thinking about the explosives and hoped the bouncing didn't somehow set them off.

I had a long time to think out my story. I hoped that I would be able to take advantage of the impending storm, which was beginning to slowly announce its arrival with blasts of furious hot wind driven over the desert heat. It took around forty minutes to cover the ten miles. I finally arrived and the road abruptly ended. Directly before me was a cliff where I could see rough camouflage around the large entrance. I beeped the horn twice and heard a grating sound as the door enclosing the tunnel slid back. There were sounds of footsteps crunching gravel and a guard's face appeared in my window.

He inquired, "Where's Paco? Has something happened to him?"

I had the small .22 clutched in my right hand out of sight. But using it would be a last resort. I smiled at him.

"*Si*. My cousin Paco had to take our sister from San Felipe to Mexicali before the storm. My name is, Luis."

He shook his head from side to side.

"*Si*, I hear it is a bad one. Everyone is leaving. I am Alberto. Do you know where to go?"

I nodded.

"I think so, Paco told me the routine."

Being a typical Mexican, he gave me directions anyway.

"Go ahead, I'll see you when you come out."

I shook my head and stated, "I don't think I can get back today. The road's been mostly washed out. I barely made it here. I'm supposed to wait overnight here."

This didn't seem to faze him.

"It's the coming storm. Everything is going to get messed up."

I drove into the tunnel, my heart rate rising and adrenalin pumping, plus my hands were slick with sweat. Everything was quiet except for the noise of the truck echoing off the walls. I was in a dimly lit tunnel that was only a little smaller than the front entrance. There was no one in sight. I could see some light ahead that must have been where the tunnel opened into the storeroom.

Driving along at about five miles an hour, I shoved the .22 into my waistband, tucking my shirt in over it, and drove into the underground parking areas. Four men stood on the loading dock watching my arrival. Apparently, they were waiting for me. They laughed at my efforts. In several jerking maneuvers, I backed the tail of the rig flush to the dock, grabbed the invoice out of the glove box, and got down from the truck, making sure I locked the doors and took the keys.

As soon as I backed the truck in, they immediately removed the tarpaulin revealing crates of vegetables, canned goods, boxes of meat chilled with dry ice, and various other staples. I had the invoice and a ballpoint pen in my hand and I was pleased that I'd gotten this far. None of them cared who I was. I made one of them sign the invoice and then helped them untie the tarp. I asked if I should help with the unloading, but they waved me away. There is job insecurity everywhere.

I asked where the toilet was and one of them wrinkled his nose and pointed across the way. I guess I smelled like I'd already crapped in my pants. I collected my pack and gear, as I left them unpacking the truck. My shoes made little squeaking noises as I walked across the concrete floor in the direction the man pointed.

I found the john and opened the door, glancing back over my shoulder to see the men carrying the supplies inside the room off the loading platform The toilet was small with one sink, a urinal, and two stalls surrounded by six-foot partial partitions. Each stall had a hinged swinging metal door.

I checked the mirror and was happy to see I was still very much appearing to be a Mexican. My kidneys felt like they'd just participated in the Baja 1000, so I took a long leak. Convinced my spray tan was going to last, I splashed some tap water on my face. It was hard to believe I was here in this hell hole again, only this time I'd come of my own volition. This time things would be different.

I entered one of the stalls and sat down on the throne breaking out my map. From it and my previous visits I knew that the elevator was in the back of the loading platform, which wrapped around the kitchen and supply storage area—the entire structure being surrounded by parking. Unless I took the elevator, there was no way to get into the upper level where I hoped Jesus was still locked away.

Common sense told me to reset the explosive timer for a shorter period, stash it someplace secure, get back in the truck and ... get the hell out of there. But my conscience would not allow me to do it that way. I put the map away and cracked open the door to the restroom. They were still unloading the truck. A Mexican in a cook's apron was now sitting on the loading dock smoking a cigarette and watching them work.

I studied the situation through the crack. Three times an armed guard appeared near the elevator and walked around the loading dock scanning the parking area. I tried to time him, but he was too erratic and after twenty minutes I gave up. I rationalized that internal guards wouldn't be too concerned about security since the two tunnels appeared to be the only way in or out of the place.

I was beginning to worry about spending so much time in the toilet, but I decided that they would just think I was a typical truck driver shirking the off-loading work. I heard footsteps coming my way. I looked through the crack and saw the Mexican wearing a white apron heading for me as he whistled a catchy Mexican tune. I scooted back into the stall and took out the .22 thumbing the hammer back and sat waiting for him. I hadn't had enough time to flip the latch on the door when he surprised me by opening the door to my stall. He had already started unbuckling his pants and held the zipper of his fly with his right hand.

We looked at each other and I squeezed the trigger and heard a little 'pfft'. I'd hit him right between the eyes. A small hole appeared in his forehead as his eyes opened wide in surprise. He didn't have time to shut them because he was dead before I caught him. I removed his apron and sat him down on the toilet. I tied the apron around his head to catch the blood flow, knowing that as soon as the blood in his head drained out, it would stop. I whipped his belt off and re-strung it through two of the back belt loops of his pants, using it to secure him to the rusty plumbing behind the toilet.

I had torn it now, I didn't know how long before this guy would be missed, but the clock was ticking. I latched on the toilet door and climbed under it. Then I cracked open the door to check the loading platform. They had finished unloading the truck and there was no one in sight.

I figured I had an hour at most to get my job done before someone found him. But, it might only be a few minutes. It was time to start exploring. I walked across the parking area and up onto the loading platform. I peered through the screen door and there was no one around. My map showed a storage room just off the loading dock in the back of the kitchen and there it was.

Outside the storeroom was a row of garbage cans placed against the wall with squadrons of flies circling them. I opened the door and entered the storeroom, flipping on a light switch near the door. It was filled with wall-to-wall shelves containing rows of towels, toilet paper, aprons, cooks' hats, light bulbs, dish soap, and other supplies. That would have to do.

I went back out to the truck and removed the explosive pack, being careful to replace my pack and re-lock the truck. Back into the storage room, after checking to make sure the timer was ticking down properly, I carefully hid it under a pile of aprons on the highest shelf. Unless someone got lucky, they'd never find it. Now, no matter what happened, in a little over three hours the place was going to go bye-bye without any further help from me. I felt good about that.

Thanks to my map, I knew where I wanted to go next. The problem was getting there without having to fight a war. I decided to become one of the lowly workers. I put on a white apron and grabbed several rolls of toilet paper concealing the .22 by shoving two of the rolls over the barrel and silencer. I went back out onto the loading platform and around to the elevator. The guard saw me coming and looked at the toilet paper. I casually shuffled along slowly and spoke low in slurred Spanish so he'd have to listen hard to hear.

"El Sol must take a lot of shits. He wants more paper."

The guard laughed. Noticing my unfamiliar face, he gazed at me curiously—then shrugged it off saying,

"El Sol isn't the one. It's Gonzales that's full of shit."

We both laughed and I headed for the elevator. I pressed the 'up' button and waited, holding my breath until the elevator appeared and the door opened. The guard was still chuckling to himself as I stepped inside and pushed the button for the second level. I hoped it was where I'd find Jesus—if he were still alive.

CHAPTER 42 – IN THE CRAPPER

I knew from the map that the prison area was down the corridor and that the rest of the level was used for storage. The elevator came to a stop and I stepped out, relieved to see that there was no one in sight. I sauntered slowly and quietly down the passageway, checking each door as I walked along. They were all locked.

The passageway curved around to my right just as the map indicated. When I got to the prison area, on my right was a door that opened into another restroom. It was exactly like the other one. I dumped the toilet paper into the sink and heard a grunt. I nearly jumped out of my skin. I looked around and sure enough, there was a pair of legs showing beneath one of the toilet doors. Not knowing what else to do. I opened the door to the adjacent toilet, dropped my pants, and sat down.

A voice from next door asked how I was.

"*Como estas?*"

I muttered lowly in Spanish. "*Muy bien, y usted*? Meaning, Good. And you?"

"Same. Are you coming on duty now?"

"Yes." I hoped he wouldn't catch the frog in my voice.

"Who's on duty now?"

"Pedro and Garcia." He grunted again and to keep the rhythm going I grunted too.

This was better than torturing someone for information.

"Is the policeman still here?" I asked.

"Yes. He's in five. I heard they are going to let the dogs kill him once the storm passes. Say, who are you?"

I grunted hard.

"Patrico—I'm new. My cousin Paco, who drives the supply truck, got me the job."

"Oh!" said the voice. "Paco is my friend. We get drunk together sometimes. I'm Fernando."

I heard him rip off some paper so I reeled off a handful myself, wadded it up, and dropped it into the bowl—flushing the toilet. I stood in the stall fiddling around as if buckling my pants. Fernando had also finished and flushed his toilet. I stepped outside and waited for him.

I said, "Where do we get our uniforms?"

"Why? Didn't they give you one? You're supposed to wear a uniform? Didn't they tell..."

I interrupted him. "Everyone's worried about the storm."

"I hear it will be a bad one. My sister lives in San Felipe but they won't let me off. Some people have already left."

He was still talking when he stepped outside the stall. As quickly as he did, I hit him as hard as I could right in the kisser with my open palmed good right hand. He flew back into the enclosure and his head struck the edge of the toilet bowl. His cranium furiously thrust forward against his chest. I had my gun out but he was slumped and unmoving. I knelt and felt his pulse. He was dead from a broken neck. Better that than a bullet I supposed. I sighed. He sounded like a nice guy. Unfortunately, he was a few inches shorter than me, but his uniform would have to do. I began to undress him.

In a few minutes, he was clad only in socks and underclothes. I took my clothes off, hoping I could somehow make his work. I removed my master key. It was almost the same color as the one he wore so I put it on. The pants were very snug in the crotch and way too short, but otherwise, fit me. I got into the rest of his uniform but kept my shoes. Then, I quickly put my pants and shirt on the dead guard and propped him onto the toilet using his belt to secure him in a sitting position. I latched the door from the inside and then crawled under it. This was a dejá vu act becoming a habit I suppose.

Their bathrooms were coming in handy. Fernando looked very much like a man taking a peaceful constitutional. I stacked the toilet paper neatly in a corner of the toilet stall and cleaned my hands. Checking the mirror, I could see that I didn't look too unlike a guard. I strapped on his holster and pistol and then stuck my own .22 inside my shirt and marched down the hall to the prison area. I came to the locked door and banged loudly on it. A guard came up and recognized my uniform, but not me. He cautiously swung the door open. I grinned at him and said,

"My name is Patrico and I am taking Fernando's place. I'm here to relieve Pedro or Garcia."

"I'm Garcia. You're to relieve me.? Are you new?'

"Yes. They let Fernando off to be with his sister, because of the storm. I'm filling in."

"You're fifteen minutes early, you know."

"I always relieve early."

Garcia smiled. "That's good, *amigo.*"

He yelled over at Pedro who was watching from a chair,

"Hey Pedro, come and meet the new man."

Pedro came strolling over, a cup of coffee in his hand.

Garcia joked, "This is Pedro Fernandez and he's a card cheat. So, don't play with him for money. He'd even cheat his mother."

I stuck my hand out and we shook.

"I'm Patrico. I've been known to gamble …. On occasion."

Pedro's eyes lit up at the prospect of a new sucker.

He said, "Ah, that is good, amigo. Too bad I have to go off watch, otherwise I'd be glad to take your money."

We laughed and another guard knocked on the door.

I opened it and said, "Here's your relief, Pedro. You may never get a chance at at me or my money."

Pedro looked at the new arrival.

"You are on time for once. You finally do so, just when I've got a new fish to reel in. This is our new man, Patrico. He came early. This pig is, Manuel Delacruz."

Manuel stuck his hand out and I shook hands with him, recognizing him as one of the guards who marched me into El Sol's office.

I strolled over and plopped down into a chair to steady my nerves. Manuel relieved Pedro and he and Garcia took off leaving Manuel and me alone to guard the prisoners. Things were working out better than I expected, but I knew my luck could turn in a hurry if I made a misstep. Manuel looked at me several times as if trying to place me and I figured that it would only be a matter of time until he realized who I was.

I quickly caught onto their routine, which mostly involved sitting on their butts and drinking coffee. I figured they worked eight-hour shifts, but I wasn't certain. Anyway, it wouldn't be long before someone discovered that the guys sitting on the thrones had more than a bad case of diarrhea.

In the cane-bottomed chair, I leaned back against the concrete wall, taking in the musty odor and watching Manuel puttering around. Rats scurried freely about, and I said loud enough for Manuel to hear,

"Why don't they poison these damn rats?"

He wandered over and cocked his head at me.

"There are too many. Besides, Gonzales likes them. She says they're good company for the prisoners. Where are you from, amigo?"

He looked curiously at me.

"You see familiar. Hav I met you before?"

I tossed a reply off the top of my head.

"I'm here because of the storm. I work for El Sol someplace else. I'm not allowed to talk about it. El Sol's orders."

That was more than adequate. He nodded his head and smiled. Naturally, he wanted to talk about it.

"El Sol is a piece of work, eh Patrico?"

I nodded my head to indicate yes and changed the subject.

"What's the routine, here?"

"The what?"

"You know, the routine? The little things a new guard should know?"

Manuel spit at a big black rat dragging his scaly tail down the hallway.

"Like what?"

"I was just wondering about eating and breaks. Do we get any breaks?"

I wanted him to think I was more interested in the privileges than the job at hand. Everybody likes to bad mouth the boss when the boss is not around.

"Shit, man. They only give us enough time to eat and go to the bathroom. We're stuck in this stinking hole all the time. One of these days..." He let it hang without finishing.

I took his side and claimed, "I hear you, man. What about prisoners? How many are there?"

Manuel stood and said, "Come! I will show you."

He took a flashlight hanging from a strap on the wall, flicked it on, and shone it down the corridor to test it. The powerful beam of light, which I remembered well from my captivity perspective, stabbed into the darkness. The corridor was about seventy feet long with six cells on each side. I studied the scene as I tagged along behind Manuel. My cell had been the last one on the right, farthest from the entrance.

We stopped at the first cell on the left and Manuel handed me the light. "This is the old man. He's been here for over a year."

Manual handed me the light and I shined it through the small barred window into the cell. The inhabitant reminded me of prisoners of war I'd seen. The man lay on the hard wooden cot, with one frail thin arm flung up over his eyes to protect himself from the blinding light. He looked every bit like he'd been in captivity a long time enduring the ravages of torture and malnutrition. His ebony eyes were deeply sunk into their sockets. Blanched and burnt wrinkled skin sagged under his ragged gray beard and he wore only a burlap sack, ripped apart to form a sort of toga. His cell stank of vomit and excrement. I gagged as I peered into the rank darkness. Rat eyes gleamed like demons in the beam of the flashlight.

Manuel grabbed the light away from me and flicked it off, realizing how much the scene had shocked me.

He proceeded to comment, "This is not a very good job, amigo. Some things a man just has to do. These two tried to run away last night."

He shined that light in the next cell and I peered over his shoulder. There were two Mexican men who I didn't recognize. They appeared to be in reasonably good condition. We continued our tour.

"This is another *gringo* they caught making too many inquiries in San Felipe. He's been here a month, but he'll die soon I think."

Manuel shined the light through the bars. I looked but had to turn away. The man's eyes had both been burned or torn out and all of the fingers on his hands were missing. He trembled in a corner, the useless stumps of his hands in his lap, while rats chewed away at the stubs of his fingers. He had no will to live and if I had the opportunity I would end it for him. I choked and looked at Manuel with disgust. He nodded in agreement and we walked down to the next cell. He shined the light through the bars. I expected to see another mangled prisoner.

I almost gasped out loud. Mickey was sitting on the hard wooden cot wearing the same clothes she'd been wearing when I'd last seen her. She looked up when the light hit her but she couldn't see me.

Manuel asked. "You know about this one? She's a tranny.

"No. I do not know her." I turned my head and tried to make my voice inaudible. I walked quickly away from the cell, making sure Mickey didn't recognize me.

"I wonder how she'd be in bed, eh?" I nudged Manuel but he looked sternly at me as if to imply he wasn't into that sort of fun.

"How long has she been here?"

"They brought ... him in last night. He helped the *gringo* escape. They will torture him pretty bad I think."

I didn't say anything as we stepped up to look at the next prisoner.

"And here is the policeman who also helped the *gringo*. Do you know about him?'

"My brother mentioned him, that's all I've been told."

I took the light away from Manuel and shined it into the cell. Jesus was naked and lay on the floor, his body jerking spasmodically, blood-encrusted lips tightly drawn back over his teeth. His body was covered with knots and bruises. There was a large inky puddle on the floor where the stumps of three amputated fingers had bled out.

I shined the light into the pool of blood where a rat was licking at the black coagulation. It looked up into the light, its eyes glowing brightly. The flashlight beam reflected onto the blood casting the image of the rat against the far wall. In my various pursuits I had seen hell and then some, but the sight of such torture turned my stomach. I felt that strange warm swallowing sensation as the saliva began to explode in my mouth and I was doing all I could to not puke. I handed the light back to Manuel.

I bent over and felt myself gag, but I kept from vomiting.

I told Manuel, "Excuse me."

Manuel came up behind me and laid his hand on my back.

"I know how you feel, Patrico. I remember the first time I saw these misfortunate detainees."

I played my innocent card and let him lead me back to the guard area and sit me down in the chair. My face must have revealed the revulsion I felt as I watched the rats scurry away. This preview only made me more determined to end this vile wickedness.

CHAPTER 43– PRISON WATCH

A little after 5:00 p.m., having regained my composure, I was considering my next move when Manuel gave me what I wanted.

"It's time to eat. We take turns. You want to go first?"

That was the opening I'd been waiting for.

"No! You go first, please. The way my stomach is, I couldn't keep anything down right now anyway. I'd rather sit here alone for a while."

"Okay. I'm going to the dining area then. I'll bring back the slop for the prisoners. "

"Take your time."

Manuel nodded in agreement, unlocked the door, and disappeared down the corridor. I waited until I heard the elevator door open before I raced for the keys hanging on a nail above the table near the entrance. I grabbed them, a flashlight, and ran back down the passageway unlocking Jesus' cell. He looked like the victim of a bad car accident. He was in a complete state of shock. He opened his eyes as the beam of the flashlight dilated.his pupils

I cradled his head in my arms and said softly, "Jesus! This is Pat. I'm going to get you out of here. Can you hear me?"

He rolled his head to the side and I saw a faint flutter of recognition on his face.

I lifted him to his feet and dragged his inert form out into the dimly lit corridor. Even the faint light of the corridor was too much after the darkness of his cell, and he shut his eyes. He tried to help by moving his feet, but they just wouldn't cooperate.

I had to drag him down the passageway and out the door. He struggled to retain consciousness and I prayed for him to become coherent. Somehow, I managed to get him into the toilet where the dead Fernando was still where I'd left him on the stool. I leaned him over the sink and began splashing cold water onto Jesus' face. He started coming around and must have felt the pain in his left hand because he stuck it under the running water. A stream of dark red flowed from his missing finger stubs into the sink. I could see that someone had made a vain effort to cauterize the wounds, probably to prevent him from bleeding out. I rubbed his unshaven neck and chin and the bristles prickled against my hand.

I had no way of knowing how much blood he'd lost, or if he would ever recover. Luckily, within a few minutes, he managed to recover some from the stupor and stand up, bracing himself on the sink. I kept talking to him slowly, repeating everything twice. I didn't know how much he heard in his state of semi-consciousness, but I kept trying.

"Jesus! Jesus! Can you hear me? Can you hear me? I know I don't look like it, but I am Pat! Pat!"

He turned away from the sink and I had to grab him. He was fighting to free himself from his state of mental shock.

He cracked his eyes open and looked at me.

"Pat? "I did not tell them ... nothing."

"I know, Jesus. I know! Listen to me, there's a guard in the toilet that I killed. Do you understand? I killed a guard and took his place. That's how I got you out. I got you out of your cell. Remember?"

His hazy eyes looked blearily at me and then into the mirror. I don't know what he saw in the mirror, but he lowered his head and said again,

"You are darker, Pat. I did not tell them."

"I know, my friend. Listen to me. We don't have much time. I'm going to take the dead guard and put him in your cell. I want you to put on his clothes and stay in here. Do you understand me?" I repeated it for him again.

He looked at me blearily and mumbled. "I unnerstan—-"

"Good. Stay in here and clean up. If you hear somebody coming, go into the toilet and sit down. Don't leave until I come back for you. I'll be back in a while. Do you understand?"

He nodded.

I repeated the explanation, "I'll put him in your cell so they will think you are still there. Please, Jesus! Do what l say, my friend, okay?" He nodded his head again.

I left him standing over the sink and climbed under the partition. I opened the door and dragged the guard out. I stripped his wristwatch and clothes off and tossed them on the floor. Jesus stood there watching me and I could tell from his eyes that he was drifting in and out of consciousness.

I handed him the guy's watch and clothes from the floor and he began struggling into them while I used my knife to cut three fingers off the guard's left hand. It was not a pleasant job but had to be done. I wound toilet paper around them to stop the blood and capped the bloody mess with some paper towels. I stuffed another roll of toilet paper under my shirt and began dragging the body down the hall toward the cell Jesus had occupied. Because of gravity, his hand leaked blood profusely and I realized I should have waited until I got him in the cell to cut off his fingers.

I put the dead man on the cot in the cell, turning his face to the wall and placing his arm so the missing fingers could be seen. Then I locked the door satisfied that anyone checking would assume it was Jesus. I made my way back down the hall, wiping up the blood that had splattered on the way. In the bathroom, Jesus was still sitting on the toilet struggling to get into the pants. "I'll help you in a minute. I have to clean up first."

I picked up the fingers from the blood-splattered sink, flushed them down one of the toilets, and rinsed out the sink. I managed to quickly get most of the blood off the floor and decided to let it go at that, hoping that no one would inspect the place close enough to detect the mess. I washed my hands and face.

Jesus managed to get into the pants and shirt, but he couldn't zip up the pants, so I did it for him. I then strung the belt and buckled it for him. While I put the shoes and socks on him, I slowly explained again what I had done and what I wanted him to do. Through his haze of pain, he seemed to comprehend. I found a paper cup from a wall dispenser, filled it with water, and gave it to him. He sipped at first and then guzzled it down.

I took the little. 22 out of my waistband and handed it to him. He laid it on the sink as he slipped the dead guard's watch on over his bloody left hand. I tapped the watch to get him to look at it.

"If I do not come back for you in an hour, try to get out anyway you can. *Comprende*?"

He picked up the gun and nodded his head that he did, but I knew he seemed barely capable of rational thought.

"I'm going back to the cell block now. Sit, rest, and be careful. I'll come for you soon."

I hurried back down the hallway and into the cell area, locking the door behind me. I ran over to Mickey's cell and shined the flashlight on her. "

"Mickey? It's me, Pat. Why are you in there?"

She ran to the small opening at the cell door.

"Pat? Are you here? I can't see you."

She couldn't see me but recognized my voice. I thought it best not to let her see my disguise, so I kept the light away from my face.

"Yes. It's me! What happened?"

"They caught me at the airport. I bought a ticket to New York and they captured me. I tried to run, but they let me get outside and knocked me out. I was brought back here and now they're going to kill me! They're looking all over for you. What are... uh... how come... how did you even get here?"

"Never mind that now! Do as I say and maybe I can get you out of this mess."

"Anything you say! Just don't let that fat pig torture me. I've seen what she does to people! She's crazy you know, and gets her jollies that way. I can't imagine what she has in store for me."

"I know! I'll get you out, somehow."

My mind raced. I knew I had plenty to do, but for some reason, I couldn't think of what. I contemplated letting Mickey out of the cell but figured she might foul things up.

"I'll get you out, Mickey. Just stay here quietly and keep your mouth shut. Don't tell anyone about me being here, no matter what happens. You got it?"

"Yes! But, please don't let her torture me!"

I heard footsteps approaching and I said quickly, "Okay, I've got to go now."

I ran back and flopped in the chair and put my head down into my hands. A rat-a-tat sounded at the door, so I got up and walked over to open it. It was Manuel. He was carrying a bucket of bad-looking boiled prunes, for the prisoners. He set it down on the floor.

"Feeling better?"

"Some, but not much."

Manuel set down across the table from me and several times he looked at me as though he remembered, but time passed and I tried not to worry, figuring that I could always dispose of him if he made any threatening moves.

While he picked his teeth, I tried to get my mind in order. All the pieces of the puzzle were there. But I couldn't quite make them fit together.

I kept thinking about the visitors that were due to arrive soon and wondering, who they were. Common sense told me to dispose of Manuel, grab Jesus and Mickey, and just get out. I was reasonably confident I could manage all that unless I ran into some unexpected obstacle. However, the same type of curiosity that killed the cat was also gnawing at me. I was too interested in the so-called *visitors*. Besides, I still had about two and a half hours before the big boom.

I appeared to be reasonably safe, at least for a little while. No one would look for me inside the prison area. I hoped that Jesus was coming around and that his will to live would bring him out of his mental mind fog. If it came to a shoot-out, I would probably have to leave him behind, but I owed him a lot.

I decided to play it by ear a while longer. We sat quietly for about a half hour, and although Manuel brought back a bucket of slop for the prisoners, he'd made no move to feed them. I decided to take the initiative and volunteer to do it myself avoiding the possibility of him discovering the dead guard in Jesus' cell.

"You want me to feed the prisoners?"

"Sure, if you want to. There's a ladle hanging behind you on the wall. We don't have any clean bowls, so just use the ones already in the cells. Only give them each one helping."

I snatched the ladle off the wall, grabbed the bucket, and flashlight in hand walked down the passageway toward Jesus' cell. I unlocked it and put only a small amount of slop in the bowl so that it would appear as if Jesus had eaten some of it. As I shut the door behind me, I heard rats scampering for the dish and realized that the little food I had left in the dish would soon be gone. I walked up to Mickey's cell, glancing down the hall at Manuel who had not moved.

I opened the door and stepped inside, peering through the crack at Manuel. She was looking in my direction and I watched as she slowly stood up and started easing toward me. Mickey was on her feet right behind me and didn't recognize who I was. I turned the flashlight off and said in a whisper. "Don't be alarmed, it's me, Pat. Keep your mouth shut, no matter what I say."

"Pat? It's you, Pat? All right, but—-"

I raised my voice so Manuel would hear me. "

Ah, you're a man, no? Let me see you."

I could hear Manuel, just a a few feet away outside the cell and listening. I shined the light on Mickey and her blue eyes looked terrified, but she didn't say anything. I started walking toward her when I heard the door swing open behind me.

"Don't mess around with the prisoners. Just feed them."

I turned around, acting surprised that he had caught me.

"I was just trying—-"

I let it hang there and walked out of the cell, dishing a scoop of slop in Mickey's bowl on the way out. Manuel was standing in the doorway and I had to brush past him on the way out. He gave me a dirty look. I was beginning to like the bastard. He watched me as I fed the other prisoners and then we walked back down the hall to our chairs.

CHAPTER 44 – BETRAYAL

The relationship between us deteriorated, and we sat quietly. I was considering taking him out and had my hand on my gun when I heard footsteps approaching. I slowly eased the leather catch off the hammer. We stood up when a knock sounded at the door. The door opened and it was another guard.

"You two take he/she to El Sol's office at once. I'll stay here."

I cursed softly under my breath, realizing I'd stalled too long. We went to Mickey's cell and opened the door, Manuel said, "Get up! Come on, fem boy! Come with us!"

We handcuffed Mickey and fell in on each side of her as we traversed the hallway, through the prison area door, and into the passageway leading to the elevator. As far as I knew, Mickey hadn't truly recognized me, not having seen me in the light yet. I squeezed her arm softly and she turned to look at me. I put my finger in front of my lips to indicate silence, but Mickey gasped in surprise when she realized who I was. Manuel thought she was about to attempt a break, so he gave Mickey's arm a sharp jerk. Still, he didn't catch on even though Mickey appeared to be stunned.

As we passed the door to the toilet where Jesus was I said,

"Wait! I can't hold it any longer. I've got to go. I'll just be a minute or two."

"Hurry up, then!" Manual cursed under his breath and shook his head, but nodded for me to go. I stepped quickly into the bathroom, leaving him and Mickey standing alone in the hall. Jesus was sitting on the toilet with the door shut.

I whispered, "Open up, Jesus. It's me, Pat."

The door swung open and he looked up at me. He was getting some color back onto his face..

He grinned and whispered, "I'm better now, Pat."

"Good! I'm going to Solorio's office. I may run into trouble. If I'm not back for you in about a half hour, or if you hear gunfire, try to get out of here. You know where the elevator is and how to get out, don't you?"

"*Si Patricio!*"

"All right. Listen, do not come looking for me. If I'm not back in thirty minutes, just save yourself."

He gave me a strange, thankful look, so I touched his shoulder. "You promise?"

"*Si!*"

"Okay then. I'll see you later."

I flushed the urinal and walked out zipping up my pants. We fell in alongside Mickey again and marched down to the elevator. It arrived and we rode up to El Sol's floor and walked down the hall to his office. I thought about making a move, but I was curious about what I would find in Solorio's office. I held my breath while Manuel banged on the door. In a second it opened and we entered.

El Sol stood talking to Gonzales. Another woman had her back turned toward us. When the other women turned around, my heart jumped up into my throat and I almost gagged. It was Carmen. A million thoughts seared across my brain. None of them made sense.

"Bring the girly boy over here," ordered Solorio.

We marched Mickey over in front of El Sol who was playing holier-then-thou and didn't even look at me. I glanced at Carmen. She had a bandage on her shoulder where the bullet had struck her. I then realized what had happened as the cog in the wheel game slipped into place inside my mind. I remembered the enforcer killing Ricardo, the one who had shot Carmen, and what he had said about them not having orders to kill the girl.

Carmen looked directly at me, which caused me to avert my eyes. I wasn't fast enough, however, and for an instant her eyes met mine. Unless I was wrong, she knew immediately who I was. She didn't say anything though, so I looked away in the hopes that she hadn't recognized me.

At El Sol's order, Manuel and I stepped away from Mickey, leaving her frightened body standing alone in front of the big desk. Solorio stood with his back turned to us, patiently staring out the window overlooking his valley. Since I'd been inside the mine, I'd forgotten about the impending storm. From what I could see, it was now raging.

Although it was daytime, it was pitch dark outside and heavy rain beat against the window making it vibrate in its frame. I could hear claps of thunder over the howling winds. Behind Solorio, I saw fiery lightning streaking in disjointed patterns across the leaden sky. It was a furious tempest.

Carmen and Gonzales stood on the right side of the desk away from me. I glanced at Carmen again and she was fixated on me intently. I was positive she knew who I was. Gonzales kept glaring sadistically at Mickey in anticipation of the thrills to come.

El Sol spoke to no one in particular.

"It is pissing bricks out there."

Then he turned toward Mickey.

"You? You've been a bad *travesti*."

Mickey glanced nervously back and forth between El Sol and Gonzales. Then she turned and looked right at me with a desperate look on her face. I glanced at the floor avoiding her stare and she turned toward Gonzales with a pleading look. Gonzales' cheeks were bright red in anticipation, and with obvious enjoyment, the big bitch slapped Mickey across the mouth. It started a thin trickle of blood running down Mickey's chin. She did not attempt to wipe it away. At the sight of blood, Gonzales subconsciously licked her lips. I noticed that Carmen had looked away and I knew she was making her decision.

Solorio said, "You knew the penalty for betraying me. Why did you do it? I took you and that big buck out of the slums and made you into something and then you had to go and be disloyal to me.

Mickey lowered his/her head and watched his blood dripping onto the thick carpet. Solorio continued, "I could take it easy on you... if you cooperate."

Mickey looked up at him questioningly.

He then added, "Just tell me where Race is and I'll let you walk out of here alive."

I could tell that Mickey was pondering the proposition. All I could do was pray she had the common sense to realize El Sol would never keep his word nor let her go.

"Or must we let *señora* Gonzales play her games with you?"

Solorio's face tightened. "Tell me, God damn it! You left here with him and you know where he is!"

Mickey lifted her head as though she had made up her mind.

Her feminine controlled voice snarled, "Go to hell, you skinny son of a bitch."

El Sol lashed out and struck Mickey in the face with his clenched fist. The blow landed with a resounding thud and I almost went for him but checked myself at the last moment. Both Manuel and I stepped up alongside Mickey, but Solorio turned his back and walked over to stare out the window again, his hands busy tweaking his mustache. No one said anything for a few seconds. The only noise was the eerie screeching, crunching sounds of the storm raging outside.

Carmen walked over to a large red couch against the far wall and dropped onto it.

She said softly, "I can tell you where Race is."

That was it! I'd had it! All eyes were instantly upon her. I knew the game was over as she pointed her index finger at me. I quickly withdrew the gun I was wearing, training it on Manuel. I backed away slowly, dragging Mickey with me and waving the four-inch .38 from Manuel to Solorio.

El Sol stared at me in disbelief. "Is it possible? I don't believe it."

Gonzales' jaw dropped open. "It really is—-"

Manuel's memory jogged. "I knew I'd seen him someplace before. I should have remembered."

I motioned for him to back up and he did.

I pointed my weapon at Solorio. I waved the gun from him to Carmen. "Over there Stretch! Right now!"

I herded them into a group. Carmen remained seated on the couch, aloof and seemingly unconcerned.

I barked at her. "Off your ass, Carmen!"

She smiled benignly and stood up alongside the others.

As usual, El Sol wanted to discuss matters.

"Race, I can assure you that you'll never get out of here alive. I have guards."

Manuel picked that exact moment to take a swing at me. I ducked and took him out with one chop of my gun barrel against his temple. El Sol ran for his desk. I put a bullet just over his head. It smacked into the wall before him with a loud thud and got his attention. He froze in mid-stride and stuck his skinny arms up so far his fingers touched the ceiling.

The shot was loud but had put me in charge. Mickey walked up in front of Solorio, stupidly getting between us. I braced myself to shoot them both if I had to, but no one moved. Mickey balled up a fist and bounced it off the end of El Sol's nose causing him to collapse to the floor. Mickey liked popping people in the nose. I'd been there myself. This time I rather enjoyed it.

As I stood there covering them with the gun, the pieces of the puzzle fell into place. Carmen was the key. She had been my Achilles heel—the one who had told El Sol about me in the first place, and the one who had sold me out. She'd been planted from the get-go. That explained a lot of things. It confirmed that Jesus had been telling the truth when he claimed that he hadn't told them where to find me. I had assumed he had broken under drugs or torture. Carmen had been the one who told them, just like she'd told them to nab Jesus.

It also meant that she would have been the one to pass the word along to Tate that I was inquiring about Mickey. I had shown her Mickey's picture and asked her about Mickey on that first night in San Felipe. I should have put it together when El Sol's soldier said what he did.

He claimed, "We had no orders to kill the girl."

As I stood there with the fog slowly lifting, I realized what a hell of a situation I was in. I wondered who was the prisoner. The gunshot had been too loud. I wished that I had kept the .22 with the silencer, but hindsight is always twenty-twenty. I didn't have the faintest idea of what to do with them, although I was seriously considering shooting everyone except Mickey. Solorio lay on the floor whimpering beside the guard, Manuel, who was out of it. I had to do something.

"All right bastards, take off your shoes and lay face down on the floor."

When they had done so, I told Mickey to secure them well using their shoelaces and pantyhose. While Mickey was tying them up, I sat on El Sol's desk. I kept my gun trained on them as I searched for alarms. I found two buttons that could have been used to summons help had Solorio been able to reach them. I was glad he had been standing up when the showdown came. Perhaps. I was going to get by with this after all.

Within a few minutes, Mickey had everyone trussed up and secure. I checked the knots and they were okay. Next, I found the circuit that supplied the power to the alarms and it was a simple matter to disconnect the power. I took Solorio's office keys and yanked the telephone line from the wall, then stopped to survey my work. They wouldn't go anywhere for a while.

CHAPTER 45 – SLAPS AND POKES

I walked over to the door, swung it open, and stood there like an idiot staring at six guards. It didn't take a mathematical genius to deduce that I couldn't kill all of them with the. 38 in my hand, but I was willing to try. I aimed it at them, but they were already aiming theirs at me. It was a genuine Mexican standoff and I knew that one word from Gonzales or El Sol would be all it would take to get them to shoot. While I still had the chance. I folded my hand and tossed in my chips by lowering my gun.

It only took Solorio a few minutes to regain his composure and set things back to his idea of the right perspective. This meant that Mickey and I now stood before him with a guard on each side and several more behind us. Gonzalez danced around with glee in her eyes that said she was going to enjoy doing us in. She slapped each of us across the face several times.

Finally, I said, "If you slap me one more time, I'll shove that fat arm of yours up your ass."

The guns sticking in my back didn't give her quite enough backbone for she stopped hitting us.

El Sol regained his composure.

"Lock them up. After the storm passes, *Señora* Gonzales can do what she wants with them."

The guards stood by watching quietly. As commanded they started marching Mickey and me back to the cell area. Manuel had come out of his stupor and walked along beside me, rubbing the bump on his head.

"I couldn't place you, but I knew I'd seen you before. Nice Mex disguise."

The poor bastard was still worried about not recognizing me.

"It's okay, Manuel. I forgive you."

He looked at me oddly and I think he took me seriously.

Four guards were dragging us, and two more with guns drawn walked slightly behind. I figured I might take them, but it was a big chance. There would be a better time. I still had my master key.

As we approached the cellblock area, I wondered if Jesus might help out if he saw us coming down the hallway. However, I saw no sign of him as they marched us smoothly past the bathroom where he was hiding. As they unlocked the cellblock door, I turned to Manuel.

"Is there any chance of putting us in the same cell, Manuel? I'd like to talk with Mickey before they kill us."

He glanced at Mickey who was nodding okay. Manual shrugged his shoulders.

"We'll lock you both in number six."

They marched us down the hall and under Manuel's direction threw both of us into my old cell. As the door clanged shut, I had a flash of dejá vu. The wretched place was beginning to seem almost like home to me for I kept ending up here. The guards walked away leaving us alone in the cell. I stared out the small window trying to determine who stayed behind and how many there were, but I couldn't tell, I waited a few minutes until I heard the cell block door slam and then I took off my belt.

It was time to use the master key.

Mickey watched curiously as I explained. "

This belt has a plastic explosive in it. I'm going to blow the door and get us out of here. A Mexican policeman is hiding down the hall in the bathroom. His name is Jesus. If anything happens to me try to make it to him. He'll help you get out of here."

I began to shove the belt as tightly as I could into the hinge crack of the door and when I had it jammed in, I briefed Mickey.

"When I set this thing, it will blow in exactly three minutes. I don't have a watch so I'll have to count. When we get down to fifteen seconds, I'll nod. I want the guards to be standing outside that door when it blows, so I can get at them through the smoke. Try to make them think I'm raping you or killing you, or something, but get them down here. Do you understand?"

This was Mickey's game. "I'll get them down here. Do you want me to count too?"

"No. I'll do the counting. You just start screaming when I give you the signal. One more thing—I don't exactly know what it'll do—so stay away and cover up the best you can before it blows."

I felt the belt in the dark. It was wedged pretty tightly into the crack of the door with only the activator buckle sticking out. I could only hope that the explosion would blow the door. I reached up and twisted the buckle starting the three-minute timer.

Then I yanked the cot over on its side and Mickey and I scrunched down behind it. It was a long three minutes. My mind kept drifting away and I had to force myself to concentrate on counting. I again told myself to stop thinking of Mickey as a man. I told myself to give Lukban and Maria a vacation when I got back. I told myself a hundred things while I counted. When I had silently counted to one thousand and sixty twice, I started the last sixty seconds, giving Mickey a signal to get ready.

"When I tap you twice, it means the door is about to blow open, so start screaming then."

At my signal, Mickey let out a loud screech and began yelling.

"Take your hands off me! No! Don't do that! Please stop!"

Then she screamed again, so loud it hurt my ears. I heard the guards charging down the passageway and I wondered if we'd jumped the gun. A key jammed into the door when a sudden shock wave threw me on top of Mickey, followed a millisecond later by a blinding flash and an ear-shattering explosion. The concussion left my head spinning and my ears ringing.

The cell was full of dust and falling debris. I coughed and tried to stand, but there was something on top of me. I pushed it off and realized it was a body. Where I had touched it, my hand came away wet and sticky. I staggered to my feet and out into the hallway ready to attack any guard that might be there, but I didn't see anyone. Then I saw the other guard lying on the floor across the hall and I stumbled over and bent down to take the gun from his hand. The world started to spin and the cold floor came up and hit me in the face.

I came to with Mickey and Jesus bending over me.

I stammered out a question, "What happened?"

"You blew the door. Don't you remember?" asked Mickey.

"Yeah. I do remember. How long have I been out?"

"Only a few moments."

Red's master key had done the trick. Thank goodness I'd known better than to return to the mine without a card up my sleeve. I sat up and everything seemed to function satisfactorily. I was still shaky but struggled to my feet with Mickey's help. I stumbled across the hall and into the cell we had been in. The thick dust was still settling and a burning flashlight lay on the floor, its beam penetrating the air. I picked it up and shined it on Manuel—lying on the floor, blood bubbling out of his mouth. I kneeled and tried to lift the back of his head, but it was all pulpy and I realized that he must have caught most of the blast.

He was still alive and somehow he managed to open his eyes. He tried to say something, but could only make a gurgling noise. Then he was silent and I knew his troubles were over. I lifted his gun and closed his eyes. When I walked out into the hall, Mickey was bending over the other guard who was still alive but unconscious. The concussion had blown him across the hall and smashed him into the wall.

I took the time to open the cell with the agent in it, but when I checked his pulse he was already dead. With Mickey's and Jesus's help, we dragged the guard into the cell and re-locked it. I shined a light in on the old man, but he was unconscious and almost dead. I didn't want to carry him so I left him there along with the two Mexican escapees. I couldn't trust them.

"It's time to go. " I started walking toward the door and Mickey and Jesus followed. We hurried down toward the elevator with me in the lead and when we got there I was surprised to see that it was moving.

"Get back against the wall." While Mickey and Jesus pressed against the wall, I kneeled in front of the elevator. As the small window of the elevator got even with me, I looked in and followed it up. Two guards were in the elevator but neither of them saw me. As the door opened, I jumped in and shoved Manuel's .38 in their faces. Holding the door open with one hand I motioned them out into the hall toward the others. Jesus took a double barrel twelve-gauge shotgun from one, and a pistol from the other while I kept them covered.

"I'm the *jefe* now?" Jesus said with a smile.

He handed me back the .22 and I gave him my .38, which he tucked into his pants. I stuck the .22 up under the nose of one of the men, fully intending to use it if necessary to get the other one to talk.

"Tell me why you're here. Was it because of the explosion?"

He was shaking uncontrollably. "We heard no explosion! We came to relieve the guards."

I breathed a sigh of relief.

"You two stay here and hold the elevator. I herded the two guards down the hall in front of me, marched them into the prison area, and locked them in a cell together. I dropped the keys in my jacket pocket and raced back down the hall to the elevator.

We got inside and I pushed the button for the fifth floor. Mickey gasped. "We can't go back there! They'll kill us!"

"The hell you say!" The elevator came to a stop and the door slid open. I stuck my head out to check, but there was no one in sight. With Mickey and Jesus reluctantly following, we walked down the hallway to Solorio's office.

I whispered to Jesus. "I'm going in there! If you hear shooting, cover the door and shoot anybody who comes out ... except me!"

He nodded and took the safety off the twelve-gauge. I grasped the handle and turned the knob. It opened and I stepped inside fanning the air with the .22. The room was empty and I motioned for Mickey and Jesus to come in.

"Where the heck are they?" I said out loud to nobody in particular.

"They could be down at the ranch", said Mickey, "or below in the printing area."

"How well is that place guarded?"

"You'd never get in and out alive! You can't even get in the door unless they recognize your face through a bulletproof window."

"Who can get in?"

"Only people who work there, plus El Sol, Gonzales, and a few others. You don't want to go there! There must be ten guards in there! There's even a command station in the middle of the room with a machine gun in it. It would be suicide to try going in there!"

I walked over to the window. I couldn't see anything except walls of water smashing against the pane. It pulsated with a creaking sound like it was about to implode. The wind beat furiously at the glass and it sounded like all the sleeping demons had come to life in the darkness.

"We'll see about that. I'm pissed, and when I get this way, there isn't much that can stop me."

"You're crazy! You'll never—-"

"You're not going in with me, so don't worry! We're making a detour first through the garage area where you and Jesus are bailing out."

We got in the elevator. I pushed the button and we rode down in total silence. I trained the .22 on the crack in the door of the elevator. When we reached the bottom, a guard was standing outside waiting for us. I pulled the trigger and put a little hole in his jugular vein. He stood there with blood obscenely spurting from the wound. He stared at us in disbelief and then turned to walk away. I put two more into his back and he fell. No one else was in sight as we walked around to the loading platform.

I left Jesus and Mickey standing beside the platform while I went into the storeroom and retrieved my two packs from the Jeep with the Ingram, spare ammunition, and explosives.

When I came out, they stood watching me, not knowing what to do or say.

"Okay, you two. There's the police car, right by my Jeep. Get in and get the hell out of here! On second thought, don't use the police car! They'd suspect something at the gate! Use a Lincoln. You may have to shoot your way past the guards, but you'll have a good chance of making it. I've still got business here!"

"You're crazy," said Jesus, "and I'm staying here with you!"

"Me too," insisted Mickey.

"There's nothing you two can do to help me. You may not have a chance if you stay. Haul ass out of here now while you can!"

Jesus touched my shoulder.

"No, we're in this together, whether you like it or not. Now, what do you want us to do?"

I looked at the two of them and realized that there are some things a man couldn't possibly ever buy.

"All right, my friends. You're in! I just hope I can get you two and me out alive."

CHAPTER 46 - THE SPEECH

From the map of the operation, I figured they stored explosives on the fifth level in a special pyro-locker in the southwest corner. I intended to set off my explosives there, capitalizing on any ordinance they might have on hand. We walked back to the elevator, skirting the guard lying in a pool of blood. Mickey gasped as she sidestepped the body to get into the elevator. I wondered if I'd made a wise decision by allowing her to tag along.

We rode in silence and got off on the fifth floor. The room I was looking for was at the end of the corridor, past Solorio's office. We started toward it. Suddenly, the door to El Sol's office opened and we quickly pressed back against the wall. I took the .22 and pointed it at whoever was coming out, almost pulling the trigger when I saw it was fat ass Gonzales steaming down the passageway like a charging rhino. A guard was with her. I took careful aim and shot him in the face three times. He fell and Gonzales looked stunned as she stared at the silencer of my .22. The gun was now empty. Fortunately, no one except me knew it.

Gonzales came out of her stupor and started to reach for the guard's gun. "Go ahead," I said. "I'd like that."

She froze like a Popsicle. I pointed the gun at El Sol's office.

"Is anyone else in there?"

She didn't say anything. I smacked her across the face lightly with the .22. It's hard to hit someone lightly with a gun.

"I asked you a question, bitch."

Her hearing quickly improved ... remarkably.

"No, please stop! There's no one else there."

"Good," I said. "Let's get going!"

I grabbed my two packs and we went into the office.

I told Jesus, "You two keep her here. Find out anything you can from her, but don't kill her."

I needed her to get me into the printing area.

"I'll be right back."

I hoped they could handle her. I slung the packs over my shoulder and reloaded the .22 as I walked along. At the end of the hall, I found the door labeled "Ordinance". It was locked and I had to pump five carefully aimed shots into it before it would open. The place was loaded. I had hoped they'd have stored some explosives, but I hadn't anticipated anything like this. They had a complete assortment including lots of dynamite and ammo. But, best of all, a small refrigerator in the corner contained quite a bit of nitro.

I took the Ingram machine pistol out of the pack along with three clips of ammo. Because of the nitro, I decided to leave the C-4 intact rather than mold it for separate explosions. I checked the detonator, which was now down to an hour and a half and counting. I sat down for a moment, as I thought and considered how much time to set on the clock.

I started turning it slowly and stopped at fifty-five minutes. I hoped it would give me enough time. I started to leave when I noticed a wooden door stop just inside. I shut the door and kicked the wedge tightly under it, but it wasn't tight enough, so I released the clip from the Ingram and used it like a battering ram, banging the wedge tightly under the door so that nothing short of a torch could get it open.

With the Ingram in my hand and the .22 in my waistband, I ran back to El Sol's office. Mickey was rummaging through the desk while Jesus sat holding the shotgun on Gonzales. Her eyes were red as if she'd been crying.

"Did the fat lady sing?"

Jesus laughed. "She sings fine with a little encouragement."

"They're all down in the printing room now," said Mickey. "They're conducting an inspection and El Sol is showing them around."

I growled, "Well, let's not keep the folks waiting."

On the way to the elevator, Gonzales slowed down and Jesus gave her an enthusiastic kick in the butt to speed her along.

We paused outside the elevator.

I explained, "I want to use this witch to get me into the printing room. I doubt if anyone will shoot at me using her as a shield, but it is a chance I have to take, yet only I'll take it. I want you two to leave now, while you still can."

Both Mickey and Jesus shook their heads 'no' and started to protest. By the look in their eyes, I knew I wouldn't be able to talk them out of it. I didn't want to waste any more time, so I gave in. I grabbed Gonzales around the neck, choking the wind out of her.

"I'll have a gun stuck up your ass the whole time. Go along and you may get out of here alive. Give me trouble and I'll shoot you several times in the spine."

Her face turned beet red and she bit her lips. She understood my warning and nodded her head vigorously to indicate she would comply. I released her and she fell away from me, as she gulped in the air. With her, I looked forward to breaking my promise. I pushed the button, the elevator opened and we got in.

As we rode down, I said, "Keep your guns out of sight, Jesus."

The elevator opened and we stepped out. The passageway was identical to the others except that it ended about fifty feet down the hall. There, two armed guards sat peacefully watching us. I poked Ingram in her back and we walked cautiously toward them. There was a red-tinted mirror on the door and I knew it had to be a one-way viewer, but there was nothing I could do about it.

The guards watched us, seemed curious, but made no move until we got to them. Then they seemed to realize that something was wrong. Gonzales was noticeably trembling. I leveled the Ingram at the eyes of one of the guards.

I instructed in clear slow Spanish, "Open the door for us and step inside, or you'll be dead by the time I count to three!"

He looked at Gonzales while I counted. At the count of two, she was nodding her head vigorously for him to obey my command. He reached over and pressed a button near the door. It opened with a hiss and I pushed through—forcing Gonzales before me—the gun pressed against her back.

Jesus removed the weapons from the two guards and made them come into the printing area along with us. Mickey tagged along behind.

Three more guards were just inside the door. One of them realized what was going on and started to reach for his weapon. I pulled the trigger on the Ingram and moved it across both guards. It made a sound like popcorn popping as the spray of bullets smacked into them. They were probably dead before they hit the floor.

Apparently, no one heard the shots or commotion. The area we entered was huge. It was filled with all kinds of running machinery and equipment, including various other background noises that made it difficult to hear. I estimated that there were about fifty people in the room, including El Sol and the visitors who were standing in front of a large press. He was jabbering away as they listened intently, completely oblivious to our presence. The room was about two hundred feet long with a slick metal floor that gleamed brightly.

Behind Solorio and the group were six rows of presses. The place was wreaked of paper, machinery oil, and ink odors. Several large gasoline generators chugged away in one corner of the room with large ventilation hoses disappearing into the walls behind them. Operators were grouped around various pieces of equipment, some of them wearing white aprons; others wore tan, ink-stained aprons, and still, others had on black rubber hip boots and heavy rubber aprons. They were cutting and arranging stacks of green stuff that, even at a distance, I knew had to be the money.

We stood waiting for them to notice us. I had the Ingram stuck in Gonzalez's ear. I felt kind of foolish as I wondered when someone would realize we were standing there. Jesus held the guards in the corner, his shotgun trained on them. In the middle of the room was the raised command station and I could see a guard with a machine gun casually perched inside. He was watching Solorio and still hadn't seen us. He was too much of a risk. I trained the Ingram on him and squeezed the trigger.

The bullets peppered him and those that missed ricocheted around the room. He screamed as he fell over the rail, and his impact smacked the floor loudly. Jesus realized I was trying to get everyone's attention and he blasted both barrels of the shotgun into the ceiling. The noise was deafening and it certainly did get their attention.

I pressed tightly behind Gonzales, sticking the hot gun up to her ear without thinking. It burned her and she let out a nerve-shattering scream several octaves higher than the roar of the machinery. Now, every eye in the place was looking at us.

I grabbed her tightly; half cutting off her scream, and holding her in front of me like a big fat siren, and marched boldly toward El Sol and the startled visitors. Mickey was so close behind me that she stepped on my heel. I paid no attention and kept my eyes on Solorio to make sure he stayed put.

One at a time, the machines began to slow to a stop. By the time we reached the platform a few feet below Solorio and his group, the room became deathly quiet. That was what I had been hoping, for now, I had the chance to make myself heard, and I took it.

> I looked at Jesus. He picked up the machine gun and was waving it maniacally around, his eyes wild and dilated. "Jesus, if anything at all goes wrong, you shoot El Sol in his gut … as I'll then blow Miss Piggy's brains out! Mickey, if you see anyone make a move—just point and scream."

I felt, rather than saw, Jesus move up beside me. I saw El Sol's eyes momentarily widen when Jesus trained his weapon on him. Solorio's lower jaw moved up and down, and his eyes darted nervously about—but no words came out. The visitors stood there big-eyed as if waiting for Solorio to clear the situation up. I could see doubt was beginning to creep into their minds as they became aware of the situation. Behind them in the presses hung sheets of money stopped halfway through the print cycle. Despite the illegality of this operation, It was a brilliant and fascinating sight.

Jesus sensed a need to introduce me to the group and shouted out. "*Atencion! Este hombre guerrero!*" Then, for some reason, he screamed it out again in English. "Attention! This man is a warrior!"

I'm not much for speeches, but I gave it my best shot. I spoke in my best Spanish as loudly as I could so all the workers would hear.

"Listen to me! I am the American who fought the dogs. I am here to warn you! You all know El Sol and Gonzales will never let you leave here alive. They kill anyone who tries to leave, and that is the truth."

The workers looked at each other and I saw a few heads nodding in agreement.

"When you leave here, you have to go in the company of his killer guards who will feed you to the rabid, mad dogs. Yes—he pays you decent wages—but look!"

I pointed at the printing presses.

"Look where he gets the money from. You make it. How many of you will ever be able to spend it? I'll tell you. None! Not a single one of you. Not even you guards will ever live long enough to enjoy all of the money you've worked for so hard."

I snarled and told them, "Listen to me, now! We have placed explosives and the whole place will be blown to hell in a few minutes. Soldiers have surrounded this place, but they have nothing against you. You're not to blame for what's going on here. That's why we are going to allow you to leave. You can all go in peace. Take whatever money El Sol has paid you ... and go now!"

They hesitated, but I could tell they were seriously considering my proposal.

"Listen well to what I am saying! Do not ever talk about this place, or what you did here. If you ever speak of this place, or what happened here, the authorities will come for you and take you and your family away. You will go to prison for the rest of your lives. Tell no one! Do not take any of this money."

I waved the gun around indicating the money in the print room.

"You only have about thirty minutes before this place will be destroyed. Don't try to take your belongings. There's no time. Tell the others to go also. This is your last warning and opportunity. Now—all of you—get out of here!"

They stood silent for a moment watching me and mulled around as if stunned. I sensed that many were afraid to believe that the door to their cage was open at last. I grabbed two fat-ringed pinkies of Gonzales and twisted her arm behind her shoulder blades.

I said softly in her ear, "Tell them that what I said is true, or I'll break your arm."

She took the pain for several seconds until something snapped.

She was in pain and cried out, "Do as he says ... It's true!"

Some of the workers dropped whatever they had in their hands and ran for the door.

Solorio, suddenly realized that his empire was crumbling before his eyes. He opened his mouth to say something.

He got as far as, "Wait, you fools!"

Then I heard Jesus' gun boom, and Solorio was thrown backward against one of the printing presses, blood pouring from his right shoulder. I turned and looked at Jesus who stood grinning at me. He pointed his gun upward and grinned.

"I didn't think you wanted me to kill him, so I only shot him a little!"

"Hell, you could have killed him for all I care."

The exodus began in earnest, as almost all of the workers were set in motion by the gunfire and were escaping now, like just-released animals from a cage. They ran for freedom and clean air and knew they'd best get out while they could. The dam was broken and all the king's horses and all of his henchmen could never hold them back, even if he somehow regained control.

In any case, I wasn't going to let him. I pointed the Mac at the command station.

"Get up there, Jesus. If anything happens, cut these bastards down, and then get the hell out of here fast."

He nodded and went up on the platform leaving Gonzales, Mickey, and me with the group of VIPs standing before us. I studied them closely. They were beginning to realize the seriousness of the situation and glanced nervously at each other, wondering what to do. El Sol managed to get to his feet.

I walked toward the group of strangers.

I asked, "Who the hell are you people?"

One of them raised his hand, asking for permission to speak, as though he were at a press conference. I pointed my Ingram at him signaling him to go ahead.

"Son, I'm Senator Jeffries. I believe you may have heard of me."

I had. He was supposedly one of the bright boys. One of the names tossed around for a high-level cabinet position in the current administration.

He continued. "I don't believe you realize the seriousness of what you're doing. We're all members of a very special group."

He spread his right arm to include the other men.

"This is a very powerful organization your messing with here, sir. If it is money you're after, we can give you all you want. Just say the word. If not money, then name what you value. Anything at all."

The Asian spoke up, using excellent English with a slight British accent.

"Please stop and consider what you are doing. You need to call your boss—let one of us speak with him. I assure you an arrangement can be worked out to your satisfaction. There need not be any more violence and no harm need come to anyone else."

I started to say something but was interrupted by a well-dressed gangster-looking character wearing a shiny silk suit and alligator shoes that decided to try and throw his weight around.

"You don't know who the hell you are dealing with, boy. You're making a big mistake that's gonna bring you a whole heap of trouble—maybe cost you your life!."

I was getting tired of the threatening conversation.

"Bold talk, fella ... do bullets bounce off you? I'm not 'dealing,' pal! I'm closing down the game."

I didn't need Dunn and Bradstreet to tell me that these were fat cats. They had the expensive suits and the brash, self-confidence of big-time city crooks. They reeked of money and politics. I'd been around the block enough to know that assholes and pricks come in all sizes and this group was an assortment of the biggest. They thought the world was theirs to screw with as they pleased. I had a surprise for them.

CHAPTER 47 – THE SACRIFICE

Mickey was standing demurely to my left, intently watching the proceedings. Jesus was in the gun tower with the machine gun trained on the fidgety group. At the far end of the room, and further most end of the area, I noticed a huge shiny bank-like door that I reasoned had to be the entrance to the money vault.

I pointed at it with the gun, "A vault! Now I wonder what's in there."

El Sol took a step toward me, clutching his shoulder, and uttered in grief-stricken anguish.

"Mr. Race, there's over a billion dollars in that vault. You can have all you want of it."

He looked desperately at the other men for support.

I smirked and declared, "Open it up, I want to see it."

El Sol smiled imperceptibly, apparently seeing a glimmer of hope.

"I can't right now. There's a timing device. It can only be opened at certain times. If you will stop the explosives from going off, we can arrange something—a very good deal for you."

Gonzales, who stood patiently by, saw a chance to score points

She blurted out, "He's a liar! I can open it! All that will occur is an alarm will ring until it is shut off from inside the vault."

Solorio lowered his eyes in disgust. I glared at Gonzales. "So, open it then," I said as she walked toward the vault.

"Watch her, Mickey," I stated.

Jeffries must have decided to take over and spoke up. "Could I inquire whom you work for, young man? Perhaps, we know someone in common—someone who could be of great benefit to you."

I winked at him and remarked, "You've been filla-bustered. Up yours!"

"I'm serious, young fella," he said while smoothly taking a pipe out of his inside jacket pocket. I almost shot him before I realized he was only groping for his tobacco status symbol. He stuck the pipe in his mouth.

He asked, "Whom do you work for? FBI? CIA? Who?"

I snarled back, "The question is ... whom do you work for?"

He curled his lip and bit into the stem of his pipe.

"It is of little matter," he continued talking to me. "I have friends in many organizations. I'm sure I can smooth things over for you."

I squeezed the trigger and several shots splintered his left leg.

He winced in pain as I repeated my question, "Mister, I asked who you work for."

He cried out and fell to the floor, grabbing at his leg.

"What about the rest of you?" I asked. "What can you offer me?'

The well-dressed Asian man started to open his mouth, but he looked at Jeffries and changed his mind.

Suddenly, Jesus yelled. "I like the show, but we'd better get out of here *muy pronto!*"

I replied, "*Un momento*, Jesus. Just hang on."

An alarm rang by the vault as Gonzales slid the huge door open and I motioned for the men to go in with her.

"All of you! Inside! Let's go! "

They started moving, except for Jeffries.

"Undisguised gentlemen as well ... meaning you too, Senator. " I pointed the gun at Jeffries. "Crawl over and into the piggy bank."

"But, I'm shot!"

I pointed my gun at him and remarked, "Would you like to be shot some more?"

He let go of his bleeding leg and began to drag and crawl toward the vault.

I stopped one of the men and told him, "You ... get hold of the senator and help into the vault."

El Sol and the rest were walking ahead of him. Gonzales held the door partly open but was not strong enough to open it all the way.

She looked at me. "It's unlocked, but I need help to open it."

"They'll open it, "I said, motioning to the men. "Open the damn door."

A full-bearded Mexican, who reminded me of Castro, and the well-dressed Asian managed to swing the vault door enough so that it was passable to the inside. Gonzales stepped in and out of sight. Abruptly, the alarm stopped, leaving a ringing in my ears. I stared at the vault, which was about forty feet deep and twenty feet wide. It was packed full of brand-new twenty-dollar bills, all stacked neatly on shelves.

I whistled as I peered in at it. "You weren't kidding, were you?"

I looked at the men standing there and then I knew what I was going to do.

"All right, gentlemen. If you'd be so kind as to step into the vault, I'd like to make you a little proposition."

The men glanced at each other desperately as they entered the vault. Jeffries crawled after them. Leaving a trail of blood behind him like snail slime. Solorio seized the opportunity and began making his pitch.

"We can fix you up fine, Mr. Race. We'll even make you one of the committee." He glanced at the others for confirmstion, "Won't we?"

Some others nodded in agreement. They were all now inside the vault. Leaving Mickey and me standing just outside it.

I turned to check on Mickey and out of the corner of my eyes, I saw someone move toward the entrance of the vault. Mickey was looking past me and her eyes suddenly grew wide with fear. Before I could react, she screamed and leaped in front of me, pressing tightly against me just as an explosion sounded, immediately followed by a second explosion. I felt the thuds of both bullets smacking into her body, slamming me with force.

I carefully eased Mickey to the floor and looked into the vault at Gonzales—who was holding a small and still smoking double-barrel derringer—which she had hidden someplace on her body. She had a crazed gleeful smile on her face. I grabbed the .22 out of my waistband and pointed it at her. My first shot struck her high in the right shoulder and she dropped her empty weapon but continued smiling.

I shot her in the left shoulder. Her smile slowly faded and she stared absently out into space over my head, seemingly unaware that I was shooting her. I aimed the gun at her once more and this time the bullet seared into her massive gut. I knew it would take her a long time to die. She seemed to realize and expect what happened, although her eyes were still unfocused and glazed over.

I tucked the .22 back in my waistband and pointed the Ingram at the group. Mickey cried out softly as they watched me intently.

"Sorry. Gentlemen. I was considering making a deal with you but this fat pig just changed my mind."

I smiled at Gonzales as I grabbed the heavy door and started closing it. Several of the men ran at me, but I waved my weapon at them and they backed up. I slowly closed the huge door and dogged it shut. Their faces said everything I wanted to hear.

Jesus had come down and was bending over Mickey. I dropped my gun and picked her up. I walked over to a table covered with money and gently laid her down. She was moaning softly.

I looked down at her. "I'm so sorry, Mickey. Damn it! I am sorry!"

Mickey put her long slender hand on mine, and her weakening voice ripped at my insides.

"Don't worry, Pat. I'd never have made anything of myself anyway. I want you to know something, although you won't understand it."

"What. Mickey?" She tried to speak, but couldn't.

Her lips were moving slowly and I knew she was dying. She didn't have to say it though, because I understood what sentimental term of endearment she meant to say.

I managed to get it out in a choking voice as the bright red blood oozed out over her pale lips.

"Yeah, me too, kid ... you're quite a woman."

She went out trying to smile. I put my hand over her lifeless blue eyes and gently closed them. A lovely butterfly had just died.

CHAPTER 48 – DASH FOR THE CASH

I don't know how long I stood there looking down at Mickey. I might have stayed and died with her if I hadn't felt a hand on my shoulder. It was Jesus.

"It is time to go, Pat." He spoke in a soft compassionate tone. I turned and looked at him and my face must have shown the anguish I felt inside. He was patiently waiting for me, expecting the place to be blown up any second.

Jesus sensed how emotional I was. "Come on, Pat. Let's get out of here. No need for us to die too."

I reassured him. "Don't worry. We still have time. I lied about the time a little so everyone would get out okay."

As we started to leave, I paused in the doorway and looked back at the silent printing presses and the piles of money. The presses sat there gleaming in the stillness. I walked across the room to the vault. I didn't think it could be opened from the inside, but I wanted to make certain. I ripped up a roller bar from a conveyor belt and using the Ingram as a wedge jammed it into the door to prevent it from being opened from the inside. It was time to go. I wagered that if there was no illumination inside the vault, the terror would be doubly bad … good, so shot at the electric wall panels before leaving the area. Sparks flew and it went dark inside the press area, and I guessed inside the vault.

As we began to exit the press area, I noticed the light switch just outside the door. I reached up and flicked it off too. I wasn't sure, but I thought I could hear the muffled screams coming from inside the vault. I hoped so. I grabbed a hefty double packet of newly wrapped twenties and put it in my jacket pocket. I glanced back inside one last time at Mickey's lifeless body, imagining all the modifications and challenges she'd faced in life … that led her to this sorry fate. I blew her kiss, and a tear rolled down my cheek.. Jesus didn't say a word. We walked down the passageway and caught the elevator.

No one was in the basement and it was beginning to flood. We splashed across the parking lot. All the Lincolns were still there plus the supply truck, Jesus' police car, and my jeep.

"Jesus, you go first and I'll meet you back in San Felipe. I've one other small thing to do before I leave."

He started to protest, but the look on my face must have told him it was pointless to argue.

"All right, amigo. It'll be tricky driving with this one bad hand, but I'll try. Go, I'll wait till you're back, then meet you back in San Felipe."

He got into his police car and started the motor.

At my Jeep, I removed the small magnetic hidden key holder from its hiding place inside the rear bumper and used it to get inside. I released the catch on the Nellie compartment and it snapped open. There was Nellie and all of my papers exactly where I'd left them. I fired the engine up and the echo vibrated through the garage. I drove slowly down the tunnel, letting Jesus precede me.

As we neared the open gate, the sound of the wind became much more noticeable. I had the driver's window open and I could feel it sucking the air from the tunnel. The gate was open and a downpour of rain fell from a blackened sky. The howling wind screeched like spirits at a banshee convention and it was hard to hold the jeep steady.

I drove slow and carefully. When I got to the ranch house, I noticed the taillights of a car with its motor running. I pulled into the driveway and parked. The surrounding trees were flapping madly. Their fronds danced like a moving landscape, rising and plunging in massive swells in cadence to the whim of the winds.

Several lights were on inside the big house, but there was no one to be seen. I grabbed the Nellie and leaped from the jeep. The wind tore at my clothing, as I ran for the main entrance. Rain fell in buckets and I clutched the Nellie tightly, using it like a machete to knife my way through the elements. I turned the front door handle and it was unlocked. I quickly stepped inside and closed the door. I was soaked. I heard nothing so I dripped quietly down the passageway until I heard someone moving about in one of the rooms to my left. I gradually opened the door.

Carmen had her back to me and she was working furiously, grabbing money from a wall safe and stuffing it into large black plastic garbage bags. She hadn't seen me come in. "Need any help?" I asked sarcastically.

She dropped the bag she was holding, stood up, and slowly turned around.

"You sure looked busy there. I was wondering if you needed any help."

"Pat! I ... I..."

"You what, Carmen?"

"I was worried about you."

"Yeah! I'll just bet you were. I can see the worry etched on your face and in your eyes."

She stood there looking at me, confusion slowly spreading over her guilty face. She already had four shopping bags three-quarters full of money. I walked over and looked into them. It wasn't the stuff they'd been printing because these were wrapped bundles of hundreds, fifties, twenties, and tens.

"What were you planning to do with all this money, Carmen?"

"I was... uh... we could go away together, Pat. As you said, we could go around the world with all this money."

I looked at her and laughed.

"I've already been around the world. Besides, I just turned down God knows how many billions of dollars up there."

She looked as if I'd slapped her in the face.

"What do you mean?"

"I mean, I just told El Sol and Gonzales to shove their money up their perverted asses when I locked them in the vault with their associates, whoever they were."

"You locked my mother up?"

It sunk in at last. "Gonzales is your mother?"

"Yes! Why else do you think I would have done the things I did to you? She made me! I had to obey her or she wouldn't have left me anything. When I heard what you were doing and saw the workers fleeing, I decided to grab what I could and get out. The safe was open—believe it or not—and I was going to clear out."

"Why were you working in San Felipe as a .... as a..."

"As a whore?"

"Well ... yes!"

"Because ever since daddy disappeared, I've had almost nothing. I had to work! I had no choice. It was only when you came into town that mother had anything to do with me."

I stood there listening to her, but only half-hearing what she had to tell me. Something was missing. Something she had said hit home. Some very important part—which I couldn't remember. Then it all fit together. I should have understood it before. Mitigoso was an acronym for Miguel, Tiente, Gonzales and Solorio. The puzzle was complete. All the pieces matched perfectly.

I sat on the corner of the desk and looked at her, wondering if I should tell her or not. She was no less the beautiful girl I once came to love.

"Carmen. Suppose I tell you where your father is?"

She looked at me in disbelief. "Father? Alive?"

I remembered the photograph of the white-haired man with sparkling eyes that Smith showed me. It looked nothing like the man in the cell, but I knew that he was her father, or at least what was left of him.

"Yes, I know where he is. Do you want to go to him?"

"Oh, yes! I thought he was dead! Please tell me!"

"He's at the mine in one of the prison cells. He's in pretty bad shape."

She looked at me and then at the money. I thought for a while she was going to choose the money, but maybe she was made of better stuff than I figured, or maybe she just assumed I wouldn't let her take it.

Without saying another word she bolted out the door and I heard her footsteps running down the hallway. I knew I'd probably never know if she had merely wanted to get away from me, or if she truly longed for her father. I sat there on the desk and suddenly remembered that I had the keys to the prison cells in my jacket pocket. I started to go after her, but her car was already roaring off toward the mine.

I guess I'm not too enamored with villains that confess and repent after they're found out. She'd sold me out one time too many.

"Oh well, "I said aloud to no one in particular, "At least, maybe she's got time to see her father ... through a small window."

CHAPTER 49 – THE EXODUS

I picked up all the bags of money and carried them out to my jeep, stashing them under the fold-down compartment in the back of the driver's seat. Then, I ran back into the house, quickly checking the rooms until I found what I was after. It was a huge kitchen with two large gas stoves sitting side-by-side. I'd also spotted a kerosene lantern hanging from a nail. I blew out the pilot lights on both stoves and turned on the burners.

I could instantly smell propane flooding into the room. I took the lantern down, carried it across the room, and lit it with a kitchen match I'd found on the stove. I tightly closed the kitchen door behind me, leaving the lantern sitting on the floor across from the stoves that were busily pumping gas into the room. As I left, I twisted the self-locking catch on the front door.

I started the jeep and headed down the road. The rain was coming down steadily. There were deep puddles in the road and the wind kept whipping me from side to side. I began passing groups of Mexicans half walking and half running away from the ranch. I honked my horn to get them out of the way, but I didn't dare pick any of them up. I had only gone a few hundred yards when the noise of the gas explosion sounded behind me. In the rearview mirror, I could see the ranch house blazing away. The Mexicans on the road moved even faster.

I took it slow and easy, choosing the best parts of the road, and avoiding the fleeing Mexicans and as many puddles as possible. When I finally arrived at the main road, a blue Volkswagen beetle was parked on the side of the road just outside the main gate exit. I recognized it and pulled in behind, flicking my lights a couple of times to get his attention. I turned the motor off, got out, and walked over to see Smith. He saw me coming and rolled down his window a few inches.

I kneeled and stuck my head in the window out of the rain.

I had to talk loud to be heard over the roar of the storm. "Just Passing by?" I asked.

He almost shot me with the .45 in his hand. But, I held both hands up in mock surrender.

I shouted. "It's me... Race... the good guy!"

He suddenly realized who I was, and began laughing.

"Holy crap! It is you! I didn't recognize you. What the hell? Nice disguise. You do look like a Mexican."

He paused and then said, "Actually, I was waiting for you."

"You were pretty sure I would come out, were you?"

"Not until the exodus started. What's with the explosion?"

"Just business."

"Fooled me! What was it that your business exploded?"

"The ranch, but that was just the appetizer. Stick around a while and you'll get the main course."

"You mean there's more?"

"That's what I mean."

"Well. Are you just going to stand there with your ass out in the wind and rain?"

He swung the passenger door open. I walked around the car, opened the passenger door, and squeezed inside.

He wanted to know, "That's quite a glow on the horizon."

I tossed the packet of twenties on the seat beside him. "That's a good old-fashioned ranch house bar-b-cue. Pretty soon you'll see a dollar factory turn into a pile of ashes along with your problems. I quickly told him about Jeffries and the others I'd locked in the vault, explaining that I still had no idea who they all were or what their agenda was.

Smith gave me a curious look, arching an eyebrow and flaring his nostrils. His cheeks flushed a little and his eyes darted nervously downward, to me meaning that what he was about to say was probably a lie.

"Never mind them ... let's just say that money can buy lots of friends and power and ... uh ... well, just let it go at that."

He threw his palms up as a gesture that I interpreted meant, 'so what'.

And that was it. He shrugged as if he didn't care. Perhaps he had known all about them the entire time. I didn't see any need to mention Carmen, Mickey, or Jesus. My biggest regret was leaving Mickey's deceased body there to be destroyed with all those other assholes. I hoped in her afterlife that she was given the female body she always desired.

A steady stream of Mexicans staggered up the road from the ranch, grasping at their clothing and possessions as the wind beat them with a fury. It was a terrible time and place to be afoot. As they got near us, they moved to the opposite side of the road and avoided us like the plague. I could see that most of them carried some kind of bag, which they clutched tightly. I'm sure they hadn't packed their clothes. They seemed happy and I couldn't help but smile realizing that they probably all carried more money than they would ever see again, and probably best of all—they were free.

As we sat there, the wind gusts rocked the little VW around like it was make-out time at the drive-in movie. Smith was beginning to get impatient.

"Are you sure the place is going to blow?"

"You can take it to the bank!"

Just as I said that the ground started to tremble. First, there was a small tremor followed by an explosion that shook the earth. It wasn't much of a surface blast, but rather a series of subterranean explosions that caused the ground to quiver and shake. Along the roadside, the fleeing Mexicans stopped and were looking back toward the mine. Some of them shook their fists in the air, and a few unanimous cheers were sent out as they became aware that their nightmare was truly over.

It felt like the ground was about to shatter apart. Explosion after explosion rocked the earth until at last, after perhaps ten long minutes of continual eruptions, the ground lay still once more. Smith hadn't said a word. His eyes were wide but vacuous as he stared at the distant orange flames licking the sky, visible even in the heavy downpour.

Finally, when things died down some, he grinned at me.

"I figured you to be a loose cannon, but never thought of you as a one-man brigade and war zone."

I still couldn't read his eyes, but I knew he was satisfied.

"There will be a nice bonus in your account tomorrow, shall we say another hundred thou?"

I grinned in the darkness but didn't say anything.

"Will that amount be sufficient?" he inquired.

I thought he probably wanted to ease his conscience, so I piled it on a bit.

"Let your conscience be your guide. It's a brutal job killing people for a living. But, I learned a long time ago to deal with the trauma and anxiety. But, when they're assholes like those people were, my conscience is clean."

Smith nodded in agreement with me, speaking slowly as if thinking out each word carefully.

"You'll never truly make sense of all this, or justify the stress. You just have to accept the calling and let it happen."

"I guess you're right," I replied.

The explosions slowly abated and the only sound was the steady pitter of rain on the roof. I had been fortunate. The rain would soon extinguish the flames and the storm covered the explosion. Had it occurred at any other time, it would have attracted a great deal of attention. Tomorrow, no one would even know about it.

We sat quietly for a few more minutes and Smith started the motor. I guessed it was time to go, so I opened the door.

I stated, "Is there anything else I can do for you tonight? If not, I need a shower and shave."

"Your employers would like to see you at the Half Moon around four tomorrow afternoon. They'll want a full report then."

It occurred to me that I still had to run the border one more time.

"See you there then. I need to go crash for a while. Oh—can you just make sure I get a clear pass-through at the border tomorrow morning with no trouble?"

"Sure thing," he said.

"Oh yeah, there's one more thing I wanted to ask you."

His eyes narrowed into thin slits as if expecting me to say something really bad.

"Why do you drive this damn bug?"

He grinned and winked at me as if he'd answered that question many times.

"It gets great gas mileage."

He gunned his motor and spun the beetle around in the road, then puttered north toward Mexicali. The wind swerved the little car from side to side. I'd only been sitting in it a few minutes, but my legs ached from being cramped. I'll never understand why anyone would drive one.

I stood in the heavy rain letting it wash me down. I still had a few things to do. and decided to check on Jesus first. I got into the Jeep and headed toward San Felipe driving slowly and carefully. Since I was wet anyway, I opened the driver's side window halfway and let the rain beat me in the face. I kept inhaling deeply. I was alive.

CHAPTER 50 – A SAN FELIPE GOODBYE

It reminded me of driving through a never-ending car wash. The wipers swished back and forth, creating a Gene Kruppa staccato as they pushed the walls of water aside. A few cars were on the road, all of them headed in the other direction running from the storm. Most had their lights on bright and refused to dim them, blinding me. The road kept disappearing under sheets of water and I could only average a few miles an hour. Several times I came upon stalled vehicles blocking the road, but the four-wheel drive let me power around them.

Every gully and dip was full of water and I was glad to be in the jeep. Few other vehicles would be capable of moving under conditions such as this downpour. I had only gotten about halfway to San Felipe when I spotted a police car with its hood up directly ahead of me. It was stalled in a three-foot-deep puddle and I slowed to a crawl as I passed around it. Sure enough, Jesus had his head under the hood trying to get it started. I honked my horn and he came running.

He was ecstatic to see me. Using my back tow hitch and a steel cable we'd soon towed his car out of the puddle and over to the right shoulder. He locked it up and climbed in with me. He had a worried look on his face.

"I must find my wife and children!"

I tried to reassure him, "Don't worry! We'll find them!"

"I hope so! We have to get to San Felipe!"

"We'll make it—this Jeep will go through anything."

I hoped I was right. I'd never seen anything like it before. The closer we got to San Felipe the stronger the wind blew and the heavier the rain fell. We were heading into the worst of the storm. It was like the great Gods Zeus and Thor were having a contest to see who was the most powerful. First, we'd see the blinding flash of a lightning bolt followed an instant later by an explosion of thunder.

Once a bolt struck so close that I could feel the heat flash through the window glass. I looked at Jesus and he was as nervous as I was. I kept thinking how ironic it would be to have survived all we went through just to get fried now by a random bolt of lightning. Jesus' voice cracked as he tried to talk.

"I heard that if you get struck, you never hear the thunder."

"If we get struck in the Jeep, the tires will ground us and we'll be okay!" I'd said it, but wasn't that sure I believed it.

We were nearing the town when the road abruptly ended and the water began. It almost looked like a boat launching ramp. I backed the Jeep about a hundred feet from the water's edge to what seemed like a safe distance and turned the motor off. We were as close as we could get without a boat.

Few people have ever witnessed the destruction that water is capable of doing. A cubic yard of water weighs 1,700 pounds and the angry ocean tossed millions of yards over the town. Before us lay the storm surge of tossing, foaming water, covering what had been San Felipe. Almost all of the structures were gone. The roadside was covered with metal roofs, felled trees, snapped power poles, and all sorts of debris from the strong winds. Broken branches and pieces of wood floated at the water's edge.

All of the boats were either capsized, swept off their anchors, or pounded onto the shore—tossed about like loose kindling. They lay in splinters where freak waves had deposited them. I could see the remains of the 'E1 Bonita' on which I'd been fishing, being smacked against the roof of a building at least a mile from where it was anchored. Where the Sun Tower Lodge had been, was now nothing but water.

As we sat in the Jeep looking through the windshield at the devastation before us, I didn't know what to say to Jesus. We both knew that if his family had been in the town, they were probably dead. I jumped when he cried out.

"Look! There's a boat."

Sure enough, a small wooden boat, propelled by an outboard clamped on its stern, was headed right for us through the maelstrom It rode the crest of a five-foot high wave. Three men were in it. We got out of the Jeep and ran to help them, catching the full brunt of the intense squall belting us in the face. The closer it got to us, the more the turbulence tossed the boat about. The small motor was revved to the max. When they got within thirty feet of us, the driver cut the power and tilted the motor up to avoid destroying the prop. The huge swell carried the little boat forward and dropped it with a thunderous clap onto the blacktopped road.

Jesus and I waded out into the water to catch them, but cutting the power raised their stern and they almost went under. We waded out a little deeper.

I heard Jesus yell, "Sanchez!"

At about that time, I slipped and went completely under. I surfaced in time to see the wave carrying the boat straight at us. I grabbed onto its side and hung on for dear life as we surfed in on the freak wave. We almost hit the front of the Jeep.

I fell to the pavement and struggled to my feet. My broken finger throbbed in pain, as did my other injuries, which while in capture, I managed to ignore most of the time. The Mexicans began leaping out of the boat and dragging it up onto the blacktop. One of them was another policeman and Jesus grabbed him by the shoulders.

"Sanchez, where's Rosita and my children?'

Sanchez smiled. "Don't worry. All the women and children were evacuated this afternoon. She's probably at your sister's in Mexicali."

Jesus looked up toward heaven and made a religious cross over his heart with his bandaged hand.

"*Que Milagro!*"

"*Si*. It is a miracle," said Sanchez.

The color returned to Jesus' face.

I asked, "This is some *chabasco*? What are you crazy Mexicans doing running around in this boat?"

Sanchez wiped his forehead on his sleeve.

"It is the worst. Our town is destroyed."

Moving directly up the Gulf the storm funneled directly into San Felipe by the warm waters. The intense surface winds exceeded 100 miles per hour as it slammed into the small Mexican town. However, the main thrust had passed over and was now spending itself over land as it changed from a devastating hurricane into a huge tropical storm. We stood there as another big wave rolled in and broke a few feet away, sending a spray of foam and water over us.

Sanchez noticed the bandage covering Jesus' missing fingers.

"What happened to you, my friend? Do you need help?"

Jesus scratched his chin with his good hand and looked out at the boiling water.

"I was injured during the storm, but there is nothing you can do. My friend, Patrico is helping me."

The other two Mexicans, a boy of around sixteen and a man in his fifties were struggling to keep the boat from sliding back into the water as another wave crashed over them and quickly receded, washing the blacktop clean and leaving the boat out of the water.

Sanchez turned to them, "Shall we go back out?"

They both voted to go back out. So, Jesus and I helped them pick the boat up and turn it around. We carried it to the edge of the water and pushed it out a few feet, timing the waves so it would be in the water before the next one broke. The men got back into the boat. Jesus patted Sanchez on the shoulder.

"Don't worry, my friend. We will rebuild."

Sanchez's eyes twinkled. "I know we will. It is home and where we live."

They had never realized that I wasn't Spanish. We sat in the Jeep and watched them fight their way out into the darkness. Then we turned around and headed toward Mexicali. Jesus hadn't said a word about what I'd done, but I knew that the time would soon come to talk about it. As we drove along, I composed my thoughts and by the time we'd gotten back to his police car, I knew how I would handle it.

I asked him if he wanted to take his car or ride to Mexicali with me. He thought about it a moment and decided he'd like to try to get his car running. I could see he was going to leave it up to me—so when arrived at his car—I took advantage of the opportunity.

I turned the motor off and we sat in the darkness. The heavy rain had slacked off to a slow downpour with occasional furious spates.

"Jesus, I'm very sorry that I got you involved in the things that have happened. You are a good man, and your friendship is deeply appreciated. I could never put a value on your friendship, or the help you've given me, but I do have something for you."

I reached over the seat, opened the compartment, and pulled out one of the plastic bags full of money.

"This is yours. You've earned it and I want you to have it. It will go a long way toward helping rebuild your town."

He looked inside the bag and his eyes grew big. He knew what it was, and he knew the implication.

His eyes got misty. "Are you sure, my friend? This is a lot of money!"

I laughed. "Yes, and it's yours!"

He threw his arms around me and tried to hug me. His whiskers scratched my cheek as he squeezed me tight.

"*Mucho gracias, amigo! Mucho gracias!*"

I put a hand on his shoulder. "I think that the less you say about the ranch, the better off we'll both be."

He grinned. "What ranch is that *señor*? I know nothing of a ranch!" He held up his left hand. "I lost these fingers in the *hurricane!*"

The battery was dead on the police car, so he dug out some jumper cables from his trunk and hooked them up to my Jeep. In a few minutes, we got him running. As he was preparing to drive away, I stuck out my hand for one final shake. "Perhaps, someday I will come back, and you and I can go fishing or something."

He smiled. "You are welcome anytime, Pat. *Mi casa es su casa!*"

He started to drive away but stopped. "You will come back, won't you?"

"I shall ... to see the rebuilt town, and you, *amigo.*"

CHAPTER 51 – THE REWARD

I followed Jesus' taillight until I came to the place where I'd had the car wreck. I parked by the side of the road and retrieved another bag of money, counting out what I wanted—being careful not to overdo it to the extent it would cause them problems.

I left the Jeep's motor running and waded through the foot-deep water in the roadside ditch to get to Rolando's shack. Even though it was pitch dark, he was up on the roof trying to nail down a section of tin that had ripped loose. He saw me coming and climbed down to greet me.

He didn't recognize me either at first, but I explained and he soon realized who I was. We shook hands, and without saying a word, I quickly handed him the twenty thousand dollars I'd counted out. He probably had no idea how much money it was, but he knew it was a lot and would change his and his family's life.

I felt good doing something nice for them. Rolando was speechless, but as far as I was concerned his warm handshake was enough. I left him standing there smiling, bewildered, and happy ... with the money clutched in his hands He was staring at it in disbelief.

It was after midnight when I arrived at Campo Rio and pulled in. The barking dogs woke the manager and he came out rubbing sleepy eyes.

"Can I help you, *Señor?*"

I answered in Spanish, holding up a wad of American money to show I had a way to go.

"The storm. I need a cabin for the night and some supplies. Can you sell them to me?"

He was immediately wide awake. "What is it you wish, señor?"

I followed him into the small country store and I began to pick out the supplies I needed. The bill came to a little over fifty-eight dollars including the price of the room for the night. I gave him four twenties and told him to keep the change. He kept thanking me ... all the way to my same old cabin door but never recognized me. When I insisted on unloading the gear from the Jeep myself, he happily toddled away to go back to sleep.

The lumpy old bed looked soft and inviting. Before turning in, I had things to do. I moved the Jeep to just behind my cabin. Then I unloaded the three remaining bags of money and took them inside. I lit a kerosene lantern and counted the cash. It took me a while but I realized there were a million, three hundred thirty-two thousand, and four hundred dollars, give or take a few counting errors. I sat there in the quietness of the cabin looking at it. An opportunity like this hadn't come along before and probably never would again.

I always do my job in the most intelligent way possible. I take as few chances as necessary and always make my best deal. I'd be lying if I said that money didn't mean anything. It did and does. Another opportunity like this was not likely to come again in my lifetime. So, after the dirt and grime was scraped away—after the job was accomplished—and after the ethics were rationalized—in the end, that's what it was all about: **the race for the money!**

I hadn't planned it this way, but there it was right in front of me. I asked myself if I could live with taking it. It wasn't a difficult question to answer. I often thought that one day, l would walk away from danger and step away from such risky work. With this large of a take, the time was mine and ripe to pick for retirement..

I packaged the money in the plastic wrap I bought. Then I wrapped it again in tin foil and packed it all tightly into one large Styrofoam picnic cooler. After it was sealed tightly with duct tape and packed away. I stripped down to my shorts and went out onto the patio. The water level had risen to within a few feet from the top of the concrete wall along the bank.

By now, the rain had almost stopped as the storm spun itself out over the land. The few falling drops made little circles on the inky black water.

I was certain that everyone was asleep except me. It was very quiet as I knelt and went to work. It was slow and tedious removing the cobblestones, but once I had them out, the earth was soft and the digging was easy.

I found some old newspaper and spread it out to pile the loose dirt on and dug slowly and easily, being as quiet as possible. In an hour, I dug a four-foot deep hole that was large enough to hold the picnic cooler, which I then covered with dirt, stopping when I had about six inches left to go. I carried several pitchers of water out and poured them into the hole to pack the dirt down tightly, let it sit a while, and then filled the hole the rest of the way to the top, packing the dirt down as tightly as I could.

I carefully replaced the cobblestones and surveyed my efforts. I was satisfied and confident that no one would ever uncover the money there. I dumped the remaining dirt into the lake and washed down the entire patio making sure that the spot where I had been digging wouldn't stand out from the rest. It was important to make sure my buried treasure would keep for a while.

I stood there looking out at the darkness. The shadows of time were creeping up on me. I'd been on the cusp too long and my adventuresome days were numbered. My sword was getting rusty and the magic didn't seem to work as well anymore. Perhaps, there just weren't enough true believers. I told myself that's why I'd disregarded the rules. I was required to operate outside the boundaries of right and wrong, providing the best solution possible as the sole judge, jury, and in this case ... the exterminator of the evil I encountered.

I remembered something I'd once heard. I'd been visiting a Mossad agent whom I developed a friendship with on a job. He was critically injured and a rabbi came to see him. They asked me to stay and my friend expressed some regret about what he'd done in the course of duty. He decided to take some lives. It was during Yom Kippur or the 'days of awe' wherein one has to fast and pray in an attempt to persuade God to change his attitude from that of judgment to that of mercy.

In answer, the rabbi quoted an ancient poem by an unknown author, which he thought was written sometime between the 4th and 6th centuries.

As best I recall, it went: 'Who shall live and who shall die? Who by fire and who by water? Who by the sword and who by a beast? Who by flood and who by drought?'

I knew my behavior had not been the righteous way and that I'd have to account for my actions one day. When I was younger and more idealistic, I required moral justification to meet the threshold of seriousness I considered necessary to initiate the seemingly unreasonable sanctions ordered by my superiors. They often had the appearance of corruption and required great sacrifice. I struggled to identify the correctness and means necessary to achieve the ill-defined objectives. In the course of such things, people often died and were sacrificed for the cause, whatever it was. That was all there was to it. It took me a long time to realize that I would never understand. Sometimes the only correct answer is that there is no answer at all. I just learned to accept it. I'd long since given up on the rules of engagement because there were no rules. There was no great list of regulations for justification of conduct, only to survive and complete my mission.

So, I didn't have any answers—only that I realized how much different my life was from that of most people. A long time ago, I decided to venture down a one-way street that would eventually end in a cold dark place. I had no right to feel sorry for myself, so I let it go, knowing I'd be different forever.

The uncertainties of tomorrow would have to wait. I now felt I'd stayed at the dance too long. It was all an ongoing experience that could only be endured—not defended. I knew I'd made mistakes and I tried to correct them when possible. I paid the price and blended the things I couldn't grasp with the realities of those I could.

There was only the 'mission accomplished' or 'mission failed' to evaluate my effectiveness. I'd put this one down as 'accomplished' and let it go at that. Only that day wasn't now. Who was to draw that thin line between survival and the reality of what I had done?

In my mind, I acknowledged that I was rationalizing my failure to disclose, which was a self-serving act—justified by the degree of danger my anonymous employers subjected me. I'd succeeded beyond any reasonable expectations and felt fully deserving of my special tax-free retirement fund as a bonus. I had to admit to myself that money played a significant role in my self-esteem. Before you put me down—ask yourself, what would you have done?

My biggest regret was not being able to save Mickey. Twice she saved me, once when I felt sure my time was up, and a second time when she took those bullets meant for me.

CHAPTER 52 - EXPLANATIONS

I'd been working for several hours and was exhausted and muddy. I slipped out of my under shorts and threw them in a nearby trashcan. I stood nude in the moonlight with a light rain falling. I heard a fish splash in the water. I stared into the darkness, feeling the water calling. I slipped off the ledge into the coldness and swam slowly, letting the water wash away the mud and pain from my body. I swam until I got to the middle and stopped.

A feeling was building up inside of me that I couldn't control. I was treading water and had no idea how deep it was beneath me. Some impulse made me kick over and dive down, swimming slowly into the pitch-dark blackness. My ears began to ache with the pressure, but I kept on going down even farther. I finally struck the soft muddy bottom at about twenty feet.

I opened my eyes and the world was gone. There was only the bitter darkness and softness of the bottom. It was as black as a mother's womb. I shoved my hands as far into the soft mud as could. When I lodged myself in up to the elbows, I surrendered and was pleased to find that the bottom held me down securely. I opened my mouth and screamed as loud as I could until I was out of breath and the mud started to flow back into my mouth. A large part of me could have just let it happen, but some stronger survival instinct made me struggle to pull my arms free.

I didn't try to swim for the surface, even though my lungs screamed for air. I just turned over and let positive buoyancy lift me to the surface. It seemed like an eternity, but at last, I popped free. I swam on my back all the way to the bank and then totally exhausted, I climbed out and stumbled back to my cabin.

I plopped down in a lawn chair and couldn't help thinking about Mickey again. It troubled me that I didn't think of her as a female Although we hadn't seen eye to eye on some things, Mickey came into my life and changed its direction. I knew I wouldn't be alive if she hadn't made the ultimate sacrifice and given up her own life to save mine. I will always honor the fire that burned in her and never forget what she did. Her loyalty and bravery were equal to that of any other man or woman I'd ever known. She was a true heroine as far as I was concerned. I knew she struggled greatly with her gender confusion and what was no doubt an immutable biological characteristic of wanting to be a female. With respect, I would forever remember her as the shield that protected me and kept me from death.

I guzzled down most of my last beer and splashed the last of it onto the patio in a silent toast to Mickey. It was time to call it a day. Before I did, I got the unregistered Nellie out of the Jeep and tossed it as far as I could out into the water. Then I went inside and flopped down onto the lumpy bed, my mind racing over the events of those past few days and what had transpired. I learned the hard way that overcoming grief is a long and difficult road. But you have to take it to the end of your journey and there are no easy exits.

That so-called 'closure' thing is a myth because it is never over emotionally. You just mute it the best way you can and accept whatever vindication you manage to get. There is no way to push out the pain because you will carry it with you for the rest of your life. Once the bullets have stopped flying—the noise of the screams has gone silent—and the blood has stopped flowing—the most difficult thing is forcing our minds to accept our flaws and acknowledge what we are capable of doing. I killed a bunch of people, who altogether hadn't mattered as much to me as the life of that one brave girl who'd had the misfortune of being born a boy. I knew I couldn't put it back the way it was, and that I'd have to file it, along with all the other traumatic memories of the violent way I had chosen to earn a living. I never expected it, but at least it paid well and I had the money now. I was a millionaire. With those thoughts boiling in my brain, I closed my eyes and utterly exhausted, fell asleep.

I awoke just before noon the next day with a pounding headache. I heard the sound of children's laughter, and then immediately checked the patio. It looked completely normal. I smiled and tapped my foot over the spot where the money was buried. It rained off and on during the night, but the storm had broken up and now the sun was out.

I went back inside and took a long, hot shower, ripped off my fake mustache and the mole. Then, I shaved away the stubble. The tan would have to wear off, but I felt like myself again. I loaded the gear into my Jeep, got out my identification papers, and took off for San Diego.

I drove at a leisurely speed and by the time I reached the border, I was feeling almost human. The radio news reported that the savage hurricane had devastated San Felipe and that the mammoth rains caused widespread destruction including many mudslides and flashfloods throughout the area.

A felled tree had killed six people fleeing from the storm in a van. The body of two young boys who had been swept away by river currents had been found covered with mud, as were those of five other victims who were killed by mudslides. The low-pressure system continued to dump rain on Northern Mexico as it weakened into a tropical storm. Authorities estimated the death toll from the hurricane at 28 but it was expected to rise. Over 43 structures had been destroyed and numerous others damaged. The entire fishing fleet had been destroyed, and one 36' boat had been tossed on top of the local police station by the storm. Scientists believed that the violent storm might have triggered a small earthquake. Others denied the possibility. There were numerous lightning strikes, one of which started a fire that destroyed a large ranch house to the North of San Felipe, and a violet explosion in an old abandoned mine was probably caused by methane gas being ignited by some unknown source.

As I heard all that, I couldn't help but wince ... and yet ... felt vindicated, for such devastating events were necessary to erase despicable humans from among the innocents they tortured and slaved.

A little later, among the many reports, the news report mentioned that Senator Jake Jefferies, his guest Dr. Fung Lee Wang, the CEO of DayWan Industries, along with several companions were overdue from a fishing trip near San Felipe. They were feared to have fallen victim to the hurricane.

As I expected, once he recognized my vehicle, the border guard pulled me aside, checked my papers thoroughly, and he, and his drug sniffing dog gave my Jeep a thorough inspection. We both knew what he was looking for. He even found the empty Nellie compartment. Finding that gun alone would have been grounds to hold me for a more thorough search.

When he was satisfied, I had no green contraband, and his dog detected no drugs, he reluctantly waved me through. So much for Smith's 'safe pass-through promise'. As usual, I was glad to get back to the land of the free. I had seen the grass on the other side of the fence, and despite the money, it was not greener. Even with all its faults, there is no place else that comes close to the United States.

Once across the border, I stopped at a Carl's Jr. and enjoyed two delicious Star Burgers, a large order of fries, and a large chocolate shake. Afterward, I took it slow and easy, pulling into San Diego a little after five in the afternoon. When I arrived at the Half Moon Inn, I didn't stop at the desk but headed straight for my room where, as I expected, Smith was waiting for me.

"You sure took your time," he said as walked in. "They have been waiting for you since two o'clock. They want to see you right now."

We walked out of the motel, and to my surprise, continued around back and down the ramp into the marina. I followed Smith, curiously wondering what the heck was up. He led me out onto one of the piers and then turned right on a finger pier where a large houseboat was slipped.

I followed him up the gangway and into the houseboat. We stepped down into a large, lavishly decorated, but dimly lit room where four men wearing business suits sat in a semi-circle around a sizeable, highly polished walnut-topped conference table. Smith motioned for me to sit at one end of the table, opposite the men. I slipped into a chair without saying a word.

The stateroom was pleasant with several overstuffed chairs, mid-Victorian paintings, and a huge bar that matched the conference table. The lighting was supplied by strategically placed lamps, arranged so that it was difficult to make out the faces of the men sitting at the other end of the table, although they could see me quite clearly.

Smith, who was standing behind me, patted me on the back and walked out of the room. I sat there waiting for someone to speak.

One of them finally said, "Congratulations, Mr. Race."

I nodded and acknowledged their platitude, "Thanks!"

"Please tell us your accounting of what occurred, from the beginning and please don't leave anything out, no matter how insignificant you may think it is."

"Sure. Okay ... well—-"

I began to recite what happened and told my story, yet avoiding things I wanted to remain private, including anything about Mickey, Jesus, Carmen, and the money I'd hidden. Belief is a blunt instrument and sometimes the truth cuts like a dull knife, especially if it is not what the listener wants to hear. Sometimes the listeners are like cowardly big game hunters wanting to bag the trophy without dodging the horns, hooves, jaws, or claws. So, I told them what I thought they wanted to hear.

When I finished, one of the men said, "Do you have any idea who those men were that you sealed up in the vault?"

"A few, but I don't care. To me they were greedy, tortuous assholes that deserved what they got."

One man rolled his eyes but agreed with me.

"Indeed, Mr. Race. To us and the world, they proved to be insignificant traitors, and in every way weren't important ... certainly not to you anyway. No doubt you've heard on the news about some of them going missing and recognizing their photos, but ignore those reports and disavow any involvement in their disappearance... understand?'

I smiled at his cliched mafioso-type answer.

"I've no idea who you are talking about."

"Yes, that's excellent. All knowledge of what you have told us here, and what's transpired these past couple of weeks is to be flushed and forgotten."

"As you wish ... it's done."

They were an enigma to me. The reality was that although I did recall the ones that tried to bribe me, I didn't know or understood the ideologies of those all of those other dysfunctional anarchists I'd eliminated in Baja. To live with myself, I had to believe my employers to be the lesser of two evils—incompetent politicians collaborating in damage control mode against the surreal entities of decadent self-indulgent destroyers of civilized society.

They questioned me for another half-hour. When I'd finished, they seemed satisfied. They expressed their sincere appreciation for my services and said they would call again if they ever needed me.

Though I truly intended to retire, I said, "Of course. Thank you, gentlemen!"

I rose and left immediately. My obscure moral compass rig justifying my actions, while they remained safely away from absurdity and danger. I had merely been their enforcer—the maintainer of civil order—the guardian of a societal alliance—the bullet for their loaded weapon.

EPILOG

I walked outside feeling pretty good. I still had no idea who l had been working for. I honestly didn't know whether I'd just carried out an important mission on behalf of the United States government, or if I'd merely gotten rid of someone's partners for them. In either case, I'd been well compensated.

The sun was just going down beyond Point Loma and all around the city thousands of rosy-cheeked young ladies were getting dolled up for the evening. I pondered if an old dragon slayer like me might have a chance.

I strolled back to my room, opened the door, and went inside. My eyeballs practically fell out. Reclined seductively on my bed, wearing nothing but a smile and a short white silk nighty—was the gorgeous redhead from the check-in desk. It was easy to see her red hair was natural.

She purred in a sultry voice. "Mr. Race, I'm sent from, Mr. Smith."

I gasped. "Are you now?"

She laughed. "Yes! For now and later if you'll have me."

I didn't believe my ears.

"You mean—you are my present ... a bonus gift of sorts?"

"That's right! For as long as you want me!"

I feigned concern, "Oh, my ... well sweetness, that could be a long time!"

She rolled over exposing her twin bosoms to me.

"That's all right with me!"

I had to know. "You're lovely, and I'm guessing your bank balance amply increased today."

Her pink tongue flicked across full crimson lips that formed into a wry smile.

"Most certainly ... Mr. Race!"

"Call me Pat, and I should like to do that to your gorgeous body. What is your name?"

"Call me ... Plenty."

By all that's holy, this gift was to be my favorite. I sauntered over to the bed and leaned down to embrace and kiss her. I could smell the sweet, sensuous aroma of her body and began to feel enticingly giddy with anticipation. I slid confidently onto the bed, yet careful to keep from falling on her. Her lips tasted faintly of honey and I pulled back to admire her beauty.

As I squinted my eyes, to me she took on a strikingly similar appearance to Carmen, then she became Mickey, and while my head spun, she became my Golden Retriever Glory and then a big fierce-looking mad dog with frothy saliva dripping over pointed, fanged teeth. I shook off those silly images and pulled her to me to make the apparitions go away. Suddenly, I remembered that I'd missed my rabies shot for the day.

The sultry redhead noticed me swoon and asked, "What's the matter? Are you okay?"

I pulled her close and held her tight.

"Sure! I'm okay. I just have something else very important to do today ... but for the moment ... it'll wait."

Somewhere deep in my mind, I wondered if everything would ever again ... be okay.

THE END

MACK MAHONEY'S COMMENTS ABOUT
"RACE FOR THE MONEY"

Before there were Private Eyes or Secret Agents behind every tree on every block of every neighborhood of this downtrodden crime-ridden world—before there were thousands of writers trying to create an interesting and entertaining character to write about—there was an era of greatness.

It was not at all like today's cadre of central characters of every conceivable nature. Nowadays, the big name can be of any ethnicity, male or female, young or old, alcoholic or drug addict, blind, fat, gay, straight, slim, smart, intuitive, OCD, or just dumb. Cutting-edge writers even have multiple protagonists in one novel.

But I cut my reading teeth in that time when a couple of dozen authors ruled. The time before the advent of spell checking and grammar correcting computers—when writers wrote their first draft in long hand or banged out their stories on an old mechanical typewriter.

The one thing you could always count on was that another escapade of that particular male hero would soon follow. Each story was different, and yet they were pretty much all the same—the sympathetic protagonist standing alone against an accomplished and unscrupulous evildoer and managing to overcome all obstacles. The villains were depraved and deceitful and the heroes were always up against seemingly unbeatable odds, which pushed them to the limits of physical and mental endurance. The protagonists were normally calm but cynical—entirely devoted to their work—with skills beyond most men. There was often a twist in that one of the hero's closest companions turned out to be a traitor.

It was a gentlemen's only club, with no dames allowed, unless they fell for the good guy and in most cases, proved it by dying for him. It was a high adventure of the first order.

There were lots of others whose adventures I went on and whose names I don't recall. I read many of them as I lay in my small berth on a nuclear submarine at sea. They were ambrosia for the mind. They captured my imagination and entertained me in a way that modern writers could never do. Many were written in first person and were more real than the technologically laced, fast-paced, bombs-and-bullets protagonists of today's fiction. The primary character was developed and perfected through each sequel their authors created. Once you got to know them, you were hooked and skewered. They were fodder for voracious reading appetites. They provided entertainment of the highest order.

If you've never experienced the thrill of such amazing characters, the books are still around, and I promise you won't be disappointed if you go back in history for the read of your life. They were wonderful! This book is dedicated to those great writers for the fond memories with genuine admiration and my sincere appreciation for all those vicarious adventures.

ABOUT THE AUTHOR

MACK MAHONEY

Vernon 'Mack' Mahoney Jr. was born and raised in Waco, Texas, and currently lives in Newport Beach, California.

Mack is a retired U.S. Navy Chief who served on nuclear submarines. After the Navy, Mack became a salesman, manager, and owner of marine retail dealerships in Southern California. He has also been the Vice President of Marketing for several new product development companies.

He has been a columnist for newspapers and magazines and for several years wrote and published boating books for marine dealers throughout the United States. He has written three fictional novels, a screenplay, and three non-fiction books.

During the last twenty years, he has created over 8,000 original greeting cards containing his artwork, photographs, and poems, recognized by Guinness as the world's largest such collection. To read more of Mack's writing, and view some of his cards, poems, photos, and artwork, simply go to **poetic_greetings.net** At that website you can make free "**print your own**" cards or send free "**E-cards**" as well as download some of Mack's writing for free.

www.ingramcontent.com/pod-product-compliance
Lightning Source LLC
Chambersburg PA
CBHW021955010726
47494CB00003B/740